Orphan of Creation

Contact with the Human Past

Novels by Roger MacBride Allen

The Torch of Honor
Rogue Powers
(above reissued in combined volume as Allies & Aliens)

Orphan of Creation
The Modular Man
Farside Cannon
The Ring of Charon
The Shattered Sphere
The Game of Worlds

Supernova (with Eric Kotoni)
The War Machine (with David Drake)

A trilogy of Asimovian Robot Novels:
Caliban
Inferno
Utopia

The Corellian Trilogy of Star Wars Novels:
Ambush at Corellia
Assault at Selonia
Showdown at Centerpoint

The Depths of Time

Orphan of Creation

Contact with the Human Past

a novel by

Roger MacBride Allen

FoxAcre Press

401 Ethan Allen Avenue
Takoma Park, Maryland 20912
www.FoxAcre.com

Dedication:
To Harry Turtledove,
fellow victim of incitement to fiction

Suppose... that one or several species of our ancestral genus *Australopithecus* had survived—a perfectly reasonable scenario in theory.... We—that is, *Homo sapiens*—would then have faced all the moral dilemmas involved in treating a human species of distinctly inferior mental capacity. What would we have done with them—slavery? extirpation? coexistence? menial labor? reservations? zoos?

—Stephen Jay Gould
The Mismeasure of Man

▼◆▼

She walked along the rows of the burned-over field, her bare feet crunching on the rain-soaked clumps of charcoal. The fire had been here; the men had brought it here deliberately to clear the jungle back and make a field for growing crops. The planting had been done, and the rains had come, and now the field was a raw sea of churned-up mud and dissolving charcoal. The sullen earth fairly steamed in the cloying humidity of the hot day, turning the field into a grim place of lurking mists beneath the steel-gray sky. Not all was harshness: the ugly browns and blacks of the field were set off here and there with the delicate, hopeful, transparent greens of the next crop.

But she saw none of that, and only looked straight down at the ground as she walked, pausing to stoop over and yank out the robust weeds that constantly threatened to overwhelm the tiny, fragile shoots of the food crop. If she had been set instead to pulling out the crop seedlings, leaving the weeds behind, she would not have known or cared.

She worked quickly, her stubby-fingered hands surprisingly graceful at their task. Most of the weeds she shoved into a bag that hung on a strap around her neck, but, now and then, she would pop one of the choicer stalks into her mouth and crunch it down to a digestible size before swallowing it.

The field was large, wide and long, but at last she came to the end of the row. She stopped, brought her head up, and stared, straight ahead, at the solid wall of trees and undergrowth that leaped up from the very edge of the field. She listened to the sounds, and smelled the scents, of the jungle and the wild places.

She stood there, a few leaves of a bamboo shoot quivering at the side of her mouth as she chewed, peering out into the jungle, as if she was searching for something in the forest. Then, suddenly, the overseer shouted. She jerked around, startled, and turned back to the field, obeying the sound of the man's voice rather than the words.

As the day wore on, the endless cloud of insects seemed to thicken

9

about her. Most of them she managed to keep off by waving her arms, but a few got through. A mosquito landed on her flat nose, and she brushed it away. Another tried to land on her chest for a meal, but instead got entangled in the hairy thatch of fur between her teats. She swatted it without looking down and went on with her weeding, leaving the tiny corpse squashed flat on her skin.

There was another weed. She stooped, pulled it out and examined the roots hopefully. She spotted a pinkish grub between the root tendrils. Making a low, happy noise, she caught it between her fingers, popped it into her mouth, and crushed it between her massive jaws. Today was like every other.

Her world was very small.

NOVEMBER

Chapter One

The house was old. Seven generations had trod its floors—through plantation times, Rebellion and Reconstruction, through carpetbaggers and cross burnings, through two world wars, through segregation and civil rights marches. Gowrie House had stood since the days of King Cotton, its lands shrinking from square miles down to a few acres as the generations of owners sold off what was no longer wanted, and its dominion of fields that stretched halfway to the horizon had retreated to a few garden plots of solemn, decorative flowers.

Dr. Barbara Marchando sat perched at the edge of a dusty chair in the attic of Gowrie House, surrounded by things that were heavy with that eventful past, things that felt *old*.

That the ages hovered here, no one could deny. But still somehow it was strange for her to think of this place, of *any* human place, as old. Barbara was a paleoanthropologist, a student of the past who worked in millennia, in millions of years, spans of time so great that the century and a half this house had existed were meaningless; flickering moments so small they could not be recorded in the scales of geologic time.

Still, time and history could be felt, hanging heavy, in this place. Innumerable events and memories were entangled in the web of the so-brief decades that measured this house. Barbara's family had owned this house for a long time, in the human scale. Twelve decades before, the *house* had owned her family, until the Slave had taken the Master's place, and started legends in doing so.

Now, it was Thanksgiving again, and for the hundredth time since she was a little girl, Barbara was seeking refuge from a loud and festive gathering downstairs by sneaking up to the attic. She loved to sift through the mysterious amalgamation of family treasures and debris there, to breathe in the fragrance of faded linens and the dry, somber scent of wooden rafters cooked by the attic heat of so many summers past. Perhaps it was in searching through its secrets that she had found her vocation. Certainly she had always loved this place.

Always, when she came up here, she dreamed of finding the prize, the jewel beyond price, that has to be hidden in this place. Now, with the last of the Thanksgiving dinner plates being clattered back into the cupboards downstairs, she decided to search in the one place she had never dared look as a child: the locked steamer trunk that had waited for her so long. She knew to whom it had belonged: the initials *Z. J.* were painted over the hasp and picked out with dusty gold leaf paint.

This trunk had belonged to Zebulon Jones himself, her great-great-grandfather, the legend-maker of her family, the bold defier of slave owners and rebels, carpetbaggers and the Klan.

As a skinny young man, he had escaped Colonel Gowrie's plantation in 1850, at the age of 25. He went North, earned his way however he could, taught himself to read while staying alive as a stable boy in upstate New York, finally owning his own stable and tavern, proudly gaining himself the franchise in 1860, just in time to vote for Abraham Lincoln. Denied a chance to join the Union army, he instead earned his fortune during the War by breeding, brokering, and selling horses for the Union Cavalry.

He returned home to Mississippi a wealthy man, in the headiest days of Reconstruction. Some crafty Northerners had meantime succeeded in forcing the bankruptcy of the Gowrie homestead, and had sought to bamboozle Zebulon and relieve him of his money in a complex phony land deal, but they found the tables turned when they learned how much law their mark knew.

Zeb bought his old master's plantation out from under them, and nailed the deal down tight in court. He settled in to plant new crops, and establish his own family. He twice shot Klansmen dead from the portico when they came to lynch the uppity colored boy and burn the place down.

He stood for Congress, and won, and served two years in the early 1870s, before the white man stole the ballot box and the promises of Reconstruction away from the supposedly enfranchised blacks.

Zebulon Jones. The family jealously preserved the heritage of his character: Every child and grandchild, unto the latest generation, knew the stories and legends of Zebulon, and all had a fair share of his gumption and pride, his courage and determination.

Knowing the trunk had belonged to her great-great grandfather made its secrets all the more alluring to Barbara. Her whole life long, even long before she was born, the trunk had sat in the attic, keeping its treasures locked away. Throughout her childhood, every time her parents had visited the family homestead, she had come up here to stare at it, endlessly. Each time she would try the sturdy lock, to see if it had yet given way to rust and decay—but she had never dared try to force it open, and always the lock was solid still.

The key undoubtedly was lost long ago, forgotten in the keepsake chest of some aunt or another. As a child, Barbara had imagined the secrets that might be locked in the trunk, and thought of the archaeologists and grave robbers from her picture books, opening Pharaoh's tomb. She had never dared try and force it open.

But now, today, finally, it was too much for her. She could not say why, precisely, but today the temptation to look inside was too great, and the pressure to stay away much weakened.

Maybe it was that she was still angry with her husband Michael, and could take it out on a poor helpless antique steamer trunk. They had separated not long before, and Michael blamed the separation wholly on Barbara—another of his endless denials of responsibility, a big part of what had driven her away in the first place. He was back home in Washington, stuck working the Emergency Room for most of the holiday weekend.

Maybe it was that she had opened tombs a hundred times as old, and her professional detachment had finally driven the sin out of broaching the old trunk.

Maybe she was silently rebelling against the relatives downstairs who still insisted on treating a 32-year-old Ph.D. like a clever 15-year-old.

Even as she invented all the rationalizations, she knew none of them mattered. Plain and simple, her curiosity had at long last gotten the better of her, and she was no longer able to resist the mystery and challenge of this forgotten family relic.

She got up off her chair, raising a cloud of dust as she moved.

Sighing, she carefully brushed every speck of the dust off her green sheath dress. She was a tall, slender, dark-skinned black woman, her oval face graceful and expressive, her startlingly honey-brown eyes wide and lovely. Her sleeveless dress showed her arms to be surprisingly well-muscled, thanks to endless hours working a shovel on innumerable digs, her hands strong and firmly callused. She patted at her carefully coifed shoulder-length hair, worrying about having to shampoo the dust out of it.

But that was for later. She prowled around until she found an old fireplace poker that had probably been retired to the attic well before World War II. She jammed the pointed end of the heavy iron bar between the hasp of the lock and the frame of the trunk, gave one good pull on the poker, and was rewarded with a loud crack and a clanking thud as the hasp fell clean off the trunk. Apparently, the wooden trunk was less well-preserved than the lock had been.

She set down the poker and knelt before the trunk, took hold of the lid, and pulled up on it gently. It resisted for a moment, and then popped silently open, puffing out a faint cloud of the dust that had lain undisturbed for generations. The hinges squeaked slightly, feebly resisting their unaccustomed movement.

As the lid swung open, she felt a half-dozen emotions flutter through her heart, like a flock of birds chasing each other through a narrow byway, one after the other.

She had felt that way many times before—on a dig when the tomb was opened, when the fossil was uncovered, when she opened the envelope holding the lab report that would confirm or collapse her theory. Excitement, anticipation, a dream of the wonderful things about to be discovered, a faint disappointment when the mundane reality was not as marvelous as the possibilities, a gentle self-rebuke for forgetting her scientific detachment, a hopeful reminder to herself that wonders might *still* be hidden if she looked a bit further.

For there was nothing in the trunk but the sort of things she should have expected—personal items and old clothes for an old man, possessions stored away with great reverence, memories redolent with the smell of old mothballs and attic-baked air, things no one could bear to throw out when the family patriarch died. A silk shirt, a pair of gold wire-rimmed bifocals in a worn case, a lacquered wooden hatbox with a browning straw boater in it, a grey woolen suit that must have been hot and scratchy in a Mississippi summer. A wizened corncob pipe, and with it a gnarled and much-smoked briar, still bright and gleaming from its last polishing sometime in the previous century.

Carefully, gently, she lifted each item from the trunk. Under the hatbox was a stack of elderly books. She picked them up one by one and riffled through the pages. A bible—not a big family bible, but a small pocket volume that a man might keep by him when he traveled. *A Tale of Two Cities*—a handsome book with a hand-tooled leather binding and illustrated with color plates, printed in 1887. *History of the Negro Race in America* by George Washington Williams, 1886. *Narrative of Sojourner Truth*, no printing date given. All the volumes were well-thumbed, much read. These had to be the books Zebulon Jones had kept by his bedside; the best-loved books—old friends he had visited often. Barbara felt it a shame that they had been packed away with the other relics, stifled in the darkness instead of being put in a place of honor in the library. Books, especially such favorites of Zebulon's, should have been put where they could live, where the family could see and touch and read the words their much-honored ancestor had loved. She set down the *Sojourner Truth* and looked back in the trunk.

There was one more book there, smaller and more worn than the others. She took it out, examined the spine and binding. There was no title anywhere. Barely daring to think what she had found, she opened it, turned a page or two, and her heart skipped a beat.

The carefully scripted legend on the first page read:

ZEBULON JONES
A JOURNAL, DIARY, AND MEMORY BOOK
of Current Occasions
and
Times Past
1891

Barbara smiled excitedly as she read the words. *This* was the prize, the jewel beyond price. No one still living had known that Zebulon had even kept a journal. *This* would have stories to tell. She touched the book to her face, breathed in its fragrance, opened it to the first page of narrative, and marveled at what she had in her hands.

Beyond any question of how one measured time, the book was old, and rich with experience. The pages were limp, worn, darkened by time. Precise, angular handwriting marched across the unlined pages with the same certainty and confidence with which it had been set down, nearly a century ago, but now the once jet-black ink was faintly brownish in places. The leather binding, softened by much handling and long years, exhaled the scents of the decades it had survived—the musk of sweaty hands, the faint hint of tobacco after being jammed in the same pocket with a much-smoked pipe, the flavor of mothballs and old wool, testimony that the book had spent many years in the old trunk with the stored-away clothes.

"Barbara? Child, you up there again?" A deep, resonant voice echoed up from the stairwell, breaking the spell of the moment. It was Barbara's mother, Georgina Jones, a solid, no-nonsense, matronly woman.

"It's me, Mama. What is it?"

"I knew you couldn't stay out of that dusty attic when the aunts started gabbing. Come on down here. The touch football game is over and they're setting out the desserts. Better hurry, or you won't get any of Cousin Rose's apple pie."

Barbara smiled in spite of herself. "Coming, Mama." She put everything but the journal back in the trunk, closed the lid, balanced the hasp back in place, and put the fireplace poker back where she had found it.

She went down the stairs, carrying Zebulon's journal book, back toward the family gathering below. She stopped off at the little corner bedroom Great-aunt Josephine had put her up in, and hid the journal away in the top drawer of the wardrobe. Sooner or later, she'd have to admit to her crime of trunk-cracking. On the other hand, the discovery of the journal would serve as a great defense against sharp tongues—but she wanted a chance to *read* Grandfather's Zeb's words before anyone else could. She had always liked finding secrets—and liked knowing them when no one else did.

But Rose's apple pie first, and Clare's brownies, and George's pecan pie, and three kinds of pumpkin pie and two of shoo-fly, and the little children racing around. The oldsters were settled into their overstuffed chairs, comfortably close to each other—and to the buffet table laid out specially for the occasion in the living room (which the Southern branch of the family insisted on calling the parlor), with their grown children bringing them their desserts and coffee. It was not just the food, of course. It was the family, the closeness, the love, the constant recollection of a proud past, a confident eye toward the future— and a real Thanksgiving celebration of a contented and comfortable present.

Barbara waited in the buffet line and got the second-to-last slice of Rose's pie, and generous helpings of two or three others of her favorites, and laughed and smiled and chattered away with everyone, and even managed to find a whole chair to herself in the crowded living room. When everyone was settled down with a plate of six kinds of dessert and all diets forgotten until tomorrow, Great-aunt Josephine led yet another grace, thanking the Lord because so many loved ones were there, because those who had "gone on ahead" (as Great-aunt Josephine delicately put it) were still honored and remembered, because those separated by distance or duty were happy and well (though Barbara had a little trouble thinking of her absent and soon-to-be-ex husband Michael as "happy").

There was a chorus of loud Baptist "amens" and the noise level suddenly dropped as everyone dug in, finding just room enough for dessert.

Afterwards, the men wandered out onto Gowrie House's wraparound porch to start playing pinochle and bridge and dominos by twilight and lamplight. A few of the more daring younger men actually snuck upstairs to get up a poker game, leaving their less rash cousins to mutter in admiration at their brazenness. Gambling, for money, right there in Aunt Josephine's house! The children raced off to play who knows where, and the women started cleaning up after the meal. Each group went to its place and activity without anyone being told what to do, or even any of the women objecting—for today, at least—about being stuck with the dishes. It was part of the expected holiday ritual, the tradition, and Barbara found something comfortable about being in solely female company, carefully washing and drying the good china and the best silver as the women shared the latest gossip about this or that absent relative, boasting about how well the nieces and nephews were doing in school. Afterwards, the women had coffee and nibbled on the last of the desserts as they talked around the big table in Josephine's roomy, museum-piece kitchen, a room exactly as it had been when Barbara had been born.

The evening wore on toward night, and Barbara slipped away from the bright-lit table, collected her sweater from the front hall closet, and went outside for a stroll in the cool night. She stepped down off the porch and went out into the calm darkness, the laughter of the card players faint and close in the freshening breeze. She walked down the winding paved driveway that led to the county road.

It had been a clear, perfect, blue-sky day, but now the last traces of sunlight went sliding beneath the western horizon and steely clouds rolled in from the south, blanking out the first stars of night even as they appeared. A distant rumble of thunder growled, a strange sound to come from a November night. Barbara stopped a few hundred feet from the house and looked back the way she had come. It was a big old place, and every generation had added onto it, the exterior of the original house nearly lost under a century of remodeling. Solid old oak trees had been planted to shade the house long decades past, and now their uppermost branches swung back and forth, thrown about by the strengthening wind.

Ghosts lived in Gowrie House, Barbara thought to herself, friendly spirits that taught the ways of family and love and remembrance. There was a comforting presence and strength in the place.

She heard a fluttering noise and a slight commotion from the porch, looked to see what it was, and smiled. The wind was starting to blow the cards about, and the bridge players were retreating inside, just as the women were finally coming out to join the men. It was the cue to wrestle the card tables into the parlor and form up into new foursomes. She walked back to see if she could get into a game.

Chapter Two

It was close on midnight before the last rubber of bridge was done and folks started thinking about turning in. Barbara returned to her tiny bedroom and changed for bed.

There was just room inside the little corner room's flocked wallpaper walls for a small dresser, a night table, and one narrow bed, but that suited Barbara just fine—with so many visitors in the house, she was one of the very few who wasn't sharing a room that night. She realized how used to sleeping alone she had become. Even before the recent split, for most of the last few months, Michael had been on the overnight shift at the hospital.

Back in Washington, Barbara usually wore something along the lines of an old T-shirt to bed, but somehow that seemed too frivolous and undignified to wear in Zebulon Jones's house. She always wore a full-length nightgown to bed when she was at Gowrie, and now, as always, she was careful to cover even that with a ladylike robe as she went back and forth from the bathroom.

A few minutes later, she maneuvered herself into the narrow bed, her face scrubbed, her teeth well-brushed, and her hair combed out. Settling into the too-small bed in the doll-sized room, with the thunder rattling the windows and the rain suddenly coming down, with Zebulon's journal in her hand and the room lit by the cozy yellow light of the lamp on the nightstand, Barbara felt as if she were a child again, secretly reading her Nancy Drew books under the covers with a flashlight after Mama had tucked her in.

And Zebulon's journal was as fine a secret as she had ever found. At last alone with no chance of being disturbed, she opened the book and began to read as the rain splattered down on the windowpanes.

The handwriting was fine, proud, and precise, clearly an old man's hand, but the hand of an old man still sure and confident, the phrases couched in the formalized dignity of the 19th-century educated man.

▼◆▼

I was born a Slave, [it began] and spent the first twenty-five years of my life in that monstrous condition. A quarter-century of such an imprisoned existence left its plain mark on the rest of my life, which I have spent in a search for all the things denied a slave—freedom, dignity, education, prosperity, property, control over one's own destiny, the chance to provide for one's family and people, the leisure to treasure the beauties of God's world.

In these endeavors, I believe I have in some small way succeeded. I am now approaching the end of a useful life, and I feel that I have made myself ready to meet my Maker. I will not dying willingly, for life is a precious gift none of us dare deny while it is offered. But I strive to be an obedient servant of the Lord, and will go when He at last calls me home.

If my life has not been Faultless, neither has it been so Blameful that a just and merciful God should deny me entrance to His kingdom. After lifelong battles with His enemies—the Slavemaster, the Lynch Mob, the Klansman, and all the other agents of Hate—I am at peace with God. I have done my duty to him, and to myself. It only remains for me to recount, as best I can, the events of my life, not as a Monument to myself, but as an Instruction to those not yet born as to what it is possible for one Man to do.

In that connexion, and with the same admonition that what follows is not a Boast, but an Example, I must commence by relating the difficulties ranged against me.

For a man to say he was a Slave, to say that he was denied a right or that he was treated inhumanely because he was a Negro, is to report so much in so few words that nothing at all is said.

To be born a Slave in Mississippi in the Year of Our Lord 1824 or 1825 (I confess that I have never known the exact date of my own birth) was to be born not merely into ignorance and poverty, but ignorance and poverty ruthlessly enforced by law, violence, murder, and terror; enforced by the forcible sundering of families, enforced by the fears of the Master and the lies told to the Slave.

I lived out my childhood sleeping on a pile of filthy rags in a dirt-floor shack, eating out of tin cups and wooden bowls, never with spoon or fork, but merely with my hands, ignorant not only of reading and writing, but even ignorant that such skills existed. I had no playmates, for we were toilers in the cotton fields, and there was no play from the moment I could walk and speak, but only endless work.

As a child, I was savagely beaten many times— beaten for such grave flaws as laughing, or being afraid, or failing to lift a bale of cotton as large as myself. And yet I was never beaten out of anger, but always in a skilled, calm, scientific manner, nicely calculated to produced the desired results— as a blacksmith might pound a horseshoe on an anvil, bending the iron to his will without anger or emotion, without a thought that the metal he worked upon could possibly feel pain or fear or want.

I believe that I would have *preferred* to have been beaten in anger. Better the furious punishment of an enraged Master than a calm man methodically forming a tool to suit his needs. Not only in the way they beat us, but in the way they fed us, housed us, clothed us, our former Masters treated us not as men and women, not even as dumb creatures, but as objects—tools to be used up, patched up if it seemed worthwhile, but otherwise discarded without a care or thought.

Yet I also believe that, when the War came, and Emancipation came, and the end of the "Peculiar Institution" came, slavery had cost the Master far more than it had cost the former Slave. It had cost the Master his Soul.

How crippling to the heart and soul for a young white child to be raised and trained and schooled to believe that a human being could be less than an animal. How vile, to force oneself to believe that pain did not hurt, that cruelty was blameless. How evil to learn—and then to teach—the techniques of stripping a fellow man of all dignity.

How horrible to know at the back of one's mind that all one's wealth, all one's peace and prosperity, had its foundations set on Blood, on the Lash, on barbarity carefully hidden from view beneath the most elaborate civility and courtliness. Guilt hung like a heavy, funereal shroud over the white man's plantation.

Perhaps it was for pity's sake, then, strange as that must seem, that while all Slaves hated their servitude, hardly any hated their own Masters, and even after Emancipation, many former Slaves stayed on in service to their old owners, those owners for the most part much reduced in circumstance by the War's privation.

To this day, it is with a strained and muted, and all but embarrassed affection, an affection not untinged with hatred, that I recall my own master, Colonel Ambrose Gowrie. No Slave of his household ever felt the lash from the Colonel directly, and his presence was sure to mitigate the severity of any beating. If the White man was debased and brutalized by Slavery, then Colonel Gowrie was far less polluted than he should have been. He retained far more of his humanity than he should have.

Perhaps that is why I hate him even as I recall him fondly. The owner of such an enquiring, open, brilliant mind should not have been so closed to the evidence of his own senses. Unlike so many of the White men in and about Gowrie town, he could not claim ignorance or stupidity as a bulwark for his beliefs and actions. He, of any of the Masters, should have realized that the Negro was a man and brother. But, of all of them, none was so certain of the Negro's inferiority. He was a barbarian, sure and certain that his own vile prejudices were the law and word of God.

So much and no more will I write concerning the general condition of my own background. Much has already been written by more skilled hands who came from similar circumstance, and it would be in vain for me to attempt any improvement upon such accounts.

I shall instead relate the unique experiences of my life, which I believe have no model in the written word, for I have been many other things than a Slave, and done many other things than bale Cotton.

▼◆▼

Barbara smiled at that, and closed the book for a moment. On an impulse, she threw the covers back off, got out of bed, drew on her slippers and robe, and stepped out into the upstairs hallway, taking the book with her. She still knew the secret children's folklore of this house, legacy of the many times she had sneaked downstairs after hours with her cousins. She knew her way around the house in the dark, knew which boards creaked, knew the quietest, safest way to go downstairs without alerting the grownups. With no other light but the far off, flickering lightning, she made her way downstairs by the old servants' stairs. Zebulon himself must have trod these stairs, in the old days before he bought the place out from under Colonel Gowrie.

She opened the door at the bottom of the stairs and found herself in the kitchen, now spotlessly clean after all the day's good cooking and eating. She went through the doorway to the dining room, out into the foyer, and through the wide entrance of the front parlor.

There was the portrait, over the mantel, dimly seen in the flickering gloom of the storm. She flicked up the wall switch, and the darkness was thrown back by warm yellow light.

She walked to the center of the room and regarded Zebulon's face—a good, strong, lean, dark-skinned face, solemn without seeming stuffy. The portrait had been made in later life; his thick shock of hair was snow white, the face weathered and mature. He was dressed in a trim frock coat and waistcoat that showed a form still slender and vigorous. His right hand held the lapel of his coat, and his left was holding a book. The artist had captured well the power and grace of those long-fingered, work-hardened hands. This was the man.

She reached up and touched the frame, the edge of the painting, then turned and sat down on the stiff old claw-foot sofa and continue her reading in the presence of the author's image. She opened the journal, flipped the pages back and forth, a few words here and there jumping out at her as the phrases fluttered past her eyes. *The fire in the cotton field burned for two terrible days . . . Though Gowrie prided himself on keeping a slave husband and wife together, he thought nothing of selling their children . . . I was twelve before I wore a pair of shoes, and those were crude, splintering wooden clogs cast off by another . . . certain strangely formed Creatures appeared on the Gowrie plantation. . . .* Barbara stopped at that last, frowned, and read it again. Creatures? She started again from the beginning of the passage.

▼◆▼

. . .One of the strangest episodes in my life as a Slave began in what I now suppose to be the summer of 1850 or '51 (at the time I was almost wholly innocent of dates and calendars). It was at that time that certain strangely formed Creatures appeared on the Gowrie plantation, supposedly to serve as a new breed of Slave.

I made no sense of the incident at all when it transpired, and could not understand why these Beasts were brought to us, but now I think I understand what was happening: the old slavers, the cruel men who carried their miserable cargoes of captured Africans across the horrible Middle Passage of the Atlantic, were making one last attempt to revive their gruesome trade.

For centuries, as many Negroes died on those voyages as survived, and at length, the traffic was banned by all civilized nations. In 1808 the United States made the importation of slaves illegal (though of course not in any way alleviating the situation of the Slaves already imported, or born here). Many thousands more slaves were of course smuggled into the South from Africa since '08. Still, the trade was illegal and risky—and that cuts into the profits. These Creatures were a stratagem to get 'round the slavery importation law. Since these Creatures were patently not Human beings, therefore, in a lawyer's logic, they were not Slaves, and therefore they were legal to import.

The slaver who imported the Creatures, and the men (including Colonel Gowrie) who purchased the beasts, made a d**ning but unknowing admission by taking part in this effort to circumvent the law, for behind the transaction's claimed legality, based on the assumption that importing non-human Slaves was legal, hid the backhanded admission that Negro Slaves *were* true men and women, not animals. In spite of all their protestations otherwise, as they bought up the Creatures, the Masters were discarding their sheltering sham belief that the Negro was not a Man. Perhaps that is why I recall the incident so clearly.

Yet it would be impossible to forget the day Colonel Gowrie brought home his new charges. Stranger creatures I have not seen before or since.

▼◆▼

Creatures? Barbara hesitated over the page as the lightning flickered outside the parlor wall. She skipped ahead to find if Zebulon had described his "creatures," and quickly found the passage.

▼◆▼

They were much of the same form as men and women, their similarities to humans accentuating rather than disguising the vast difference between our kind and theirs.

They stood erect, and had well-shaped hands

(which were not so graceful or clever as those of a man, however). Their heads were quite misshapen, and they were weak-chinned, with such bulging jaws and large fierce teeth that they offered an altogether ferocious aspect that was in marked contrast to their timid behavior. Until they became used to us, the smallest child could startle them quite out of their wits.

They could not speak, but they could convey their wants and desires with astonishing clarity, by means of pantomime, hoots and grunts, grimaces and faces.

As I have observed, their heads were most strangely misshapen, with a large shelf of bone above the brow, and a sort of crest along the center of the skull, running from the highest point of the skull toward the back.

Barbara read further, fascinated. It sounded very much like some of the local gentry had taken to importing gorillas, or perhaps chimps, as farm labor! Zebulon must have revised their appearance in his memory, made them seem to look and act more like humans. None of the great African apes were well known before the 1800s, and the gorilla wasn't described until 1847. They would not be well known on a sleepy Southern plantation, especially to an uneducated slave.

Their bodies were dark-skinned, and covered rather sparsely with coarse black hair. They wore no clothes willingly, and when the White men would try to force them to cover themselves decently, they would tear the rude shirts to shreds and insist upon their lewd nakedness.

These were the Creatures, the animals, that the latter-day slave traders would present to Gowrie and his friends as the equal of the Negro in all things—intelligence, ability, skill. I have said that the importation of animals to circumvent the slave import laws was a tacit admission that the Negro

Slave was indeed human. How doubly d**ning then, how hypocritical and two-faced, for those same White men to expect us to live with and accept these Beasts as our equals, in huts next to our own, as if it was nothing more than housing a donkey alongside a horse. And how foolish. The Negro Slaves, needless to say, were, all of us, every man, woman and child, disgusted and horrified by these unnatural creatures, beasts in the form of men. I remember well the first time I saw them. I worked as a stableboy then, and it was as the cart brought their cage up from Gowrie Landing . . .

Barbara suddenly felt as if she were no longer simply reading this story. Some part of it gripped her soul, as if she were seeing it, *living* it. It had happened to her a thousand times as a child. She felt again the sensation of being drawn down into the tale, the words transforming themselves into sights, smells, sounds. As the words marched in front of her eyes, with the stern countenance of the writer staring down at her, with his very blood coursing through her veins, with the wild storm chasing itself madly around the darkened landscape outside, the images of those elder days flashed before her eyes. She *knew* how it must have been . . . .

Young Zeb looked on the beasts in outright terror. They seemed huge, monstrous, the denizens of a nightmare. They were perhaps no larger than a grownup, but their shrieking, screaming, maddened yelling, the wild way they flung themselves at the bars of their cage, the banging and clanging of all the bars and locks that set the cart to bouncing wildly about, all this made them seem far larger than they really were.

The pair of horses drawing the cart were just as fearful, snorting and whinnying, pawing the ground in their fright, the well-muscled sinews rippling beneath their perfect chestnut hides. Zeb found himself staring at the horses instead of the beasts, for at least the horses seemed real, normal, of this world.

But real or not, the horses too were terrified, and it was all the ostler could do to keep them from stampeding. The cart was backing and starting, threatening to pitch over on its side altogether. Finally, the drayman, adding to the chaos with a stream of shouted curses, brought his team to a full halt, and leapt gracefully down from the rig and stood at a respectful distance. At least the horses suffered themselves to stand still, wild-eyed, with their nostrils flared, their flanks twitching and flecked with foam. Zeb didn't know where he got the courage to step in and hold the leads, but he did, and stood between the heads of the frightened horses, speaking soft soothing words to them as he watched the proceedings at the back end of the cart.

Gowrie himself was there, a tall, rangy man with a small black goatee and a fierce enthusiasm of expression. He was standing by the rear of the cart, grinning wildly, looking over his new chattels with great pleasure. "Joe, Will, let's get that cage open and welcome our new friends," he said, holding out the key to the cage and gesturing to two of his slaves.

"Massah Gowrie," Will said in his soft plantation creole, "This ain't no time to let them things out." Will worked in the stables and barns, caring for the farm animals, and knew a lot about most live things. "Let 'em set a bit, calm down a mite. They's scared half to death from the ride, and someone sure to get hurt if they come out now—else they just go over the horizon in a flash."

"Will, I said to open the cage!" Gowrie growled. "You fixing to get whipped?"

"No suh. But I'd druther be whipped than bitten and clawed. Them things is *fierce* right now!"

"Joe—get up there and—" Gowrie began, but Joe just shook his head. "Damn you both, then!" Gowrie shouted, and leapt up on the cart bed. He set the key in the lock—and two hairy arms reached out for him.

He suddenly found himself thrown to the ground, his clothing ripped and the flesh in his arm badly scratched. He was shocked, infuriated, swore incoherently. He got up, grabbed a whip from the drayman, and lashed it savagely against the bars of the cages, setting the beasts into new paroxysms of hysteria, panicking the horses anew. Zeb was almost thrown off his feet and trampled before the drayman came to his rescue and helped calm the animals.

"To the devil with all of you!" Gowrie thundered ineffectually, flinging down the whip. "Leave them there caged up on the cart overnight, then, and see how they like it!" He stormed off, leaving the ostler to chase after him, protesting about having his cart standing idle all night.

Will, Joe, and Zeb chocked up the cart and gingerly got the horses out of harness and into the stable to be fed and watered.

The beasts they left to themselves, and the air that night was filled with an endless, terrifying hooting and calling.

▼◆▼

The lightning flickered again, and Barbara came back to herself with a start. She had a vivid imagination, and had always managed to scare herself gleefully half to death by reading ghost stories. She read on, trying to keep her imagination in check if she could.

▼◆▼

Gowrie had had a slave hut newly fitted with stout bars and a locking door, though none of the other Negro huts had a door of any kind—an irony that was hard to miss. The night in the open seemed to soothe the beasts somewhat, and Gowrie managed to get them out of their cage and into their new quarters without much incident.

In the days that followed Gowrie started to work teaching them their duties. New shipments of the creatures arrived, every other day or so over the space of a fortnight, a pair at a time. Gowrie worked them all as hard he could, but in spite of all his efforts, all his coaxing and cajoling and threatening and whippings, he still could get but little work out of them, and that only after such endless training that it would have been less bother to do the job himself.

And, after all that effort, the creatures did not last long. Three were dead in a month, of influenza.

Gowrie House Plantation had (and still has, for that matter) a small plot of ground that served as a graveyard for the Slaves. Of course, not a grave there had a proper headstone, but the survivors would fashion a wooden cross out of picket fence staves and place it over their loved one's grave, and perhaps add a smooth, round, whitewashed stone. The place was most carefully tended and maintained, and if any one thing on Earth could be said to belong to Gowrie's Slaves, it was that graveyard, held as joint and common property by all of us, the final resting place of those who had finally died under the lash.

And it was here that Colonel Ambrose Gowrie proposed to inter those three dumb beasts, laying them beside the honored and ancient bones of our grandparents and the remains of children lost in infancy. If Mississippi had ever been close to a slave revolt, it was on that day. . . .

Almost unwillingly, Barbara let the story steal over her again. She could *see* the Colonel in the midst of his predicament—the fear in his heart, the anger of the mob around him.

Ambrose Gowrie himself stood with the reins in his hands, the cart stopped dead right where the main plantation road intersected the path to the slaves' burying ground. None of the white overseers had been willing to do the job, and even his own sons felt it was foolhardy to try this thing. Behind him, on the bed of the wagon, lay the three wooden boxes, packing crates renamed as coffins for their final service. Black men and women, his own slaves, surrounded the flat-bed wagon, a straining, silent, surly, dangerous mob. Gowrie thought of the lash, the bullet, and realized with a sudden, sick feeling in his gut that such things would be worse than useless.

The sky was steel, a flat sheet of sullen grey that murmured with the rumblings of a nascent storm. The wind tossed the cotton plants about and lashed at the trees surrounding the plantation house, and a loose shutter on an upstairs window banged angrily.

Behind him, silent in their boxes, lay the causes of all his troubles. His slaves had hardly ever offered a bit of difficulty, but they had been close to open revolt from the first moment those accursed creatures had arrived. This now-dead trio of beasts had done nothing for him but cost him money, effort, and pride.

Gowrie did not dare to so much as glance back at his cargo as he thought about the dead creatures. He could not risk looking away from this roiling mob. He felt a trickle of sweat slide down his face, and suddenly realized his armpits and back were soaked with the perspiration of fear, his hands clammy in the reins of the cart.

With a conscious effort, he drew himself up and shouted, almost screamed at the crowd. "The corpses must be buried! Make way and let me into the graveyard, damn you! Make way or you'll live to regret it!"

The crowd did not move. Fearful and uncertain, he sat down in the driver's seat and swallowed hard. From the rear came quiet mutterings, the briefest flickerings of movement. The press of bodies inched forward slowly, quietly, until the closest of the myriad solemn faces were only a foot or two from his own. Gowrie suddenly found himself making calculations of how far he could get if he ran.

But he had to do this thing, get those bodies below

ground before they began to rot . . . and yet that was impossible. He might drive the cart into the graveyard, but how could he possibly dig the graves and move the heavy crate-coffins into the earth by himself, with this mob about him? He realized with a wrenching knot in his stomach that they weren't afraid of him. What were they capable of if they weren't afraid?

The rear of the cart suddenly bucked and swayed, and Gowrie let out a wild yelp. They were overturning the cart! They were going to tear him—

He looked behind to see a number of the burliest black men pulling the packing crates off the cart. Shovels and picks appeared from somewhere. The earth sprouted holes by the crossroads. Shallow graves suddenly gaped open.

Gowrie sat in the cart, powerless, speechless. Will came up to him, and that little stable boy Zeb trailed behind. "Them dead will rot and smell same's any other, Massah Gowrie," Will said solemnly, "and they mus' be buried—but not in our place. Not in *our* place."

Gowrie watched in silent, fearful awe as his slaves openly, willfully, jointly disobeyed him. Even if their revolt was in the form of a compromise, burying the corpses near their graveyard, and even though all his slaves quietly returned to their tasks the moment the last shovel of dirt was atop the graves, he had witnessed the beginnings of something—the primordial act of peaceful, determined defiance.

He had seen how fragile his control was. And he saw the changes coming, saw that his world would never be quite the same again. This moment would be at the back of his mind every time he gave an order.

▼◆▼

So the first of the creatures died and were buried. The rest soon followed. Some number more were lain to rest in that small crossroads. A few escaped and terrified the vicinity until they collapsed from illness, privation, or the gun. The remainder died, in secret and quiet, at the Negro's hand, the bodies never to be found. They were animals, we were not, and we did not suffer lightly being equated with them.

Colonel Gowrie was much affected as well, and from that time on, he would never willingly speak of the creatures that had cost him so much. As the town's leading citizen—and the owner of most of it—he also saw to it that few others spoke of them again. The Negroes who traveled to town on errands reported to the rest of us that what should have been the grandest story and scandal of the day was scarce ever mentioned.

Barbara closed the book and sat there for a long moment. Even then, no one had known. Today, the secret of those unmarked graves was as dead as the corpses within them. The secrets of that story had waited a long time for her. She rose and looked out through the flickering lightning toward the slaves' old burial ground. The creatures, the gorillas, were still waiting out there, bones moldering in the ground, proof of a brief, peculiar, and never chronicled sub-chapter in American history.

She looked to the sky, and saw a star or two flicker to life on the horizon as the storm clouds retreated. Tomorrow would be clear.

Those bones would not have much longer to wait.

▼◆▼

They locked her in at night with her kind, in the strongest, best-built hut in the village. She lived with the others in squalor and filth inside the well-made walls and solid roof. It kept the night out, kept them out of the night.

She wanted to be free. That much was in her, a solid sure thing, a part of her. Endless times she had tried to escape; endless times they had stopped her. The hut was made as well as it was, thanks to her.

Perhaps she should have been no more aware of her bondage than a fish is aware of the water it swims in. Bondage was her element, the old and only heritage of her line, back through the mists of all half-remembered times. She and her kind had never known anything else. But fish can sense the water—the currents, the smells, the temperature. And she sensed and resented her enslavement, knew it to be wrong, even if she could not understand it. She had no idea but away, no plan but now, no real awareness that time had a past, a present, a future, that today and tomorrow were different. She had only slowly developed the craftiness that taught her to wait until she was unwatched before she tried to run, that made her bide her time, that forced her to scheme and be secret in her efforts to be away.

Tonight, she would try the door again. It was a heavy wooden thing, made of vertical logs set close together with only the slightest of gaps between, hung on stout leather hinges and held shut with a series of thick leather straps firmly tied off from the outside. In the pitch blackness of the cell, she groped for the door, found it, and started chewing at the leather straps.

Part of her knew it wasn't going to work, that dawn would come long before she finished, that the overseers would see what she had done and beat her again. She didn't care. She closed her eyes and worked her massive teeth over the salty leather.

Away. Now.

Chapter Three

Dr. Michael Marchando staggered into the on-call room and flopped down on a bunk. He was exhausted. The Emergency Room had been a madhouse his whole shift long, an endless parade of car-wreck victims and gunshot wounds, seasoned with the usual Thanksgiving catastrophes—allergic reactions to unusual holiday dishes, burns from cooking fires, turkey bones lodged in the throat, excruciating indigestion and cramps brought on by massive overeating, and an upswing in drunk-driver injuries.

He shut his eyes and tried to sleep, but sleep wouldn't come. Here he was up in Washington, while Barb was down with that damn family of hers in Mississippi. This was the first Thanksgiving since Barbara and he had split up. He thought back, remembering the holidays they had had together, and wondered what she was doing. Right now, she was probably sound asleep, just about to wake up after a happy day with her family and a peaceful night of rest. Mike had bolted down his turkey early in the day, and left his mother's place to rush to the hospital and get up to his armpits in the sick and injured. It wasn't fair.

He thought ahead to Monday. Barbara had agreed to meet him for dinner. He smiled humorlessly. He had managed to get a date with his own wife. They still spent the occasional night together, whenever Michael could pressure her into it, whenever he could escape from the hospital. It wasn't any kind of a life. The more he thought about it, the more he saw how unfair it was.

He opened his eyes and stared into the darkness. It wasn't fair at all.

▼◆▼

Barbara woke, not with the sort of disorientation she usually experienced when she found herself in a strange bed, but instead with a preternaturally precise knowledge of where she was. Without opening her eyes, she knew exactly how the covers were wrinkled, precisely how far down the window shades were drawn, just how far the sunlight had made its way into the room, just how many children's voices she could hear outside.

She opened her eyes. The near-antique clock on the nightstand read 6:25. Good. Plenty of time left in the day. She had set the alarm for 6:30, and now she reached out to switch it off, pleased that she awakened before it went off. Nice to have a sense of minor accomplishment without even getting out of bed. But today was full of big plans. She wanted to get started on disinterring those one-hundred-thirty-odd-year-old gorilla bones. Today was Friday. She had the weekend to work with before it was time for the long ride back to the airport and the endless flight from Mississippi to Washington. There was little time, and she would need all of it.

Barbara threw back the covers, swung her feet out of bed, sat up, and looked out the window at the new, fresh-scrubbed morning. She heard laughter, looked down, and saw the children, four or five toddlers, tiny nieces and nephews and first-cousins-once-removed, wandering about on still-unsteady legs in the magically dew-brushed lush green of the lawn.

It was barely light yet, and the sunlight swept in a low, golden fan across the clean, bright day, all of it lovely. Barbara suddenly realized there was a lump in her throat, and she looked back to the tiny children, laughing gleefully because they were alive.

Barbara had no children, and never would. The doctors hadn't quite come out and said that, but they had came as close as they could. Michael and she had tried everything before the collapse of their marriage. Probably, trying too hard had contributed to that collapse. Mike had not liked the thermometers or the precise timing that eliminated spontaneity, and, later, had liked even less the idea of storing his seed in the sperm bank for tries at artificial insemination. His sperm was still there, on ice, another relic of the ruined marriage no one quite knew what to do with.

But children. She watched the children play outside, discovering the marvelous world. Suddenly, the old sorrow washed over her, and it was suddenly one of those times, one of those brief moments, when she felt a sense of grief and loss for a person who had never been brought into existence. It made her world emptier.

But the toddlers' bright laughter wafted up toward her window again, chased her regrets away, and she found herself smiling at their adventures.

She looked out toward the old slaves' graveyard. Today was go-ing to be *her* adventure. If she got away with it. If—If she dared go through with it. She drew herself up short. If she dared? She stopped, thought for a moment, and realized she was *scared*. Of what, pre-cisely, she could not say. She suddenly felt as if she were on the edge of a precipice, stepping out on a bridge that might not hold. She looked again at the graveyard, and told herself quite firmly that there was nothing there to harm her.

She scooped up her dressing gown and bathroom gear, stepped out into the hall, and headed for the shower before any other early riser could beat her to the hot water. She moved briskly, decisively, through the rituals of morning, as if that could banish her misgiv-ings.

But what was it that was bothering her? Barbara had always found the shower a good place to think. The routine and privacy of the moment, the luxury of steaming hot water, let her mind relax enough to focus in on the problems at hand. So what was it? True, there were several difficulties to be surmounted before she could get at the go-rillas' burial site—chief among them Great-aunt Josephine. Maybe Barbara was just reacting to Aunt Jo the way she would have as a child, a little girl who knew she was in big trouble and had to work up the nerve to face the music. After all, Barbara had broken into an old trunk—an offense that would have gotten her a tongue-lashing and a real hiding as a kid.

No, Barbara thought to herself, she definitely was not looking forward to admitting her break-and-enter into Zebulon's chest—and she was not looking forward to the endless fuss the relatives would make over the journal book. But that all paled before the formidable figure of Aunt Jo. How to get around the strong-willed old lady?

And if she did win Aunt Jo over, what then? Barbara would have to come up with tools, assistants, figure a way to pinpoint the burials and log them in . . . She grinned to herself. Politics and logistics, soothing the local potentates, scrounging up hardware and help. This was going to be just like a regular dig. It occurred to Barbara that maybe she could use some advice. Well, if Aunt Josephine cooper-ated, she might try a phone call to one of her Washington colleagues.

By the time she was out of the shower, dried off, dressed in work clothes, and had her hair in some sort of order, Barbara had decided the best way to handle Aunt Jo was head on. Time to take the bull by the horns, so to speak. Subtlety would be lost on the strong personalities around here. She glanced at the clock. 7:05. Aunt Josephine would be down in her kitchen working on breakfast by now.

Barbara picked up the journal book and nervously headed downstairs, into the big, sun-bright kitchen. The warm, clean smells of fresh, hot breakfast being made flooded the air—biscuits, flour, bacon, coffee, milk, the tang of orange juice—all mingled with the comfortable fragrance of a kitchen cleaned and polished until it shined. The gurgle of the percolator and the sizzle of the frying bacon seemed the perfect background accompaniment to it all. Aunt Josephine was standing over the kitchen table, busy with her rolling pin and biscuit cutter, vigorously making up another sheet of her buttermilk biscuits.

Aunt Josephine looked up, her dark, round face framed owlishly by her gold-rimmed glasses. "Well, come on in, child, and give a body some help here. If you're going to stand around my kitchen, I might as well get some work out of you."

Barbara almost protested, but then decided it would be good politics to follow the path of least resistance. She carefully set the journal book down on the sideboard. The spare rolling pin was in the third drawer down, as always, tidily wrapped up in its canvas rolling cloth. She pulled a mound of dough out of the mixing bowl, dredged it with flour, dusted the rolling pin, and set to work.

The fresh, warm fragrance of the dough took her back to her own childhood, to the first romantic days of her own marriage, when even making breakfast was special; to the early morning bustle she had even forgotten she missed. But this was not the time for such thoughts. She had to face that damned music.

"Aunt Josephine," she said slowly, "I think I might be in big trouble with you."

"You're never too old for that, child. What is it?"

"Well, I was up in the attic yesterday——"

"And you broke open the lock on Zebulon's chest," Josephine said matter-of-factly. "I was up there after you, to put away the Thanksgiving platter until Christmas. I could see it had been fussed with, and the lock hasp fell away in my hands when I touched it. I knew it had to be you."

"And you weren't going to say anything?"

"Well, I was plenty mad to begin with, but I got to thinking just how foolish it was to have a trunk full of memories up there, locked up and forgotten about. What's the point of having things to remember a body by if no one can remember what the remembrances are?

"Besides, heavens only knows where the key to that trunk has got to—someone was going to have to break it open sooner or later. It might as well be the family's professional grave robber." Josephine gave her great-niece one of her best stern looks for a full half second before breaking into a broad smile.

Barbara smiled back and breathed a sigh of relief. She never knew what would happen when she crossed Great-aunt Josephine. The tough old girl might decide to let you get away with it, if your motives were pure or you were on her good side. Then she would struggle valiantly to find a good reason to forgive you. But she was just as likely to turn mule-stubborn in defense of *her* way of doing things, and then—watch out. Barbara guessed that Josephine was pleased enough by the rediscovery of Zebulon's effects that she had decided to overlook the offense of burglary.

Aunt Josephine went on with her work, setting down the rolling pin, cutting the biscuits out of the dough with the biscuit cutter. "After you were so careful to put everything back the way you found it, I looked through that trunk myself, you know," she said mischievously. "There are some real heirlooms there. His glasses, the books he read. Some splendid things."

Barbara swallowed hard and set down her rolling pin. "There are more than just books he *read*, Aunt Jo." She wiped the flour off her hands, took the journal down off the sideboard, and solemnly offered it to her great-aunt.

The older woman cleaned her hands on her apron and took the leather volume. She opened it and gave a little gasp as she read the title page. She stood there, not reading further, but simply staring at the words on the page for a long time. Finally, she put the book back down, took off her apron, looked at her niece with shining eyes, and spoke with a strange little catch in her voice. "Barbara, you're going to have to tend to the rest of getting breakfast for everyone. Mind the bacon doesn't overcook. I'm going to sit and *read* this book for a bit."

Josephine picked up the book again and smiled to herself, at nothing at all.

Barbara offered up a silent cheer. If Aunt Josephine stopped their conversation to read the book, that might cost Barbara some digging daylight, but the lost time would be more than made up if it got the family matriarch on her side when it came to the question of turning spade to earth.

Josephine poured herself a good strong cup of coffee and headed out to the front porch with the journal, a very thoughtful expression on her face. Barbara busied herself in the huge kitchen, and got the last of the biscuits into the oven in time to tend to the bacon and keep it from vaporizing. About fifteen minutes later, just as she had finished putting the rolling pins and mixing bowls away, four of her cousins, each with a baby or toddler in tow, appeared through the back door. By getting cousin Shirley to agree to watch the biscuits, Barbara managed to hand off kitchen-management duty, and went outside looking for Aunt Jo.

The solid old woman sat in her rocker on the south side of the porch, the splendid morning sky framing her in pale blue. She sat reading the journal, rocking slowly, her face a study in solemn concentration, her eyes hidden behind the light reflected off the well-polished lenses of her wire-rimmed glasses.

Barbara went to her and leaned against the railing, watching her, waiting.

Finally, she closed the book and looked up with a smile, her face happy, her eyes gleaming. "He was quite a man. A very good man. Thank you for finding this."

"Aunt Jo." Barbara knelt in front of her aunt and took the journal. "I found something in here, late last night. I need to show it to you." Barbara turned to the pages that dealt with the creatures Colonel Gowrie had brought to the plantation. "Read this part, starting here."

Aunt Jo adjusted her glasses and studied the writing on the pages carefully, almost reverently, as if she was considering the full worth of each word before moving on to the next. Barbara sat back against the railing and hugged her knees up to her chest, watching her aunt's face for some sign of surprise, or bafflement, or shock, but her expression remained fixed and solemn, with only an eyebrow twitching now and again as a sign of her emotions. It was as if she were reading the holiest of holy tracts and was determined to maintain her dignity while doing so.

Finally she closed the book and looked to Barbara. "That's a very strange story, child. What on earth does it mean?"

Barbara stared off across the field, and felt a cold weight in her stomach. "I think it means that damned old Colonel Gowrie tried to import gorillas or chimps to work alongside our ancestors, and it didn't work. Then Great-Great-Granpa Zebulon remembered them as more manlike than they really were," Barbara answered, her voice hard and cool. "Does that make sense to you?"

Josephine knotted up her mouth for a moment and thought. "When I was just a young child, there were stories, the sort of thing you might tell around a campfire to throw a good thrilling scare into a body. All about wildmen lurking out by the river and in the hills, ready to gobble up bad little girls and boys. When I was a bit older, I remember Papa saying that there was something to it all, but even back when he was a boy, no one would ever talk about it."

Barbara turned back toward her great aunt. "Maybe the stories were about the creatures Zebulon saw." She almost shuddered and her voice softened. "Brrr. Can you imagine, wild gorillas wandering free around Gowrie? The poor things would be frightened out of their minds, and sick from weather they weren't used to, but they'd still scare *me*. But—Aunt Josephine—the truth behind legends isn't what I'm interested in."

"What *do* you want, child?"

This was it. The bull by the horns. Barbara felt her shoulders tense, the cold weight in her gut tighten. None of the older generations of her family had ever altogether approved of her chosen profession, and now she had to put them face to face with it. To a family of hard-edged black Southern Baptists, even to Baptists who wanted no truck with what the white fundamentalist preachers had to say, there was something clearly sacrilegious about the whole idea of digging too deep into the past. And Barbara knew only too well their attitude toward what many of them still referred to as "Evil-oution." Aunt Josephine had been teasing, mostly, when she had called Barbara a grave robber, but Barbara knew that many in the family felt she was just that, nothing better, and possibly something much worse.

It was only the Jones family's rock-ribbed, unshakeable faith in the value and dignity of education and book-learning that made Barbara socially acceptable. She was a Doctor, and Doctors were to be respected. *That* was the tack to take. "I'm a paleoanthropologist, Aunt Josephine," Barbara said, hoping the long word sounded impressive and learned. "That journal says the gorillas, the chimps, whatever they are, were buried by the crossroads. If that's true—well, it could be very important. It could say a lot about how our people were treated, how slaves were regarded. If it's true, it implies whole chapters in history—*our* history—that no one even knows about. Who traded for them? How? Was this the only place they tried it? Now, I know you won't like it, but I want to dig for them, prove it all really happened. *If* you'll give your permission."

The old woman turned and looked out toward the old burial ground, gazed out on the whitewashed marker stones turned golden ivory by the light of the rising sun. She seemed preoccupied, as if the history she held in her hands and the dead whose graves she looked upon were far more interesting than anything the present and living might offer. "I suppose those are good reasons for *you*. It might make you famous, let you announce a big science discovery. And it would be good to learn more of the history around here. But if you'd stop thinking like a fancy Washington *scientist* and started thinking like a member of the Jones family of Gowrie, you'd know *I don't want some herd of monkeys buried out there right next to my relations.* So you go right ahead and dig up your monkeys. They're too close to where our kin lie. Just clean it up when you're done, and don't bother me with it if you don't have to. I've got more important things to spend my thoughts on. Like my grandfather's journal." She reopened the book, found her place, and recommenced her reading, dismissing Barbara with a wave of her hand.

Barbara had thought *this* would be the moment she would stop being afraid. It wasn't. She felt a chill wind blow across her soul, colder than any November. She was getting close to the fear, but she was not there yet.

She suddenly realized how much she needed some advice. Without another word to Aunt Jo, she headed inside toward the phone.

Chapter Four

Barbara sat by the phone in Aunt Jo's lavender-scented old lady's bedroom, her address book at the ready, her bits of paper with her personal long-distance codes, so the call wouldn't be charged to Aunt Jo, scribbled on them, her note pad and pen handy to jot down any advice she got. But for the life of her, she could not think of whom to call.

It was not really *advice* she needed, although it would be welcome, as much as she needed a bit of hand-holding, some words of encouragement before she went off and spent time and hard-earned money on chasing an old family legend. She finally admitted to herself at least part of what was bothering her: The idea of gorilla or chimp slave-laborers dead and buried in Aunt Jo's backyard had seemed a lot more believable in the middle of a driving midnight rainstorm than it did in the clear light of day.

But that was just the problem. Who could she dare call at eight in the morning on the day after Thanksgiving to talk about such a crazy idea?

She thought first of her husband. But it was safe to say that Michael would not be at his most supportive today, after spending Thanksgiving patching up people in the ER. Besides, they were separated now, and it wasn't right to go to him for advice. Her boss, Jeffery Grossington? A kindly old man, but a very careful, conservative one. He was the one she would call if she wanted to be talked *out* of doing the dig. Besides, she would not *dare* call him at this hour, and she did not want to waste any part of her brief digging daylight waiting for what Grossington would think of as a civilized hour for the phone to ring.

By process of elimination, that left her with Rupert Maxwell. Smiling to herself, she realized he was the one she had wanted to call all along. She shared office space with Rupert and two other paleontologists at the Smithsonian. Rupert was the new kid on the block, just arrived at the Smithsonian from his previous job at UCLA. He had named their jumbled-up, overcrowded office the Diggers' Pit the day he had moved in, and the name had stuck. Rupert was that one person in every workplace who knew instinctively which rules he could safely ignore, who somehow got away with flouting the tribal laws without ever actually annoying anyone.

Barbara and Rupert had had a few long lunches commiserating over each other's divorces. Their talks had been the sort of personal discussion that was easier with a stranger in the same boat than it was with a close old friend. On the subject of unhappy personal lives, they spoke the same language. Maybe, Barbara hoped, they would also speak it when it came to work. Besides, Rupe lived his life off to one side already. He would surely lend a sympathetic ear to Barbara's off-the-wall problem.

She grabbed the handset off its cradle and dialed.

The phone rang, or more accurately gave off a small electronic *bleep*. Rupert looked up at the wall clock, noted the time, marked his place in the book he was reading, hit the PAUSE button on the VCR to freeze the action on the football game he had taped yesterday—he had bet and won money on the game and wanted to analyze the plays for future betting reference—turned down the compact-disk player that perched atop the VCR, shutting off Bartok's string quartet in mid-note—he was watching the game with the sound off—and reached around the mouse cage behind the computer—which was dormant, for once—to shut off the answering machine before it could cut into the call. Chairman Meow, snoozing atop the mouse cage, woke slightly to see what was going on, then closed his eyes again to dream of catching the mice once more. Rupert shoved the computer keyboard out of the way and pulled the phone forward, front and center. It was a crowded desk.

"Hello, Rupert Maxwell."

"Rupe? Barbara." The voice came through the miles, clear but slightly faint.

"Hey, Barb!" Rupert grinned. "Happy Turkey Day or so. But I thought you were home visiting family."

"I am, Rupe. But something's come up. I need your advice." To Rupert's ear, she sounded a bit hesitant about asking for it. "Nothing personal, this time," she added with a note of hurry in her voice. "Professional advice. Digger to digger. Hey, I didn't wake you, did I?"

"Nope," he said cheerfully. "Been up for a while, just puttering around. So talk to me. What's up?" Rupert opened a desk drawer and fished out a pen and paper. He liked to keep notes on conversations related to work. *FRIDAY 8:03 A.M. Barbara M. Re: pro question. B. sounds embarrassed.*

"Well, I found something, Rupe." She quickly told him how she had come across the journal, and what she had read in it. Rupert started listening more and more attentively, taking more and more notes, speaking only to ask an occasional question on one detail or another. He immediately noticed that she was only telling him what she had discovered, not what she was *doing* about it.

"Anyway," Barbara concluded, "what with schedules and money and whatever mood Aunt Jo gets in to change her mind, what it really comes down to is that this weekend might be my only chance to do the dig and see what's down there."

"And you've got permission to dig if you want to?" Rupert asked, doodling with his pen.

"That's right."

Rupert made a sort of harrumphing noise into the phone, tossed down the pen, and thought for a minute. "Well, it's a real interesting story," he said, in a studiously neutral tone.

"But what should I do about it?" Barbara's voice asked, sounding almost querulous over Gowrie's tinny, small-town phone lines.

Rupert knew what to say, what she needed to hear, what *he* would need to hear if the roles were reversed. But he paused once again, not sure of *how* to say it. "Look, Barb. You and I are diggers—grubbers in the dirt in search of all the old truths, walkers on the past, whatever you want to call it. Call it something grand, call it grave robbing, it's what we do. And we do it because we're *curious*, no other reason, in spite of what we tell each other about history or knowing ourselves or whatever. You know and I know you *want* to dig those old ape bones up. What else could possibly occur to you when you stumble on a story like that? What you really want to know from me is if it's worth the cost, the risk to go for it. Right?"

There was a silence on the phone line for a long moment. "Well, yes, I suppose," Barbara answered.

Rupert sighed and stretched out a long arm to scratch Chairman Meow behind the ears. "Well, you know as well as I do, you're the only one who can answer that question. But, look, you and I— we're associates, just met, not bowling buddies or best friends yet. I don't know you so well. Something's bugging you here, I can tell that, but I don't know what. So let me ask, try and save some time: You afraid of being wrong or being right?"

"Huh? Why should I be afraid of being right?" The voice on the phone sounded surprised, a little defensive.

Aha. Rupert raised his eyebrows, picked up his pencil, and began a small, tight patch of doodling on his note pad. "'Cause what it sounds like to me, to make a quick prelim dig might cost you a few hundred bucks in equipment and labor. That's cheap for knowing, one way or the other, every morning when you wake up for the rest of your life, that you did the right thing. And if I'm not getting too personal, if you take a chance and it costs more than that and you get a bit in debt—right *now*, no one else gets hurt. Take it from a fellow ex-married type—it's much safer to take chances when you're single. It's no one else's money, or time, or problem. So it's no great shakes, really, to be wrong. You'd blow your weekend making a big damn useless hole, and maybe look a bit silly in front of your relatives. Are you afraid of that?"

"Nooo. Not really. I wouldn't like it, but I could live with it," Barbara replied.

"Then," Rupert said gently, "that leaves being scared of being right. Are you?"

"I—" Rupert listened intently. He could tell, from that one syllable, that she had been ready with a quick, unthoughtful "No." But now she was pausing, reconsidering.

"Barbara," he said quietly, "are you really prepared for the grand fuss and scare that digging up gorillas imported for slaves will produce? Especially if they're dug up by a black woman? This won't be some piddly little scientific thing, a few huffy letters in *Nature*. This could raise six kinds of hell and get every newspaper and television station in the world down on your neck. I was small-time controversial at UCLA, you know. Sometimes I wonder if the real reason I came back East was to escape the heat. Being at the storm center can get rough. You *ought* to be afraid of it. Are you?"

"Hell, of course I am!" she almost shouted back. "Who wouldn't be?"

"Everybody *should* be afraid of it. You shouldn't go into it lightly. Good. Then all you have to ask yourself is: Are you more afraid of not knowing the truth about this wonderful story for the rest of your life, or more afraid of handling the truth for the rest of your life?"

This time the silence on the phone lasted much longer. Finally there came a sigh, half resignation, half happy release. "Rupert," Barbara said, "For a pain-in-the-neck know-it-all, you sure are a smart guy. I gotta go."

"Just keep me posted, Doctor. That's all I ask."

They said their good-byes and Rupert hung up. He sat there and stared at the phone for a long moment, as if it held all the answers. Then he leaned forward in his chair, pulled a manila folder out of the desk, labeled it MARCHANDO DIG, and put his notes of the conversation in it. If anything came of Gowrie, he'd already have a start on a record of it.

"Let's hope that file gets much thicker," he said to the cat, who purred back in reply. One of the mice started to climb up the bars of the cage, and the Chairman took a hopeful but unsuccessful swat at it.

Rupert reached out a hand to switch his various machines on and get back to what he had been doing, but suddenly the football game, the music, and the book seemed a lot less interesting.

He looked around his too-quiet efficiency apartment, as crowded and tightly packed and necessarily neat as a submarine. He suddenly wished he could be down in Gowrie. Down where the action was.

Barbara hung up at her end, and felt much better. Yes, she was still afraid, but at least she knew of *what*. There was a strange, edgy thrill to seeing the danger clearly, heading straight for her from a far horizon, rather than lurking in shadows. Now, at least, she knew what she was up against.

She also knew she needed help. Digging a real excavation, even a little prelim job, was no job to tackle single-handed. So who around here could she draft? Who around here would be any use at all?

Livingston. Livingston Jones was the one relative who could be of even the slightest help. She headed back downstairs and started hunting for him. By now it was 8:15 and the various members of the family were starting to filter downstairs in force, but no sign of Liv yet.

Barbara swore to herself. She needed time to think, to plan, but she was already suffering from the paleontologist's greatest fear—losing the light. The days in late November were short enough at best, and an appreciable fraction of today's working light was already gone—and she only had today and Saturday, and whatever tiny sliver of work she could get out of Sunday before it would be time to fly back. She knew that she could *never* get official permission to mount a dig on Smithsonian time—who outside the family would believe a nutty story based on the hundred-year-old report of an old man's recollections, set down decades after the event?

It could be months or years before she had this chance again, and by then Great-aunt Josephine could have changed her mind, and whatever bones there were left would be decaying even further all the while. This brief Thanksgiving weekend was definitely the magic moment, and Barbara did not want to waste a second of it.

She tried the porch, the living room, and the dining room before getting smart and checking for Livingston in the kitchen. Bingo. There he was, digging into the bacon and scooping up big mouthfuls of scrambled eggs someone had cooked up. In the half an hour or so she had been gone, the kitchen had lost its air of quiet, domestic peace. It was a cheery madhouse now, with too many people cooking, laughing, talking, drinking coffee. The children were racing around, the littlest ones seemingly competing with each other to see who could put the largest fraction of breakfast on their faces instead of in their mouths. The sound of conversation now and again swelled up to a dull roar for a moment as half a dozen people raised their voices to be heard over each other, then faded away as fast as it had started once everyone talking had got his or her point across.

Barbara launched herself into the sea of bodies, steered herself in next to Livingston, and managed to find a seat next to him. "Hey, Liv, how's it going?"

She had caught him with a mouthful of food, and he smiled and nodded at her in lieu of answering. She considered her younger cousin for a moment, sizing him up before making her sales pitch. He was twenty-three, and youthful-looking even for that age. He was big—six foot three, with a massive body, a wall of muscle. He was wearing a short-sleeved pullover shirt that threatened to burst at every seam, accentuating a solid, powerful body that didn't need any accentuating. He looked as if he should have been playing ball somewhere. In fact, Liv had ridden a football scholarship to Ole Miss and played left tackle well enough to scare off plenty of guards.

Back when Liv got the scholarship, Barbara had been concerned. Suppose he focused so hard on football that he ended up out of college when his five years of football eligibility were up, with a make-work degree in basket weaving—or maybe no degree at all? Suppose he was equipped to do nothing but play football, one of ten or twelve thousand graduating college players chasing the three or four hundred available jobs as pro ball players? Too many young men, especially black young men, were left fighting for too few football jobs—football jobs that quickly left most of the players out on the street with bad knees and no job skills after only a few years anyway. And left tackles didn't get much glory.

Maybe it was because of a stats course Barbara had urged him to take freshman year, but in any event, Liv had figured out the odds against him and avoided the football trap. He had played hard, but never so hard that it got in the way of his major in biochemistry. He had graduated the summer before, and now was working at some sort of part-time job, waiting for his master's degree program at the University of North Carolina to start up in January. He was going to do okay.

But at the moment, he could undoubtedly do with a few bucks. He finished his food and pushed his plate back with one massive hand as he hauled in his coffee mug with the other, every movement setting massive muscles to rippling in his arms and under his shirt. "So, Barb," he said. "Haven't really had a chance to talk with you this time around. What's up?"

"Plenty, Liv. Grab a refill on your coffee and come outside where it's quiet. I need to talk with you."

He shrugged. "Sure. Just let me hack through this crowd to the percolator. You want one?"

"Yeah, cream, no sugar."

"Okay, see you on the back porch in a minute."

▼◆▼

A few minutes later they were settled in on the porch swing. Livingston leaned his feet up on the porch railing and sighed contentedly. It was a good morning, and it was nice to have a private visit with Barb. She had always been one of his favorite cousins. "So what's the situation?" he asked.

"Liv, I've got a business proposition for you. I've stumbled across old Grandpa Zebulon's diary. Aunt Jo's around the other side of the house right now, on the front porch, reading it. It'll be passed around all day, I guarantee that. But in it, there's a mention of something really weird being buried on the family property here. I want to excavate, now, this weekend, and I need some help from someone who has some sense. It'll probably suck up most of the weekend, but I'll pay eight bucks an hour."

Livingston looked at his cousin and thought for a minute. "Aunt Josephine says okay?"

"Yup."

"Then I'm in. I could use the bread. What are we digging for?"

"Gorillas."

Liv raised his eyebrows and tilted his head to one side. "Okay, that's different." That was the nice thing about the Yankees—the Northerners—in the family, he thought. They could come up with a ring-tailed doozy of a story, like digging for gorillas, and at least you knew they were for real. The Southerners were another kettle of fish. If one of *them* had handed him that story, he'd be waiting for the punch line right now. But Barbara was for real. Nuts, maybe, but for real.

"Okay, you're on the payroll—and on the clock." Barbara stood up and pulled her wallet out of her back pocket. Livingston could see how she seemed suddenly pleased to be in charge, in command of a team, even if it only had one member. She always had loved running things, even back when he was the little kid and she was the bossy teenager. "Here's my American Express card," she said. "We'll need some stuff." She dug a crumpled piece of scrap paper and a pen out of her pockets and handed them to Livingston. "Here, you'd better make a list. Hit the Radio Shack in Gowrie and come back with the best metal detector they've got."

"*Metal* detector?"

"These gorillas are in caskets."

"Now that's *real* different." Maybe, Livingston thought, North-erners knew how to tell a tall tale too.

"Well, they're in packing cases, anyway," Barbara conceded. "I hope with nails and hinges. If they were put together with wooden pegs, we'll have to think of something else. Also, hit Balmer's Drugs and pick up four or five rolls of Kodachrome. Thirty-six exposure, ASA 64 if they have it, but ASA 25 will do. Get me some graph paper and a clipboard too. Then stop at Higgins' Hardware and grab a compass—the kind for finding north, not for drawing circles—and a tape measure, the longer the better—and marked in metric if they have one. Also a meter stick—I'll settle for a yardstick. And some string and tomato stakes."

"This is starting to go past interesting to weird. All this on the level, Barb? I mean, I'm not going to end up at the end of this in some crazy practical joke, am I?"

Barbara laughed. "No, 'fraid not. That's all just stuff for digging a real professional-style hole."

Livingston shook his head. Well, it was her money he'd be spend-ing. "Okay, boss. What will you be doing while I'm on the scavenger hunt?"

"Surveying the site. Now go. The stores should be open by the time you get into town."

Livingston gulped down the last of his coffee, fished his car keys out of his pocket, gave Barbara a mock salute, and got moving.

▼◆▼

Barbara went back to her room and grabbed her camera bag and tripod, brought along to take a group portrait of the family. She rooted around in her oversize pocketbook until she found a serviceable note-book and pencil, feeling happy and excited, at the start of doing what she did best. Just before she left the room she looked out the window at the kids who were back playing in the yard, and suddenly found herself thinking about her first dig, so many years ago. Back when she was twelve years old . . . .

It all began one spring with her pet hamster, a rather surly brown-and-tan rodent by the name of Fuzzball. The foolish little thing es-caped from its cage one day while Barbara was at school, and the cat caught it and killed it. Her mother didn't want her child to see the broken little body, and by the time Barbara got home from school, her mother had gotten the tiny corpse away from the cat and had unceremoniously thrown it in the trash can out back.

If her mother had hoped an invisible corpse would ease Barbara's feelings, she was mistaken. Barbara was not only heartbroken at the death of Fuzzball and shocked at the cat's homicide, but infuriated that her own mother could just throw Fuzzball away.

Barbara insisted on giving Fuzzball a decent burial. Her mother, who had never much liked hamsters, and who had wasted the entire morning chasing a live hamster around the house and then lost the afternoon trying to pry a dead one out of the cat's mouth, was exasperated enough to do whatever would give her some peace and quiet. She dug the hamster out of the trash, wrapped it in tissue, put it in a shoebox, and presented it to Barbara.

Barbara, with a little girl's ghoulish delight in the theater of it all, dug a hole in the little plot of untended ground behind the back garden, put the box in it, buried it, put a cross made out of two popsicle sticks over it, and said a prayer over the tiny grave. Then she laid a few dandelions on the little hump of earth, and went inside to dinner. By the next morning she had all but forgotten Fuzzball. She didn't think of him for months. Summer vacation came and went.

The following fall, Barbara returned to school and one fine day got a book on archeology out of the library. Its title was something like *How We Know About Prehistoric Man.* She picked it because of the scary-looking skull on the cover, next to the pickaxe and shovel. As soon as her father tucked her into bed that night, she dug out her flashlight, burrowed under the covers, and began reading all about the famous scientists who dug up the bones full of secrets. Lying with her head buried under the covers, she read by the weak and flickering yellow gleam of dying flashlight batteries, all about the grand, romantic discoveries the great diggers had made. Her thoughts inevitably returned to the dead hamster buried under the brown earth of her own backyard.

In her mind's eye blossomed the image of that tiny grave, a smooth, rounded hump of earth, with no weed or blade of grass growing on it. She imagined the popsicle-stick cross still new and perfect, the pencilled inscription on it absolutely legible. She imagined the hamster's earthly remains, and his intact, white-polished skeleton safe under the sleeping earth. She saw him there, sheltered from the elements by the shoebox, every impossibly tiny bone in place, gently pillowed in Kleenex, the minute bones of his forepaws folded on his chest, his gleaming skull grinning into the darkness of the grave. It was a perfect, compelling vision, and Barbara had to struggle with her imagination's tendency to put in little ear-bones and whisker-bones, too.

The next morning was Saturday. She dressed and ate breakfast in a hurry and rushed to the garage for a trowel, then to the rear of the back garden to dig up her prize, just like a real archaeologist—only to discover there was not the slightest trace of the grave. By thinking very hard, Barbara could just about remember roughly how far from the back fence and the dogwood tree she had buried the box, but there was no smooth mound of peaceful earth there, just a wide, weedy patch of mulch and dirt.

She made her best guess as to where she had buried Fuzzball, and dug twice as deep as she recalled making the grave months before. There was nothing there. She dug another hole a little farther left. Nothing. She tried digging farther to the right, then closer to the fence, then closer to the house. Nothing. Maybe she had missed the grave altogether in the areas of ground between her excavations. She traded in her trowel for a full-size shovel that was far too big for her and merged all her holes into one huge, sloppy pit. Her hands were getting sore, and swelling with huge blisters.

By that time, she had churned up such a huge swath of ground that it was impossible to tell where one hole started or ended, or where the piles of dirt lay atop undisturbed earth. She surrendered to a fierce grumbling in her stomach, and retreated to the house for lunch—after first muddying the bathroom sink with the first layers of dirt off her face and arms. Perhaps recognizing the gleam in her daughter's eye, her mother allowed Barbara to go back to her searching after eating.

The search for Fuzzball was not a game anymore, but a challenge, a quest. Barbara, faced with the daunting, cratered mess that had been a little strip of ignored waste ground that morning, forced herself to sit down and *think*. She fought the temptation to pitch back into digging wildly. By now she was sure she *must* have dug in the right spot. How had the body vanished? What could have happened?

Dirt was a lot messier, a lot damper, a lot *dirtier*—and a lot more alive—than she had imagined. The body could have simply rotted away altogether, or been gobbled up by the bugs and worms and creepers scuttling to escape the disturbance her excavation had made in their world. Or perhaps a larger animal—a possum or raccoon or a dog—had nosed out Fuzzball the same night she had buried him and dug him up for a quick snack. Maybe her father or mother had jumbled things up with some forgotten gardening chore in the intervening months, spading up the dead rodent in the act of putting some extra topsoil on the tomatoes. The shoe box would have been no protection: one good rain would have collapsed it, and it would have quickly rotted away.

Or maybe, Barbara realized, she herself had dug up Fuzzball hours before without recognizing his few tiny, muddy-brown slivers of bone for what they were. There was not and could not be anything clean and ivory-white in this sea of brown. She could have reburied his bones as she threw her dug-up dirt to one side, trod them down and crushed them to nothing, then dug them up again when she started a new hole. She could be staring right at his invisibly small remains in the churned-up heaps of dirt in front of her.

She looked over the huge mounds of dirt she had thrown up, and realized that she would need not a shovel, not a trowel, but a set of tweezers and a magnifying glass to sift through it all carefully enough to locate whatever bones were left to find. A squirrel scampered past along the back fence, and Barbara suddenly realized that squirrel bones had to go somewhere when *they* died. In all probability, there were dozens and dozens of small animal bones in this one patch of earth. Even if she did find *some* bones, she wouldn't have the slightest idea whether they belonged to Fuzzball, or a squirrel, or a chipmunk, or a bird.

She sighed, threw her shovel back down, and trailed disconsolately back into the house—only to be sent out by her mother to fill the holes back in and put her tools away properly.

She never found the slightest sign of the hamster's grave.

That failure was a pivotal moment for her, the event that marked her, sparked her interest, told her what she wanted to be.

In some strange way, she felt as if she were *still* looking for that silly rodent's body. The small mystery of its disappearance was her first attempt to peer into the ground and the past. It was the first stage of her quest, the first clue that led her down the trail she was still on, tracking the endless mystery of life and its history, the great questions of how and why humanity, and life, and the world itself, were here.

As an adult, she had often wondered what would have happened if she *had* found Fuzzball, if some series of chances had mummified his body, had hidden it from scavengers and insects, had led her to dig in the right place to find the grisly little souvenir. It was altogether possible that success, digging up such a smelly and grotesque little carcass would have disgusted her, made her throw the little body into the leaves, run away to wash the cooties off and forget all about digging up yucky things from the ground. Or maybe such an easy win would have bored her, and she would have gone on to find some other, seemingly greater challenge. Certainly success would not have inspired her to go back to the library and get out better books on paleontology and archaeology. Success would not have goaded her into asking her science teacher how bones vanished, how fossils were born, how to tell one bone from another; would not have led her to learn more than her teacher knew and go in search of more knowledge; would certainly never have pointed her toward archaeology and anthropology as a career, a life. The challenge of failure, the fascination of a whole little body being magically swallowed up by the earth, was what drove her on. Until the magic died out of it, she would never turn back.

She had once held a three-million-year-old skull in her hand, had seen the marks left on the fossilized bones by the folds and convolutions of the long-vanished brain, had seen the seat of a mind that had smelled, looked, touched, tasted, listened, perhaps even *thought* thirty thousand centuries before. She had peered through a microscope at the marks on ancient hominid teeth and learned how to read them, and so had known what the creature had eaten all the endless years before. She had made the pilgrimage to Laetoli, seen the upright, bipedal footprints left in the sands of time by gracefully-striding creatures two million years before their distant relations would call themselves *Homo sapiens*.

Such magic would never, could never, die.

Chapter Five

If the magic had started for Barbara with the Fuzzball dig, so had the lessons. Site survey, site preparation, careful record keeping, designing a precise grid-location system so every artifact could be precisely positioned relative to a prominent landmark, selection of a dump site for the overburden—the dirt removed to get at the study-objects—to allow for convenient sifting if need be; all of this required careful thought. Without planning and record keeping, a dig in *this* backyard would be no more professional than the dig in that other backyard, so long ago.

Barbara stopped in the still-crowded kitchen for another cup of coffee and a yardstick. Then she left the house and walked the few hundred yards to the entrance of the burial ground. It was surrounded by a carefully tended picket fence, long and low, with a wide entrance made of two gatepieces hinged to swing open in the center. A worn gravel road led from the burial ground's entrance to what had once been the plantation's main internal road. It had led from the public highway around the main house and then to the working buildings, the storage rooms, stables, the blacksmith's forge, the plantation's depot for arriving goods and departing cotton.

None of those buildings survived, but Barbara knew where they all had been. As a child, she had many times joined her cousins in scrambling around the slumped-over foundations, searching for old horseshoes and other bits of ancient ironmongery. Now the plantation road was merely a long driveway, paved over in dusty, aging asphalt, that terminated in a two-car garage, with a large garden shed set down next to the garage some years ago. A line of cars from half a dozen states were parked along the plantation road at the moment, relatives having cautiously pulled off the asphalt onto the soft, narrow, gravelly shoulder. Fortunately, the line of cars began at the front of the main house and worked its way back to the county road. None of them were blocking the excavation area. Barbara was eager to avoid explanations as long as possible. She didn't feel like going through a big involved song and dance just to get Uncle Clem to move his Buick.

Barbara crouched down by the side of the present crossroads, sipped at her coffee, and thought. The gorillas had in theory been buried at the crossroads, at the point where the plantation road met the path to the burial ground. She had to determine the exact burial sites from the clues in Zebulon's journal, and from her reading of the land.

The gravel road down from the burial ground was only a hundred meters or so long, and it ran straight as an arrow. Barbara smiled at herself. She was thinking in scientific meters already, instead of civilian feet and yards. Translating between the two systems was an automatic reflex for most American workers in the sciences.

Though the burial ground road was straight, the old plantation road curved here and there, meandering over its leisurely present-day route from the house to the garage.

That was the tricky part. Small country lanes and roads have a habit of moving around, shifting their beds in much the same way a river does, moving to one side for a rock or a tree or a building that might not be there ten or twenty or a hundred years later, the next time the road was rebuilt. A road might develop gullies or potholes, forcing traffic to shift left or right in a temporary move that might accidentally become permanent as erosion washed the gully out further. A flash flood might wash the road out altogether, to be replaced in more or less the same place, if at all. Then—as was the case here—a casual modern-day road builder might simply slop some asphalt on the beaten-down gravel, effectively sealing over many of the clues as to how the road had evolved, until erosion began its patient gnawing at the edges of the asphalt, and the newest road slowly sank into the old, beaten down and punished by the weight of traffic.

The gravel road from the burial ground was strictly the shortest distance between two points and nothing else. It was too short, too straight, to have shifted much. Clearly, then, Barbara's first task lay in figuring out where the plantation road had been in antebellum days. Then she could zero in on the crossroads of the past and know where to dig.

She set her half-full coffee cup on the ground by the edge of the asphalt and stepped out onto the low crown of the road. She laid her aunt's kitchen yardstick athwart the plantation road at the present crossroads, dug out her camera and tripod, and spent twenty minutes carefully photographing the undisturbed site from a half dozen angles, thoroughly describing each photo in her notebook. She finished off her remaining stock of film.

Next step: ground survey. Read the earth and see what it had to say. But the grass was overgrown, making it harder to read the ground. There was an oversized rider mower in the garden shed.

▼◆▼

When Livingston arrived an hour or so later, slowly threading his car past the line of visiting relatives' cars parked on the side of the narrow plantation road, his cousin Barbara was just about finished with the mower. An area about the size of a baseball diamond was cut down to a pathetic stubble less than an inch high. The ground that had looked so smooth and level when hidden by the grass was revealed as rough and hummocky, much littered with road gravel, broken twigs, and other debris. It was a quick-and-dirty mowing job, with some narrow strips of grass simply trampled down or missed altogether. Barbara was by the garden shed, emptying the mower's grass-catcher into the garden compost heap—for the fourth or fifth time, judging from the heaps of cuttings. Livingston parked his near-antique '73 Dodge by the shed, got out, took his purchases from the back seat, and set them on the rear deck of the car.

Barbara dusted off her hands and came over. "Welcome back, partner. Just about ready for you. Get everything?"

"Sure did, Barb. But you won't like it when that American Express bill hits."

"That's tomorrow's problem. Let's see the haul." Livingston extracted the metal detector and shoved the batteries into it. Barbara took it from him and ran it over the grass by the shed until it started beeping. She bent down, scrabbled in the grass, and produced an old bottle cap. "Okay, that works." She walked back to the car and checked the rest of the bags. "Film, notebooks, string, compass. Even a metric tape measure. Good. Okay, let's get to work."

They found a good-sized hammer, a wheelbarrow, shovels and trowels, dumped everything into the barrow, and wheeled it over to what cousin Barbara was already calling "the site." Livingston thought they would be getting right to it with some spade work, and was relieved to learn that evil moment was to be put off for a bit. Barbara explained briefly to him how a road could shift, and how the first order of business was finding the line of the old plantation road. So he relaxed at the edge of the cleared area, sitting on the upended wheelbarrow, happy to be getting paid by the hour, while she walked over every square inch of the ground, rarely taking more than one step at a time, frequently crouching down to examine a bit of stone or a handful of pebbles, scribbling down innumerable notes.

Livingston watched her as she worked, and got the distinct feeling that she had forgotten him altogether. There was something almost otherworldly in her concentration, as if she was looking at a place that was not there anymore, a place no one else could see. With a start, he realized that was precisely her job description. He watched more intently, wondering what the rocks and clay and topsoil of Mississippi told her that was hidden from him. He started to follow her about, a pace or two behind, trying to see what it was she saw.

She looked behind herself suddenly, realizing he was there. She smiled, and her face lit up with the light of some special secret inside. "Careful, Liv. You're walking on the past." She knelt abruptly and patted the ground with the flat of her hand. "The past is buried right here, if you know how to read it. All this dirt *came* from somewhere. The pebbles and rocks were part of mountains; the soil itself used to be trees and animals and air and rain, churned up and recycled again and again. The bones of creatures no human has ever seen, from a hundred million years ago, are beneath our feet somewhere, locked up in sediments that were formed before this continent was here."

There was a long pause, and Barbara seemed to be staring *into* the ground, through soil and rocks and strata made clear as glass, to look upon the ultimate secrets of yesteryear.

As last she shook herself, stood up, and smiled again, this time in embarrassment. "I'm sorry. It's just that I get so focused, so involved, that I forge t everything." With a visible effort, she brought herself back to the job at hand. "Listen, load up the camera and photograph the whole area. I shot the whole site before it was mowed, and I might as well have a record of what it looks like now. What I'm looking for is the shape of the land—where the road is in relation to the burial ground and the house, that sort of thing. Grab a notebook and write down a description of each shot."

Livingston got busy with the camera, and shot most of a roll. He felt as if he had seen something meant to be unknown, hidden from view under the sheltering mantle of professional decorum. Barbara must be pretty spooked to open up that way. He got on with his picture taking.

Now and again, Barbara would call him over to snap one little patch of gravel that looked like all the others to him. She was very excited to discover a little washout—evidence, so she said, of an intermittent stream that had run alongside the present road some years before. She traced the stream bed, wholly invisible to his eyes, right through the length of the site, and carefully noted its location in a sketch map she was making.

Finally, she seemed satisfied and put away her notebook. "Okay, Liv, let's break out the metal detector." He got it from the barrow and handed it over. She started working the detector at one edge of the site, and Livingston followed behind. Almost immediately, she got a strike. She pulled her trowel out of her hip pocket and dug up an old masonry nail.

Livingston bent down eagerly. "That it? You found it already?"

Barbara didn't answer. Instead, she shoved the nail in her pocket, stood up, and started again with the detector. She got another immediate find, this time an old bolt. In short order she had dug up a broken hinge, two more nails, a crumbled piece of wire, and a rusty tin can, all from a few square meters. She shut off the detector, squatted back on her haunches, and sighed. "I was afraid of this," she said. "Junk. J-U-N-K junk. The whole topsoil is riddled with whatever fell off the cart going past for the last hundred and fifty years. I've got the metal detector set at minimum sensitivity as it is. We'll never find the caskets with all this garbage over top of them."

Livingston groaned to himself. She was going to want all the topsoil scraped off, that was next. He very definitely didn't want to dig a hole eight inches deep and a hundred yards across. He thought fast. "Look, Barb. Can we get rid of it with the rider-mower? I thought I saw some sort of tiller attachment, and maybe we could rig up some sort of drag-plow for it."

Her face brightened. She didn't think removing topsoil was fun either. "Hey, good thinking. Let's get to it."

They actually got halfway to the garden shed before Barbara remembered all her early lessons about being overeager. "Wait a second, Liv. We're about to make more work for ourselves."

"Huh? What do you mean?"

"I've got a space maybe thirty meters on a side mowed down over there. That's nine hundred square meters of topsoil, say 10 centimeters thick, to clear off. Do *you* want to move 90 cubic meters of dirt, even using a jury-rig plow?"

"Ah." Livingston had done some landscaping work as a high school kid. His muscles started to ache in advance. "So what do we do?"

"We find the old crossroads point *first*, and just clear the area immediately around it."

She turned around and led him back to the site. Consulting her sketch map, she relocated a part of the old washout she had found before. She stood in the middle of the broad, shallow depression and turned to her cousin. "Okay, Liv, my guess is that *this* is the old road."

"C'mon, Barb," Livingston protested. "This is a stream bed. You said so yourself."

"Yeah, but how did it get to be one? Where's it running from? The land here is as flat as a pancake. I figure that the road was here—just a dirt road at the time, of course—and the wheel traffic wore down the ground level, scraped away the topsoil. Then the rains would come and the waters would funnel down to the lowest ground. A flood or two, erosion, and the road keeps sinking lower and lower. Happens all the time. When they first paved the road, maybe fifty years ago, by the looks of things, they said the hell with it and moved the roadway over twenty feet or so. Over the years, with no more traffic to keep it worn down, the gullied-out road filled itself back in. Most of it is already filled in completely. That all make sense?"

"Yeah, okay, I get it," Livingston said, his voice betraying a hint of excitement. He was getting caught up in the mystery-solving, the detective work of the job. "But let me guess. We can't see where the old dirt road crossed the path to the slaves' burial ground because they—I guess *we*—kept the path in repair, filled in the washouts as they happened. Right?"

Barbara grinned, squinting a bit. "Right. We'll make an archaeologist out of you yet."

"So what we've got to do is locate every inch of the washout we can to get the best fix we can on the crossroads, *then* start scratching away the topsoil," Livingston said.

"Go to the head of the class. So you grab a bunch of those tomato stakes and walk the washout south of the burial ground path. Mark both sides of the washout every two or three meters or so, every place you see it. I'll do the same to the north side."

Livingston went to the wheelbarrow and collected an armload of the tomato stakes, then walked to the far end of the site and started searching for the faint marks, the slight depression in the earth that betrayed the old course of the road.

At first, he couldn't see a thing, and was frustrated to look up and see Barbara pounding stake after stake. College football left a man with a real competitive streak, and falling behind goaded him to greater efforts. Finally, he spotted a flattened little notch in the earth about in line with the stakes his cousin was driving, and drove home one of his own. He bent low over the close-cropped grass and studied the earth. With a little grunt of triumph, he spotted the other side of the washout, and drove in a second marker.

Suddenly, his eye seemed to know what to look for, and he was reading the ground, pounding in stake after stake. Even as he spotted another trace of the road, he marveled that *he* was seeing Barbara's lost world, the signs of ways people had lived before his grandmother was born. He was catching the same bug Barbara had caught twenty years before, in search of a vanished hamster.

Finally, the last of the stakes that could be set was pounded in. Barbara examined his work and was basically approving, though she adjusted the position of two stakes slightly. She drew the stakes-points into her rough sketch map, and then photographed the entire area yet again.

Livingston was getting a bit tired of such relentlessly methodical procedure. "Barb, why are you working so hard to document all this? What's the point of taking three pictures of everything?"

Barbara picked up the tripod and moved it to a new position, Livingston trailing behind. She thought for a moment and spoke. "Liv, suppose you thought you were going to break the class record for, say, the fifty-yard dash—run it a half-second faster than anyone else in your school that year. A coach and a pal with stopwatches would be enough. Everyone could accept that. But suppose you were a complete unknown in track, just one guy out of thousands, and thought you might take *three* seconds off the all-time world record. Would two guys with stop-watches do it? Would the *Guinness Book of World Records* or *Sports Illustrated* settle for that?"

"Hell no. There were a couple of guys chasing *state* track records back at Ole Miss. They arranged to have the attempts filmed, got the watches calibrated, and made sure the judges were impartial."

"Okay, then. If there really *are* gorillas buried here, I'm going to turn a lot of American history upside down. I want every step of the effort nailed down. I don't want anyone to say that there was any way I could have faked it, or gotten it wrong, or spoiled the evidence. So let me take my pictures."

Livingston smiled. "I get the point. Tell you what, though. It's getting kinda warm. I'm gonna see if I can scare up some lemonade or something. You want anything?"

"How 'bout a Diet Coke?" Barbara said absently as she peered through the viewfinder and fiddled with the focus.

"Right." Livingston turned and headed back to the house.

He came back about ten minutes later, drinks in hand. "Took me a while to escape," he said. "The whole mob is gathered around Aunt Josephine, listening to her read aloud from that journal you found. They all wanted to know what you were up to, and Aunt Josephine skipped ahead and read the passage you showed her this morning. I think we'll have an audience in a minute."

Barbara shook her head. "Wonderful. Nothing I like better than sidewalk superintendents. C'mon, let's get back to it while we still can. I've sketched in all the markers. If you sort of connect the dots and extend the line from the places you can still see the washout, it looks as if the old road curved a bit, sort of looped a little bit closer to the burial site than the present one does. Grab a few more stakes, will you?"

They walked down the present-day plantation road to the point where it crossed the burial-ground road. "Okay, partner," she said cheerfully. "Now we work from the sketch map and the line of the old road we've staked out and figure out where it crossed this path. Wish I had a surveyor's transit, but I think I can manage on eyeballs.

Gimme one of those stakes." She stared back along the lines of stakes running north and south, muttering to herself, tracing the old roadline. She took the stake and walked to the closest south-side stake, then backed up the way she had come, dragging a stake in the dirt. She marked her line across the burial-ground path and met up neatly with the closest stake on the north side, then repeated the performance with the line of stakes marking the other edge of the old washout road. She had now, she hoped, relocated the shifted landmark of the crossroads, under which the gorillas were supposedly buried. "Grab the tape measure, Liv," she said. They used the measure, four more stakes, and a few tricks in geometry to mark out a square exactly eight meters on a side, with the theoretical fossil crossroads at its center. "That's it, Liv. Our prime search area. *Now* let's get that rider mower out here and see if we can't rig up some sort of bulldozer blade."

Either Aunt Josephine had an altogether exaggerated fear of southern Mississippi snowstorms, or the mower salesman was most persuasive, but they didn't have to jury-rig anything. Put neatly away in the rear of the garage was a perfectly good, purpose-made, never-been used 'dozer blade attachment for the mower. In twenty minutes, they had the old crossroads scraped clean of the top ten centimeters of soil, and, hopefully, clear of most of the casual litter that would jam the metal detector.

Aunt Josephine, sitting on the far side of the wraparound porch from Barbara's work site, surrounded by a crowd of relatives listening to her read from the journal, was growing more and more restive. For starters, she had been sitting in one place, reading to herself or aloud, for hours now, and she was an active, busy person. Her excitement over finding the treasure trove in the attic was expressing itself in the form of nervous energy. She felt a great need to bustle, to *do* things, not so much for the sake of doing them, but more as a way of soothing herself. Not only that, but she had gotten a constant stream of reports from some of the teenagers who had wandered over to watch Barbara and Livingston at work. She could hear the growl of her brand-new power mower again. In point of plain fact, she was getting a bit worried about just how big a hole that fool girl Barbara was fixing to dig. It sounded like they'd be halfway to putting in a swimming pool by the time it was all over. It was high time she got over there and took a look for herself.

With a start, she realized she had been reading aloud without hearing the words herself for a page and a half. The same thing had happened back in her teaching days, when she was preoccupied. That settled it. She closed the book, looked up, and spotted someone to whom she could give an order. "Leon, take over, honey. My voice is getting tired and I need a stretch."

She handed her middle-aged nephew the book and stood up. Taking a shortcut through the interior of the house, she passed through the front parlor room where a squad of the more sentimental aunts was going over the other things—the bedside library, the clothes, the glasses—that Barbara had found in the trunk. Aunt Josephine made her way into the foyer and back outside. She shielded her eyes and peered out across the yard.

There the two of them were, crouched in the middle of a huge patch bare dirt that sat like the squared-off bulls-eye in the center of an even larger patch of ground that had been mowed—no, *shaved*, within an inch of its life. Lord help us all, Josephine thought, this yard was *never* going to look the same again. Now the two of them seemed to be spooling out lengths of string across the plowed patch, working carefully with a tape measure as they paid out the taut lengths of twine. She shook her head and headed out across the lawn. She stalked over to the two kneeling figures, and glared down at them. "And just what are the two of you doing *now*, as if you haven't done enough damage already?" she asked in her best school-marm voice.

Livingston looked up, his voice bubbling with enthusiasm. "Setting up a reference grid, Aunt Josephine." He pointed to the stakes at the corners and along the sides of the plowed-up area. "Those are exactly a meter apart. We run these lines from one side to the other, ten centimeters off the ground, and we can get an exact grid reference on anything we dig up."

"You two aren't planning to dig up this whole yard, are you?" Josephine asked, getting a bit alarmed.

"I sure hope not," Barbara answered. She looked up from her notebook and grinned. There was a big smudge of dirt on her nose and another on her forehead, but she didn't seem to notice. "We've got a metal detector that should let us zero in on the caskets, if they are still here. We're just about ready to get to work with it."

"Hmmph. I see. Well, before you do one more thing to my poor side yard, Livingston Jones, you run and fetch me a chair. I'm going to set right here and keep an eye on you two before you put a whole underground subway in here."

Livingston stood up and brushed the worst of the dust off his trousers. "Yes, ma'am," he said, and got going.

Livingston felt a distinct sense of relief as he headed toward the house. Aunt Jo was putting up with them. The *words* might sound a bit severe, but Livingston had caught the slight tone of indulgence in Aunt Jo's voice. It was the voice she had used back when he was a kid visiting during summer vacation, when she had caught him reading a *worthwhile* book after bedtime. When he had been caught with a comic book, there was hell to pay.

He found an unused garden chair on the porch, but before he could make his escape, Barbara's mother captured him and demanded to know what was going on. He confessed that they were getting to the interesting part.

The result, of course, was that a whole parade of aunts and uncles and children and parents were soon on their way to the site, carrying chairs and parasols and cool drinks, settling down to watch Livingston and Barbara at work, peppering them with questions, making jokes, then wandering off to watch a frisbee tournament or a pick-up football game between the younger set, or check on the progress of the Big Game blaring from the sitting room television, then wandering back to ask the same questions and make the same jokes. The dig quickly turned into the focal point of a family carnival.

Barbara looked up from her work and suddenly realized just how many of her relatives had gathered around. It was all too familiar to Barbara, though she would never dare say so to anyone here. At every dig she had ever been on, the locals had wandered in to make a nuisance of themselves.

Every anthropologist knows that all groups of humans have words, idioms, phrases, contexts, that identify members of the group as the insiders, the true people—and that there is always a second set of words and ideas that define the outsider as something lesser, foreign, foolish, dangerous, ignorant. It held true even for the cosmopolitan, egalitarian world of the paleoanthropologists, where half the greatest names were not formally trained in their craft, where the very nature of the work absolutely forced one to know that all humans are one kind, the same marvelous breed the world over, that all men and women are the same in their uniqueness within the kingdom of life. Even the paleoanthropologists had the names—for them, it was the "diggers" versus the "locals."

Barbara remembered the Spanish Neanderthal caves where the local Basque separatists had popped up. At first, they apparently were concerned that the diggers were with the *Guardia Civil* searching the caves for weapons caches. They had stayed on as self-appointed guards against no known threat—they themselves being one of the primary dangers of being in the region, getting the locally-hired diggers, and some of the foreigners, drunk on the local wine every night, keeping everyone up with their loud singing, and, on at least one occasion, using a dig-site cave as a campsite, seriously damaging the excavation.

There were the Kenyan villagers who had reached the conclusion that the rich white people were crazy, far from an uncommon reaction. They could not make Barbara out at all. The diggers' camp cook had single-handedly wrecked the local economy by buying a goat a day for the camp workers' meals, thus inflating the price of goats, pumping too much cash into a primarily barter economy, and all but wiping out the local meat and milk supply.

There were the South Africans and their endless supply of police enforcing apartheid, one or another of them barging into the decades-old Sterkfontein cave sites to check on the reports of a black woman there without a passcard. The local blacks prized their access to jobs at the site highly. They complained constantly about the outsider, obviously a big-city person, and worse, a woman, who was working there, seemingly taking one of their jobs. Barbara nearly wore out her passport and visa papers proving she was an American and a legitimate scientist. The police always ended up very nervous and deferential. Everyone knew a *foreign* black was a person of high status. In other words, they could get into deep trouble harassing an American.

Hilarious tales of how one dealt with the locals was always one of the prime topics when a gang of diggers got together over a beer. Somehow they always got around to the half-legendary, huge, impressive, flowery, colorful, and quite meaningless certificates and requests for permission some diggers allegedly would produce in order to convince the local leaders, who nine times out of ten couldn't read English anyway, to cooperate. "Dago-dazzlers," the things were called. One tale that never died was of the high school diploma pressed into service as a dazzler. The digger in question was from Tennessee, and he had swiped a blank somehow on a visit to his alma mater and filled in the appropriate name. The illiterate chief to whom it was presented kept it and hung it proudly on his wall, much to the confusion of later visitors who wondered, but dared not ask, how the chief had come to be a graduate of Daniel Boone High School.

But the locals, anywhere, anytime, were more than just the butt of the diggers' jokes. For this far-flung tribe of paleoanthropologists, paleontologists, archaeologists, and all the other kinds of diggers and diggers' allies, the locals were the outsiders, the strangers who did not speak the language. The locals did not understand the diggers' hidden dreams, did not understand the diggers' fiercely competitive clan, and did not realize how abruptly the intramural backstabbing could end when the diggers needed to close ranks against an outside threat.

And now Barbara's own family were the locals, the foreigners, the barbarians.

It made for a strange feeling inside, strange as the knowledge, when she felt alone in the world, that her own name was rooted in the word "barbarian." She tightened up the last of the grid-mark lines, and heard Aunt Josephine and her own mother laughing at some joke about the grid lines being the perfect height for string beans.

The jokes ran both ways, for all people laugh away the discomforting feeling of seeing what they do not understand, what they are not a part of. Barbara felt a strange, deep sensation in her gut. It was the first, faint crack, splitting the scientist in her away from the person. She found herself wondering which side would win.

Chapter Six

The metal detector's meter quivered again, just barely. "Make that a point oh-three, Liv," Barbara said. She pointed down, and swung the detector's head out of the way, then picked up her clipboard and carefully marked the point on her graph-paper grid-map of the site. Meantime, Livingston knelt down and poked a small stake into place where the detector's head had been. Using the meter stick, Livingston carefully noted the distance from the edges of the grid block and logged that and the metal detector's reading-intensity into the notebook. Finally, he bent over to write the same figures on the side of the stake itself. Relentlessly thorough, endless record-keeping.

Dr. Barbara Marchando wiped the muddy sweat from her forehead with the back of a grimy hand and considered their handiwork so far. She had marked out the grid square in columns A to H labeled east to west, and rows 1 to 8 numbered north to south, then had started a survey of the entire grid with the metal detector. They were now finishing up in H8, the last of the sixty-four grid-squares that defined their eight-meter-by-eight-meter prime site.

Livingston had logged in 37 hits from the metal detector. A glance at the grid map showed that three-quarters of those hits were clustered in two zones—the squares B2, C3, B3, C4, and another cluster spread somewhat more diffusely through F3, F4, G3, G4, H3, H4, with some slopover into Row 5. She took out her pencil again, circled the two concentrations of hits, and named them *Alpha* and *Beta* respectively. Barbara had done her best to center the prime search site on the crossroads itself. Her best guess was that the burial ground road had run pretty much straight along Row Five, as it presently did, and the old plantation road had run at a slight diagonal from D1 to E8. It looked more and more as if she had spotted the fossil roads correctly. If she *had* gotten that part right, it would put Alpha to the northwest of the crossroads, and Beta to the northeast. She noted the far vaguer collection of hits in the southeast edge of the grid and

70

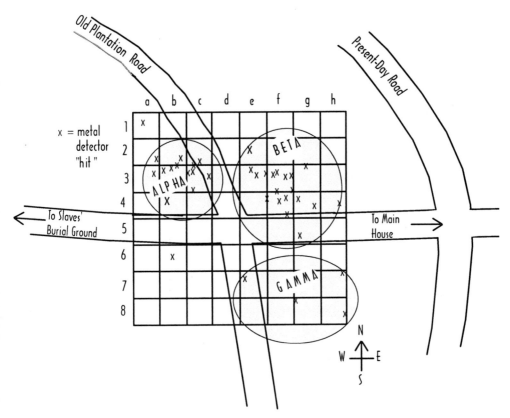

marked it *Gamma?* The odds were perhaps fair-to-good that at least one of those three clumpings of points on the grid represented the partly rusted-out nails and hinges that had once held together the packing cases Zebulon's gorillas were buried in—unless they were the dump sites from the blacksmith shop, or even just random collections of rocks with extremely high iron contents.

Or maybe there were never any burials in the first place. For all she knew, Zeb had been kidding all of them, or had unwittingly injected his first-person recollections into someone else's tall tale. He could have heard the story a hundred times, each time a little grander, a little greater, his child's imagination working on it, until the tale took on every bit as much strength as genuine memory. It happened all the time.

She shook off her moodiness and doubts. They always hit her when she got close to the moment of truth on a dig. When it was time to make the decisions that would steer the rest of the project, Barbara invariably came up with plausible theories that showed her every premise was fatally flawed and that they might as well pack up and go home. It was her version of stage fright. She did her best to put her doubts behind her and *think*.

Careful not to get tangled in the strings that marked out the grid, she crossed over to the now mostly empty lawn chairs and sat down. The only observer still present was her own mother, and she was fast asleep, a light blanket tucked around her feet, her faced calm and untroubled as she quietly snored in the gentle afternoon sun. The rest of the audience had drifted off to more exciting entertainments, though certain of the younger boys had extracted a promise from Barbara to let them play with the metal detector when she was done with it.

And, for the moment, she *was* through with it, though none of the kids was around to lay claim to it.

She knew that she had accomplished a great deal that day, though no one outside the profession would realize it. Using improvised materials, and procedures invented to make the best of the situation, she had avoided some traps that would have thrown the amateur or journeyman (such as assuming the road would not move), eliminated ninety-nine percent of a dauntingly large search area before she started to dig, and kept a record of her work that should silence any nit-pickers later on.

But what to do now? She took a look at her watch, and at the sun. Two-thirty p.m., in late November. They were going to lose the light in another hour or two. The tedious work of digging out a grave, assuming every conceivable effort to preserve an accurate record of stratification and protect any possible additional artifacts could take a week, a month, easily. She had *three* potential grave sites, and at best two days—plus these two hours of daylight—left in which to deal with them. Obviously, she would have to concentrate on one potential grave, do it fast, and pray it would pay off.

She looked again at the grid map. Alpha was the most obvious bet. It was by far the most concentrated and tidy grouping—but something made her shy away from it. Maybe just that it *was* the most obvious. But then she put her finger on what bothered her about it. Alpha was the closest of the three to the slaves burial ground. If the point of the crossroads burial had been to protect the sanctity of that hallowed ground, then it seemed to Barbara that the slaves who had done the burying would have wanted the psychological distance and barrier of the plantation road between the gorillas and their ancestors' resting places.

Livingston stood up from the last of his labors and stretched, his massive muscles straining under the fabric of his shirt. "Break time, by any chance, Barb?" he asked. "Haven't eaten all day here."

Barbara suddenly realized that her stomach had been rumbling for hours. On the other hand, she knew what kind of eating her cousin could do. There had been jokes the night before about serving him his own turkey. Right now, there wasn't time for that. "Okay, Liv, but we can't waste the daylight. I want to be back out here in twenty minutes.

Livingston moaned. "Come on, Barb, have a heart!"

"Don't you go starting a union on me, Liv. You can eat all you want after sunset. Let's hurry." She turned and gave her mother a poke. "Momma, we're heading in for dinner. Don't stay out here too long or you'll catch yourself a chill."

Her mother shifted sleepily and opened her eyes. "Find any monkeys down there yet, child?" she asked with a smile.

Barbara grinned back. "No, Momma, but we're hot on the trail." They all went back inside, Barbara and Livingston to eat, and Barbara's mother to a more comfortable nap on a bed upstairs.

It was a wash-the-first-layers-off, stand-up, eat-the-leftovers-fast meal, but even that sort of eating was better than a sit-down dinner in most houses, when you were in Aunt Josephine's kitchen. The turkey sandwiches and apple pie were perfect. And with a generous helping of stuffing, they were filling enough for Liv to stop grousing. Then they were back at it, at the moment of truth. Barbara discovered that she had decided on a strategy during pie. Over a quick cup of coffee, she showed him the grid map and told him her plans.

"Okay, partner, let me tell you how I see it. I figure this Beta area, a rectangle from E3 to G4, is our best bet at finding a grave." She pointed at the area on the grid. "With the stuff we shaved off the surface this morning gone, we're probably already below the 1850-era horizon—that is, the ground level for the time period we're interested in. It's purely the intrusive burial that we have to worry about anyway—there shouldn't be much else down there of interest, so we don't have to run every bit of dirt through a microscope just yet. I'm assuming that if our gorilla friends are down there at all, it's in some pretty shallow graves—maybe only half a meter or so deep. I doubt a bunch of slaves who just wanted to get some rotting bodies underground and away from their ancestors would dig the regulation six feet down. So let's go." She was already halfway out the door, eager to get back to it. Livingston had to hurry to catch up with her, downing the last of his coffee so fast he burned his tongue.

▼◆▼

Barbara stepped nimbly over the strings marking the grid marks. "I want to see if I can hit the center of the grave first. We're going to dig out the square formed by F3, F4, G3, G4 to thirty centimeters below current ground level, using spades, but going very slow and gentle, and saving all the overburden," she announced. "We dump all the overburden into the wheelbarrow, then dump the barrow onto that tarp over there."

"Why save the old dirt?"

"So we'll be able to sift it later if we have to."

Liv thought that was going a bit far in planning ahead, but he heard a bit of his old college coach in her authoritative, confident tones and knew there wasn't much future in arguing.

Barbara went on. "Once we're at thirty centimeters, we do another metal detector sweep and see if we've accounted for any of the hits. If we find out we've dug right past some ferrous rocks that fooled us, we can quit while we're ahead. But assuming we're still on track, we switch to trowels and go down as far as we can before nightfall. Hand me a shovel."

"Finally, we're digging," Livingston said as he walked less gracefully across the string lines. "I thought pick-and-shovel was all you guys did, and we've taken all day to get started on it." He picked his spot and pushed his spade into the earth, almost relieved to get to the hard part after dreading it for so long. "Y'know, somehow or another, this whole thing reminds me of the old triangle trade. The traders went from Africa with slaves for the West Indies, bought rum and sugar there, then went to Europe with those goods, and back down to Africa with guns and trinkets to trade for more slaves. Slaves, rum, and guns. All those vices going around and around in a circle. Aunt Jo would love the symbolism for her Sunday School class."

Barbara looked at her cousin with an odd expression. "What's all that got to do with digging a hole?"

Livingston pointed down at the hypothetical bones beneath their feet. "Slavers brought these gorillas to Mississippi from Africa. You'll take 'em from here to Washington if you find 'em. Then somebody or other will get all stirred up and head back to Africa looking for sources, clues. Same damn old triangle, except the products are gorillas, bones, and curiosity. I bet Aunt Jo could teach the congregation some very apt lessons from that."

"You are a very weird guy, Livingston," Barbara said. "You get back to your digging before you think of something else strange."

He grinned and stabbed the shovel back into the earth.

With Livingston's strength and Barbara's experience, the first phase of digging went quickly. They paused once, to open up a few of the grid lines so the barrow could get through, and took turns doing the digging and running the barrow back and forth to the overburden tarp.

Barbara's biggest worry was keeping the sides of the little excavation from caving in. Livingston was better at getting the hole deeper than he was at keeping the side shored up. Albeit with a great deal of fussing, she managed to keep sides square enough to satisfy her professors.

They found nothing more exciting than rocks in that first part of the dig, which made Barbara feel better. If the upper soil had been full of artifacts. the odds against the coffin nails being what had registered would have gone down. But with the dig a blank slate so far, there seemed no other possible explanation for the hits, except that something metal had been buried far deeper than people buried casual trash.

The sun was showing signs of lowering alarmingly by the time they were near the thirty-centimeter level. When they ran a metal-detector sweep at the 30 cm. horizon, none of the previous hits vanished, meaning that whatever had made them was still *below* and not thrown up on the overburden tarp. Indeed, all the readings had strengthened and two more faint ones registered. A few of the readings had shifted their apparent positions, and seemed to be clustering in a bit closer to each other. Barbara was pleased, but not surprised. A lot of things could throw a detector off: moisture in the overlying soil, a misreading of the peak on the gauss meter—or Livingston getting his big feet in their metal-toed work boots too close to the detector head.

As afternoon wore on into evening, Barbara had to use the flash on her camera to photograph the thirty-centimeter horizon with the restaked hits marked in.

By an act of sheer self-discipline, Barbara decided to knock off for the day. It was a hard call because they were close. Both of them could feel it. Just below their feet, secrets waited to whisper their truths after more than a hundred and thirty years of silence. It was tempting to dig out just one more trowelful, because whatever-it-was might be waiting below the surface, a handbreadth away. But that could be disaster in the tricky, failing light of sunset. The shadows of twilight were filling the excavation, and a vital bit of bone could be missed. A precious, irreplaceable bit of the past could easily be stepped on unknowingly, thrown away in the gloom of on-coming night. Barbara even considered scaring up whatever lanterns and flashlights were about the place, and working that way, but eyes dazzled by a flashlight could be worse than useless, and light was no help when it merely turned shadows into glare.

Reluctantly, they cleaned their tools, returned them carefully to their places in the garden shed and the garage, and took their sore muscles in to dinner and the last of the endless Big Games on TV. Barbara crept upstairs to a much-wanted shower and an early bed time—but she might as well have been eight years old on Christmas Eve, for all the sleep she got.

▼◆▼

The next morning, Saturday, she was in the excavation, shoring up the walls where they had slumped over in the night, before the last star had left the sky. Her muscles were sore from yesterday's work, but that just felt good, a real sign that she had done something the day before.

Livingston stumbled out of the house soon afterwards, carrying two steaming cups of coffee. Barbara took hers gratefully.

The two of them started with the back-wrenching, tedious, careful work of peeling back the surface of the excavation. She drummed into his head just how fragile what they were digging for was. It would require exquisite care to remove whatever remains they might find.

Livingston listened carefully as Barbara told him how to dig gently, and he set to work alongside her.

It was long, slow work. They would dig down ten centimeters along one side of the excavation, no farther than a trowel could cut. Then they would work back toward the far side of the excavation, slicing down that same ten centimeters and no farther until they reached the far side, and the floor of the hole was exactly level at the new, ten-centimeter-lower level. Then they would start again. Over and over again, they cleared every bit of the work face to the new horizon—Livingston was picking up the trade-talk—before going farther down at any point.

Start at the east side of the work face and work toward the west. Cut back the overburden east to west, whittling down a low ridge of dirt that slowly melted before their trowel blades. Slowly fill a bucket with dirt, slowly fill the wheelbarrow one bucketful at a time, empty the barrow on the tarp, and be glad for the chance to straighten up for a moment and get out of the hole.

They were about halfway across on their sixth horizon, the excavation now about waist deep on Livingston, the sun high in the ten a.m. sky—

When Livingston's trowel hit something.

Something, he knew instantly, that wasn't dirt.

Something that *gave* a little.

▼♦▼

"Barb!" he cried out, and threw down the trowel. Working with his bare hands, he scrabbled away the dirt, his heart pounding, fingers almost trembling with excitement.

"Stop!" she cried out. "Don't use your hands. Run and get a brush."

"A brush?" his hands stopped in midair over the whatever-it-was, and he looked up at her for a split second, as if he had never seen such a thing as a person before. Then he looked back down toward the ground. All he had eyes for was the invisible something beneath his feet.

"A brush! A paintbrush! It's the best way to clear the dirt away. Didn't I remember to tell you to get—oh, the hell with it! Come on, there must be some in the garage!"

Livingston got the idea. They scrambled out of the hole, and both of them nearly tripped over the grid lines on their way out. They broke all records getting to the garage, but there wasn't anything remotely like a brush in any of the neat cupboards. They drew another blank in the garden shed, and pounded hell-for-leather through the breakfast crowd in the kitchen to get down to the basement to go banging through all the storage bins. In the last cabinet they tried, Livingston came up with a treasure trove of perfectly kept, good-as-new, soft-as-could-be brushes. Probably they had been right there since Great-uncle Will had last put them away before he had died, ten years before. Never mind. They were already outside again, racing for the site, leaving a trail of curious relatives following in their wake.

They scrambled back over the grid lines again, and Livingston made ready to jump down into the pit—but Barbara grabbed at his arm and yelled "Stop!"

Livingston looked back at her. "But—"

"But nothing! We're standing right here for a second until we catch our breath and calm down a bit, or we'll screw it up for sure! Liv, you almost jumped right on top of whatever you just found—and I nearly let you! We're really close, so let's not foul up."

Livingston put up his hands in an apologetic gesture. "Okay, okay." He turned away from the hole and squatted down on his haunches, doing the breathing exercises he had used to calm himself before a big game. Barbara leaned over and patted him on the shoulder.

After a long, silent moment, she said, "Okay, let's do it. Calm and cool." Slowly, carefully, they stepped down into the excavation. Barbara handed her cousin one of the brushes. "Go for it, Liv."

Almost in a pose of reverence, he knelt down in front of the thing he had found. Barbara retrieved her camera and started to shoot. He started to brush away the dirt, and slowly exposed a tiny patch of a grimy, chewed-up-looking something, something with an oddly familiar, patterned surface. He drew back his hand and stared at what he had found. His imagination tried to fit what he saw into some sort of pattern, tried to see it as mummified skin or something even ghastlier, something horrid and unknown dredged up from the past. His stomach quavered, and the excavation's normal odor, the moldery smell of long-buried earth, suddenly seemed the stench of some evil thing long forgotten, something best left alone. "What is it, Barb?" he whispered.

"Canvas, Liv," she replied just as quietly. "It's dirty, rotted-out old canvas. But what the hell is it doing here?"

Almost reluctantly, Livingston resumed his work with the brush. The patch of canvas grew from a spot the size of his thumb to an area larger than his huge hand. A spot of red appeared, and he brushed away the dirt around it, to reveal a long, rusty nail lying atop the canvas, a few crumbling bits of wood barely attached to it.

"That's one of our hits, kiddo," Barbara whispered. "That's what led us here. One of the coffin nails, and what's stuck to it is what's left of the coffin itself. Here, let me see the brush. You take the camera and get some close-ups."

"You two finally find something?" a booming voice shouted down.

Barb and Liv almost jumped out of their skins. They looked up to see the site surrounded by a row of expectant faces. "Yes, Aunt Josephine. Yes, we have," Barbara replied. She turned back toward her work. "Take the camera, Liv."

With surprising speed, she worked the brush over the surface and cleared the dirt from a whole hump of pitted, crumpled, flattened, worm-eaten canvas, large enough that she could begin to trace the outlines of the body below it. "Looks like the grave subsided a bit toward the west," she muttered in a fast, breathy voice, not pausing in her work. She found more and larger bits of wood, some still clinging to their rusty nails, and places where the canvas was crumbling away to nothing, barely held together by a few surviving threads. "They must have wrapped the body in the cloth before they threw it in the packing case," she announced in a louder voice to no one in particular.

Her heart was racing, and she felt as if all her senses were working in overdrive, amplifying all the messages that went to her brain, making her vision clearer, her finger more nimble, her ears alert to the sound of every grain of dirt as it moved. To her, the damp, dismal odor of the excavation was bracing, an invigorating wind to a sailor too long apart from the sea. The moment filled her with the gladness of coming home to her own world. She felt more alive than she had in years.

It was again a distinct effort to stick to the job, to use approved procedure, to remember that rushing could still ruin this dig, that there were very good reasons for the dull, relentless routine of standard digging. She forced herself to be calm.

Livingston, watching her, was plainly astonished that she wasn't digging the find out, but simply clearing the overburden from over and around it as far down as the base of the current horizon. She finished quickly, and then, even more incredibly, turned her back on the find and started clearing the rest of the horizon.

"Aren't you going to dig it out, after all that fuss, darling?" Barbara's mother demanded as she leaned in over the hole.

"Not yet, Momma. If we just go straight down, we might miss something, or stab a trowel through it. We have to dig *around* it on all sides, make sure we've got the whole find cleared before we go any farther."

Livingston set down the camera and silently shook his head. He could see how excited she was, how much this meant to her. How could she be so controlled? Well, if she could . . .

He picked up his trowel and knelt down beside her again, and the two of them carefully cleared the last of the existing horizon.

A half-hour later, there was at least the satisfaction of knowing the careful procedure was worthwhile. The excavation was rather small, two meters by two meters, about twice the area of a good-sized dining room table. It did not entirely encompass the find. Once the horizon was completely cleared, they could see that the hump of canvas extended well past the grids they had been digging out, and seemed to be pitched downward a bit as well, as if it were a submarine diving down into the E3 grid. The top of the canvas was a mass of knotted wrinkles. To Barbara, who had seen such things before, it looked as if they had dropped the body onto the tarp, then used the tarp as a sling to lift the body and drop it into the coffin. Once the body was in the coffin, the remaining canvas had simply been shoved down on top of the body any which way and the lid nailed down.

Barbara sent some of the younger kids for an old bed sheet, and they came racing back in record time. Barbara and Livingston gently laid the sheet down over the grimy hump of canvas, and Livingston set to work opening the E3 and E4 grids. Working as fast and as carefully as he could, he dug it out, doing his best not to dump too much dirt onto the grimy treasure he had found. He even took a perverse pleasure in keeping a professional-looking side and corner on the new dig. In short order he had brought the new digging nearly down to the level of the old.

They pulled the sheet and its dusting of dirt off Livingston's discovery and set to work again, first with trowels and then with the brushes again, clearing the dirt around the pathetic little mound. Finally, they had a two-meter by three-meter grid cleared, with the find lying more or less at its center.

The canvas was not as well preserved over the parts of the body that had sunk into the ground a bit, mostly in the E3 grid. As Barbara brushed the dirt from one patch, it crumbled away, and the dirt that had seeped under it generations before collapsed.

There, exposed to her eyes for the first time, was a bit of leg bone, the lower end of a femur.

She looked at it, cried out—and her heart worse than broke. It felt as if she had been flying and had suddenly crashed into a brick wall.

It was a *human* femur, not a gorilla's. It was all for nothing, nothing in the world.

She had dug up some perfectly ordinary human burial, one of millions, billions in the world, an old grave some poor bastard had been thrown in, under the crossroads where they buried murderers and thieves, and a story had grown up about it. That one glimpse of bone meant all her work, all her planning—all her Christmas money spent on hardware and on paying Liv—had gone toward making a fool of herself in front of her family, a wild goose chase after a fable some old man had scribbled down a hundred years before.

She dropped her brush, squatted down, leaned against the wall of the excavation, and fought back the tears.

"Barbara!" her mother cried. "What's the matter, baby?" The old woman, unmindful of the dirt getting on her good clothes, let herself down into the excavation and reached for her child. "Baby, what's happened? What's wrong?"

"Oh, Momma, it's a *human*. Look at that bone. Human as you or I are. It's not old Zebulon's goddamned imported gorilla, just some regular person they put in the ground here. I've wasted the whole weekend, and spent all that money, and torn up Aunt Josephine's garden, and it's all for nothing."

"How can you tell from that little bit of ugly bone sticking out?"

"Momma, I went to school for *six years* learning how to tell the

difference! Damn, damn, damn." By now the family members standing along the edge of the dig were shifting around uncertainly, not
quite sure how to respond.

Livingston looked at her for a long moment. "Come on, Barb,"
he said. "Let's get back to it." He went back to work. Barbara watched
him for a long moment. How could he just shrug off the failure and
keep going as if nothing was wrong? She shook her head, tried to
clear her mind. He could do it because he was right. She rose and
picked up her own tools again. He was right because there was nothing else to do but finish the job, follow the same careful procedure,
stick to the precise rituals that had gotten them this far. They had to
behave like the sort of soulless automata people thought scientists
were supposed to be.

Maybe that was what the utterly false stereotype of the emotion-
less scientist moving coolly about in his lab coat was all about—a
shell to slip into, a shield when failure hit.

Working with the brush was soothing work, she tried to tell herself when the tears threatened to well up again. Gracefully, almost
tenderly wiping the dust of ages off the corpse, she managed to find
her composure in anger—silent, unrevealed anger at the robot-scien-
tist tradition. How had it gotten started? How, when real scientists
were so emotional, so mercurial, so impassioned about their work
and the competition from their colleagues? Who, without the backing of strong passion, without the goad of the desperate need to know,
would mix chemicals that could explode, would tickle the dragon of
nuclear fire with bare hands to find the point where a critical mass
was formed, would dive in a fragile bubble of iron into places in the
ocean where the pressure rivaled Jupiter's atmosphere, just to look
around?

Who, without that burning monkey-curiosity, without incredible
self-confidence and self-doubt in the face of million-to-one odds,
without the thrill of the chase and dreams of glory of the misty past,
would be a paleontologist, a digger? Who would roam all the barren
and desert places of the earth, scrabbling in the dust and the muck
and dirt to find such tiny scraps of bone, scraps the hyenas had passed
over a million years before?

Barbara shook her head, thought again of all her own crazy
dreams, and forced back the tears. Why weren't scientists allowed to

be people?

Never mind. She kept on with the blissfully mind-numbing work of unearthing a worthless skeleton. At least the relatives had the good taste to wander off.

God bless Liv. He stuck to it, never saying a word, just doing the grunt work.

Finally, the rotten canvas shroud was completely cleared, and they had their reward for their work—a flaccid, rotted-out bag full of bones lying at the bottom of a hole.

Livingston grabbed the Nikon and photographed their find, and not a halfhearted job either, but a thorough documentation.

Barbara did her best to match his brave front. It was easier that way. She knelt down beside the shroud. "This stuff is just rotting away anyway," she said, careful to keep control of her voice. "I think we can just sort of peel it away in strips." She pulled her Swiss Army knife out of her pocket, opened up the scissors blade, and began to cut away the worm-eaten canvas, one delicate snip at a time.

The old fabric parted easily, or collapsed altogether when the blade even got near it. She worked from the bottom to the top along the right side, opening a cut. She crouched down by the body and signaled for Livingston to kneel beside her. The two of them slid their hands into the slit and pulled about a handbreadth of cloth back before it collapsed into broken thread and dust. They stepped around to the other side, reached across, pulled back the cloth from that side, and cleared off the bits and pieces of canvas that had fallen back.

Over the decades, the soil had sifted down through the fabric of the canvas, trickling down onto the decaying corpse inside. With the canvas stripped away, they had a mound of packed-in dirt, with a few bones poking out here and there.

The dull hurt of failure still in her heart, Barbara sighed and reached for her brush again, began sweeping the dust away. Livingston started at the foot of grave, and Barbara began at the head, where the dirt seemed to have packed in deeper and harder.

Livingston worked up toward her end quickly. The small foot and ankle bones had of course disarticulated completely. A profes-sional would have stopped the basic clear-off long enough to make sure all of these were uncovered, but Livingston continued up the legs, rapidly and incompletely uncovering the pelvis and torso. The corpse had obviously been buried lying on its back, and Livingston decided to clear the arms. He found the right shoulder, and worked from there down, moving toward the elbow joint, dusting them off. Barbara glanced idly over at his work as she uncovered the first bit of the skeleton's head.

Suddenly it registered that there was something odd about the elbow joint—in fact about the whole arm. The upper arm was too long, the forearm too short, the joint itself not quite normal. For that matter, the leg bones weren't altogether right, now that she could see them in their entirety, though there was nothing she could put her fingers on precisely.

She thought for a second, a new and wild idea flickering through her mind as she realized the difference between what she had assumed and what Zebulon had written. A sudden sense of numb shock grabbed at her stomach, and the emotional roller coaster she was riding took a hard, swooping turn up. A strange, exciting thought; a terrifying suspicion; a wild-eyed idea suddenly dawned on her. What if he *hadn't* meant gorillas? What if he had never seen such a beast in his life? The idea led directly into another impossible question—and the answer was literally beneath her very hands. Back, forth, back, forth went her brush, and the last layers of dust melted away.

The eyeless face from the past hove into view, clearing the foggy horizons of the sea of time, a lost vessel arriving safely, sailing majestically into home waters, long after the last hopes for her had been given up.

The massive, jutting teeth grinned blindly up at her; the heavy brow of bone over the eyes shadowed the deep sockets into blackness. She knew what this was, and knew it could not be. Her heart suddenly gone cold, Barbara reached out a trembling finger to touch the one-hundred-thirty-seven-year-old skull of a hominid that she *knew* had been extinct for a million years.

▼◆▼

One of them died in the fields the next day. She did not know it at first; she was too far away to pay any mind to the cries and howls, and the sting of the punishment lashes she still felt was too great. Her attempt at escape had failed, of course.

It was only when the man overseeing her turned and looked toward its source that she became aware of the noise at all. The overseer looked concerned and trotted toward the outburst, and she followed behind, unbidden and unnoticed.

It was on the far end of the farthest field, there, a knot of keening, gesticulating, furry figures, crouched low in a circle, anxious men standing uncertainly about the mourners.

She cried out, the fur on the back of her neck bristling, and ran forward, forcing her way into the ranks of the death-criers. She shoved her body forward to see, jostling her way through the wall of bodies. Then she saw the corpse, and she too cried out, her own anguished voice altogether lost in the wild pandemonium of those surrounding the body.

It was an old, silver-backed female, the thin fur along her shoulders and spine long since gone grey. She was lying on her side, twisted up as if in great pain, her face a frozen, manic mask of agony, her eyes already glazed and filming, a line of spittle hanging from her lips. It was the shocked and painful face of one whose body has died, stopped, collapsed in the flicker of a heartbeat. The corpse's arms and legs sprawled out in unnatural directions, limp and horribly motionless. Death seemed to have stolen not only movement, but also substance; the whole body appeared thin and useless, as if it were far more fragile in death than in life. The corpse seemed shrunken, child-sized, far smaller than the living being.

She turned, twisted her head to look at the face, and then bared her fangs and shrieked anew, louder, more fiercely. It was her mother, the one who had held her, carried her, fed her, groomed her, protected her, loved her.

Hysterical, desolated, she cried out again and lunged for the too-still body, dove down onto her knees and hugged the unbreathing chest in her arms. She gathered her mother's body to her and rocked it back and forth, keening and moaning.

The others backed away, and their cries faded away as all eyes drank in her sorrow, and shared it, and would not intrude upon it.

After a time, hands, furry hands with callused pads on their palms and nails like chipped, broken claws, hands of her own kind, reached out to pet her back, touch her arm, smooth the bristled fur along the back of her neck.

At first she pushed away the hands and snapped at them, but at last she allowed the contact, the reassurance, the silent condolences.

The men finally acted, moved in, prodded their charges to move, to get back to their work. With a muted symphony of growls and grunts, the crowd around her allowed itself to be led away. The men and their beasts drifted back to their work, all save the dead one and her mourning daughter. The men had learned long ago, at the cost of not a few fights, escapes, injuries, and deaths, not to interfere at such times. The miserable creatures owned nothing but their grief, and that was the only thing the men would not, could not, take from them.

They left her there, and she lost herself in attendance on the dead—stroking the too-cold flesh, straightening the limbs into more natural positions, closing the eyes, trying in vain to wipe the hideous pain from the face.

For a day and a night, she stayed there in the furrowed field with the corpse. She hugged the body, feeling it stiffen into rigor as if her dead mother was drawing back, retreating from her touch. She slept there, for the first time in memory without thought of escape—though she could sense a man nearby, keeping watch lest she take advantage of her grief-freedom. She woke next morning, huddled by the body.

At last, on the second day, when the criers called them to the evening feeding, hunger and thirst drew her away, and she went to the feeding cages to eat and drink her fill, and she suffered herself to be locked up for the night with the others.

The next morning, she broke away from her overseer to the place where her mother had died, but the men, or the jackals, had dragged the body away.

Chapter Seven

Dr. Jeffery Grossington, Associate Secretary for Anthropology at the National Museum of Natural History and Man, Smithsonian Institution, Washington, D.C., was a man well-suited to a position with such a long and ponderous title. He had the character traits a man engaged in the study of the long-dead past needed: slow, deliberate, careful thought processes; the patient willingness to sift through the minute bits of evidence and fragile shards of bone for the one tiny fragment of meaning; the capacity to build knowledge out of mystery; the imagination and vision to understand what the rare, tiny clues scrabbled out of the earth could tell of human ancestry. But of all his skills, virtues, and talents, Jeffery Grossington was certain that the greatest was patience.

Students of other scientific disciplines might feel compelled to compete in a race against time, against constrained budgets, against colleagues who might be hot on the trail of the same discovery, but not Grossington. Though many of his colleagues in the field would have disagreed, he felt quite strongly that such nonsense had no place in paleoanthropology. After all, the persons of interest to Grossington's studies had all died thousands or millions of years ago; their bones could wait a day or a year or a decade more before revealing their secrets. Rush made for errors; cautious deliberation and painstaking care were the hallmarks of his work. There was simply no *need* for a good paleoanthropologist to scurry maniacally toward conclusions.

Indeed, he strongly disapproved of rush, or commotion, or *any* sort of urgency—and suspected that hurry was not only mostly unneeded, but quite often detrimental. Outright frantic activity infuriated him.

Fortunately, he was also slow to anger, or else when Barbara burst into his office at eight A.M. on the Monday after Thanksgiving, there would have been hell to pay.

She all but bounded into the room, grinning ear to ear, and charged straight toward his desk. He should have immediately given her a good tongue-lashing, ordered her out of the office, but she had the element of surprise working for her. No one in the history of Grossington's tenure had ever dreamed of barging into his office like that. Dr. Grossington opened his mouth to offer an infuriated rebuke, but he never got the chance. Before he could react to the intrusion, Barbara compounded her offense by scooping up his coffee tray and placing it none-too-carefully on a side table, sweeping all the papers from the center of his desk, and vanishing back out into the hall, only to return a moment later carrying, of all things, an old-fashioned wooden hatbox.

Suddenly moving with great care and deliberation, she set down the box, most gently, on the exact center of his desk blotter, and stepped back to stand in front of his desk, like a student waiting for the teacher to examine her science project.

"Dr. Marchando, what the devil is the—" But Dr. Jeffery Grossington stopped himself in mid-outburst and finally took a good hard look at Barbara. She was flushed, excited, and her dark brown face was alight, exhilarated. Her eyes gleamed, her hair was disheveled, her makeup was blurred and smeared. Her clothes, which she normally kept up so carefully, were wrinkled, mussed-up, and looked as if they had been slept in for a day or two. All of which was totally out of character for the prim, careful Dr. Marchando.

"Well, open it, Dr. Grossington," she said. "Aren't you going to *open* it?" she asked breathlessly. "I've been travelling all last night and the whole day before—bus, train, plane, taxi—to get it to you. *Open* it!"

He looked at her curiously, and his big, callused, well-manicured hands moved involuntarily toward the cord that held the lid of the box on. He hesitated, much unnerved, and looked hard at the hatbox, as if he feared it might contain a bomb. He looked again to Barbara. He had a nasty feeling things in his world were about to turn upside down. "Barbara, what's *in* here?"

She grinned, almost wild-eyed, and leaned over the desk, her whole face shining with enthusiasm. "The end, Jeffery, the goal," she said, daring to use his first name. "The end of so many searches. *That's* what's in there. Maybe the collapse of every existing theory of human evolution. *Open* it."

Grossington swallowed hard and undid the cord. He lifted the worn black-lacquer top off the octagonal box and set it aside. There was a layer of shredded bits of foam rubber hiding the contents proper. Grossington removed the bits of padding carefully, one by one. Years of field work had made slow and careful work a matter of reflex action for him. He wanted to make sure there was no danger of his damaging the whatever-it-was by moving too fast.

Just as Barbara had done two days before, he gradually uncovered the prize. As he dug it out from under the bits of padding, he saw more and more details of what it was, and his years of practice told him what the whole was before it was fully uncovered, before he had really seen it: a skull, a human skull, a fully intact cranium with a complete upper dental arcade, all the teeth intact, every detail fully present and preserved.

And then he removed the last of the padding, and looked again, and saw what was truly there, not what was expected. His eyes widened in shock: hominid, yes—but it was not human.

Grossington could feel his heart starting to pound, the sweat coming out on his forehead as he carefully, oh so carefully, removed the prize from the hatbox.

The prominent sagittal crest, the huge, flat molars, the large but human-like canine teeth, the box-shaped dental arcade, the obvious positioning of the skull's balance point to allow for an erect, bipedal gait. The prominent, exaggerated brow ridges—a dozen, a hundred things that spoke, even shouted, the impossible. This was an australopithecine, a member of a hominid species that had died out a million years ago.

But this was no fossil. This was *bone*, not the mineralized shadow of bone; none of the once-living material of this skull had leached away to be replaced by other matter. What he held in his hands was the actual, true, once-living matter, browned and stained and weakened by time, but still bone—and of recent vintage. Not so long ago, these bone had been as alive as Grossington himself was.

Like Hamlet with Yorick's skull, Grossington held the cranium in his hand and stared into its empty eyes, fascinated, for a long time.

▼◆▼

Barbara stood there, in front of Grossington's desk, for what could have been a minute, or could have been an hour, watching him examine the impossible find. Finally the old man spoke. "When and where, Dr. Marchando?" he managed to ask at last, very quietly. "How old is this, and where in heaven's name does it come from?"

"Sir, that cranium—and the well-preserved *complete* skeleton found with it—were buried—deliberately, ritualistically buried— about one hundred forty years ago. In Gowrie, Mississippi, U.S.A. My home town."

Grossington sat there, stunned. "How? How could that possibly *be*?"

"I don't know, sir. I honestly don't know. But I have a very strong hunch that our friend here might have some living relatives still around, if we knew where to look."

That much she had realized on the endless bus ride through the Mississippi darkness, rushing for the Jackson airport. It was plain bad luck that she had had to hustle for the fastest route she could manage in the overbooked chaos of Thanksgiving Sunday, when all America was headed home. At least the endless delays had given Barbara the chance to think, to consider, to contemplate—to let her imagination run away with her.

"If these creatures survived up to the 1850s, why couldn't they still be around?" she asked in as nearly a conversational tone as she could manage. Then, for the first time, the excitement went out of Barbara's voice, to be replaced by something else, something mixed of awe, and fear, and wonder. She reached out and touched the face of the musty skull that Grossington still held. "I think we've got some company. Out there. Somewhere."

Grossington set down the cranium, bafflement plainly overwhelming him. This was as incredible to him as a dawn in the west would be to an astronomer. His face was blank, expressionless, the face of a man who had no adequate reaction.

For a terrible moment, Barbara thought he had suffered a stroke or a heart attack, but then he seemed to come back to himself a bit, at least enough to replace the precious cranium in its nest of foam rubber. But still he said nothing, and Barbara found herself talking on, the words rushing out for the sake of something to say, something to fill the silence. "I left my cousin down there to watch over the rest of the skeleton. The rest of it is still *in situ*. Once I realized what I had, I didn't dare try and work the area without professional help and equipment. I just removed the cranium and headed back here as fast as I could. We've got the dig roped-off and tarped over, but we still need to get back down there and recover the rest of the specimen. It looked as if there was still some skin, even fur, left on parts of it. It'll be very delicate work, and we'll need the best diggers in the house for it." She paused for a moment, looked down at her boss again, reached out and touched his hand. "Dr. Grossington?"

He jerked away, startled, and looked back at her from whatever place his mind had been. "Hmmm? Diggers? Field workers? Yes, yes, in due time, Dr. Marchando, in due time. This—this requires a great deal of thought." His eyes drifted back toward the timeworn skull, and he seemed to forget her once again. "I simply cannot believe this."

Barbara winced inside. She should have thought of this, should have taken Grossington's personality into account. She had imagined him pushing the buttons on his phone, pulling all his people in, issuing crisp orders that would set the needed work in motion. That was the way she would have responded—but instead, she was dealing with a man who seemed suddenly lost. His life was no longer the well-ordered place it had been ten minutes before. He had to be prodded into action, and there was no time to guide him into his course gently. She knew Grossington hated knee-jerk reactions to the press of events, but now he had no choice. It was time to bully the old man a bit.

"Dr. Grossington, you *must* believe it—and you must act quickly! The rest of this skeleton is lying, partially excavated, under a tarp. It's more or less protected, but it's at least potentially exposed to weather and extremes of temperature. One good rain, one good cold snap that embrittles the bones, and we could lose it all. We *have* to get a team down there to recover and catalog all the bones. There are very likely other sets of remains buried nearby that must be uncovered . . ." Her voice trailed off as she watched him. Her boss was acting most strangely.

"Yes, yes," Grossington said, nodding vaguely, barely aware that she had stopped talking. He reached down into the hatbox and softly stroked the weathered brow of bone over the blank eye sockets. "Yes, of course," he said to no one at all. A strange eagerness seemed to steal slowly over him. His face lost its customary reserve, and he pulled the horn-rimmed glasses off his nose. He massaged his own forehead with his right hand as the left caressed the mysterious skull. "This is—is quite incredible, Dr. Marchando. I have not felt this way in years." He looked up at her abruptly. His breath seemed short, and his eyes gleamed with excitement and pleasure. "I cannot recall feeling this *alive*."

He stared down at the dead, grinning enigma that challenged him, and quite uncharacteristically grinned back at it. "I cannot recall feeling this *young*."

And Barbara chided herself for underestimating Jeffery Grossington.

▼◆▼

Livingston Jones sat at a table on the back porch and stared out at the crude canvas top staked down over the excavation. He knew himself to be a man with a mission, though he did not exactly know what that mission was. Clearly, someone had to stay here and keep an eye on things, just in case—but just in case what? Until Barbara called with news, or unless it rained, or animals started prowling around the tarp, or some nosy neighbor started poking around the dig, there was very little to do.

The last of the Thanksgiving guests had left that morning, and Great-aunt Josephine had the huge old place to herself again, except for Livingston, of course. She was busily at work, cleaning up after her relations, tidying up and setting to rights what was already neat as a pin. She had chased Liv out of the way more than once, convinced that neither he nor any other male could possibly get anything polished or straight or ironed or clean or put away well enough to suit her.

Livingston sighed and picked up Zebulon's journal book again. It was not the focus of reverence to him that it was to the older relations, but it was something to read. It would have been interesting enough even it hadn't led to a shocking discovery in the backyard. At first he had thought there might be more in the old book about the creatures or their burial, but there didn't seem to be any further mention. He opened it again at random, and found himself in the days when Zebulon had first returned home, after the War, and was struggling to buy out the bankrupt shell that was Gowrie Plantation.

▼◆▼

It is scarce worth mentioning the difficulties of the project I described. Any Reader who has traveled so far along in this Journal, indeed, any Person who has ever witnessed the behavior of the White Race toward the Negro, knows full well the catalog of indignities, the discourtesies and acts of violence both committed and threatened; the insidious and endless Legal tangles that might be thrown up in the face of a Negro audacious enough to purchase his former owner's home. I had returned to my native town intent only on setting up a commercial stable, but when, on my arrival, I learned that Ambrose Gowrie had recently died a bankrupt and his lands and home were the court's to sell as a means of satisfying the creditors, it occurred to me that I was the only person with a purse large enough to buy.

Indeed, I think it safe to say that scarce any Negro ever dared try any such a thing. Few to my knowledge did, and grim though the fact is, of that small number, I believe only I myself succeeded— or even survived.

The period of Reconstruction was a time of such great and heady chaos in this land that I myself can scarce credit all that I saw in my travels, both good and ill: Proud Negro soldiers of the Union cause; Shattered towns; Landscapes that, years after the battles that made their names immortal, were strewn with bleaching human bones, like so many hideous and infertile seeds sewn by the Reaper of Death.

I rejoiced to see the Slaves' Auction Block destroyed, but the Northern Carpetbaggers were swarming over the land, forcing whatever agreements they wished on Southerners compelled at the point of a Federal bayonet, to the detriment of all citizens of either race. The Kuklux Klan ran wild, meting out its own rabid mockery of law and justice. In somewhat later years, Negroes (among them myself) from half a dozen Southern states were elected to Serve in the Congress of the United States, a body which could never decide whether to Govern the former Confederate States or simply to wreak vengeance against them. Then the Poll Tax, and the maliciously impossible Literacy Tests, the Klan's intimidations and a thousand more subtle threats drove the Negro from the Poll, from the schoolhouse, from the Seats of government.

But I digress into bitter topics. Suffice it to say that it was against such a background of a world turned upside down that I bought Gowrie, and secured it. It took the entire fortune I had amassed in trading horses, and recourse to the hiring of a private army made up of discharged Negro soldiers eager to tangle with the Klan's cowardly night riders.

And it also took an ally, one that I found in a most unlikely place—in the offices of the *Gowrie Gazette*. The local news paper was in those days a biweekly affair published by one Stephen Teems. Teems was that rare combination, a Southern native and an Abolitionist, a believer—at least in principle—of the equality of the races.

It was Teems, who was not only a publisher and journalist, but a lawyer trained before the War at Harvard, who searched the land titles, cleared my deeds, made each legal document a paragon of perfection, and used the law to compel the Federal occupiers who were not altogether willing to help.

▼◆▼

Livingston closed the old book and thought for a moment. Documents. That was it. Somewhere, somehow, in the old family records, maybe there were the deeds and receipts that would mention the creatures. One thing they were sorely lacking at this point was information. Maybe there were more surprises concerning those old bones lying around among the old family papers. He went off to find Great-aunt Josephine and pester her until she showed him where to look.

When people think of the Smithsonian, they usually think only of the grand museums that bear that name. But the public areas of the museums are the smallest part of the whole. Behind the vast exhibit halls are endless scientific, scholarly, and artistic endeavors, from astronomy and stamp collecting to puppeteering and violin playing.

Even when people *do* think of the scholars and scientists who work in those grand museums and in the labs and offices behind the scene, they have a natural but totally erroneous tendency to assume that the grandeur extends beyond the public view. They think of gleaming labs full of astonishing equipment, of serene scientists in their ever-present lab coats, toiling over their experiments on acres of shining formica. They imagine imposing offices, control panels full of quietly blinking lights, and reading rooms of polished oak.

Barbara couldn't speak for the whole endless establishment, but she knew just how far from the truth that image was for the Department of Anthropology. Anthro was jammed into part of the overcrowded third floor of the cavernous Natural History Museum.

There were strange things there, behind the scenes at Natural History. Somewhere in the building was a carefully caged and isolated colony of *Dermestidae lardarius*—alias museum beetles, alias larder beetles. Those strange and voracious bugs would swarm over a corpse and eat *everything*—except bone. They used the museum beetles for cleaning small animal skeletons. A dead carcass would be left in with the beetles for them to swarm over like insect piranha, and in a day or so nothing would remain but the gleaming bones. The staff taxidermists lived in dread of the beetles escaping into the exhibits and devouring all the mounted specimens.

Anthro had its own strange features. Long rows of shelves lined the hallways of the third floor there, running floor to ceiling. Endless identical wooden boxes the size of a small suitcase lined the shelves—each with a disarticulated human skeleton inside. All told, there were thirty thousand skeletons in the massive reference collection, packed away wherever they might fit.

The living, breathing scientists were packed in nearly as tight as the dear departed. The lower-ranking scientists were crammed in with each other, four or five desks stuffed into rooms intended for two.

The main workroom was even worse, the desks there even more banged up and crowded together. A small, dusty table was wedged up by the window for the sorting and organizing of specimens. Bookcases sprouted everywhere, reaching for the old-fashioned high, white-painted ceilings, their shelves filled to bursting with papers, boxes full of bones from the reference collections, and of course, books. Books were everywhere. Books neatly put away, books stacked up precariously, books left open to a key page, books closed up and waiting forlornly for someone to come along and remove dozens of improvised bookmarks.

To such a place—scruffy, untidy, disorganized, full of the fruits of learning and learning yet to be sown, grown, and harvested, Barbara took the precious cargo she had carried from Mississippi. She set down the hatbox on the papers that hid her desk and started trying to clear some sort of work space on the sorting table. She paused for a minute and looked over the overheated, drafty, musty, dusty place. They called it the Diggers' Pit, and it deserved the name. She smiled. It was nice to be back.

▼◆▼

Fifteen minutes later she was balanced on a rickety revolving-seat stool, perched in front of the sorting table. She was most carefully working a compressed-air gun over the pitted surface of the cranium, the compressor's motor humming and throbbing a demented background rhythm. She wanted to be sure to blow out as much dirt and crud as possible before treating the fragile bone with a toughening preservative. The tricky part was in emptying the braincase, which was full of loosely packed dirt. It was slow, delicate work that required pure, focused concentration. That sort of work was good therapy, just what she needed right now. Small details drove the grand issues out of her mind. When she was trying to break up that last big clump of dirt, she couldn't think of what finding this fellow meant, or what Grossington was deciding back in his office. The skull was lying upside down in front of her. She carefully eased the nozzle of the air gun into the foramen magnum, the hole at the base of the skull through which the spinal cord reached into the brain.

She hit the trigger, and with a rattling sigh, the cranium gave up a big cloud of compacted dirt. She lifted the cranium up, poured the loosened dirt out, and decided to work on the teeth. She re-arranged the soft cloth she was using to support the skull and set the cranium back down right-side up.

Once again she stared into the expressionless grin of the skull, and felt a warm, happy feeling inside. The search for a good specimen can take a lifetime, and luck is a tremendously important part of the job. A few shards of bone can be the only concrete results of a career, the sole source of a reputation, the single reward of a life of work wandering the world in search of our ancestors. Diggers develop an emotional attachment to their finds, and at times become rather sentimental about them.

There was a long tradition of nicknaming famous fossils. The Leakeys and his "Dear Boy" and "Mrs. Ples," Johansen with "Lucy," so named because someone in camp played a tape of the Beatles' "Lucy In the Sky with Diamonds" the night she was found, all the way back to the first australopithecine ever found, Dart's "Taung Baby." It struck Barbara that *this* fellow needed a name. Her first impulse was "Zebulon," but she realized that her family would take a dim view of naming some monkey after their ancestor. Then she thought of the perfect name: Ambrose. After Ambrose Gowrie, the slavemaster who had bought the poor creature. She could make a monkey out of Ambrose safely enough. That settled, she happily went on with her work.

She switched back and forth, between the compressed-air gun and a soft, worn toothbrush, as she cleaned all the convoluted surfaces of the teeth. It was her first real chance to get a look at the teeth of her new friend here, and for a paleoanthropologist, it was a breathtaking view. Because the teeth are the hardest part of the body, they are generally the best preserved—often they are all that a scientist has to work with.

Since they are frequently all that Mother Nature will surrender up, the teeth are the most commonly and thoroughly studied hominid remains. At times, a canine or a molar or two is all that has been known of a hominid species. Because teeth are scratched and worn as their owner lives his or her life, a scientist can read a large part of the owner's biography off the pits and grooves worn into the enamel of a single tooth. Roughly how old the specimen was at death, what sort of diet it had, patterns of chewing, the power of the jaws that moved the teeth, whether chewing was side-to-side or up-and-down;

all that and more can be divined from a single tooth.

All too often, those are the only clues available at all, for the rest of the creature—fur, skin, muscle, small bones, long bones, skull—is usually washed away in the currents of time, leaving but a few bits of enamel, a few grams of worn, grimy bone, as the only proof that any such animal ever lived.

And Barbara, working with her worn-out toothbrush, was face to face with the crown jewels of australopithecine teeth. By the size of the canines, their owner had probably been a male; by the notable degree of wear on the massive wisdom teeth, indicating they had erupted sometime well before death, a male of about, say, twenty-two, twenty-six years old. That much she knew at a glance. She longed to get these teeth under a microscope and examine the wear-marks, literally read the menu of Ambrose's diet there.

It was a quiet, special, warm moment, in its own odd little way, a time of intimacy between Barbara and Ambrose the empty skull, the dead shards of bone whispering their secrets to the live person. It was such moments that made diggers say the bones could talk to them, as if some remnant of life, some fragment of spirit, clung to the fossils to converse with the stifled romantics who freed the fossils from their imprisonment in the earth.

It was slowly dawning on Barbara that Ambrose would take her into the history books. She stared at the relic of the past and saw the promise of a bright future. The naked bones and teeth seemed to take on a welcoming, benevolent expression. She touched that massive brow ridge again, and it was almost the sensation she had often felt as a child in church; of a kindly presence close but unseen, near at hand but unspeaking.

But then, suddenly, the door at her back bounced open, slammed shut, and the moment was shattered. "Good morning, Doctor!" a loud voice boomed out from behind her.

Barbara almost visibly drew into herself, winced, her stomach muscles tightening. She took a moment to compose her face before she spun around on her stool to face Rupert Maxwell, Ph.D., P.I.T.A. That was how she had thought of him when he had first arrived a few months before—as such a massive Pain In The Ass he *must* have studied, earned a degree in it. The more winning aspects of his personality had taken a long time to shine through, and his usual booming entrance was enough to make her forget everything nice she had ever thought about him. She forced herself to calmness, determined not to let his brashness destroy her good mood.

She put a smile on and turned to face him, keeping her body between the skull and Rupert. "Hello, Rupert. How was your Thanksgiving?"

He grinned from behind his mirrored sunglasses and laughed. He was a big, tall, birdlike man, with a surfer's tan and short-cropped blond hair that stood up from his head bottle-brush straight. He was dressed in a white sport coat, a dark blue shirt and a microscopically thin red tie, black slacks, and cowboy boots. Barbara often wondered if his outfits were the result of careful thought in the art of clashing, or simply random selection from his closet. "Great Thanksgiving," he said as he threaded his way toward her through the labyrinth of desks, "except for three leftover turkey TV dinners. Ended up eating Chinese with some friends instead. Only people in the restaurant."

He always dressed that way, in fragmented outfits—and always seemed to *talk* that way, in partial sentences and telegraphed syntax. He was the sort of person who unfairly made other people hate Californians. His years at UCLA may have rubbed off, but Rupert was from Nebraska.

Rupert Maxwell got away with a lot because of his reputation. Still in his early thirties, he was the author of a number of flawlessly scholarly papers whose learned prose seemed to have nothing to do with the language their author spoke. All those around him, from Grossington on down, agreed he was apparently good at his work— "apparently" because it was very rare to catch him actually doing any. The studies, the reports, the data, seemed to appear magically, effortlessly. It was as if he had a secret supplier who hid by the coffee maker he seemed always to be at, or perhaps the waiters where he took his long lunches delivered information with the check. "Anyway, a fun weekend. Played some touch, went canoeing on the C. & O. Canal, caught the ball games. Nothing too special." He flashed his grin again and started to shrug off his coat. "But never mind that stuff. What's the news from the Gowrie excavation?"

All at once it was no effort for Barbara to smile. "I made a new friend. Rupert Maxwell, say hello to Ambrose." She stepped off the stool and let her office mate see the cranium.

But he was looking at her instead. His eyebrows shot up from behind the mirrored shades and he cocked his head to one side. "Who . . . ?" he began to ask, as if he thought she was trying to introduce him to some imaginary friend hovering over her shoulder. Then his eye caught the skull.

His mouth knotted into a frown, he pulled off his shades, whistled low, and leaned in close to the unbelievable sight. There was a long silence, a longer silence than Barbara had ever heard from Rupert. At last he spoke. "Hello, Ambrose," he said, addressing the half-cleaned cranium. "Nice to meet you. Where've you been all my life?"

Jeffery Grossington was a wanderer, a fidgeter. It was as if his brain were attached to his feet and his fingers. He had to be fiddling with something, or walking, or neatening his desk, or doing *something*, anything, while his brain worked. He had to get rid of the nervous energy churned up by the adrenaline of thinking about a grand idea.

He was rarely aware of events outside the limits of his own skull at such times. He would often come to himself with a start and find himself with his fingers tangled up changing a typewriter ribbon that did not need changing, or down in the public cafeteria sitting over a cup of tea that had been empty for an hour. Mostly, however, he walked.

The worst of it was that his secretary Harriet likewise had a tendency to concentrate too much. She would sit in his outer office, absorbed in whatever report she was coaxing out of the computer, or preparing a summary of events paleontologic around the world, and she would not notice the stocky figure quietly easing out of the inner door and into the corridor. A call would come, or a visitor, or Harriet herself would have a question—and Dr. Grossington would have vanished altogether, perhaps not to reappear for hours.

At least this time Grossington told Harriet he was going for a walk, so even if she didn't know where he was, she at least *knew* she didn't know. Grossington made his way downstairs to the public areas of the museum, into the grand, musty, sweeping vault of the rotunda, with the bull elephant in its center, his trunk raised forever, trumpeting a silent salute to the massed herds of a long-passed era.

The crowds and the hordes of schoolchildren surged about, talking, laughing, rushing to see the dinosaurs, calling to one another.

Grossington navigated his way through them, through the main entrance of the museum, down the wide granite stairs, and onto the wide expanses of the National Mall. The red brick of the original Smithsonian Castle stood directly across the Mall, flags waving jauntily from its cheerful parapet.

Grossington crossed to the middle of the Mall, out from under the line of massive trees that bordered it. He breathed in the crisp late-November air and looked about him. The Capitol Building sat in majesty, a lord of creation, at the east end of the great space, and the Washington Monument speared skyward in the west, pointing upward toward all aspiration. Lining both sides of the wide tract of greensward between the two were the buildings of the Smithsonian Institution, proud monuments to learning and knowledge. It was an inspiring place to be on a perfect fall day, a place of great ambition and beauty built by generations of men and women who were not afraid to dare or dream.

The trouble was, at the moment, Grossington *was* afraid to dare. If that excitable Dr. Barbara Marchando had burst into his office with, say, a Mayan headdress pulled from the Mississippi ooze, or a stone tablet covered with Viking runes she had excavated in California, he could have accepted it. It would have been incredible, startling, but not something that threatened to turn the world upside down. Certainly Barbara did not, could not, realize how much turmoil her discovery would create—how much turmoil the possibility of finding that mankind had "company," as she put it, could raise.

And yet, how could he blame her for her excitement, when he shared it himself? He thought again of that impossible skull, and it was as if a light had gone on inside him. He grinned, his pace increased, and he rubbed his hands together in pleasure. It was gold— a gleaming fragment of scientific gold chipped out of the wall of the past, pointing the way to a rich vein of discoveries.

But—his pace slowed, and he looked up to realize that he was nearly at the Capitol. On impulse, he turned toward the greenhouses of the Botanical Gardens, tucked incongruously into a corner of the Mall. He always enjoyed a stroll through the hothouse plants, always delighted in the eccentricity of the place. He found the entrance and went inside, the humid, peaty warmth of the hothouse air wrapping itself around him.

But—was this a Piltdown or a Coelacanth? There. That was what it came down to. That was the focus of his uncertainty. He grunted to himself, pleased that he had spotted the trouble.

Was this skull Barbara had dug up a second Piltdown, a brilliantly manufactured fake, a hoax? He liked and trusted the impetuous Barbara, but he had to consider the possibility that either she was duping him, or someone was duping her. Suppose the skull and the allegedly related remains had been "salted"—craftily buried by a hoaxer in anticipation of their later discovery?

The original Piltdown Man had survived undiscovered as a fraud for forty years, and the perpetrator had never been identified with any certainty. All that was really known for sure was that a few bits of human and ape bones had been doctored and presented as parts of the same individual. The resultant forgery had made fools out of the greatest names in paleontology—Keith, Woodward, Smith and—wrecked reputations. Far more seriously, it had skewed, warped every study of the human past for two generations.

Or was Barbara's skull a Coelacanth? That strange, bone-headed genus of fishes had been confidently marked down as extinct for millions of years—until a specimen of a Coelacanth was pulled up, spluttering, flopping, and very much alive, from the waters off Africa.

Whether or not Barbara's skull was authentic, it was certain to set off a tidal wave of controversy. It upset too many theories, rocked too many boats for too many people. Real or fake, it would inevitably be challenged. Grossington knew he had to expect that, be prepared for it from square one. Barbara had done a good job of preparing for challenge already, if her careful site notes and photocopies of the journal that had offered the first clues were any indication. The film she had shot would be back from the lab in a day or so, delayed a bit by the holiday rush, more than likely, and it should provide more convincing documentation. It would back up a superb paper trail.

Of course, a good hoaxer would *have* to leave just as superb a paper trail.

Grossington found a bench and thought for a moment, and decided that Barbara had not perpetrated a hoax. It was not in her character. Yet he knew perfectly well that if she had salted that skull, a key part of the plan would be to convince him that she was not capable of any such thing. But be that as it may—he could not and would not operate on the assumption that his people were lying to him. If they called you a fool for trusting people, he preferred to be a fool.

That didn't solve his problem, however, for it made no less likely the chance that *Barbara* was being hoaxed. Still, *she* was no fool. It would be hard to trick her, and the trap that had been laid here would have required some enormous efforts.

How could it possibly be a fraud? He had *seen* that skull, had touched it, smelled it, seen on it the endless minute details that shouted out its authenticity, its unhuman-ness.

Grossington knew he was an expert, that he could not be fooled in such things. Which was no doubt exactly the same sort of thing Keith, Woodward, Smith, et. al., had said about Piltdown.

Even so, he simply could not believe that skull was a fake. He would *know* if it were. Just as he was forced to have faith in his people, he was forced to have faith in himself.

In a scientist, faith was supposed to be a rare commodity. Ideally, it did not exist. All opinion, all thought, all judgment and theory, were supposed to rest on the evidence. Did he have enough faith in Barbara's skill and skepticism tucked away to commit his department to an enterprise that would certainly expose it to controversy, and quite possibly (if his faith was indeed misplaced) destroy it in scandal and fraud?

Well, the only concrete evidence was what his senses told him about the skull—and his senses said it was real.

Was that enough to commit on? Or should he tell Barbara to forget it, go back to her current research, and risk losing history's greatest discovery in the hunt for the human past?

He knew, deep inside, that he could safely say no without stifling the discovery, especially with Barbara Marchando involved. She would go across the figurative street to the competition—the American Museum of History in New York, or that team in Cleveland. Word would get out, the site would be excavated, the lead followed up without Grossington putting himself at any risk. It was too big to squelch forever.

It came down to whether he, Jeffery Grossington, was willing to take the chance, risk his career and his reputation, on this incredible find. All it took to be safe was to say no, let Barbara go elsewhere and drag the coming storm clouds of controversy off with her and leave his quiet life alone. A very simple, easy thing...

A loud, bright noise made him look up. A child, a little girl in pigtails and pinafore, raced past his bench, down the hallways of the Gardens, laughing and shouting at the joy of being alive. Then Grossington heard a muttering grunt from quite close at hand. He turned and discovered for the first time that he was sharing his bench with a sour-faced old man who was clearly annoyed at the child's happiness, displeased with the gardens, fed up with the same world that so delighted the child. It was as clear a symbol—and a warning— as Grossington could want. It would be sinfully criminal to throw away the gifts Gowrie and Barbara were offering up.

He got up and walked out of the building back toward the museum, moving with a much faster, brisker gait. Once he had made up his mind, he walked fast, in a straight line, directly toward his goal.

▼◆▼

Come. Go. Pull weeds. Carry. Bring. Stop. Follow. Out. In.

She knew those hand signs, and all the dozen or so more, the ritualized pantomimes the men used to command her kind. So far as she was concerned, all the words in the world were commands, orders, countermands, and things the commands might be about—the crops, food, water. She signed them to herself, taking an inventory of her tiny collection of words. But now, today, for the first time, she had found a new way of telling, or thought she had: the noises the men made, the shouting, the calling. She had always taken the man-noises as just one more sort of noise, meaning no more or less than her own calls, hoots, cries, and snuffles.

Her own cries could signal distress, or pleasure, or warning, or welcome; they were just one part of the great soundings of the forest, where one animal recognized the calls of its fellows, and could understand and take warning from the meaning of the barks, the yips, the growls of many other animals.

She had always taken the sounds of the men to be such, just noises to urge on and emphasize the hand-commands. The meanings, the commands, were all in the hand signals, not in sound. The man signed them to her kind, and far more rarely, her kind used them among themselves—a skill she was most proficient at.

And yet, she knew another thing. No man ever used hand signals on another man. She had seen human children make the mistake and be severely punished for it. Yet she knew from the endless drudgery of her own life just how needful words were. And she sensed she was close to a great understanding.

For today, she had chanced to see a thing. Huddled together with her kind, locked into their prison-hut, she thought again of what had happened. A man had commanded one of his work-creatures to bring him water, just as another had man called the creature to some other task. She had seen the command gestures—a cupped hand pulled toward the body, and then a hand raised to the mouth and tilted to-

ward the face as if pouring something in.

But the man had seen the second man call the creature, and waved his hand as if to brush something away—the sign to ignore the previous order. The creature had gone away without doing the thing. A minute later, the man saw a passing human child, who had not been there to see the hand signals, tapped him on the arm, and made noises at the child. The boy had run off and brought back water!

It was clear the noises had meant the same thing. Bring-Water. *Thinking as hard as she ever had in her life, signing to herself in the darkness and grunting to help make things clear to herself, she puzzled over the facts.*

Man Never-Sign—Never Man. Bad Man—Sign No Never. *She repeated the signs, emphasizing the point.* Man noises Man. *She grunted, and tried to make some man-noises. Even to her own ear, they did not sound quite right.*

But then she made the connection that had been eluding her in the dim recesses of her mind. Her fur bristled, and she bared her teeth to the darkness in her excitement. Man Do Big Together. Huts. Crops. All-Make Fire. Eat-time. Man Noise-talk. Hand-talk Not...

Frustrated, she growled and grimaced again. She did not have the words to tell herself what she knew inside—which was precisely that *hand-talk didn't have enough words to tell how to do all the men could do.*

This was by far the most painfully complex thinking she had ever done. Already, she was struggling to make the symbols she had fit beyond their capacity.

She tried again, unconsciously inventing *words as she needed them, adding a growl to the sign for talk to mean noise-talk, an extra wave of the palm to mean hand-talk.* Man Noise-talk Do Big, *she signed rather tentatively.*

That *was it. The great revelation. She sat up straighter and snorted with pleasure.* Man Noise-talk Do Big, *she signed again to the dark.* Hand-talk Do Small-Small.

If she listened, she might learn what the noises meant. And then— Do Big. Big-Big.

She huddled herself up in a ball and went to sleep, dreaming of vague and great powers.

Chapter Eight

Ambrose the skull, newly cleaned and coated with Bedacryl preservative, lay gleaming in the center of Dr. Grossington's desk blotter, staring out across the wide expanse of the desk toward Grossington himself. The last hints of daylight were fading from the late-autumn sky framed in the window. It had been a long day all around. "We shall have to hold this rather closely, of course," Grossington said to Barbara and Rupert, calmly puffing on his pipe. Somehow, a few hours of thought was enough for him to feel comfortable, literally face-to-face with evidence that proofed everything that he knew to be false. Grossington sat at his ease, leaning back in his leather chair, surrounded by his office and all its pleasant accouterments. It was a soothing, calming place for him, though many visitors had been put off by the stuffed owl glaring down from the shelves, and the plaster busts of various human ancestors. "We shall need our ducks neatly in a row before we *let* this out."

Barbara nodded her agreement, but Rupert objected. "Dr. Grossington, I have to disagree," he said. He was sitting with his rumpled accordion-pleat briefcase on his lap, using it to support the legal pad he was keeping notes on. He shifted his weight to get the pad to a more comfortable writing position and gestured with his pencil, pointing at the skull on Grossington's desk. "This is the most important paleo discovery in, in—hell, in *history*. People have the right to know. This is *big*. We can't just sit on it until we're good and ready, pretend nothing's happened in the meantime. We have to make an announcement."

Barbara shook her head. "I don't think so, Rupe. Back when we thought this was just imported gorillas, you yourself said this could spark a very public debate. Now, with *this*," she said, nodding toward Ambrose, "things will be ten times worse, a hundred times. We'll be hit by everyone from the fundamentalist Christians to other paleontologists."

Grossington pulled his pipe out of his mouth and looked at Barbara. "Why on Earth would the fundamentalists get involved?"

"We're going to announce that we've dug up a creature that is supposed to be an ancestor of man dead and gone these past million years, and yet here he is less than one hundred forty years old," Barbara said. "Has it occurred to either of you that the Creation Science crowd couldn't ask for a better target?"

That made the two of them sit up. Barbara went on. "They'll say this proves that the australopithecines couldn't be our ancestors, or our evolutionary cousins. They'll say it proves that the Earth isn't very old, that the other hominid finds can't be more than a few thousand years old, either. It'll all be nonsense of course, but can you imagine the *damage* they could do?" As she spoke, inexplicably, Michael popped into her mind. She thought of him and suddenly recalled she was supposed to meet him for dinner tonight at The Childe Harold in Dupont Circle. It was not a comforting thought, and gave an extra twist of angry frustration to her mood.

"*Every*one is going to have an axe to grind," she went on. "*No* one is going to want to believe this. Everyone will have a vested interest in proving us wrong. So we have to be ready, have all the loose ends tied up, be prepared with a complete, orderly presentation of all the facts, rather than springing it prematurely and losing control of the situation. Announce today and there will be pickets marching through the dig site tomorrow. At the very least, we have to hold off until the rest of Ambrose and any further specimens have been safely excavated—unless you want to buy the bones back from souvenir hunters." What sort of fight would Michael pick tonight? Keep your head straight, girl. That didn't have anything to do with the matter at hand.

"Okay," Rupert said. "You've made your point. I still don't like it, but it sounds like we don't have much choice."

"It also strikes me that we should keep the list of people who are informed about this to a strict minimum," Grossington said. "Again, for reasons of security."

"Wait a second," Rupert said. "Just how minimal are you talking?"

Grossington shrugged. "Quite frankly, Rupert, I would have preferred excluding you and keeping it down to Dr. Marchando and myself. No reflection on you, of course, but just following the rule of keeping the numbers down. You are in, obviously. And of course that cousin of yours, Barbara. What about your other relations? Do they know what's going on?"

She would just have time to get home, drop her stuff, shower and change before it was time to meet him. Barbara made a deliberate effort to force thoughts of Michael out of her mind and shook her head. "Not really. Obviously, they knew I was excited about digging something up, but they weren't really clear about what it was—and frankly they've seen me pumped up about so many obscure discoveries over the years, I don't think they much care by this time. The girl who cried wolf, that sort of thing. My digging a hole was entertainment, that's all."

Grossington nodded in approval. "Good. But that still makes four who know, which is three more than the best number for keeping a secret. I propose we *keep* the list that short. The three of us will go to Gowrie and complete the excavation ourselves."

"Whoa. No way," Rupert objected. "We've got a major dig site here. We'll need *at least* three or four more warm bodies to do it right. And this job, we *have* to do right. No half measures, for all the reasons we've discussed. And with all due respect, you haven't done a field season in years. You're not in any shape to do the heavy spade work. Sir."

Barbara nodded vehemently at the mention of shovels. She could still feel how sore her arm muscles were. "I've got to agree with Rupert, Dr. Grossington. There's going to be too much work for just two or three people. At least let us raid some of the interns and grad students around here. We *need* some skilled diggers—ah, excuse me, skilled field workers for this one." For the second time that day, Barbara remembered too late that Grossington hated the slang "diggers."

For the second time that day, Grossington let her get away with it, merely glaring at her severely.

Rupert, it would seem, chose that moment to take a risk all his own. "There's another point," he said, doodling in his sketch pad, deliberately not looking up. "Maybe it would be smart if we had someone back in the home office to watch out for us, able to supply us quietly without raising questions, that sort of thing. Perhaps, Dr. Grossington, you ought to be back here instead of straining against a shovel."

Grossington snorted angrily and looked fixedly at Rupert, forcing the younger man to return his gaze. "You can offer up all the logical, sensible reasons you want, Dr. Maxwell," he said. "But I am going on this little outing."

Barbara hurriedly jumped in and spoke before Rupert could reply and turn things into a full-scale argument. It was getting to be a pretty tense meeting. "Fine, we're all going. Can we get back to the question of who else is going? We definitely will need more staff."

Grossington slowly turned from Rupert to Barbara, obviously forcing himself to calm down. "But how can we keep the situation quiet if so many people are involved? And what about accommodations for all these people? And work space? What budget will that come from?"

"Aunt Jo will put them up, for a very reasonable fee. She enjoys having some bustle around that old house. And I'm sure we can squeeze our lab space into the basement. As to security, this is an isolated house on the outskirts of a very small town. It'll be more like the African brush than being in Washington, as far as contact with the outside world is concerned. Sure, if this leaks, the place will be hip-deep in reporters, but as long as we're careful, that won't happen."

"Mmmmph. I suppose you're right. And I must admit that my back is not as strong as it used to be, either. Very well, do some very quiet, discreet recruiting among the grads and terns," Grossington said, slipping into some slang himself. "And be sure not to tell them anything substantive until they're signed up."

Barbara shrugged. "That won't be easy, but I can try."

Rupert had started scribbling notes to himself, a sure sign that he was taking things seriously. "Hold it hold it hold it," he said, rattling the words off one right after another. "Before we go signing up our team, let's decide what it is they are supposed to be doing. We'll need some specialized skills. First, obviously, excavate Ambrose, clean and preserve the bones, and search in the immediate vicinity for any more of these creatures. You said that journal suggested at least two or three more might be buried there?" Barbara nodded and Rupert jotted the figure down. "Let's remember that we're all paleo here, and we're getting into an archaeo kind of situation. Rupert looked at his two listeners, and was rewarded with a pair of blank looks. He sighed. "Look, none of us is used to working in anything less than thousands of years. Most of our work predates the wheel, and a lot of it goes back to before our ancestors made any artifacts at all. We need an *artifact* person, an archaeologist who knows more than bones. And we may need some help in local history. Just stuff we need to keep in mind. Okay?"

The two of them nodded and he went on. "Right. Now, the digging things out of ground part is pretty straightforward, but *then* what? We know more or less when these beasties arrived, but from where? So, second job, track source of the creatures, presumably in Africa somewhere. Don't ask me how, but that needs to be done. Third, analyze whatever bones we recover. We'll need to compare Ambrose and company as closely as we can against every scrap of australopithecine fossil material available."

That was not as much of a challenge as one might suppose. The entire genus of *Australopithecus* was known from only about a hundred individuals, many of the specimens little more than a scrap or two of tooth. The fossils themselves were, for the most part, far too precious and fragile for everyday study. Many were stored in bomb-proof vaults, jealously guarded by their owners, and but rarely removed for examination. There simply were not enough fossils to go around; indeed, there were probably more paleoanthropologists in the world than australopithecine fossils for them to study. Most scientists relied on studies of high-quality casts for day-to-day work. "As far as security goes, we can't spring any original fossils from their owners without raising a fuss."

Barbara broke in. "That means either moving all our casts of the material down to Gowrie, or bringing all of the Gowrie specimens back here to compare to the collection."

Dr. Grossington relit his pipe and thought. "Damn it, this is rapidly getting too complex. But you're right, we'll need the reference casts. We'll have to take them along, I suppose. But taking the casts with us is bound to get the people using them now a bit annoyed." He shrugged. "Can't be helped."

"Okay, we're agreed on that," Rupert said. "So, number three, analyze the Gowrie samples and compare against present knowledge. Just incidentally, and not losing our scientific detachment, if we can isolate the Gowrie population phylogenetically, find enough differences to call it a new species of the family *Australopithecus*, instead of deciding it's a member of one of the accepted species, that might slow the Creationists down a bit." Grossington shifted his chair and opened his mouth as if to speak, but Rupert held up a hand to stop him. "Yes, Dr. Grossington, I know. We mustn't let such concerns warp our scientific judgment and detachment. But wouldn't it be nice all the same? Then, four, we have to *explain* all this. How did these australopithecines survive into the modern era? Where the hell have they been? How could the species have been found and then lost in the 1850s? Should I keep going, or is that enough questions for now?"

Dr. Grossington smiled. "I should say that's enough." He glanced at his watch. "Nearly six o'clock. Well, completely upending the study of man's past by close of business isn't a bad day's work. I expect I shall see you both bright and early tomorrow, and we can start planning in detail. I have a date with some gentlemen over at the National Geographic, and it seems to me that this would be a good moment to pay court to our sources of funding, tell them we have something interesting on tap." The Smithsonian Institution was, of course, a government operation, but it did accept private funds and occasionally cooperated with the Geographic on research.

Barbara looked up sharply. "Remember, Jeffery, we need to hold this close."

"Don't worry, Barbara. I've a great deal of practice in being vague. Until tomorrow, then."

Barbara left the meeting wishing she had that sort of practice. Her dinners with Michael usually seemed to get a bit too bogged down on specifics.

▼◆▼

Dr. Michael Marchando checked his watch for the fifth time in as many minutes. It was still fifteen minutes until Barbara was due, of course, but that didn't make him any calmer. He picked up his martini and sipped it carefully, sedately, temperately. Tonight was no night for drinking too much. Drunks didn't win their nearly ex-wives back. He shifted on his bar stool so he could watch both entrances. The Childe Harold was an all-right place, but it was not the spot he would have picked. It was a friendly, almost boisterous neighborhood tavern, not a romantic hideaway. No doubt Barbara had chosen the place for just that reason when she had reluctantly agreed to the date the week before.

Michael was twenty-nine, a year or two younger than Barbara. He was a dark-skinned, lightly built man with a thin face and moody, brown, deep-set eyes. The lines of his face fell most naturally into sad expressions, or hurt ones, or fearful ones. Perhaps because of that, his unexpected sunburst smiles were all the more winning, all the more charming. He was a surgeon—or, more accurately, a surgical resident—at Howard University Hospital on the other side of the city, and he had the long, graceful hands surgeons were supposed to have.

He caught a look at himself in the mirror behind the bar, and, as always, was baffled at what he saw there. Michael Marchando was as much a mystery to himself as he was to everyone else. He *knew* how much he had accomplished, how far the poor kid from the tumbledown public housing project had come. He *knew* how far he was likely to go yet. He *knew* he had nothing left to prove.

He might know it, but he did not believe it.

Barbara hurried up the escalator from the subway entrance, and checked her watch as she reached the top. She would be just in time, barely. She bit her lip took a deep breath, and hurried across the street to the restaurant. Damn him for making this date, damn herself for agreeing to it, chasing this marriage long after it had already failed. She stopped for a minute, got her anger under control, and then walked down the block at a far more deliberate pace. Here was the restaurant. Down the stairs and into the lower-level bar. Scan the room and search for—

And there he was. Such a beautiful man.

And all of it melted away again, dammit. All the anger, all the frustration, all the infuriating arguments dissolved into nothingness as she felt her face forming into an unbidden, unwelcome smile, a joyous grin as warm as any summer.

She had known this would happen to her. Dammit. But then he saw her, and came to her across the crowded floor, and their arms were about each other.

She knew it couldn't last.

She stepped back, still smiling, still warm inside, and looked at him. "Hello, Michael. How you been keeping?"

He smiled back, an uncertain, nervous expression. "Pretty good, Barb. Pretty good."

The waiter led them to their table. They ordered quickly and then sat there, staring at each other, almost afraid to speak. Finally, Barbara broke the silence. "So how was your Thanksgiving?" she asked, for want of a better way to begin.

"Good, good," Michael said with a trifle too much enthusiasm, as if he were grateful for something to talk about. "Momma had a lot of the family in. She did some fine cooking. I had to share my room over the weekend with Billy and Gordon. We had a full house."

Barbara shook her head and made a noncommittal noise. Twenty-nine years old, a full-grown man, a respected doctor making good money—more than Barbara would ever make—and the best he could do when his marriage broke up was to move back in with his mother in her half-slum neighborhood. Back to the room he had occupied as a child and a wild teenager. The McKinley Tech High School pennant was still hanging over the narrow single bed, the under-sized desk still waiting in the corner, the gouges carved in it aging evidence of his model-building days. The model airplanes themselves still hung from the ceiling, floating in dusty flight, suspended on faded threads of the past. And who of all the visiting relatives did he choose to spend the weekend with? Billy and Gordon, two no-account drinking buddies. She could just imagine the three of them tiptoeing out after the house was asleep, in search of every bar that was open, pointless foolishness and debauchery.

Michael Marchando could cure the sick, diagnose a thousand diseases, ease the pain of endless hurts, and yet he seemed wholly incapable of cooking for himself, or doing the wash, or caring for himself. He had always depended on the women in his life for that, expected their care and attention as obviously, unquestionably *his*, the pampered male's unquestioned and unspoken birthright. It was as if he was incapable of fending for himself, and such incompetence was some strange evidence of his rights as a man.

The old mystery of it all clambered for her attention once again. *Why?* Barbara had walked out on *him*, left him in possession of their apartment. He hadn't even needed to move—all he needed to do in order to have his own place was remain where he was. But back to

Momma he had gone, and his mother had welcomed him back as unquestioningly as he had gone to her. There could be no other place for him.

She was starting to remember, as she knew she would, why, exactly, she had left. Why couldn't Michael be like her cousin Livingston—adventurous, independent, unafraid of taking a few knocks now and again? Then she looked into Michael's eyes, and remembered why she had longed to stay. There was so much good there, even so.

She discovered that the two of them were holding hands across the table. She almost jerked her hand back, but then made herself leave it where it was. No sense upsetting him, rejecting him, hurting him that way. She always felt she had to walk on eggshells around him. She spoke again, launching her voice across the deep silence between them.

"I had quite a weekend myself," Barbara said lamely. "Good to see the family." *This must be closely held,* she told herself in Grossington's words, knowing full well that it was a ridiculous excuse for keeping the story from Michael. But there was some very clear part of her that didn't want to tell him. It was *hers*, not some piece of community property they'd have to sort out some day. "How's work going?" she asked, wondering how long she could keep the small talk going.

"Barb, it's time we talked about getting back together."

She had known that was coming, but still it hurt. Always, it came to this. Would it keep happening forever? Would she spend the rest of her life trying to force this man-child out of the nest, out into the world where he could become a whole person, instead of a dependent little boy? She lowered her eyes and did not speak.

Thankfully, their food arrived, and the two of them ate, in silence at first, until Michael managed to say something, anything else, and they could talk about inconsequential things.

And Barbara never noticed how often she touched his hand all through the meal.

▼◆▼

How, why, she could not say, but he ended up at her place that night. She had known, they had both known, he would. His presence was so comforting, warm and safe the night before she set off again in the adventure of that impossible skull.

Why, after what purpose, she did not understand, but they made love that night, with great urgency. Afterwards, Barbara slept, slept more deeply than she had in weeks, as if her body and soul were finally willing to admit she was emotionally drained, physically exhausted.

But Michael was restless at night, a wanderer. He got up, wandered about the still only half-furnished apartment, raided the refrigerator for a glass of milk, sat down at the kitchen table, and happened to notice her voluminous briefcase, lying half-open on the table. Idly curious, he opened one of the folders, and began to read.

▼◆▼

He was still there when Barbara awoke in the morning and shuffled her way into the kitchen. "This is great news, very exciting stuff, Barb," he said cheerfully. "Why didn't you tell me about it?"

She looked down at the papers spread out on the table. A flicker of anger went through her, but then she shrugged her shoulders and sat down next to him. "I don't know why, Mike. Maybe it was just too complicated, mixed up with seeing you again. Maybe I just wanted it kept private, to myself. I don't know. Besides, Grossington wants it all kept very quiet for now.

"Hell, maybe I left the papers out on purpose, knowing you'd read them. Maybe force of habit. We always let each other see our professional papers when we were married." She hesitated for a long moment, and looked straight into his beautiful eyes. "But I guess we're not really married any more," she said sadly. "I wish you hadn't looked."

Michael took her hand and gave it a squeeze. "I'm still glad for you, but I wish you had told me face to face."

She smiled unhappily and stood up to start making coffee and breakfast. "Sorry about that, Michael. I guess you're right. I'm glad you know about it—but I don't really want to talk about it right now."

He looked surprised, as if he was expecting some whoop of joy from her, now that he knew the great news. She sighed and turned toward the coffee maker on the counter.

He hesitated, then stood up and kissed the back of her neck. "It's okay, sweetie. But just the same, it's great news. Listen, maybe we can celebrate with a nice dinner tonight, okay?" he asked, a bit distantly. He gave her an affectionate little hug from behind, then went off to retrieve the newspaper from the front door without waiting for an answer. He came back a minute later, sat back down, tidied up her work papers, put them back in her briefcase, and started reading the newspaper. Magically, the old silence had descended, the affection of a few moments ago vanished into a studied remoteness.

Damn him! He snoops in her private papers, and here *she* was apologizing it *him* for it. And here she was, unquestioningly cooking him yet another breakfast while he sat there and read the paper.

She remembered why she had left, all right. Now she was trying to remember why she had stayed so long. It didn't matter. In a few days, they'd meet up with Liv in Gowrie again.

Livingston Jones woke up, opened his eyes, stared at the ceiling, and sighed. All those neat stacks of old papers were waiting for him downstairs on the dining room table. Time to face another day of reading century-old, overly precise handwriting on the subject of everything else under the sun but what he was interested in. It was truly astonishing how many bits of paper they had cranked out back then—and how many had survived. It had taken him most of the previous day to get them into some semblance of order.

He got out of bed and began his morning calisthenics. He could still smell the musty smell of the old paper and ink on his hands from yesterday, and was not looking forward to more of the same.

He *knew*, with the sharp, clean certainty of an unproved hunch, that there were no further clues to the origins of the australopithecines in the plantation papers. He had no logical reason for so believing, but he knew. Of course, Barbara would tell him that wasn't good enough. He'd have to dig through all the papers and *prove* there was nothing—and keep careful enough notes to demonstrate that he had searched thoroughly. And then what? Nothing. A dead end.

Amazing, he thought as he began his sit-ups, just how boring science could be.

He headed through the empty house toward his shower, his breakfast, and a very dull day of work.

DECEMBER

Chapter Nine

Josephine Jones stepped out onto the porch and looked out across her yard toward the excavation. She shook her head and smiled, annoyed and delighted by it all at the same time.

They had been back at it for over a week now, a whole swarm of them: Barbara, this Rupert fellow, that funny old walrus Dr. Grossington, and an indeterminate number of younger ones who never stood still long enough for her to count them, or get their names exactly straight. They all seemed interchangeably bright, eager, polite, and industrious.

However many of them there were, they certainly knew how to dig a hole. It was huge, and getting bigger and deeper all the time—and the pile of dug-up dirt wasn't exactly shrinking, either. Every now and again, another bit of bone would be discovered, cleared of dirt, and ceremoniously removed from the still earth. Wrapped in cloth like a babe in swaddling clothes, laid carefully in a padded box as if it were the most precious jewel, each load of bones was carried from the excavation to the "laboratory" in the basement. There were three nearly complete skeletons down there now, and the diggers had found a few bones that were probably another one of these new creatures, though it was hard to say if these bones were another ape-man or just some poor human soul who had gotten buried in the same spot. Even so, the bones from number four went down into the lab.

Josephine still thought "laboratory" was a pretty grand name for a bunch of trestle tables covered with boxes of bones, but she had to admit her visitors worked tirelessly at their mysterious tasks down there. She did not claim to understand all they did, but even so, some of the excitement over this inexplicable find had spread to her. She knew, in a vague way, that the scientists said that people had descended from creatures that were somewhat ape-like. She was proud of her great-niece, and at least flipped through *National Geographic* articles on fossils, so as to keep up on Barbara's field a bit. She even knew that these particular skeletons didn't belong where they had been found.

But what a fuss they made over some musty old bones! Brrr. She didn't *like* bones one bit, and it troubled her a bit at nights to think of the skulls in the basement, being worked over. Still, it did a body good to see so much busyness about the old place again. Shaking her head and smiling, she went back inside to get another look at the basement bones. She always believed in getting a good hard look at what scared her.

▼◆▼

With a sense of resigned frustration, Livingston closed the cover on the last musty bound volume of the Gowrie *Gazette*. His hands were covered with the powdery dust of old books, and he wished not for the first time that the Gowrie Library had heard of microfilm. He had been through every page of every extant issue of the *Gazette* from 1850 to 1860. Nothing. He had been through every period letter, memoir and diary in the Gowrie library's surprisingly extensive local history section. Nothing. He had contacted the local folklore society and asked about "creature" stories and got nothing better than Aunt Jo's vague recollections of stories she had once heard as a child.

On the bright side, he was getting to be an expert on Gowrie history. That and a quarter would get him a cup of coffee most places. But he had no doubt that there wasn't a single shred of documentary proof for Zebulon's tales of strange creatures. If the bones hadn't still been coming out of the ground, Livingston would have long ago concluded that there was no basis in fact for the stories at all.

There was one last card left to play. A few runs of the newspaper were missing from the library collection—scarcely surprising after one hundred and thirty years. It was just possible his missing clue could be found in those runs.

The flaw was that the only place likely to have the editions in question were the present-day offices of the Gowrie *Gazette*. Which meant dealing with the proprietor. Just as in Zebulon's day, the paper was run by a man named Teems, a descendant of the man who had helped Zeb buy the plantation. Unfortunately, this Teems was as much of a throwback as Stephen Teems had been ahead of his time. Joe Teems was about seventy years old and an unabashed racist and segregationist, who would stand in Livingston's way as much as possible, out of sheer cussedness. Liv had worked one summer as a paperboy for Teems, and remembered him in sheer hatred and terror.

But it couldn't be helped. Livingston got up, replaced the book in its shelf, collected his notes, and went in search of a place to clean the dust off before dealing with Teems. Liv did not have much hope for a successful outcome.

▼◆▼

Dr. Rupert Maxwell, on the other hand, was deriving the most satisfactory results from his researches. Under the baleful glare and angry hum of the basement's harsh fluorescent lighting, Rupert was busily working over Ambrose's molars, carefully measuring a dozen features of each tooth. He was logging the values into a portable computer that sat in a shadowy corner of the workbench, its high-contrast screen a glowering blood-amber against the background of the relentless whitewashed walls. Every number he fed to that brooding screen was a tiny victory, a minute piece of the proof he was searching for. He set down his calipers for a moment and sipped noisily at his tea, a thick herbal brew made from a special blend he had brought along with him to the wilds of Mississippi.

He heard the slow, careful *clump-clump, clump-clump* of an elderly person's tread on the steep cellar stairs and looked up. It was Mrs. Jones, Barbara's Great-aunt Jo, wandering down for a visit. "Good morning, Mrs. Jones," Rupert said. "Welcome to our dungeon away from home."

"We missed you at breakfast, Dr. Maxwell," she said in a gently accusing tone as she reached the bottom of the stairs. "Weren't you feeling well this morning?"

Rupert grinned weakly, shifted in his seat, and set his tea down guiltily, like a small boy caught sampling his father's beer. "Ah, well, no, I felt fine. Just sleeping in a bit, that's all. Worked late last night," he offered lamely. "Again."

"Again," Aunt Jo repeated, her severe horn-rimmed glasses and formidable bulk making her seem positively unnerving to Rupert. "What is it exactly you're doing down here, anyway?" she asked suddenly. "I see you people measuring and measuring these old bones and skulls down here in the basement, day after day, night after night. The whole thing gives me the creepies, I tell you. What're you *doing* it for?"

Rupert shrugged awkwardly. "Jeez, Mrs. Jones. It's so complicated to explain."

"I've got the time, child. You just do your best and I'll make sense of it."

Rupert picked up his calipers, fiddled with them for a second and sighed. "Maybe I'd better start at the beginning, then. Okay, you've heard a lot of talk about australopithecines from us around here, right? That's sort of a generic term that refers to a whole family of species— *Australopithecus robustus, Australopithecus boisei, Australopithecus africanus, Australopithecus afarensis*. And then there's WT-17000."

"W-T what?" Aunt Jo asked.

"WT-17000. Sounds like a miracle ingredient in toothpaste, doesn't it? It's the collection number of a weird australopithecine skull. It happens to be dark-colored, so they call it 'the Black Skull'— which sounds like something out of Robert Louis Stevenson." He dropped his voice and scrunched his shoulder over into a pirate imitation. "'Kiss the Black Skull, Jim, harr, harr, harr.'" He looked up and caught the look Aunt Jo was giving him. "Sorry," he muttered, slightly embarrassed. "Anyway, WT-17000 doesn't fit in *anywhere*. It's possible that it represents a new species, *Australopithecus aethiopicus*, which is just what we need. I don't really believe in *aethiopicus* myself. The Black Skull is early *boisei*. But, back to the main point, all 'australopithecus' means is 'southern ape,' and each of the southern apes has a second name to distinguish it from the others, sort of like a Christian name and given name.

"Except. Australopithecines aren't just apes, of course. They are hominids, very closely related to mankind, to us, to *Homo sapiens sapiens*. Maybe some of them are ancestors to us, maybe some one of these australopithecines gave rise to the various species of *Homo* that led to us. Or maybe all any australopithecine is to us is a sort of evolutionary cousin, and we haven't found the common ancestor that our kind *and* theirs sprang from. We don't exactly know, for certain, what our relation is to these creatures, or even which australopithecine descends from the others, in all cases."

"But even if I buy this evolution and take it home, how could they be our ancestors if they were still around when Granpa Zeb was alive?" Aunt Josephine asked.

"Just because someone has children doesn't mean they're dead,"

Rupert said. "There are plenty of cases of an ancestral species existing, living and breeding, right alongside a descendant species. Obviously, Ambrose here," he said, patting the skull, "had to have a mother and a father, and he might even have fathered some pups of his own. Just as obviously, he isn't my ancestor." He was going to add "or yours," but decided that would be impolitic. "*But* it's absolutely certain that he and I did have a common ancestor, somewhere back a zillion years or so. My arm bones and leg bones and toe bones and general headshape and so on are very much like his. The family resemblance is very strong," he said cheerfully.

"What worries me is that when this comes out, someone is going to say Ambrose himself being alive when he was proves that neither his *species* nor any related species could be an ancestor to ours, and so all of human evolution is a crock, and therefore the creationists are right.

"Which brings me back to what I'm doing. Remember I rattled off the names of the australopithecine species? The differences between those species are actually pretty small—and we have so little fossil evidence that it's hard to say for sure which differences are important. According to some people, the differences are so small that there weren't four species, just one or two that survived a long time, with some of the creatures in those species bigger than others, or with somewhat different teeth. Just based on size, if you saw the bones of a jockey and a basketball player you might say that each represented a separate species of *Homo*. We might be doing that with the australopithecines. Now, as far as the various alleged species of australopithecine are concerned, we have remains representing maybe a hundred or so individuals, and most of them have been very carefully measured in all sorts of ways. What I hope to find out with Ambrose and his friends here is that there are a whole range of small but significant differences between them and the other australopithecine specimens. Wide enough that I should be able to establish a series of diagnostics for a new species based on these bones here."

"Diagnostics? What does that mean, you can tell what it died of?"

"Huh? Oh, no. To a paleoanthropologist, a diagnostic is a set of tests you can run to see if a given specimen is a member of a given species. One diagnostic might be, say, the angle between the point where the spinal cord enters the skull and a given feature on the cranium. That sort of thing."

"So you can just look at one little tooth and say what kind of—of australopithecine it's from?"

"Nope," Rupert said cheerfully. "Can't be done. Sometimes we can't even tell for sure if it's australopithecine or *Homo*. Remember our jockey and our basketball player? The sizes and proportions between those two extremes will contain most, though not all, of the range of human variance. Now suppose we had just dug up, say, this." He carefully picked up one of Ambrose's leg bones and turned it over in his hands. "A little odd in some respects, but this bone falls well within that human range. But one look at Ambrose's head and you *know* he ain't human. There can be ambiguities if you only have part of the skeleton.

"But what makes it even worse is that we have never found a complete australopithecine skeleton until now, and rarely have we found much more than a partially complete cranium and mandible—that is the main part of the skull and the jaw—and it's rarer still that we've found a complete and *undamaged* skull. Some of the ones that have been found we dug up were shattered into a hundred pieces. They were put together all right, but you can't ever be exactly sure that the angles *between* the pieces were right, or that you've guessed the size of the missing pieces correctly.

"The point is that our sample base of data for the entire genus *Australopithecus* is so scrappy that it's almost impossible to get any hard comparative figures out of it. There are guesses piled on guesses piled on estimates based on probable reconstructions based on what might as well be tossing a coin. Which in turn means my proof that these australopithecines aren't the same as one of the known species will be shot down by someone who interprets the figures differently, and we'll all be arguing about it for years to come. That's the thing about paleo—you're never quite *sure* about anything."

Aunt Jo frowned. "I thought you scientists were supposed to be dedicated to truth or something. But this is what you do all day, what you do with your life? Stare at piles of bones and measure them and argue over them even though it won't prove anything? That's being a scientist?"

Rupert smiled. "Next you'll be telling me that I should be out in the fresh air and sunshine instead of playing inside. Seriously, though, this"—he gestured to the piles of bones—"this isn't what I do with my life—it's what I have to do to get to my *real* work. I'm not in this racket because I like bones. What I'm really interested in is *hands*. Motor dexterity. How did we and our hands come to be able to make things—and when? We've *never* gotten a decent set of australopithecine hand bones until now.

"I've always wondered just what it was that set off the first wave of hominid toolmaking. After all, tools are one of the things that make a human human. Try to imagine getting through a day without using an artifact, a made thing. We aren't the only tool-making and tool-using creatures on this earth, but we are the only ones who *need* tools, who use them for all the jobs of staying alive all the time. You could say tools define us, make us *us*.

"We know you don't have to be smart to use tools.

Sea otters and those ditzy little birds in the Galapagos use tools, and *they* aren't all that bright. Chimps not only use natural tools, but *make* tools. And there is some evidence for non-primate toolmaking. It might be as crude as snapping off a twig to get it the right length, but it *is* toolmaking. And if some damn little idiot tweetie-bird can do it, why not Ambrose and company? He had to be at least as smart as a chimp.

"Besides, the australopithecines had better hands than chimps. Chimp hands don't have as good a precision grip, and the thumb doesn't oppose as nicely. It's clumsy. Ambrose, though—very nice hands. If he were smart enough to spell, he would have been a pretty fair typist.

"Ambrose and company should have been perfectly capable of toolmaking. But we've never found any incontrovertible tools that were unambiguously associated with australopithecines. There are some chipped pebbles that *might* be tools that *might* have been made by an australopithecine—except they might belong to *Homo habilus*. Except a ways back White and Johanson dug up a largely complete *habilus* skeleton—and the postcranial bones are more apelike and much less human-like than Ambrose's. Go figure."

Aunt Jo was definitely getting confused. "But if there aren't any tools, doesn't that proves the australopithecines didn't make tools?"

"It's awfully tough to prove a negative. Besides which," Rupert picked a wooden ruler off his workbench and gestured with it, "you have to ask, will *this* be around in a million years? Three million? Would the tools the chimps make—twigs stripped of leaves, and leaves mashed up into a water-sponge—would they last? It's very fashionable to think that *Homo* is the only toolmaking hominid genus, but I think it's possible that the australopithecines did it too. I think it even more possible since I've seen these hand bones. But before this, I didn't have any tools, and I didn't have any hands, so I started examining endocranial casts for clues."

"Endo—wait a minute, casts of the inside of the cranium—inside the *head*?" Aunt Jo knit her brow in some alarm. This boy could talk about the most ghoulish things in the most matter-of-fact way.

"Right. All you do, more or less, is pour latex into the hole in the base of the cranium that the spinal cord comes through. Slosh it around until it covers the interior, let it dry, and very carefully pull the mold back out the hole. Tricky, but it can be done. See, the brain leaves traces on the inside of the skull. You can *see* the folds and lumps and bumps of the brain that used to be there. So I got a bunch of casts together, and looked for signs of pronounced development of the areas responsible for motor dexterity. Got a lot of good measurements and shot 'em through a lot of statistical programs, compared 'em to human and chimp endocasts so see which the australopithecine motor-dexterity regions resembled more closely."

"And?"

Rupert shrugged. "And I got a big maybe—but at least an intriguing maybe. No proof, no definite conclusions. There almost never are such things in this business. You just try and pin down one microscopic corner of the big picture."

He paused, and a strange, thoughtful look came over him. "The studies we make almost seem trivial, but the weird thing is that paleontologists start out asking the biggest questions of all—where did mankind come from, how did we get to the point where we could turn back and look the other way? How are we so like the other primates, all other animals, and yet so weirdly, wildly different?" He held up two fingers very close together and showed them to Aunt Jo. "There's *that* much difference between a chimp's DNA and mine, less than the distance between a horse's genes and a donkey's—and I'd bet the farm that Ambrose's genes were even *more* like mine. We start out asking how that could possibly *be*, where the change came and what it was—and we end up in tiny corners of inquiry, measuring old teeth and waiting for skullfuls of latex to dry. We learn more all the time, and yet the big answers seem farther off than ever."

He picked up the ruler again and slapped it thoughtfully against his other hand. "And at times, I have to admit that digging up bones is never going to answer the real question, because we'll never dig up the fossil of the first soul, and know who had it and how they got it. We'll never know, exactly, what made us human and Ambrose something else, something less."

Aunt Jo looked hard at Rupert and frowned. "Young man, I have understood every word you've said—but the whole thing put together confuses the life out of me."

Rupert raised an eyebrow, tilted his head to one side. "Join the club," he said wistfully.

▼◆▼

The wizened old face looked as if it had not faced the sun for a generation, and the wispy stubble on the old man's cheeks was grey, dismal, half-hearted, as if it could not grow properly for lack of light. The air itself was cloudy grey in the editor's private office of the Gowrie *Gazette*. Smoke tendrils slithered up from the cigar wedged into Joe Teems's hand. The gloom and dust wrapped around the office like a web, as if the old man were a greyish spider sitting in the trap he weaved, waiting for a victim.

The color had long since gone from Teems's hair, his face, his clothes. The only hints of something beyond grey were in the rheumy yellow of his eyes, and the unhealthy redness of his wound-like mouth, which hung half-open in an evil-looking grin, a moist, dark cavern full of teeth as ragged as a row of old tombstones.

"What you want here, boy?" Joe Teems demanded of Livingston, and eased his damp cigar back into his mouth.

Livingston swallowed hard and clenched his fists, resisting the urge to swat down this nasty, ugly, hateful old man, resisting the urge to run away from this horrifying ruin of the tyrant who had terrorized Liv that whole long, miserable summer. Liv focused on the word "boy" in his mind, concentrated on what it meant, and got angry. Suddenly he felt no fear, no anger, no anxiety, but only cold contempt for this shambling wreck, this smelly old man who treated Livingston as an inferior.

"I need to look at some back issues of the *Gazette*, Mr. Teems," Livingston said, his voice level, calm, controlled. "Some issues are missing from the library collection."

"Is that so? Is that a certifiable fact?" Teems stood up from behind his desk, his rumpled suit a sea of cigar ash and faded stains. "And just who the hell might you be, to come barging in here like this," he demanded, his husky voice suddenly angry and sharp. "Why should a busy man like myself let some stranger—some uppity colored boy who talks real pretty—snoop around in the newspaper's archives?" He stretched the last words out grandly, and made a broad, sweeping gesture with his hand, as if indicating some palatial storehouse full of back issues. "Who the hell do you think you are?"

Livingston kept his voice steady, but he could feel his heart pounding as he struggled to keep in his anger. "It's Livingston Jones, Mr. Teems. Josephine Jones's nephew. I delivered papers for you one summer, when I was a kid."

"Delivered papers? Years ago? For *me*?" Teems asked as he touched his hand to his chest theatrically, his voice dripping with sarcasm. "Well, then, sir, I must be eternally in your debt. Just because your family has been a thorn in my side my whole life, just because I am even now recalling just how useless a paperboy you were, that's no reason for me to say no. I'll say no just because I don't like you." He took a long drag on his cigar and glared at Livingston. "Now get out of here."

"But—"

"Go away. Now. I got work to do."

Teems sat back down at his desk and shuffled idly through a stack of papers he didn't really care about, pointedly ignoring Livingston.

Liv stood there for a moment trying to think of something to say, and finally spun on his heels, opened the door leading to the tiny newsroom, stomped out of the dismal office, and slammed the door behind him. The missing newspapers were a wild goose chase anyway—nothing more than the last and most unlikely place he might find some sort of mention in print of the creatures. Not worth getting upset about, not worth begging a sour old cracker like Teems for help.

Liv found himself standing in the well-lit, slightly scruffy but clean and tidy, perfectly ordinary newsroom of the *Gazette*—a room so different from Teems's gloomy *sanctum sanctorum* that Liv felt disoriented for a moment, as if he had stepped out of his bedroom door and found himself in an airline terminal. All the people in the room—the two or three reporters, the receptionist, even the guy who had come in to drop off a classified ad—looked up and stared at Livingston.

The *Gazette* building was a low, single-story structure, a converted glass-front store on Main Street, with the newsroom at the front of the place, Teems's office tucked in one rear corner, and the entrance to the print shop in the other. Livingston had to parade down the very public aisles of the newsroom, very obviously having been kicked out. He shrugged and walked across the room toward the outside door and the street, staring straight ahead so he wouldn't have to look anyone in the eye.

"No luck, huh?"

Livingston glanced down involuntarily as he passed the last of the desks to see an improbably cheerful-looking young white man grinning up at him. Liv stopped. "Nope."

"Not surprised. Old Man Teems hasn't said yes to anyone for years." The young man offered his hand. "Pete Ardley. One of the *Gazette*'s tame reporters. You're not from around here, are you?"

Liv shook his hand. "Livingston Jones. No, I'm visiting out at my Aunt's Jo's place."

"Right. Well, what can we do for you?" Ardley swiveled his chair around to face Livingston.

"But what about—" Liv cocked his head toward the editor's office.

"Him? Just because he said no? Relax. He doesn't care about what people do. He just likes being mean, especially to blacks. Besides, he never comes in here—not even to go in and out of his office. He has his own rear entrance. So what do you need?"

Liv shrugged. "I just wanted to get a look at some back issues, old ones the library didn't have. Pre-Civil —ah, Pre-War Between the States." Liv almost forgot to use the term preferred in the South.

"Piece of cake. C'mon back here." Ardley stood up and led Livingston through the newsroom to a door marked *Library*. Ardley opened it and they stepped into a small, windowless room hidden in darkness. Ardley flicked a wall switch and the overhead fluorescent flickered on with a quiet hum, throwing a flat, shadowless light over shelves of bound volumes that went from floor to ceiling. A single table with a couple of chairs sat in the middle, taking up most of the floor space in the tiny room. "This goes from about 1920 on back. The more current issues are in the next room, but I guess this should cover you. Keep the door shut and Teems will never know you're here. See you later."

Ardley stepped out of the room and closed the door behind him. Liv looked up at the wall of shelves, the books that contained the raw materials of a small town's history. He sighed, pulled his notebook out of his pocket, and started looking for the volumes the library didn't have. This looked to be one wild goose chase he couldn't get out of.

▼◆▼

Two hours later, Liv had lost the last shred of enthusiasm for the project. It was a struggle to force himself to turn over every sheet. His eyes were tired and strained from reading the tiny lines of type, the crude efforts of a half-amateur typesetter one hundred and thirty-plus years before. Each time he turned over a page to confront a new sea of type, it felt not as if he were closer to the end of his task, but as if he were pushing farther out into the tractless depth of a job that had no end.

He did not know what, exactly, he was looking for, and so felt compelled to read every word of every four-page edition of the ancient paper. Time and again, he found himself paying no attention whatever to what he was reading, the words seemingly drifting in his eyes and fading away to nothing before his brain comprehended them. He would shake his head, force himself to concentrate, and with infinite reluctance backtrack and reread the parts he had tuned out on. It all made him long for the good old days of cramming for exams.

But then, finally, he found it. Found *It*, and felt again the way he had when his trowel had first poked into Ambrose's rotting canvas shroud, knew what Barbara must have felt like when she had read over old Zebulon's diary two weeks and a lifetime ago, and found the words that had started this adventure. This was it. Paydirt. One hundred percent unadulterated paydirt. He flipped hurriedly through the rest of that issue, and the next, and the one after that. Nothing. No further mention. But that didn't matter. This was enough. Livingston got up and headed for the door.

▼◆▼

Pete Ardley heard the door to the morgue open and turned around in time to see the big guy, Livingston Jones, waving his arm to get his attention. Ardley stood up and went over.

"I've got it!" Jones said excitedly. "Listen, is there any way I could run off a set of Xeroxes?"

Ardley immediately noticed that Jones still had not told him what he was looking for, or what he had found—which suggested (a) Liv wouldn't tell even if Ardley asked straight out and (b) it might be worth finding out. "Sure," he said, thinking quickly. So how to find out? "But maybe it'd be smarter if I did it for you. They're kind of persnickety about who uses the Xerox machine."

"Great!" Jones said. He stepped back into the room and handed Ardley the bound volume for 1851. "The June 13 issue, okay?"

"The whole thing?" Ardley asked.

"All four pages," Liv said cheerfully. "I want to sort of have the background, the context."

"Okay, wait in here," Ardley said. He took the book and went across the newsroom to the copier while Jones went back inside the morgue room and gathered up his notes. Five minutes later, Ardley watched Jones step out of the newspaper office and into the street, carrying photocopies of the old newspaper's pages. He climbed into an old Dodge, gunned the engine, and took off.

Pete Ardley watched him go. Pete was a good guy, but he was also a newspaper reporter—a slightly devious breed Livingston Jones plainly had no experience with. And Ardley was curious about what could have gotten Jones excited about a newspaper one hundred thirty-something years old. He picked up the spare set of copies he had made and started reading.

"Food." Now she knew that word; in fact, many words for "food." She had listened and listened, straining to learn something, anything, in the noises the humans made, but they babbled on so fast, so incessantly, that it seemed impossible that any of it could truly be like hand-talk, and used to tell things.

And then finally, one night, when she had all but forgotten her plan to learn the human talk, she noticed that the women calling the men from the fields to their meal were making one noise over and over. She pricked up her ears and listened at the call she had heard every day of her life.

The sound stuck in her mind, and the next night the sound was the same—and the next, and the next. Then she noticed the call in midday was different from the call at night. Eagerly she listened to the human talk whenever she dared, and experienced, again and again, a thrill past anything she had ever known when she heard a word she knew. But even that thrill was surpassed when she watched and listened and learned the words for "plate," "spoon," "crop," and many more. Eavesdropping on the unsuspecting humans, who would have thought it just as likely for a cow to be listening to them, she was learning more every day—learning how to learn, how to guess and make mistakes and try again, how to remember, and how to use what she had learned.

In the midst of the new world she was finding, her meaningless life went on. Most of the work she did, she simply did, mindlessly, endlessly, emotionlessly—but always she had hated the task of going into the dark forests for firewood. The men did not trust their creatures so far from the village, and shackled their legs with heavy chains, making it painful to walk, leaving their ankles bloody and painful at the end of the day.

And then she watched, and learned the words for "go" and "firewood." When those words were spoken, she knew to shuffle to the back of the stockade, duck down out of sight of the overseer, try to vanish altogether.

And she never had to go for firewood again. It was a tiny victory, the tiniest spark in the darkness that surrounded her—but it was a victory, and she had never had such a thing before.

Chapter Ten

"Jeffery, I don't care what you say—down in the basement we have four examples of a hominid unknown to science. My numbers prove that." Rupert got up from the kitchen table, went up to the window, and looked out at the excavation. Three of the interns were hard at it, dropping the work face to a new horizon. They were the newest kids, and Rupert wanted to keep an eye on them.

Grossington glared at Rupert. "We argued about this until two in the morning last night, Rupert, so by now you might have registered that *I* believe what we have in that basement is *Australopithecus boisei*—a form which may be unknown to you, but which science has been aware of for some time. We simply did not know it was still extant. But Ambrose is *A. boisei*, beyond question."

"An empty taxon, Jeffery!" Rupert said, shaking his finger. "A name without a species to go with it. *Boisei*, or what you choose to call *boisei*, is merely a name for variant members of a highly variable species, good old *A. robustus*. This is a new type! Call them *A. nova*, or *A. americanus*, or *A. gowrenus*, or even *A. marchando*, but one look at the teeth tells you Ambrose and company are certainly not *robustus*—"

"Both of you! Take a break, please!" Barbara cut in. "The whole house heard this until the small hours; we don't need to hear it again." She shut her eyes for a moment, sighed, and went on in a gentler voice. "We have to settle this sooner or later, but we won't do it by seeing who shouts the loudest."

There was a sudden noise from the front side of the house, the sound of a car swinging into the drive a little too fast. Rupert watched from the window as Livingston's aged Dodge swung around the corner. He was out of the car before it had stopped moving, waving a paper over his head and running toward the house. A moment later he burst into the kitchen. "I have *got* it!" he announced triumphantly.

He set the paper down in front of Barbara. "That's the front page of the June 13, 1851 Gowrie *Gazette*. Read the ad at the bottom."

Rupert and Grossington stood up to read it over Barbara's shoulder as Livingston stepped back, giving them room to examine his prize. Rupert peered closely at the narrow columns for a moment before finding the ad.

▼◆▼
I M P O R T A N T N O T I C E

Captain Josiah Wembly, a native of Gowrie and a noted mariner, has returned here after completing a long and hazardous Expedition that took him across the perilous Atlantic and far up the course of the most mysterious and feared of the great African Rivers. He is offering for sale the fruits of that voyage, a new breed of African, superior in every respect to the breed offered heretofore. These creatures, imported to this country in full accordance with all Laws and Regulations regarding the Importation of Labor, were purchased by Captain Wembly directly from the Chief of the savage Yewtani Tribe in the far interior of The Gabon. Through solemn and secret agreements with the Chief of the Yewtani, Captain Wembly has become and will remain the Sole Agent for the Importation of these creatures. Captain Wembly has obtained and will display the Legal, Medical, and Scientific opinions of the most Learned men, who confirm that no Current or Proposed abolitionist law would prevent, or interfere with, the importation, purchase, or ownership of these Creatures. Fine specimens of this new Breed of Slave are available for inspection through enquiries with Captain Wembly, who is now resident at the Blue Star Hotel.

▼◆▼

"Fantastic, Livingston, just plain fantastic," Rupert said gleefully. "All of a sudden we have some hope of tracking these creatures down. You've given us a date, a name, a place to look—everything we could hope for!"

Barbara picked up the paper and examined it closely without

saying anything for a long moment. "This is wonderful, Livingston. It's every bit as important as finding the skeletons was."

Grossington took the photocopied page from Barbara and read it over to himself again. "I am impressed by your determination, Mr. Jones," he said at last. "Very few people would have stuck to the paper search long enough to find this." He set the paper down carefully, and felt a slight twinge in his arm as he did so.

He would never admit as much to the younger ones, but working in the excavation these last few days had been quite a strain. But aside from using long-unused muscles, the dig had been as easy as shooting ducks in a barrel. Grossington was used to the usual run of luck in paleoanthropology, where even in a promising site, rich in hominid fossils, you might have to take a whole season and move half a hillside to find a few teeth. Here, they now had four virtually complete skeletons in only a matter of a week or two.

For Jeffery Grossington, the truly exhausting part had come in the basement lab, considering, measuring, comparing, *thinking* about their new prizes. He had been putting in some exceedingly long hours down there—many of them spent in fruitless arguments with Rupert Maxwell. Grossington blinked and forced his tired mind back to the matter at hand. "What you have found, Mr. Jones, is indeed immensely important. But I'm afraid we can't act on it at the moment. There is simply too much work to be done here. We have just begun the job of measuring those bones, and comparing them to what casts we managed to bring with us. What analysis we've done has been back-of-the-envelope. We need to do much more, and much better."

Rupert slammed his chair back down onto all four legs with a loud banging sound. "What!? Are you nuts? We've *got* to follow this up! Ambrose very possibly has some live friends and relations scampering around in the jungle somewhere. This tells us where to look. We ought to go and find them. Live australopithecines have been a possibility since Barbara brought that hatbox into your office. Jeffery, we *have* to go after them. What's the alternative? We just sit around for a few years staring at these bones and contemplating our scientific navels?"

Grossington spoke. "Calmly, Rupert, calmly," he said. "I'm afraid we may be forced into just a bit of 'navel-contemplating,' as you put it. Obviously, we *should* try and find these creatures in Gabon. There's no need to bludgeon me with the point. However, we lack a few things needed for the job: time and money. Right at the moment, we're tapped out. I have to go work the fund-raising circuit again. With what we've found so far, I'm sure we can raise funds—but it will take a little time. At least we're close enough to the end of the year that people might be thinking about tax-deductible contributions. Plus, as I was saying, *we* need to study the material we have, and decide what it is. One last point: Does anyone here have more than the vaguest idea where Gabon is? And who and where are the Yewtani? Do they still exist? Are they actually inside the borders of modern-day Gabon?"

Rupert drummed his fingers on the table and shifted in his seat. "You've got something there, Jeffery," he admitted, backing down just a little. "I've been to Gabon, but I can't give you any answers on the rest of your questions. We can find it out, sure—after all, we're part of the Smithsonian's anthropology unit. But I guess it will take time. We have to track down the West Africa experts, find out what they know, probably head back to D.C. and rummage around in the files a bit." He brightened just a little. "Come to think of it, I know a guy in our embassy in Gabon. I visited a chimp research center there a while back and this guy Clark White was a big help. He seemed to know the interior pretty well."

Rupert paused for a moment. "I'm sorry I snapped at you, Jeffery. I think maybe we've all been working too hard. We've had disagreements before without their turning into shouting matches."

Grossington stretched his tired back out. "It's me who should be apologizing. I haven't behaved well either." He turned toward Livingston and smiled. "I'm afraid you're seeing the dirty side of paleoanthropology. Rupert and I have been tearing our hair out trying to make sense of the skeletons in the basement. There's a lot of pressure on us, and I'm afraid none of us have been at our most civil. What makes it worse is that we know it will *get* worse once word gets out. It'll be a madhouse. We're all scared of that—and I think we're all having trouble believing in Ambrose ourselves. The initial excitement has worn off, and now we're sort of in a state of shock, I think. Those old bones in the basement turn our world upside down. I know I've had a few moments when I've stepped back and realized what a mess we're making of paleoanthropology, and wondered if a few scraps of bone are really all you need to do that."

"But those bones are *there*," Livingston protested. "They are *real*. They are *true*. They are hard evidence that has to be faced, and if the theory doesn't fit, then the theory has to go!" he concluded with just a touch of sermonizing in his voice.

"Hey, don't tell *us* the rules," Rupert said wearily. "We *know* the rules. But Liv, this is like we've just found out we're adopted, that our mothers didn't give birth to us. It takes some time to accept it. We were all trained to believe humanity was alone, that the last australopithecine died a million years ago. We've worked our whole adult lives believing that. We *knew* it the way you know who your parents are. So let us jaded old pros have some time so we can get used to what Ambrose does to our world view."

Livingston jumped in. "Even if that's all true, Dr. Grossington, what about Gabon?" He stabbed a finger down on the photocopied page. "There it is, in black and white—right where we can go to find more of them, whatever they are. We've gotta go after them. This is the chance of a lifetime for me. Go or not, I'm going to postpone grad school to stick with this job—but we've *got* to go to Gabon!"

Barb grinned. "Don't blow a gasket, Liv. We'll get there, sooner or later," she said. "Come on, let's talk outside. I could use some fresh air, and I want to check and see if they've had any luck on the sifting box. C'mon, grab your jackets." The four of them collected their outdoor clothes and headed out toward the work site.

▼◆▼

The sifter itself was simply an old screen window with wooden handles screwed onto it, lying atop a wooden frame. So far they had a fine collection of pebbles and rusty nails, but no metatarsals or phalanges. Still, the sifting was necessary. There were definitely a few hand and foot bones missing, and they weren't going home with skeletons that were merely 99 percent complete if they could help it.

Barbara shoved her hands into her jacket pockets and scrunched up her shoulders. Even Mississippi could get downright nippy in December.

Grossington watched the dirt sifting down for a moments before turned to the interns. "Sally, Walter—why don't you two take a bit of a break." The two 'terns dropped their shovels eagerly and hurried back to the house. It was a little too cold for that kind of work.

Barbara watched them go, then picked up one of the abandoned shovels and started back at the job. "Rupert—you and Jeffery aren't likely to agree on what species Ambrose and company are any time soon, are you?"

Rupert grabbed the handles of the sifting box and started pushing them back and forth, encouraging the dirt to fall through the mesh. "Nope. I don't think we are." He gave the handles an extra-hard shove. "Not any time soon, anyway."

"Watch how hard you shake that thing, Rupe. You're slopping some dirt over the side. I didn't think so—but does it really matter if you two agree?"

Grossington, still staring at the screen, spoke up. "How could it *not* matter, Barbara? Surely it's important to decide the species of this find."

"Liv, don't just stand there—grab a shovel." Barb stabbed her shovel deep into the overburden dirt and puffed out her cheeks. It felt good to use her muscles. "Yeah, but who's going to agree with either one of you? No matter who wins your argument, there'll still be an unholy row when this comes out. Me, I can't vote either way. I don't think it's possible to decide anything when we haven't analyzed the data yet. So *I'd* be dead set against *either* of you winning. Right or wrong, you'd be judging on insufficient analysis. We've probably got a few months at best before this hits the papers, and that still won't be enough time to do it right. I think it's the time pressure that's making you both so adamant, and that pressure is real, no doubt of that. We have to get ready fast." She tossed another shovelful onto the screen, then leaned back on the shovel handle. "But maybe we can agree to disagree. We write a strictly descriptive paper, simply setting down the features of the skeletons—their very low age, their similarity to 'classic' australopithecines, their completeness, the strange place they were found. Get a coherent draft written *fast* and put it in the can, ready to release immediately if we're forced to do that. Write that first, *then* the pressure eases a bit and we can all sit back and examine these bones properly."

Liv reached out with his shovel and spread the dirt out on the sifter. "What about my clue? What about Gabon?"

Grossington cleared his throat. "I've been thinking about that," he said. "We'll need time to get ready, but, yes, we should go soon.

And I've been thinking about money. I can get it quietly—at the Geographic, at the American Museum of Natural History in New York, maybe even at the Smithsonian. What we've got is big enough for me to go right to the Secretary and cut out all the middlemen. I can get it. We have to get clear of the holidays, of course, but you need to do your researches on these Yewtani first anyway. Let me wade through all the Washington Christmas parties and come out the other end with a check. I expect by the time you're ready, I'll have the money you need." He looked at Rupert, looked him straight in the eye. "Maybe we were a little reluctant to accept the new facts," he said. "Maybe I still am. But you're right, and Livingston is right. We've no choice but to follow this wherever it goes."

Pete Ardley had sensed something worth chasing in Livingston's old newspaper, in Liv's reluctance to explain himself. Besides, it was a slow day anyway, and the weather was nice. He finished up his routine assignments early, tidied up his desk, and left the newspaper office. Almost on impulse, he drove out to Gowrie House and parked out of sight of the house. He got out and pulled his camera case out of the trunk. Strolling casually back along the road toward the house, he noticed a few odd things. Three or four cars with out-of-state plates were parked in the driveway. That was rare in a small town, right there. He heard a noise and looked toward the rear of the house. There seemed to be a lot of activity in the backyard.

Then he bent the rules a bit, and peeked into the roadside mailbox—an old reporter's trick in rural areas, almost a standard operating procedure before interviewing anyone off the beaten track. You could learn a lot about a person from what sort of mail they got.

Pete got his second surprise. There were a number of pieces of personal mail, including what looked like Christmas cards, forwarded from Washington, and two or three pieces from the anthropology department of the Smithsonian Institution, addressed to some guy named Grossington.

That was enough to make him wonder about that activity in the backyard. He circled around to the back of the property to get a better look.

Five minutes later, his trousers covered with burrs, Ardley was crouched down below the low, slat-wood fence that surrounded the old slaves' burial ground, and reflecting on the absurd melodrama of the moment. Hiding in a graveyard, spying on a bunch of people digging a hole, his heart pounding for fear of getting caught—this was ridiculous. Ridiculous enough that he was tempted to call an end to the hide-and-seek, stand up straight, call out to the diggers and announce his presence—but he didn't, because that wasn't how the game was played. They were hiding something down there, something to do with a century-old newspaper, and he was a reporter, so he was supposed to find out what it was.

There wasn't a lot of substance to occupy a reporter in Gowrie. State and national news, what little the *Gazette* ran, came off the wire. City Hall and county seat stories were big news when they came, but they were few and far between. The police beat was usually sleepy as well. School board was considered a major beat. There were three full-time reporters to handle it all. Like thousands of reporters on thousands of tiny local papers across the nation, Pete wanted a shot at a *real* paper, in a big town, working up stories that meant something—the thrill of the chase after quarry worth pursuing.

So now here he was, staring in fascination at the busy crew of diggers. He pulled his camera from its case and took a few shots. Were they burying something? What could be big enough to require a hole that big? No, not burying, digging something up. Look at how careful they were of the dirt, the people clustered around that frame thing. Livingston, a black woman, two white guys, one young, one old. They were *sifting* through the dirt, *looking* for something. What? The old cliché answers from the Hardy Boy books of youth popped into his head. Buried treasure? Prospecting for gold? What could it be?

Then, suddenly, there was a shout, a flurry of commotion from one end of the huge hole. He could hear a voice shouting out, "Another one! Another one!" The figures around the sifting gizmo dropped their tools and hurried over to the edge of the pit. A youthful figure stood up inside the hole, holding something. Pete quickly switched lenses on his camera, attaching the telephoto for use as a spotting scope. The figure in the pit handed the something up to the older white man. Pete put the camera up to his eye, twisted the enlarged image into focus—and suddenly remembered he was in a graveyard, even as he clicked the shutter.

The 'something' was a skull.

There are perhaps a thousand Dew Drop Inns across the nation, the vast majority of them well south of the Mason-Dixon line. One of them, almost inevitably, was in Gowrie. Its interior was seedy; cheap-pine-paneling-nailed-over-cinderblock. The fake wooden ceiling beams made out of painted styrofoam were threatening to collapse down on the patrons, who huddled up around the mismatched tables randomly scattered across the scruffy grey linoleum floor. The lighting was dim and brown, and there was a whiff of something in the air that suggested that dried patches of spilled beer might be found in some of the darker corners. The speaker on the jukebox had something terminally wrong with it. At the moment, it was sobbing out a muffled rendition of Bing Crosby and *White Christmas*. A string of wizened old Christmas lights was nailed up over the bar, but there were no other concessions to the season of the year. The Dew Drop was a place for a man to get beer and get drunk if he wanted to, alone or in groups, quietly or noisily. There was no nonsense, no pretense about the place.

The Dew Drop was also the closest watering hole to Gowrie House, which was what drew Peter Ardley to it. He wasn't a regular by any means, which made the waitress suspicious; he ordered scotch instead of a beer, which stunned her; and he told her to bring and leave the bottle, which astonished her. Beer they served in an endless torrent, but the Dew Drop went through less than a bottle of bar scotch a night—most of it consumed by the bartender.

Pete poured three stiff fingers into his semi-clean shot glass, lifted it to his lips, and knocked back the whole thing in one wretched gulp. He made a face and looked at the label. Terrible stuff. But maybe it would settle the nerves enough for him to think.

Murder. That was the thought that came to mind, the idea that popped up into his imagination. Buried bodies, private exhumations. What else could it be? But they were taking the skull *out* of the ground. It didn't make sense. He had photos. Maybe it was already time to go to the cops—but why exhume the bones? And why treat them so carefully? He had seen them wrap the skull as carefully as any babe, seen them carry it across the yard and into the house. He had seen lights go on in the basement, then a constant stream of bones carried into that basement. They were doing something to those bones down there. What? And what the hell did the Smithsonian have to do with it—or a hundred-thirty-year-old newspaper?

He pulled a wadded-up sheaf of papers from his jacket pocket and smoothed the pages out on the table top. It was almost impossible to read in the crepuscular gloom of the Dew Drop, but Peter peered hard at the pages and managed to make out the old-fashioned type. It didn't help that he had had to set the copier to *reduce* in order to fit a whole page at a time. He downed another—and smaller—dose of the bar rotgut and puzzled his way through the photocopy of the old paper. Could the disinterment be related to some genealogical question? That was the usual reason for combing through old newspapers. But certainly no event in a slave's life would have been reported. Were the black Joneses trying to find some family link with the white gentry of the time, a dalliance between master and slave that had resulted in a child? It certainly would not be unusual. White or black, the average American likely bore genes from both races, admit it or not—and that was doubly so in the deep South.

But there just wasn't anything there. No earth-shattering event was reported that would be important today, or even anything that would have been of interest a week later. No obituary, no social note, no engagement or birth or death announcement. Nothing but the idle gossip of a sleepy southern town, and the quaint old wordy advertisements of another age.

The ads . . . His stomach knotted up, and it wasn't the work of the scotch. Grossington, Smithsonian, anthropology. It fit. He read over the ads again, suddenly stone-cold sober, and sincerely wishing he was not. That slave-sale ad on the front page. He fumbled for it in the near-darkness. *A new breed of African, superior in every respect to the breed offered heretofore . . .*

Sweet Jesus. It fit. It fit all the facts. But it was just too wild an idea.

He had to get a look inside that cellar.

Chapter Eleven

Livingston looked out across the wintering sky. Christmas was only a few days away now, and that was a deadline for everything. It was unspoken, obvious, that Aunt Jo would want her house back by then. Besides, everyone was eager to get home themselves. The plan was for the team to be packed out, lock, stock, and bones, by the 24th.

Grossington had declared the job of excavation complete, and no one was ready to argue. They had: a single one-hundred percent complete skeleton, Ambrose; three skeletons with only one or two bones each missing and presumed decayed away; and the last, Tail-End Charlie, seventy percent complete, most of his leg bones apparently destroyed when the road gullied out and a flash flood washed into his grave decades before. There was nothing left to find. The first of the grads and 'terns were already heading back home—each of them sworn to secrecy, each a potential leak. That was the pressure now, for digging up bones was just the first step. Livingston looked over his shoulder, back at the house and the cellar full of bones. They were still deciding in there, the place full of tension and frayed tempers. Liv was glad that checking on the 'terns gave him an excuse to get out into the fresh air. But after so many long, angry nights, they *seemed* close to some kind of conclusion.

Rupert stared intently at the super-massive cheek molars protruding from Ambrose's maxilla, or upper jaw, as if he were memorizing every feature of the overgrown teeth. Then he turned equally intent concentration on Beulah's somewhat smaller teeth, on Trio's, on Mr. Butler's, and Tail-End Charlie's. The skulls might properly be referred to as Gowrie Exhumation Project #1-5, but the nicknames had already stuck.

Barbara and Jeffery watched Rupert every bit as closely as he examined the skulls, weary and hopeful that the long fights and debates were over. If they had finally convinced Rupert, then it was all going to be all right.

Rupert picked up his precious calipers and rechecked three measurements, compared them against the printout and the glowing display of his portable computer, and grudgingly conceded a minor error. Then he set the spreadsheet through its paces once last time, running a series of statistical tests that flashed and flickered across the screen. Finally, a simple bar graph appeared on the screen, a range of values, a mute, simple statement of the facts, a display of values from every australopithecine specimen ever found. And the Gowrie samples fitted in perfectly right where they should have.

Rupert sighed. "Okay, *Boisei* is a valid taxon, and these guys are *Australopithecus boisei*, not a new type. No question about it. Ambrose *looks* mighty different, and some of his measures are outside the established range—he was a big, mean dude—but obviously, he has to be conspecific with the other four skeletons found with him; and none of *them* are outside the extreme range of what we know about *boisei*. It's just that they are so well preserved that they don't *look* like the bashed-up, weathered, crumbly *boisei* we know from all previous fossils."

Jeffery Grossington reached over the trestle table and patted Rupert on the shoulder. "Thank you, Rupert. I'm glad, very glad that I couldn't convince you—that it had to be the evidence, the bones on the table, that did that. I was wrong to try and browbeat you."

Rupert shut down his computer, stretched his arms to get the kinks out, then folded down the cover of the portable computer. "So let's get the hell out of here, get home, get that descriptive paper written, and give them something to attack."

▼◆▼

Everyone was startled by the speed with which they managed to take things apart and pack them up. As the specimens had come in from the dig, each had been placed in its own special niche in its own special box, so even the laborious job of packing up the precious bones of Ambrose and company went rapidly. Within forty-eight hours of shutting down the excavation, the team was ready to break up.

Barbara watched Livingston's old Dodge pull out of the driveway from her tiny bedroom window as she packed. He was taking another batch of 'terns into Gowrie to meet the Greyhound. The bus would take them up Route 61 to Jackson, to the airport, where they would scatter to the four winds, home for Christmas.

She folded up the last of her own clothes and sighed. She looked about the tiny room and felt once again that dread of going home, of seeing Michael again, especially at this time of year. She pulled out his letter and started reading it again.

Aunt Jo made her way up the stairs to the room Barbara was using, and gave a gentle tap came at the door before she turned the knob and went in. "Just about packed up, child?" she asked. "Got any of your bones stuffed into that suitcase of yours?" Aunt Jo sat down on the bed and smiled at her niece.

Barbara laughed in spite of herself and shook her head. "No, Dr. Grossington is taking care of all that. Believe it or not, there's nothing but clothes and books in there." Barbara sat down next to Aunt Jo and threw her arms around her. "Oh, Aunt Jo, I'll miss you."

"Heavens, child, you've been so busy rooting around in my back yard I didn't even think you'd noticed I was still here." Aunt Jo wrapped Barbara up in a big bear hug and rocked her back and forth. "I noticed the return address on that letter you got the other day. Another one from Michael?"

Barbara released her aunt from the hug and waved the letter she still had clasped in her hand. "Yes. I was just rereading it. He says such lovely things in it—"

"And don't you go believing a single one of them," Aunt Jo said firmly. "Michael has already hurt you so much I don't see how he could do any more damage—but I'd bet he'd be willing to try. Are you thinking of giving him another chance, or some fool thing like that?"

"Yes," she answered simply, plainly not trusting herself to speak further. Barbara's face was buried in her aunt's shoulder, and her voice was muffled, but still Aunt Jo could hear the sadness in it.

Aunt Jo went on stroking Barbara's hair, rocking her back and forth, humming quietly to herself. It was amazing to her. This little slip of a girl was going to go off and turn the entire scientific world upside down, and that didn't worry her one bit. And a no-account, cruel, petulant man-child could break her completely to pieces. "Now you listen to me, Dr. Barbara Marchando," she said in her most severe voice. "This is no way for you to be acting. This is schoolgirl stuff.

You're a grown woman. You're supposed to know what you feel inside. It's downright *wrong* to let this man mess you up so bad."

"I know, I know, I know," Barbara said, sniffling a bit as she sat up to reach for a Kleenex. "But I don't even know how I feel. I tell myself I don't love him anymore, but his letters come and they're so beautiful, and then I want to go back to him—even though I know it'd be just like before. Then I look at myself again, and realize I *do* still love him."

"Child, loving him isn't the solution, it's the problem. He is what he is, and that's what he always will be. People don't change, not on purpose. He might tell you otherwise, might even mean it, but he is *always* going to manipulate you, twist your words to suit himself, use his own helplessness to make you take care of him."

"All of that's true, Aunt Jo, but it's not all there is to him. You've never seen him at his best, at the hospital, caring for people, curing them, taking charge, doing everything *right*, saving lives."

"None of that matters, and things aren't always what they seem. Barbara, if you don't mind my saying so, Michael is not the sort of man who cares about anything or anyone but himself. I've seen his kind before. Not in a hospital, not as a doctor, but I've seen them. Now, maybe he's forever doing the best things in the world, curing the sick, whatever. It's not good acts, but good will, good thoughts, good intentions that are important. It's not enough to do good things— you have to do them for good reasons."

"Aunt Jo, Michael—"

"Is such a good doctor because it's good for his ego. He acts the way a good doctor is supposed to so he can prove himself. And then he comes home to you and acts the way all the men from his nasty little slum act, like they are God's gift to the world and just showing up is reward enough for any woman. I've been around to this big city and that, visiting relations and so on, and I *know* how it works. His momma's to blame for Michael, if you ask me. I saw the way she treated him when we stayed at their place for your wedding. Waiting on him hand and foot, doing everything for him. She taught him to be the way he is. That's the way it always happens."

Hard, clear anger came into her voice. "And we've done it all to ourselves in the cities. We didn't need any white man's help to destroy ourselves. A man's a rare thing in the projects, a man who isn't in jail or run off or gotten himself killed. So the women pamper the ones they've got left, treat 'em like the most precious little fragile things to be cared for and nurtured. It's the women that have the jobs, the work, the money—and the men who take it all just as a bribe for staying."

Aunt Jo stood up and looked out the window. "*You* were brought up in the right side of town, and your father was a good father, a good man, a hard-working provider who brought you up right. The men you grew up around—uncles, teachers, your older cousins—*they* were brought up right. That's all you ever really saw, so you didn't really expect people to be any other way. That's the kind of man you keep expecting Michael to be—but he never, ever can be that, not the way he was brought up!

"A few years ago, after I retired from teaching, I decided to spend my summers working with the inner city kids up in Chicago. My church and some others ran some programs for them. I went up there—I *saw* what it was like. There aren't any families left anymore. And I don't care how far out of those slums you get, it *scars* you for good. Michael is a product of how he grew up, just as much as you are.

"From Michael's point of view, treating you wrong, and seeing you take it—that's what proves to him he's a real man! He's not a good doctor to be good—he cures the sick to prove how clever he is. That's why he does *everything* he does."

"*What's* why he does everything?" Barbara asked. She wanted desperately to defend Michael, in spite of it all, even knowing that if she defended him, it meant he had won.

"Haven't you been listening at all, girl? I'll tell you one more time, as clear and as clean as I can: You remember this one thing about Michael, and *maybe* you'll be all right. *Everything* he does, *everything* he says, *he does for the sake of his pride.* Not self-respect, but pride. And that's the dangerous thing about it, because there's nothing stronger than self-respect, and nothing as fragile as pride."

Aunt Jo looked down at her niece and shook her head. It didn't do any good to tell her these things. The only hope Barbara had was that she might finally learn them for herself.

▼◆▼

Pete Ardley happened to look up from his desk and through the plate-glass of the *Gazette*'s storefront just as Livingston's old Dodge pulled up in front of the Greyhound station across the street. He watched as suitcases, duffel bags, and sleeping bags sprouted from the trunk. So they were pulling out. Dammit.

Ardley opened his file drawer and pulled out a slender manila folder. He opened it and flipped through the photos. The shots of the skull being taken from the ground. The little knot of figures examining the find.

He flipped through the file and found the second series of shots, taken later that night through the basement windows of Gowrie House. *That* had been a spooky little assignment, made no less so by the not-so-steadying effects of Dew Drop Inn bar scotch. On the other hand, it seemed unlikely that he could have worked up the nerve stone-cold sober. He had made his way back around through the slaves' burial ground and crawled the hundred or so yards from there to the house to avoid being seen, ruining his pants, muddying his coat, and earning a full set of scratches and bumps as he ground his knees into unseen rocks, fell into holes that shouldn't have been there, and found a whole forest of brambles to scrabble through.

But that second set of prints—they had been worth it. He had dragged himself up to one of the brightly lit, well-cleaned cellar windows—and found himself a few feet away from not just one, but a whole *row* of misshapen, grinning skulls. They were just lying there, leering up at him. Creepy was scarcely the word. But he shook that off, set up his pint-size table-top tripod, and took a whole set of long exposures, two or three seconds each, then switched lenses and got close-ups of each skull through his telephoto. Once he had what he wanted, he didn't try to be subtle. He just stood up and ran like hell away from the house back toward the burial ground—and nearly broke his ankle in a chuck hole. But no alarm was raised, and he had the pics. Two hours and a pot of black coffee later he had been steady enough to process the film and print the photos in the newspaper's lab.

He was justifiably proud of the final products. The photos were just a trifle grainy, but all of them were sharp and clear, well exposed and perfectly focused.

That satisfaction had been short-lived—for then he had been faced with the question of what to do with the things. The photos by themselves were weird, but were not enough by themselves to print in any paper except the tabs, the papers Pete mentally filed under the generic term *The National Perspirer*. He had to know what they were pictures *of*. It had seemed a simple enough question.

He looked again at his perfect, perfect pictures, and then sorrowfully at his stack of library books on evolution. He had *thought* it would be a simple matter to match up the obviously non-human skulls with their pictures in the books and go on from there. Easy.

Instead, he had been reminded of his first attempt as a birder. He had been completely lost then, unable to tell the nuthatches from the finches in the book, never mind comparing the little pictures with a ball of fluff seen for a few seconds at a hundred yards.

Skulls were—*skulls*, one very like another. He had no idea *what* he was looking at. The books he had weren't much help, either. It was slowly dawning on him that the libraries and bookstores of rural, Baptist, evangelical, born-again Mississippi were not the best place to find good books on what most of the locals pronounced 'evil-otion.' There weren't that many librarians and booksellers in the area to start with, and what few there were tread softly around issues on which the church had strong feelings. Pete shook his head. It was frightening what a book-banning, or even the threat of a book-banning—a protest, a letter to the editor—could do to the sources of knowledge. And he needed help. He was a newsman, wholly innocent of paleoanthropology, not even entirely sure what the term meant until he had looked it up.

The few books on the subject he *did* find were years or even decades out of date, and the illustrations consisted mostly of artistic and contradictory reconstructions of what the authors were pleased to call ape-men, shambling about the landscape. What few illustrations of bones and skulls there were seemed to be little more than crude line drawings or badly reproduced photos that were too muddy and dark to see properly. Pete's photos were clear, but his shots at the excavation were all from far off, and the shots into the basement were looking *down* on the skulls from an oblique angle that wasn't shown in any book. Worse, Pete had no idea which shapes and features of a skull were important and which were meaningless variants.

But Pete had plugged grimly on, trying to match his photos up with the pictures in the books. At one point or another, he convinced himself of matches with the chimp, the gorilla, *Homo erectus*, and *Sinanthropus pekinensis*, until he discovered that science had long since decided that last species did not exist. Then he thought the skulls might be orangutans, Neanderthals or even just some sort of big monkey. He had even found an ancient book all about *Eoanthropus dawsoni*—Dawson's dawn man—and thought *that* might be the match, before he realized *Eoanthropus* was nothing more or less than a forgery, the Piltdown Man.

Leafing through the book, he found some cold comfort in the oft-repeated tales of trained scientists who had studied this skull or that endlessly before clearly and confidently misidentifying it. But if *they* all got it wrong so often, how could he hope to get it right?

It was impossible for him to decide definitely what this crowd from Washington was up to. What was it all about? Had he stumbled on to a bunch of eccentrics digging up some old monkeys some nut had buried there, or was this what his hunch told him it was—the biggest story of his life, bigger than he could ever dream of? Suppose he treated it like a mega-scoop and it blew up in his face, turned out to be an unstory not worth wasting newsprint on? It had to be one or the other; there was no middle ground.

He looked up again through the plate-glass window and watched Livingston waving goodbye to the others. Now it looked like they were all going home. *That* suggested maybe it was all a bust. Why would they pull out if it was a big deal?

The damnable thing was that doing nothing was so *safe*. If he left the story alone, nothing bad would happen to his career, no risk would accrue. And it seemed like such a far-off long shot ...

Regretfully, he closed the folders, shoved them back into the files, and shoved the drawer shut with a bit more force than necessary.

He sat there for ten solid minutes, staring at that drawer, telling himself over and over again all the reasons for letting it alone.

Then, quite abruptly, he stood up and went into the row of reference shelves that lined one side of the newsroom. The phone books for the whole state were there. He pulled down the book for JACKSON, brought it back to his desk, and began riffling through the pages, looking through the entries for Mississippi State University.

Working the phones was second nature—or maybe first—in the newspaper business. In ten minutes he had the name of Dr. Roberta

Volsky of the anthropology department. Unfortunately, her receptionist said, Dr. Volsky would be unavailable until after the Christmas holiday. Pete shrugged that off. Those skull had waited underground a long time—they could wait a bit longer. He settled for a January 11 appointment at ten a.m.

He felt better afterwards, and spent the afternoon happily working on a soppy little holiday feature about the animal shelter's annual adopt-a-pet campaign. Front page stuff for the *Gazette*, with a shot of a puppy with big soulful eyes alongside. Pete didn't care anymore. Maybe on January 11 he would be through with all that.

Rupert rattled his keys into the lock, wiggled them this way and that until the catch caught, stepped into his apartment—and was jumped from behind, grabbed hard in the leg, his shin exploding into red blossoms of pain.

He dropped his suitcase and cried out in alarm, then caught himself and bent down to disentangle the yowling Chairman Meow from his blue jeans. He should have been expecting it. The poor guy had been left all alone for three weeks, with just Blanche from next door coming in once a day to feed him. No wonder he was happy to see Rupert come home. Rupert had his hands full for a minute, trying to calm the excited cat. Finally, he managed to settle the Chairman down enough to hold him in one arm, leaving the other free to switch on lights and so on. The Chairman snuggled down into his chest and began buzzing loudly, pumping his forepaws into Rupert's sweater.

Rupert sniffed the air suspiciously. Yup, the apartment definitely smelled of used cat. Well, he couldn't blame Blanche for not changing the box more often—that was no one's favorite job. Rupert sighed and started opening windows. It smelled like time to clean the mouse cage as well. Getting home was always such a blast.

Two hours later the place was aired out, the mail was sorted, and the apartment, to Rupert's eye, was in some semblance of order. To anyone but Rupert, the place would have seemed immaculate, but to him it was just barely tolerable.

He switched on his desk computer and fiddled with it for a bit, transferring files from the portable. But that was just stalling, and he knew it. He had some writing to do: his portion of the paper on Ambrose and company—and a letter. Rupert hated writing, hated the endless fiddling with phrases and adverbs to get things to come out right on paper. Scribbled notes and quick jottings were all right— it was formal writing that he couldn't bear. Everything he set down always sounded so stilted, so formal in the first draft—and the second, and the third. The final results were always quite satisfactory, but getting to that point was endless pain—so tough for him that he never let anyone at the office see him in the act of writing, but did it all in the privacy of his own home. Setting down words always made him long for the clear precision of numbers, charts, graphs, solid facts.

Across town, he knew, Barbara was already hard at work on the section dealing with the discovery of the skulls. Harrumphing old Grossington was supposed to do the comparative section, once he had scared up the money needed for the trip to Gabon. All of that left Rupert to do the actual *description* of the bones. It was a logical division of labor, and gave Rupert that part of the job that made best use of his talents, but he hated it all the same. He had that all-important letter to write as well. And no one else could do that job.

Chairman Meow vaulted up from the floor onto the desk and bounced up to his accustomed place atop the mouse cage. Rupert reached up and scratched him behind the ears. "Don't get too comfortable, partner," Rupert told him. "With any luck, I'll be off on another trip before long and leave you on your lonesome again. Let's hope Blanche can still put up with you."

He sighed and started in on the letter first.

JANUARY

Chapter Twelve

Clark White carefully eased his broad rump down into his superannuated government-issue swivel desk-chair, and set the chair to creaking loudly as he leaned back and cleared his throat with a heroically noisy *harrumph*. He rubbed his fleshy chin, or chins, to be more accurate, where the razor had nicked him that morning, folded his hands over his expansive potbelly, and stared glumly at his in-basket.

Every morning it was the same, here in Gabon or at any posting he had ever held. Paperwork. Somehow, somewhere, he knew, all these bits of paper got things done. Nothing would happen, could happen, without the bits of paper. But how or why that was so, he could never explain. He glanced out over the thrumming window air-conditioner through the flyspecked window at the streets of Libreville, just to be sure the foreign capital was still there. For all the excitement and exotica of his job, he might as well be back at his desk in Foggy Bottom, Washington, D.C.—or back home in Des Moines for that matter.

With infinite reluctance, and with more than a passing thought for the pastries calling to him from the shop around the corner, he pulled out his scruffy old reading glasses and started his daily quest for the bottom of that damned in-basket. It was all routine stuff, of course. Urgent requests for emergency supplies from the Howfritz expedition, a panicky note from the Museé de l'Homme in Paris requesting transport for one of their primatologists who was stuck in the back of beyond in some God-forsaken village north of Booué in the central region of the country. A squabble between two American scientists over charges for trans-shipment of equipment. Rush visas for three graduate students needed by the lepidopterologists in the south, near Franceville—undoubtedly told to bring their own butterfly nets; that group was strapped for cash.

The job of science attaché usually had more to with lost luggage than with great discoveries. It was all stuff he could do in his sleep.

156

He knew it all by rote—which Gabonese office to call, who owed whom favors, who in which embassy was cooperative only after a lengthy liquid lunch, who knew where to get Land Rover parts, all the minutiae of running science in the jungle. And that was just one part of his job. In a small embassy like this one, everyone wore more than one hat.

It was getting on toward eleven and coffee-break time before Sam, the embassy clerk, came around with the mail. Mail was always the high point of Clark's day. It might just be more bits of paper, but at least it was bits of paper specifically for *him*, not some bureaucratic rigmarole.

Clark's mail was delivered straight to the embassy. It got there faster and more reliably than anything sent to his home through the local postal system. Besides, the embassy would know where to find him after he left Gabon. This was his seventh or eighth posting, and he still got mail forwarded to him from every former address—stuff forwarded again and again, circling the globe to get to him.

A grown daughter in Washington saw to it that mail to his home address was forwarded just as diligently—not just letters, but junk mail, magazines he had never gotten around to canceling, bills, the whole beautiful, domestic, pedestrian stacks of mail every American got every day. Getting a dozen notices screaming You May Already Be A Winner from Ed McMahon made him feel a bit less cut off from life in America. He trashed it all, of course, but even so, it was satisfying to retain some tiny shred of the way they lived back home. In fact, it was strange, but mail from home was the one thing that made him *feel* far from home. This dull, paper-pushing existence took place in Limbo, not in a real foreign place.

Some of the bigger embassies Clark had served in—especially the one in Bonn—made that Limbo by contriving to create a tiny island of Americanism in the midst of the foreign capital—American food: American furniture, American-style telephones, musty American banged-up government furniture and dismal linoleum, an American school for the Embassy kids, American products in an American-style embassy grocery store. All the unreal, inappropriate American-style this-and-that served not to comfort the staff, but only to remind them how cut off from local life they really were—how *alone*, how *alien*. Going through the rituals that made sense only in office buildings found half a world away made day-to-day embassy life seem otherworldly, unreal.

Here in Gabon, it took the whole tiny diplomatic community working together to create a different kind of Limbo, a microcosm not out of place, but misplaced in time. It was the French, in their far larger embassy, who did most of the work. There was still a weird, dated paternalism to French dealings with their former colony. The colonial-era buildings, the school-book French everyone seemed to speak, the various peculiar adaptations of Western-style formal attire to the tropics, the institutions the Gabonese borrowed, all seemed to make the past realer, clearer, sharper than the sleepy present. It all had an air of unreality about it, like the forced hominess of a divorced man's lonely bachelor apartment. It formed a shroud of protective, cloying cotton wool, serving only to make the staff feel even more cut off from the rough, bustling, baffling world of an overcrowded African coastal city baking between the Equator and the Atlantic.

But mail from home was of the present day and *real*, proof that home was still there, and operating in the present day. Today the mail was a satisfyingly thick stack that *thumped* down solidly on his desk, a fat bundle strapped together with thick rubber bands. Most of the envelopes had been travelling some time: they looked worn, much used, and their original addresses were scratched out, with PLEASE FORWARD scribbled on them.

Clark White happily threw away the ads from stores a world away, the invitations to sign up for credit cards he could never use here, laughed over postcards from Foreign Service pals scattered about the globe, frowned over a note from the IRS, skimmed over the late-arriving Christmas cards from here and there, and, saving the best for last, eagerly read and reread his weekly letter from his daughter. All was well at home, it seemed, and his Christmas package had arrived in time. At least, he thought that his daughter's letter was the last of the mail. But there was something else he had overlooked.

At the bottom of the stack was that rare thing, a piece of personal mail that had been sent directly to his current address. He looked at the postmark. Smithsonian Institution, Washington, D.C. He ripped the envelope open, pulled out a thick wad of paper, spotted a reference to Mississippi, and wrinkled his brow. He checked the name on the return address. Rupert Maxwell? What the hell had he been doing in the back of the bayou beyond?

Clark harrumphed to himself and examined the letter. That was Rupert's style all right—classy paper, obviously written on a computer, a perfect print-out job. With a sorry glance in the direction of his worn-out old Royal Upright, he wished, not for the first time, that the Embassy budget would allow for some hardware like that. Then maybe people would take his correspondence seriously. He sighed, adjusted his glasses, and began reading.

▼◆▼

Dear Clark—

Greetings to you! I expect that Libreville is even more like it was than ever, and I hope you're doing all right over there.

I am writing in hopes that you can scrape up some information in preparation for a trip over there. Some friends of mine and I are interested in getting a look at a tribe called the Yewtani. (That is an old and possibly corrupted spelling—as you and I both know, such things are bound to get garbled in transliteration.)

At the moment, we have but a single reference to them, which reports them to be in 'The Gabon.' I am writing you in some haste, and prior to getting results I am expecting from other sources. Since we don't know how much information our in-house people will have, and since any duplicated information will also serve as a valuable cross-check, I would ask you to research the tribe as completely as possible. We are eager to know where the tribe is, what language (or dialect) they speak, what trade languages we might be able to use for communication with them, how large their population is, what sort of life they lead, how many villages they live in, and so on. I would further ask that you include any anecdotal information—gossip, if you will, concerning the tribe—the details that could give us the 'feel' of the tribe.

By this time you are really starting to wonder about me, I'm sure. None of this is in my field, or even remotely connected with it. Not only that, but you are wondering why on Earth you should bestir yourself over the question of some diddly-squat tribe over in East Nowhere. Okay. I have been hesitating since the beginning of this letter for a way to explain this, but I guess the best way is to tell you a story. It began when a friend of mine found an old diary . . .

▼◆▼

Clark kept reading, with an increasing sense of astonishment. As always when he was intent over his work, he forgot himself in his reading. A far-sighted hostage to glasses with a too-weak prescription, he held the page out almost at arm's length, his head tilted back to make the lenses magnify a bit. That posture in turn made his jaw slump open, an invitation to wheezy mouth-breathing and mutterings. These lunatics were claiming to have found what amounted to humanity's ancestors, still living in the goddamned African jungle! The double-damned missing link!

Inside the prison of his fat old body, he could feel his heart beating strong with excitement.

He finished the letter and carefully put it away in his personal safe. Three minutes later, his overflowing in-basket joyously forgotten, he was on his way out to see a certain gentleman at the Ministry of Culture.

▼◆▼

Jeffery Grossington rolled a fresh sheet of paper into his venerable old electric typewriter and glared at it. He was still a man who hated haste. Now he was remembering just how much he hated succumbing to it himself. But there was no choice, no choice at all. This paper *had* to be ready as soon as possible. Rupert's and Barbara's contributions lay in their folders on his desk, and the two of them were busily preparing for the trip abroad, assuming they got some sort of favorable reply from that Clark White person. It was agreed that the paper had to be ready before anyone went anywhere, that all three of them would have a chance to look over the words on the page and agree on every nuance of phrasing *before* the team left for Africa.

Even with the paper complete, of course, there would be delays in publication. There were still the drawings to do, for example, and Grossington had not so much as hired an illustrator yet. They would have to submit to a journal and have the paper reviewed and juried before publication, a process that would take weeks or months.

That sort of routine work Grossington would handle on his own. But the words themselves were too delicate, too important, to be delegated to just one member of the team. They had to stand together on this, not just in name, but *actively.*

At least the money side of the problem was resolved. The coffers of the National Geographic Society were always open—once you were already successful. One look at Ambrose, and the president of the Society was reaching for his checkbook. There was a quid pro quo, of course—the Geographic would want a popular article for the magazine. They could worry about that later.

Of course, now several people at the Geographic knew about Ambrose. And all the scattered grad students. And, soon, a freelance technical illustrator, and the editor and staff of *Scientific American.* Oh, it would leak. It would leak, and soon.

He flexed his fingers and started pounding away at the keyboard, with the too-hard touch of a typist who learned on a manual machine. There were a *lot* of things they would have to worry about later on. Now all that mattered was getting the damnable words on paper.

It was a cold, crisp, January day, and the city of Washington was at its splendid best. The C & O Canal was just about iced over. If the cold spell held, there would be skating in a day or so. Barbara breathed in the sharp, clear air and felt the satisfying crunch of gravel under her feet as she walked along the canal towpath. Her work was done for the moment, and it felt good to get out of the apartment and the office.

She stopped as she saw him. There Mike was, by the canal lock, right where she had told him to meet her. He looked good, handsome, solid, yet somehow a little lost. It took an effort of will for her heart not to go out to him. Instantly she knew she had been right to meet him outside, in public, in neutral territory. No chance for hysterics, emotions, no cozy restaurants. It was the only successful way to deal with Michael. Keep her gloves on, wear her heaviest, bulkiest coat to ward off the touches, smother the physical attraction for him in layers of clothing that kept her from really feeling his body if he should chance to hug her. It was even a deliberate tactical decision on her part to say yes the *first* time he asked to see her, rather than saying no a half-dozen times, letting him wear her down, make her feel guilty, let him get in control and pick the time and place when he finally talked her into it.

She knew, even as she made her plans and took her precautions, how paranoid, how close to insane it was. But she felt *good* as she walked toward him in this public spot, felt in control, safe, shielded from whatever he might throw at her. She forced herself to remember everything Aunt Jo had said. It helped.

He saw her and walked a step or two toward her. She stopped a good five feet away from him, backed up a step when he moved toward her. "Hello, Mike," she said, smiling. "Nice to see you." The weird thing was, she *did* feel good about seeing him. It was almost as if she were winning a skirmish this time. She had enough guards up to feel safe. She could relax behind her sturdy defenses.

"I missed you over Christmas," he said. "You never came over. I tried to call, but the answering machine was always on."

She laughed for no reason she understood exactly. Already he was needling her. "I was very busy. Just got finished writing a big paper. Besides, it was only Momma and me, a very quiet Christmas with just the two of us."

"But you could have come over, or called."

"Michael, we're separated, not really married anymore. I'm not in charge of how you spend your holidays. Come on, let's walk." She stepped wide around him and started north along the towpath, taking long strides, forcing him to hurry if he wanted to walk alongside her.

"But you came today," he pointed out as he stepped into pace alongside her.

"Because I wanted to," she said. "Not because of any duty, not because *you* wanted me to."

He was silent for a long minute. "What was the paper? About that skull you found in Mississippi?"

"That's right." She looked up along the towpath, watching a cyclist a long way off, wheeling toward them. He came closer and rushed past a moment or two later.

"Aren't you going to tell me about it?"

She stopped and turned to face him. "Michael, you only know about it in the first place because you went snooping through my papers and then made *me* feel guilty about it. It's all very delicate, sensitive stuff and I'm not supposed to talk about it just yet—and I don't see where you've shown yourself to be a reliable confidant."

"What you're saying is, you don't trust me," he said petulantly.

"Have you given me any reason to?" she asked.

"I'm sorry. I won't go snooping anymore," he said in a hard voice. "But I wish you'd tell me what you've been doing."

She happened to glance over at him just then, and it was almost her undoing. The firm voice was at odds with his expression. He looked so helpless, so put-upon, it was all she could do not to reach out, touch him, tell him it was all right. She caught herself and realized he had done it again, made himself the aggrieved party, made her feel she should apologize, given her the power to make him feel better—all in a sentence or two. Undoubtedly, he didn't even realize he had done it, it was all reflex. That wasn't the sort of skill you learned overnight. It took years of practice to get that unthinkingly *good* at it. Could he ever hope to get over it? Why would he ever want to? It worked so well for him.

Michael spoke, breaking into the silence of her reverie. "But that's all right," he said, pardoning her imagined offenses against her. "I just wanted to see you again. I want to be with you."

She wanted, on reflex, to *say yes, of course, let's try again, let's have dinner.* She could feel her hand moving toward him, felt it reach half the distance to take his hand. Just in time, she stopped herself. She opened her mouth to speak, closed it, finally started over and got the words out of her mouth. "It's too late for that," she said. "I'll be leaving again, very soon."

And she marveled at how good it felt to say those words. As if she had finally won a victory, was finally in charge of something.

But there was an ache in her heart, too. She looked Mike in the eye again. Running away, abandoning the man she loved, giving up, choosing loneliness. It was a strange sort of victory when you lost so much.

Chapter Thirteen

Pete Ardley shifted uncertainly in the hard, wobbly wooden chair. It was the sort of chair that is always relinquished to the hallway at a college, kicked out of the classroom for being too rickety. He looked at the clock and sighed. The long, echoing silence of the corridor he was sitting in magnified the sound and made him feel even more uncomfortable. He looked at the clock again, knowing full well he had checked the time 30 seconds before. Quarter to eleven. He had been waiting here for three quarters of hour now. The reason for most of the delay could be seen posted right on the office door, hung on the glass part of the door with yellowish scotch tape. Professor Volsky had class from 9:30 to 10:30 on Monday mornings. Her secretary had muffed it when she had made the ten o'clock appointment.

Just then the bright, precise *clip clop, clip clop* of wooden-heeled shoes on a hard floor started in at the end of the hall, and a lean, brisk looking white woman of about fifty turned the corner. She noticed him at once and smiled as she hurried toward him. She was a cheerful looking person, with grey hair piled up in tight, neat curls on her head. She was dressed in a plain blouse and skirt and flat shoes that looked more comfortable than stylish.

Pete stood up and took her hand. "Professor Volsky? I'm Pete Ardley, Gowrie *Gazette*."

"Yes, Mr. Ardley, of course. My apologies over the mix-up. They changed the schedule during the Christmas break and I'm afraid I only discovered my class and your appointment conflicted when I was already in class this morning. Please come in," she said as she worked the key in the lock, pushed open the door to her minuscule office and gestured Pete into a chair. It was a small bright, airy room, stuffed full of books and papers. Pete looked out the high window onto the wide lawns of Ole Miss.

Professor Volsky maneuvered into the tight corner between her desk and the window, set her papers down on the desk, poured water from a pitcher into a tiny coffee maker perched on the windowsill, spooned coffee into the grounds basket, opened the top of the window just a crack, scooted her desk chair out and sat down—all in a smooth, graceful flow of movement that made it seem she wasn't hurrying at all. "Now, then, what can an anthropology professor do for a newspaper reporter?"

Pete pulled a manila folder out of his briefcase. "I'd like you to take a look at some pictures."

She pulled her glasses out of her purse and perched them on her nose. "Pictures of what?" she asked.

"That's what I'd like you to tell me," Pete said, handing the folder to her. Now he was sharing the secret, on the first step of the journey that would get the story—if there was any story—out. He watched with sweaty palms and butterflies in his stomach as she opened the folder. She took one look at the first photo, closed the folder, and looked up sharply. "Where did these come from, Mr. Ardley?"

"Please, Professor, I'd prefer not to say at the moment. I'd like you to look at the pictures—look at the objective evidence, you might say, and interpret *that* without any word of explanation from me. I don't want to cloud the issue. Afterward I'll be happy to tell you everything I know."

"Indeed," she said. "I must say you ask a great deal of a person, but I see your point. Obviously, however, they can't be what they seem to be." She reopened the folder and slowly looked over each picture, her face expressionless.

A tendril of cool air looped into the room, wandering down from the open top of the window. Pete felt his nose begin to itch, and found himself resisting the urge to scratch it, as if he were back in grammar school and was being made to stay after class with a strict teacher. Pointlessly embarrassed, he reached up furtively and rubbed it for the briefest possible moment. The coffee maker giggled and burbled, and a thin stream of coffee flowed down into the carafe. Professor Volsky pulled a magnifying glass out of her desk drawer and examined the photos more carefully. Pete became aware of the loud ticking of a clock, somewhere in the shelves over his left shoulder.

The coffee maker finished its work, and a little puff of steam rose up from it with a chuffing noise. The professor looked up distractedly and said, "Help yourself to coffee, Mr. Ardley."

Now Pete found himself in a new quandary. Obviously, he should pour coffee for his hostess as well, but how did she take it? Dare he interrupt her concentration and ask? He had forgotten the way a teacher, any teacher, put the fear of God into him. Forget it. Best not to pour for her at all.

She stood up abruptly, turned around, pulled a book down from the shelf, and sat back down with it. Pete poured his coffee into a styrofoam cup, sat back down in his chair, and tried to drink it without slurping as the professor flipped through the book, comparing the photos against its illustrations.

Finally, she closed the book and the folder. She stared at Pete for a long while before she stood up and got her own coffee. She sat back down and stared at him again, hard.

Pete cleared his throat nervously. "Well?"

"It would *appear*," Professor Volsky said carefully, "that those are photographs, taken surreptitiously through a window, of a collection of superbly preserved nonhuman hominid, probably australopithecine, remains. There is also a series that would appear to be of the moment of discovery of one of the skulls. The skulls are *so* superbly preserved that I am tempted to say that either you are the intended victim of someone else's hoax, or else I am the victim of yours." Her voice was cautious and precise.

Pete started to speak, but thought better of it.

"Adding to the unlikelihood of the photographs being real are various details—the house and the cars in the background of the outdoor shots are clearly not only American, but I'd venture to say they are local. One of the cars appears to have Mississippi plates, for example, and the young black man is wearing a Mississippi State warm-up jacket. Since the photos are apparently local, and since you are a reporter for a small-town Mississippi newspaper, I assume that you took these photos. That would tend to make believe that you are the hoaxer.

"The one thing, the one detail in any of these photos that makes them at all believable is this," she said, pulling one of the long-range exterior shots out of the stack. She leaned across the desk and pointed to the older man in the photo. He was grinning broadly as he held the strange skull in his hands. "*That* is Dr. Jeffery Grossington, of the Smithsonian Institution's anthropology department. I cannot believe he would be a willing party to any fraud. If he weren't in that photo, you'd be out in hallway right now, with these ridiculous photos thrown in your face. But, with Grossington involved . . ." Her voice trailed off for a minute, and she seemed to realize the significance of what she was saying. She spoke again, with a sudden eagerness, a new excitement in her voice. "I've kept my side of the bargain. Now you keep yours. Tell me about these photos—tell me about those skulls!"

▼◆▼

The 747 jetliner eased to a final halt in the middle of the endless, sun-baked tarmac and pulled up short with a slight jerk. Livingston peered out of his hazy plexiglas window at the tiny slice of Africa he could see rippling through the heat-addled air. The jet engines sighed to a halt, and that helped a little, but even so, the air would not stay altogether still. The sun beat down on the asphalt and concrete, set up rippling towers of air that seemed to turn the world into a congealing, gelatinous fluid that wobbled and bounced at every touch. The control tower twisted and bent over, and the baggage cart and mobile stairs transmuted into a thousand incredible shapes as they rolled toward the plane.

Barbara nudged him in the ribs and grinned at him. "Welcome," she said, "to darkest Africa."

Livingston grinned right back at her, and reached up to rub his arm where she had nudged him. The inoculations against twelve kinds of God-knows-what were still a collection of sore spots. Three weeks ago he had never even had a passport, never been any further from Mississippi than a hotel room for an away football game—and now he was in *Africa*! Passports, visas, inoculations, customs, duty-free shops, the shifting time zones and jet lag, all the tedious minutiae of travelling to foreign parts were new to him, almost as great an adventure as the goal of the journey itself.

He blinked hard and tried to make his head stay on straight. The wild sixteen-hour layover in Paris where Barbara and Rupert had taken him to every nightspot they could think of still left a residue of hangover, but even that was almost something new and special.

Seventy-two hours ago he had been hugging his mother and father goodbye in Jackson, and now he was hung over, disoriented, jet-lagged, queasy from the last of the inoculations—and in *Africa*.

The cabin door sighed open in the front of the aircraft, and the bright light of an equatorial sun poured into the plane, the steamingly humid air sloshing in behind, chasing out the cool, sanitary, lifeless air of the jetliner. The moist, sultry air, full of the tang of the tropical sea and the ripening life of the great inland forests, was almost intoxicating after the sterility of airports and airplane food and airplane air. Almost immediately, he could feel sweat springing up on his face. The heat of Africa. Livingston couldn't wait to get out in it, escape from the over-orderly, impersonally perfect world of modern travel and out under the sun of his native land.

—Or what *might* be his native land, anyway. Livingston had gotten full of romantic ideas about Africa and homecomings and discovering his past once it was certain they were really going to Africa, but he had no idea—and no real way of finding out—where *his* people had come from. What tribe, what land, what country had been carved out of the territory his ancestors had trod—all of it would be forever unknown and unknowable, a heritage lost in the slave raids and the forced marches and the torments of the Middle Passage and the long generations of servitude.

His people might have lived over the next hill, or two thousand miles from here. But none of that mattered. He was *home*. The stewardess went through her spiel about overhead luggage racks in French and then in English. Livingston pulled out his carry-on bag and lined up behind Rupert and Barbara as they shuffled down the narrow aisle toward the door.

The full force of the equatorial sun and heat was a shock when Livingston stepped out onto the platform of the mobile stairs. He had to pause for a moment and blink his eyes into adjustment with the *brightness* of it all. He stood there and looked around him as he dug his sunglasses out of his shirt pocket, vaguely disappointed to see nothing more than an modest-sized airport-shaped airport, not much more than the little field at Natchez, near Gowrie. He wondered what he had been expecting. Lions and zebra wandering around on the runway?

Once inside the chaos of the customs building, a big quonset hut attached to one end of the main terminal building, he felt a little better. Hundreds of people in African and Western dress were swarming this way and that, mobbing the baggage carts and shouting in languages he didn't understand. Maybe it wasn't exactly exotic, but at least it was different. He retrieved his bag and got in line for passport control, slowly becoming aware of the sweat that was gradually adhering his light cotton shirt to his skin.

The small band of customs inspectors phlegmatically ignored the shouting, the pushing, the masses of people, and calmly went through each passport and visa, each piece of luggage. Livingston got through in fairly good order, quickly followed by Barbara—but then it was Rupert's turn.

Rupert, it appeared, was the quintessential over-packer. Very few of the things that bulged from his backpack and carry-on bag were clothes, however. Cameras, lenses, his portable computer, a two-way radio set, batteries, binoculars, a machete, pens, notebooks, a rock hammer, a lead-lined bag full of film—endless gadgets, each packed carefully away. Inevitably, the customs inspector's suspicions were aroused by all the mysterious bits of hardware.

Instantly, Rupert and the inspector were engaged in a spirited shouting match in French—and to Livingston's monolingual ears, it was soon clear that Rupert's French was communicated more by shouting and gestures than clear syntax. It struck even a neophyte traveler like Livingston that it was a mistake to antagonize a customs inspector. Sure enough, the inspector insisted that each item be unpacked and thoroughly examined.

The shouting continued, along with a great deal of passport waving and general commotion. Finally, the inspector had had enough and rather firmly escorted Rupert through a door into some sort of office.

Barbara, seeing what was happening from the other side of the barrier, moaned out loud. "Hell's bells, Rupert's going to be there all day." She dragged her duffel bag over to a bench along the side wall and sat down. "Might as well settle in for the long haul, Liv. It looks like we could be here a while."

Livingston looked longingly toward the far end of the quonset hut and the swinging doors that were the entrance to the terminal proper. He sighed, dropped his duffel bag, and sat down on it next to his cousin. Every time anyone was cleared through customs, he or she would hurry through those doors, and Livingston would get a glimpse of hustle and bustle, brightly-clothed people carrying huge loads on their heads, cab drivers shouting for passengers, people selling all sorts of things. A whole new country, a whole *continent* just outside that pair of swinging doors, and he had to sit here while Rupert Maxwell unpacked his luggage.

The crowds of people coming off the plane gradually melted away, and the stifling-hot customs-shed terminal grew more and more quiet.

Suddenly there was a bustle at the entrance to the main terminal. A short, paunchy white man in a baggy suit, a straggly necktie, and a strange, decrepit-looking snap-brimmed straw hat came bursting through the swinging doors. He stopped just inside the entrance and looked about for a moment at the people still in the customs hut. Then he shrugged and shouted out "Marchando Party! Calling for the Marchando party!"

Barbara was on her feet in a moment. "Here!" she shouted back.

The paunchy man hurried over to them, moving faster than it looked like he could. He put out his hand and took off his hat. "Dr. Marchando. How do you do. I'm Clark White, from the Embassy." His voice was a bit reedy and winded, quite in contrast to the shout he had offered up a moment before.

"Mr. Clark, it's very kind of you to meet us," Barbara said.

"Quite all right. It's a pleasant break from the routine. As a matter of fact, your researches sounded so fascinating I did something I've never done before—I invited myself along, if that's all right."

Barbara smiled happily. "It certainly is! We need someone who knows the country. We'd be delighted to have you along."

"Excellent. In that case, I'll really have the chance to get out of the office." White turned to Liv and offered his hand. "And Livingston Jones, I presume," he said—and then hesitated, obviously concerned that he had given offense. "Oh, dear. Forgive my extremely small joke," he said, awkwardly putting his hat back on his head.

"It's okay," Liv said easily. "I've been getting Stanley and Livingstone jokes ever since I was a kid. Worse since I announced I was going to Africa."

"That's most kind of you. But what has happened to Dr. Maxwell? Wasn't he to travel with you?"

Barbara hooked a thumb at the customs inspector's office, where a threatening silence had replaced the loud voices. "I'm afraid he's already having trouble with the natives. Some difficulty about his luggage."

White sighed. "Oh Rupert, Rupert, Rupert. Some things never

change. If you could wait here a moment, I'll see what I can do."

White marched up to the customs barrier, waving his credentials at the inspector, who let him through into the office area. The previous shouting resumed for a moment before settling down to calmer tones, led by White's reedy, smooth-voiced French. Finally, the voices quieted down enough that Barbara and Livingston couldn't hear them anymore, and a few minutes later White, Rupert, and a gaggle of customs workers popped out of the inner office, if not in good spirits, at least calmed down a bit.

Clark hustled Rupert and his baggage through the gate, gestured to Barbara and Livingston to follow, and hurried them all through the entrance to the main terminal. "That's done with," he said happily. "I wanted to get you clear of there before Rupert and his friends could think of anything else to argue about." White turned and looked up at Rupert, who stood a full head taller. "That last thing, the pith helmet. That was the limit, that's what really got them mad, you know. What the devil are you doing with a *pith* helmet, for God's sake?"

Rupert, still rather angry, glared back down at the diplomat. "They're very practical in this climate. Keep your head cool and protected, and your sweat doesn't come pouring down your back."

"Oh, for God's sake! Didn't it ever occur to you that a pith helmet is a symbol of something here—the great white hunter, colonialism, native bearers, all the stereotypes. When you went to visit Barbara's family in Mississippi, did you bring watermelon as a visitor's gift?"

Barbara laughed out loud. "No, Mr. White, we talked him out of it. Come on, I want to see more of Africa than an airport."

White shook his head and peered owlishly up at Rupert. "Pith helmet. Well, come on, let's see if there's a decent taxi left. The passengers on your flight who came out a half hour ago like regular people probably cleaned them out."

▼◆▼

Livingston was feeling disappointed again. The train banked a bit to round a sharp curve, then settled back to its smooth progress, swaying back and forth just as it streaked over the smooth rail. They had left the capital of Libreville on the coast a few hours before, and were about halfway to the inland city of Booué. Liv had imagined their trip inland on a chugging steam launch, like Humphrey Bogart's boat in *The African Queen*. He had seen it all in his mind's eye—the doughty little craft heading up the endless, winding reaches of a mysterious jungle river, crocodiles sunning themselves, hippos diving out of sight, weird noises from the jungle as they surged upstream ...

Well, there was a river all right, the Ogooue. He could see it peeking through the trees every now and then as the rail line rolled alongside it. But he might as well be riding Amtrak for all the romance of it. He wasn't really that clear on whether there were crocs or hippos in the river, but there certainly weren't any on the train. Okay, the lady sitting on the other side of the compartment had a cage full of live—if scrofulous—chickens on her lap, but that was more smelly than colorful. And rather than anxiously watching for attacks from the shore, Rupert, Barb, and the guy from the Embassy, White, were all calmly reading paperbacks.

In honor of the trip, Clark White had traded in his rather rumpled summer-weight suit for a very sensible-looking set of khakis that made him look a great deal more impressive and authoritative. He looked up from his book and seemed to read Livingston's thoughts from a glance at his face. "Sorry we're not more like the movies, Mr. Jones," White told him. Barbara and Rupert looked up to listen. "But it can't be helped." He looked out the window and blinked happily at the westering sunshine streaming through the walls of the jungle. "A train ride might seem dull to you as opposed to a river trip, or bouncing around in a Land Rover, but the Transgabonais railroad is a dream come true for the people here, their ticket into the present. It's binding the country together, making it a real nation instead of a bunch of isolated villages—just the way our railways did. For the locals, *this* is the romantic, exciting way to travel. Besides, we'll get all the Land Rover bouncing you want a bit later on." White and the others returned to their books.

Livingston grunted, looked back out the window, and sighed. He heard the chickens' fussing get louder for a moment. He glanced over and noticed that the woman holding them was giving him yet another sidelong glance. She realized he had caught her at it and shifted her attention to Barbara. The woman looked intently at Barbara's hair and then reached up to pat her own kerchiefed head. She was clearly fascinated by Barb's hair, her black woman's hair, in a Western style.

The chicken woman had scarcely even noticed Rupert or White, but had spent the entire trip staring at the two black Americans. That had been the pattern of the entire journey in Gabon so far. The porter at the hotel, the waiters at the restaurants, the taxi drivers, the railroad conductor, everyone seemed fascinated by the sight of this huge black man with his football player's physique, his American clothes, and American-accented English. It didn't take long for Liv to realize that *everything* about him—his mannerisms, his shoes, his haircut—tagged him as an outsider. And a *black* outsider, who looked like an African and acted like a European.

Livingston had expected Africa to feel like a second home, like the land of his birth, and yet he had never felt more like a foreigner, a stranger, in his life—not even when he had first stepped onto the virtually lily-white campus of Ole Miss.

He had expected to be a black man among black men, but instead he was a freak. And he wasn't even the right shade of black. The locals were far darker-skinned than he was, jet black instead of chocolate brown. Was is that a lifetime of equatorial sun had baked their black skins blacker, or were they *really* blacker, more purely black, than he was? Livingston had always known that a lot of masters had lain with their slaves, but he had never really thought of it on a personal level. He knew, more or less, who most of his ancestors were for the last hundred years or so—but how many of *their* ancestors had been white?

Uncomfortable questions, uncomfortable ideas. Instead of helping him get in contact with his roots, Africa was making him question them. He caught that damn woman with the chickens staring at him again. This time he decided to ignore her.

▼◆▼

They spent that night in a stiflingly hot hotel in Booué, sweating under mosquito netting in rooms where whole herds of cockroaches scuttled for cover when the lights went on. To Livingston, the jungle noises coming from outside the small town seemed as loud as any city traffic for the purposes of promoting insomnia. Maybe it was the noise, maybe it was the heat, maybe it was the last gasp of jet lag, but none of them slept well that night. Except Clark White, of course.

Nothing ever seemed to bother him. Fat, old, and balding though he was, Clark was endlessly active and energetic, unfazed by the intemperate climate. When Livingston and Rupert staggered down to breakfast the next morning, they found Barbara in sole possession of the run-down hotel restaurant, with Clark nowhere to be seen. The hotel had seemed full of people the night before, but now it was deserted.

A waiter who seemed to regard them all with some suspicion served them strong, bitter, black *cafe noir* without being asked. Rupert and Barbara had dealt with espresso before, but Livingston thought his tongue would blacken and fall out. He had never tasted anything as bitter or as strong.

Rupert grinned when he saw the face Livingston was making. "Suffer through it, cowboy. No milk to be had, so you have to take it straight. But I guarantee it'll get you awake."

Livingston shuddered. "Yuck. I can see why they serve it in such small cups. So what's the plan? And where's Clark?"

"Up and out hours ago. He left a note saying he was heading out to make some sort of arrangements for the next leg of the trip," Barbara said. She managed to catch the waiter's eye and gestured him over. "Rupert, you're the one who speaks French. Order us something shaped like breakfast."

Livingston winced a little less over his second sip of *cafe noir*, and by the third was used to it. Rupert and the waiter spent a good five minutes discussing what on the menu was actually available. Finally some sort of negotiated settlement was reached, and the waiter shouted the order to the kitchen in what was presumably Fang, because it wasn't French. Five minutes later, a slab of greasy ham and half a canned peach was set before each of them with an appropriate lack of ceremony, accompanied by rather frugal glasses of orange juice that had the taste of being in a can too long.

The check appeared magically, with *service complet* scribbled in the corner and twenty percent added to the bill. Livingston remembered it was about three hundred *Communité Financial Afrique* francs to the dollar, converted in his head, and compared the price to the dinner they had had in Libreville. He decided they were being overcharged because they were foreigners, even if you accounted for their being in the backside of nowhere, but on the other hand, breakfast in a diner back home would have been cheap at the price. He shrugged and ate his ham, then helped Barbara and Rupert finish theirs.

Clark came in just as they were finishing, carrying a rolled-up map. "Morning, all, morning. Congratulations on setting a record this morning. The desk clerk just told me he won a bet off a bellboy that you three got down to breakfast later than anyone else. All the other guests were up and out hours ago. The perils of jet lag." He pulled out a chair, sat down and gestured for the waiter. "*Garçon, cafe, s'il vous plait.*" Clark glanced about at the remains of breakfast on their plates and chuckled. "I see they are giving you the royal treatment, though. Canned food. Nothing but the best for our European visitors."

"I couldn't understand it," Rupert said. "They didn't seem to have anything fresh on the menu."

Clark laughed out loud. "Ah, but they were no doubt scandalized that you wanted fresh things. They have a very different point of view about such matters. Fresh things rot so fast around here, in this heat. Besides, everyone can afford them. No snob appeal. But canned stuff, preserved stuff that won't rot if you leave it on the shelf for two days, *that's* the height of modern, convenient luxury and elegance in these parts. Right now, freeze-dried stuff is all the rage. Incredibly expensive, but the height of sophistication." The waiter appeared at Clark's elbow with coffee, and he took it gladly.

"Well," he said, taking a sip. "It took me half the morning, but I tracked down the fellow in town who hires out his Land Rover. He can drive us to Makokou, northeast of here. Here, clear away some of these things and I'll show you where we are and where we're going."

They cleared the dirty plates and the salt and pepper and so forth to an empty table—scandalizing the waiter anew in the process—and Clark unrolled his map, a large-scale chart of the region. "All right, this is where we are, in the sub-prefecture of Ogooue-Invido, as if that mattered to any of you." He stabbed a plump finger down at the map. "Here's where we are, Booué, and here—" he traced his finger along a prominent dotted line on the map "is the future route of the northeastern branch of the Transgabonais. They've already cleared a good piece of the right-of-way and laid some of the track, and we should be able to follow it most of the way to the next and final major town we'll see, Makokou."

"Then what?" Barbara asked.

"I don't know," Clark said cheerfully. "Your Smithsonian people and the reports I got from the locals both place a tribe called the Utaani, whom I assume are your Yewtani under a different spelling, as being somewhere in the vicinity of Makokou, without any further details. We have to ask about, find them somehow."

"How tough could that be?" Livingston asked.

"Pretty tough," Clark said. "They are semi-nomadic, slash-and-burn farmers. Slash-and-burners tend to move around fairly often, and most of the neighboring tribes seem to make it a point to have nothing to do with the Utaani. Also, they're a small tribe, which should also make them a bit hard to find. *But* the interesting thing is that they are also the center of a lot of nasty stories and legends around Makokou—stuff about their dealing with goblins, black magic, lost souls, that sort of thing.

"When a person vanishes, lost in the jungle somehow, they say the Utaani have taken him and turned him into one of their *tranka*. That is a word that translates badly, but it means something very like 'goblin' or 'ghoul,' and it got my attention. Think about it—what would one of your australo-whatchamacallits look like to a person if he stumbled across it in the jungle? Mothers use the Utaani and the *tranka* stories to scare their kids into being good. All very suggestive, no?" Clark asked with a sly little smile, his glasses hanging low on his fleshy nose. "Leaving folklore to one side, the Utaani are also supposed to be extremely secretive, strange, and unpleasant people."

He scooped up the map and rolled it into a tight cylinder. "One last thing: the Utaani were also one of the last tribes to give up kidnapping their neighbors and selling them down the river as slaves. Put all that together and I feel pretty confident that they are the ones we are after."

"You mean, they can lead us to the australopithecines?" Livingston asked.

Clark shrugged. "In theory, yes. In practice, who knows? We're dealing with rumors and a Mississippi newspaper ad from the last century. But I chased around every library and archive and ethnologist I could find in Libreville, and they seem to be the most likely lead by far. Let's be on our way."

▼◆▼

They were packed and out of the hotel in fifteen minutes, Clark leading the way, carrying a small, professional backpack that didn't seem to match the years or bearing of the fussy little man they had met in the capital. But in his khakis and hiking shoes, a brown canvas bush hat plopped down on his head, carrying an improvised walking stick that had once been a broom handle, the neatly packed backpack an unnoticed burden gracefully balanced on his back, he seemed a transformed and far happier man.

Rupert walked alongside him, all but staggering under the weight of his far heavier pack. Liv and Barb brought up the rear, returning stare for stare with the curious locals. Booué was a railroad boom town, just in the first stages of growing from a collection of near-shacks strung out along a single road into a real town. The four of them had to cross an enormous rail yard, far larger than the town itself, to get where they were going. It was a frantically busy place, full of men and equipment bound for the northeast spur that was still abuilding, and freight and passenger cars switching back and forth for the runs to Libreville on the coast and Franceville in the southeast interior. It all seemed wildly out of proportion to the still-sleepy village next door. At the edge of the rail yard they came to a small garage, a weathered but well-cared-for Land Rover parked out front. A wiry, middle-aged man with white hair, skin the color of ebony and the texture of leather, dressed in shorts and a much-washed white cotton shirt was squatting on the hood of the Rover, polishing the windshield.

Clark called to him, and the man stood up on the hood, turned around, and grinned broadly, an expression which made his entire face fold up into a series of wrinkles. "*Bonjour, M'sieu, bonjour!*" he called and jumped down from the Rover.

Clark returned his greeting in French and then made the introductions. "This is Monsieur Ovono, who owns this fine vehicle. *M'sieu Ovono, j'presente Monsieur Rupert Maxwell. Monsieur Maxwell parle Francais aussi. Et, j'presente Mademoiselle Barbara Marchando, et Monsieur Livingston Jones.*"

Monsieur Ovono helped them load their gear onto the roof rack, very carefully laid a tarp over the luggage, and tied it down firmly. In fifteen minutes they were jouncing along on their way, grinding through the rubble and red mud of the railroad's right-of-way, plowing through the raw, unhealed slash sliced through the surrounding jungle.

The stumps of dead trees lay everywhere, some of them uprooted, torn from the muddy red soil. The right-of-way was 300 hundred feet wide, but the narrow service road—little more than a rough path in places—ran almost in the shadows of the great dark trees that stood, brooding and sullen green, alongside the empty rail line. The jungle, its massive trees rearing up to block out half the sky, seemed much displeased at the invasion.

Rupert found himself in the front seat of the Land Rover next to Monsieur Ovono. "So, you four are driving to Makokou," Ovono said in rapid French. "What takes you to such a place?"

"We are looking for a certain tribe who might know something about an animal we wish to study," Rupert said, choosing his words carefully. He had no idea what Ovono might think of the Utaani, but from what he had learned so far, it wasn't likely to be favorable.

"What tribe is that? I'm Fang myself, of course."

"One of the smaller ones."

"Which one? Eshira? Bapounou? Okande?"

"No, no. They are called the Utaani," Rupert replied, fearful of the response.

Ovono laughed out loud. "That mob? What could they know about animals? A bunch of dirty farmers they tell foolish tales about."

"You've heard of them in Booué? I thought they were little known far from Makokou."

"No, no. Not from Booué. I am in Makokou many times, and they tell the same mad tales about the Utaani every time, having fun frightening the railroad workers who come to drink."

Clark White leaned forward from the back seat, holding on to the back of Rupert's seat to keep from being thrown about by the bone-rattling ride. "Then you have no concern of the Utaani, M'sieu?" he asked, shouting over the noise of the Rover.

"No, not at all," Ovono shouted back. "Every town has its ghost stories. If you believed them all, it would not be safe to step outside your house for fear of six kinds of monster leaping from the forest to eat you. I am a good Catholic," Ovono said proudly, pulling a small crucifix on a chain out of his shirt, "not one of those damned animists who sees spirits in every tree and twig." He gestured grandly at the ruined strip of landscape. "Look, it is a hundred meters wide and hundreds of kilometers long. If every tree had a spirit, could they have sliced down all these trees without being cursed forever?"

Rupert looked out at the huge trees that marched alongside the right-of-way, with the dark, murky clouds of a rainstorm suddenly gathering above them. He shuddered, for the moment quite ready to believe the trees, the jungle, all of nature, could be angered at this affront and ready to strike back.

The cloudburst exploded over their heads, an impenetrable, torrential rain that made the world ten feet away from the Rover invisible. Ovono simply rolled up the windows, switched on the windshield wipers and the headlights, and drove on, not slowing down at all.

They rode on, the noise of the storm making speech impossible.

They camped by the side of the maintenance road that night, with that same angry jungle rearing over them, a deeper blackness blocking out the stygian darkness of an overcast, moonless night sky. Ovono said there was little danger of more rain and they shouldn't bother with a tent. He took two long bamboo poles and slipped them through rings atop the roof rack, so that the poles hung out over the side of the Rover. Then he draped a huge piece of mosquito netting over the whole rig, Rover and all. He quickly built a fire outside the netting and got dinner going. The sun set abruptly, as it always does in the tropics, but by the time it did, Ovono had them ready for the night, a can of stew heating on the fire. Everyone was hungry and set to the meal eagerly. They ate off tin plates balanced on their knees, sitting on rickety folding camp stools. Rupert pulled a tiny short-wave radio out of his backpack and, after great fiddling with the dial, managed to pick up a music program on the Voice of America broadcasting out of God-knows-where. It made for a pleasant background to dinner. Ovono had the plates gathered up the moment everyone was done, wiping them off and packing them away before any insects could be attracted. Rupert shut his radio off to save the batteries, and everyone discovered how tired they were.

Without the noises of the Rover or the radio or the bustling around of making camp, they could really hear the sounds of the jungle for the first time that night—screams, shouts, murmurs, crashes, scraping noises, rustlings in the underbrush and the scratches of claws on bark in the trees overhead. Ovono seemed quite unconcerned, and placidly stared into the campfire, smoking his pipe. **Rupert and** Clark, who had at least been in the jungle before, seemed, **if not at** ease, at least ready to deal with the situation, and Barbara **was too** exhausted by jet lag for anything to keep her awake.

But Livingston, named in a misspelled way **for** a great jungle explorer, eager for so long to be in his idea of the real Africa, far away from civilization, yearning for the romance of the jungle—Livingston and his imagination listened, wide awake and wide-eyed, to the endless ravings and stalking of homicidal maniacs in the forest all night long. He didn't get a wink of sleep until daybreak, and Ovono nudged him awake all too soon after that.

▼◆▼

They were all beginning to fear her, hate her. Her own kind sensed, somehow, that she was becoming different, growing apart from them.

It was the things she was learning—language and the power of words, of symbols—that set her apart. Because she knew the words, she had the power to know many things. She was always first to the food, last to the work. She learned craftiness, learned how to avoid punishment.

As she grew more confident of her ability, she seemed to need the approval and reassurance of her fellows less. She gradually stopped taking part in the grooming sessions. She ceased to take an interest in the constant fussing and scrambling over who would get the most favorable sleeping spot in the hut. The males began to avoid her, and she did not care.

She grew more silent as well, hardly ever making a noise on her own, and rarely responding much to the grunts and growls and shouts and hoots of her fellows. Perhaps she was losing her skills at that sort of communication as she was gaining new ones, or perhaps she had learned to be quiet in order to listen. It became easier and easier for her to think in the new way, and it was no longer taxing or diffi-cult to concentrate. She no longer forgot what she was doing. Now she rarely slipped back into the old habits of dull obedience and con-formity.

Those of her kind gave her a wider and wider berth, and began to resist orders from the humans to work next to her. The younger ones especially would bare their teeth and chitter at her, or simply run away.

The humans grew to fear her as well. This was not the first time one of the tranka *had behaved strangely, and it had often ended badly in the past. The keeper had seen it before, had been warned of the dangers by the old keeper, his father. A* tranka, *usually one of the less docile ones, would suddenly change, would grow more and more uncontrollable, upsetting the other slave-beasts, disrupting the work* schedule. *No one knew why it happened, but it did. Sometimes the* tranka *would seem to forget whatever it was that upset it, begin to behave normally again, and things would get back to normal of their own accord. It was worth waiting for a time to see if such a thing would happen;* tranka *were hard to breed, hard to train, and not to be lightly discarded.*

But if things did not improve with this one, and soon, the keeper knew what he would have to do. It would have to be done quietly, so as not to upset the other tranka, *but it would have to be done.*

This rebellious female would have to be destroyed.

FEBRUARY

Chapter Fourteen

Pete Ardley had a first-rate view of the top of Joe Teems's head as he stood over his editor's desk, watching the old man slowly read Pete's story.

Teems had a pencil in his mouth and was chewing it methodically as he read, making small crunching noises when he bit down, and an odd little irregular clicking when he rolled the pencil around on his teeth. Every now and then he would pause in his reading, refer back to a previous page, and then shift his position just a trifle, making a small *uffing* noise as the movement forced the air out of his lungs and squeezed it past the pencil. Then Teems would snort to get some air back in his lungs and go on with his reading. Pete ignored the small noises and concentrated on examining Teems's head, noting the sparse little wisps of hair and the mottled liver spots that dotted his bald spot, which appeared surprisingly large from this angle. The old blowhard was sure as hell taking his time reading the piece. Was that a good sign or a bad?

▼◆▼

HUMAN-LIKE MYSTERY SKULLS
UNEARTHED IN GOWRIE

by Peter Ardley, Gowrie *Gazette* Staff

Skulls of a species of hominid previously known only from African fossils millions of years old have been excavated in secret on the outskirts of Gowrie, throwing many firmly held ideas about the human past into confusion. The five skulls, along with an undetermined number of post-cranial ("below-the-skull") bones, were removed from the site by a team of scientists, apparently led by a prominent anthropologist from Washington, D.C.

Professor Roberta Volsky of the Department of Anthropology at the University of Mississippi, working from photographs obtained by the *Gazette*, has identified the skulls as being of the genus "Australopithecus." She described the discovery as "absolutely incredible. I can't imagine how those bones got there. This whole area of Mississippi was underwater when these creatures lived, and australopithecines have never been seen outside Africa. I can't imagine how these skeletons got here. We may have to write a whole set of theories to account for this."

The skulls were dug up from the grounds of Gowrie House, on the outskirts of the town, over the last month. Gowrie House is the home of Mrs. Josephine Jones, a retired school teacher. Mrs. Jones declined to be interviewed for this article.

Citing various details of the skulls visible in the photographs, and noting features of the photographs themselves, Professor Volsky discounted the possibility of a hoax. "I can't imagine anyone trying to pass off this as real if it wasn't," she said. "This discovery is such an unlikely occurrence that it will inevitably be subjected to the most severe scrutiny when it becomes public. Any possible phony skulls or other fraud would be instantly obvious." Professor Volsky also cited the reputations of the persons in the photographs of the site as an argument against fraud.

Identified in the photographs taken at the excavation are Dr. Jeffery Grossington, Dr. Rupert Maxwell, and Dr. Barbara Marchando, all of the Smithsonian Institution in Washington, and Mr. Livingston Jones. Dr. Marchando and Mr. Jones are relatives of the owner of the house, Mrs. Josephine Jones.

Professor Volsky discounted the secretive nature of the work as evidence of fraud, and said the secrecy could be attributed to caution, the scientists confirming their work before revealing it to a skeptical world. "I expect that Dr. Grossington will reveal everything in due course. It simply takes some time to analyze what you have found. Many important features of a skull aren't immediately obvious. But I have full faith in Jeffery Grossington."

According to Professor Volsky, four species of *Australopithecus*, all closely resembling each other, are generally recognized by science. They are (in chronological order) *Australopithecus afarensis*, *Australopithecus africanus*, *Australopithecus robustus*, and *Australopithecus boisei*. A possible fifth species, *Australopithecus aethiopicus*, has been proposed but not yet generally accepted. The oldest australopithecine remains are about four million years old, and the genus was believed to vanish from the earth about one million years ago. Professor Volsky believes the skulls uncovered in Mississippi are either robustus or boisei, two species that are so similar that some scientists regard them as one species erroneously given two names.

Although *australopithecus* means "southern ape," Professor Volsky pointed out that this is misleading. In taxonomic terms all australopithecines are members of the family "hominidea," the scientific grouping that includes all fully upright bipeds. Taxonomically, human beings are called *Homo sapiens sapiens*, of the genus Homo, also of the family hominidea. The australopithecines are related far more closely to own our species than to the apes, which are not included in the family hominidea. Taxonomy is the science of naming species and relating them to each other.

Professor Volsky said the species to which the newly found skulls belong is not ancestral to man, but instead shares a common ancestor with us. "In evolutionary terms," Professor Volsky said, "the robust australopithecines are our long-lost cousins, not our grandparents."

According to the theory of evolution, a species of plant or animal can respond to changes in its habitat, or adapt to a new habitat, by changing, or evolving, into another species. However, the ancestral species need not die out—it may survive, and even flourish, side by side with the descendant species. Many do not believe this theory, and instead point to the creation story of the Bible to explain the appearance and diversity of life.

However, most scientists believe the earliest australopithecines (i.e., *afarensis*) were ancestral to two branches of descendants, one leading to own species, *Homo sapiens sapiens*, perhaps through *Australopithecus africanus*, and the other leading to the late australopithecines before dying out. Other scientists, such as the noted paleontologist Richard Leakey, believe that the human and australopithecine lines may not share a recent common ancestor, and *afarensis* is not so closely related to man. In this theory, *Australopithecus afarensis* led only to the later australopithecines, and the human line will eventually be found to be more ancient when more fossil are found. According to this idea, even the earliest of the australopithecines are thus humanity's "cousins," not its ancestors.

Whatever ancestors they shared with modern man, it has been generally agreed that the later australopithecines, *boisei* and *robustus*, left no evolutionary descendants and that their line became extinct one million years ago. . . .

▼◆▼

Pete sweated it out. There was nothing more miserable for a writer than watching someone else read his work. Pete decided a dozen times in ten minutes that Teems would kill the piece, and decided just as many times that he would let it run.

Either way, it didn't really matter. Pete had already decided to quit if Teems turned down this story, didn't let him run it and put it on the wire. If Teems said no, Pete could hawk the story elsewhere, no question. This story was his ticket out, and he was taking that trip whether or not the Gowrie *Gazette* cooperated.

At long last, the pencil stopped rattling around in Teems's mouth and the old man tossed the last page of the story on his desk and looked up at Pete. "Are you actually expecting people to believe this hogwash?" Teems asked. "You expect *me* to believe it? The folks around here don't even believe in evolution—*I* don't believe in evolution. Why the hell should I run the piece?"

"Because it's a hell of a big story that will put this town on the map!" Pete said eagerly. "And even if you don't believe it, dammit, we've got the *pictures*! And not just of the skulls—I've gotten IDs on three scientists from Washington, D.C. It's all there in the story."

"Mmmph. And I notice how you've cast the story so it'll all fall on this Grossington's head, and then you put in a plug for creationism, as if that would keep the locals from going crazy. Nice fence sitting. Did you call Grossington up for comment?"

"No sir, I didn't. I don't want him to know anyone is on to him until the story hits. He's been keeping this whole thing secret for some reason—why should we give him the warning he needs to put the kibosh on it?"

Teems reached out to the story on his desk and tapped it. "Do you think it's a hoax in the making?"

Pete shrugged. "It's possible, but I don't believe it. Right there in the story, Professor Volsky says it's quite normal for scientists to take the time to do some thinking and analyzing before they report their findings publicly—sometimes it takes as much as a year or more. But if it *isn't* a hoax, he might well *ask* us not to publish until he's ready. If we went ahead and published anyway at that point, he might have grounds for a suit, claiming he had only agreed to talk because we agreed to delay. And this thing is sure to leak again sooner or later. If we do get asked to delay, and politely wait until Grossington says it's okay to print, someone else will break the news and we'll lose the scoop. Besides, if it *is* a hoax he's preparing, we want to catch him with his pants down, don't we?"

"The point being that, in either event, you don't think it'd be such a swift idea to talk with him," Teems said. "Okay, fair enough. What about this Volsky woman?" he asked. He picked up the best photo of the skulls. "Your story flat out says she identified the skulls as some kind of ape-man. Was she really that certain? They're strange-looking skulls, but was she really that positive?"

"All she wondered about was if the pictures were genuine. She checked the pictures against a lot of sources, and she was flat-out certain by the time she was finished."

Teems dropped the photo on the table. "I want to know how you got on to this," he said suspiciously. "You haven't actually admitted to taking these photos, and I'm not going to ask if you did. If the sheriff decides to arrest you for trespassing, I don't want to be in the middle of it. So we'll leave the photos. But you'd better tell me how you knew to go looking for this."

Pete Ardley shook his head. If Teems didn't remember Livingston Jones coming into the office, didn't recognize Livingston in the little group examining the skull in the outdoor shots, couldn't put two and two together, that was his problem. Pete intended to write follow-ups on this story, but he didn't plan on writing them for Teems. "I'm sorry, I can't tell you just yet. I've got to protect that source for a while."

"You've been seeing too many movies about reporters on TV," Teems said irritably. "But don't think for a moment you're fooling me for a moment, boy. This is the biggest story ever to come out of Gowrie—if it's true—and I'd bet anything you like that you've got your resignation all typed up if I spike this story. You'd be in Jackson trying to freelance it this afternoon. No loyalty. Which means I can't really trust you, can I?"

Teems glared at him and then went on. "That's bad for you, because it's up to me to decide if it would be good for the *Gazette* to run this story, up to me to decide if it's true. And I've just concluded I can't trust you. And I'll tell you something else. You've got more information than you put in this story. You're holding back, hoping to parley it into a big follow-up, maybe keep other reporters from getting ahead of you on this story." Teems smiled abruptly and nastily, exposing his scraggly yellow teeth in all their ugliness, and Pete felt as if the old man were staring right through him. Suddenly the smile vanished, replaced by an angry, suspicious glare. "Except it's your ass on the line too, and *you* couldn't have put a hoax like this together by yourself, and if you *did* put it together, you fooled that lady professor, and you ought to be able to fool the rest of us for long enough so it won't look bad for me when it blows up in your face. And I don't want to force you to quit so I have to break in a new reporter. Cut the last two 'graphs and run it. Page one. And then recast it for a non-local audience, get rid of the weasel-worded creationism fence-sitting stuff so that we sound like big-city folks who believe in evolution, and put it on the goddamn wire, while you're at it."

But Pete had bigger plans than just getting on the wire. Two hours later he had packages mailed off Express Mail to the New York *Times*, the Washington *Post*, and the Jackson *Clarion-Ledger*. He wanted this story to break wide. He sent a third package to Dr. Jeffery Grossington, care of the Smithsonian Institution. He also wanted to *control* this story.

▼◆▼

Livingston leaned back in his unsteady chair and stared at the far wall of the tiny café. Makokou was like Booué, he decided, only more so—smaller, rougher, smellier, rawer. It was also duller, if such a thing were possible. And it was a rotten place to do the one thing he was able to do at the moment—wait. So far as finding the australopithecines, nothing further was possible until they learned the present whereabouts of the Utaani tribe. Livingston, who spoke no French, was of no help in the researches. Rupert and Clark, accompanied by M. Ovono to translate the tribal tongues for them, were busily scouring the countryside for miles around, following up this rumor and that. Barbara couldn't speak French either, but she at least had brought work along to keep her busy. She was constantly borrowing Rupert's portable computer, finishing up a routine paper she had been working on before Thanksgiving had brought so much excitement.

There was little for Livingston to do but wander the town and drink too much *cafe noir* at the two grotty little restaurants and this depressing little café. The only other amusement was to be astonished at how fast the plants grew, how heavy the rains were, how humid and muggy the nights were, how ferocious the mosquitoes were.

The jungle seemed closer here, more powerful and determined, as if it would conquer the town overnight if humankind turned its back for a moment. It was a point driven home on the ride here, when they reached the rear guard of the rail-building crew and then had slowly driven past the army of men who were cutting back the jungle to lay the steel road. They had passed the supply wagons, the camps, the mess tents, the supply dumps, driven past the track-laying machines—the whole elaborate army needed to fight through the jungle. M. Ovono had maneuvered his Land Rover past bulldozers and the earthmoving gear, huge machines grinding and hacking away at the sinews of the forest, a nightmare noise of diesel engines and trees falling and men shouting—and then they were past the head of earthmoving team, ahead of the lead work gang.

M. Ovono followed the old dirt path to Makokou, driving straight into the wall of trees. In the moment they entered the trees, the sound of men working on the railroads stopped, abruptly, sharply, like a switch being thrown, the world of men swallowed up by the jungle and its own sounds.

When they had started out on the trip, Liv had been shocked by the railroad's violation of the forest, the cruel clear-cutting. He had given a silent cheer when he saw some evidence of the jungle's fighting back—a stand of saplings popping up inside the clear-cut line, a wall of bamboo growing back where it had been cut down, new-growth vines and creepers swarming over the felled trees, reaching out tendrils toward the track.

Not anymore. Not after they arrived in Makokou and M. Ovono pointed out an abandoned house with trees growing *through* the porch, sprouting up out of holes the branches had punched in the roof. The foundation of the house had collapsed, churned up and thrown over by termites, so that the entire structure twisted and sagged drunkenly. The remains of the roof were barely visible under heavy mats of moss and tangles of vines. Birds and lizards lived in it—and M. Ovono told them the house had been occupied eighteen months before! Liv had always thought of Nature as the underdog, a subdued and fragile entity, and thought of humanity as having her on the ropes. But slogging through the virgin rain forest, wandering the overgrown streets of Makokou, living in a world where it seemed all light was filtered to dark green by the endless foliage—all of that had changed his mind. Nature was no delicate and fading thing of beauty here, but a tough, vigorous opponent who could defeat and destroy all humanity's work in a moment if she so chose.

It was, Livingston decided as he finished his coffee and dug out a wad of CFA francs to pay for it, one hell of a depressing town.

Barbara was concentrating hard on writing her paper, not really listening to the world around, not registering the banging noise behind her. Finally she came to herself enough to realize that someone was pounding on her door. She turned around. "Come in!" she said.

Rupert, Clark, and Ovono came bursting into her room. "Found 'em!" Rupert announced triumphantly. He dropped gratefully into a chair and sighed. "At least we've got directions that should bring us to them. Mister Ovono found these guys who were hiking along about a month ago and stumbled into some slash-and-burn fields. They saw their camp and were able to find the spot on a map."

"And you know how to get there?" Barbara asked.

"Piece of cake. Drive three blocks, come to the traffic light, and turn green. About three days from here."

"Perhaps less, depending on how far M. Ovono can get his Land Rover," Clark said. "But our informants were very sure it was the Utaani. They didn't know until they asked the tribesmen, and they were plenty scared when they found out. These fellows we talked to wander around trading, selling pots and pans and so on. You can bet they got the devil out of there as soon as they could, didn't even try to make a sale. One of them even claimed to have seen a *tranka* on the way out, though since he claimed the thing was hovering in mid-air I'm not sure I'll believe that part. Probably just a lemur that they spooked. But I'm thoroughly convinced they saw the Utaani village. Too many details matched—the language the villagers spoke, the slash-and-burn farming. Besides, after all the research we've done around here, the Utaani were just about the one tribe we hadn't accounted for. And the village site they pointed out is nowhere near any of the other tribal villages around here. We've found them. If we can get packed up and ready, we should be able to leave tomorrow at first light."

Barbara shut off the computer and stood up. "Then let's get moving. This place is driving me nuts." She turned to Monsieur Ovono and smiled. *"Merci, M'sieu Ovono,"* she said carefully, using up a significant fraction of her store of French.

Ovono grinned delightedly. "You ess welcome much!" he replied, using up all of his English.

They both laughed and Barbara shook his hand. "You guys start packing up," she said. "I'm going to go find Liv and give him the good news." She took her leave of her friends and hurried out into the night.

▼◆▼

M. Ovono yanked the distributor cap off the engine and slammed the hood shut. There was a hasp set into the front of the hood. Ovono closed it, put a heavy lock through it, turned the key, and pocketed it. He wrapped the distributor cap up in a bit of clean rag, then put it in a drawstring bag with the sparkplugs.

"People in the jungle can be quite honest, but now we are certain no one will find my Rover and drive off with it, eh?" he asked Rupert in French as he handed him the bag. Ovono walked once more around the Rover, making sure all the doors were locked against thieves, all the windows were sealed against the weather. The exhaust pipe was plugged to prevent anything from making a nest there, the radio aerial was stowed away, the spare tire and other external gear were locked up inside the Rover. Ovono took the bag of parts back from Rupert, placed it carefully in his backpack, and put the backpack on.

They had gone a fair distance along the road, which had slowly dwindled to a trail, a game path, and now, finally, to a single-file track through the jungle. The rest of the party shouldered their packs and set off down the trail, following Ovono.

This was it, Barbara thought. The last leg of the journey, the end of the road she had started down when she had broken open Grandfather Zebulon's trunk. She rearranged her pack straps more comfortably and kept on walking.

▼◆▼

This might be the last leg of the trip, Barbara thought, but it was certainly also the longest. So far it had been three days of slogging through the jungle, making barely perceptible progress down the overgrown path, swatting flies, pulling off leeches if they chanced to cross a stream, sweating endlessly, their backpacks growing heavier with every step, the virulent-green jungle reaching out with its endless leaves and thorns and vines and mud to stop them. The dim light would suddenly darken, a sign of thick clouds forming overhead, and the heavens would open almost without warning, drenching the miserable travelers. When the skies cleared, they could scarcely tell under the blanketing foliage, and when the rains were over, the water would drip and pour off the trees and leaves long after the downpour had ended, so they could scarcely tell sunshine from shower.

The nights were more miserable still. Ovono, knowing with how little warning the sunset came, would stop them in the day's march when it was still full light, as soon as he found some sort of clearing. He would set them to work clearing the underbrush and setting the mosquito netting while he built a fire. No sooner was the blaze going when the dim, shadowless daylight, filtered and diffused through the interminable layers of green above, gave way to impenetrable darkness, and the night cries of the forest began. Each night passed with infinite slowness, one person on watch, the others curled up in their sleeping bags in exquisite discomfort, restless on the hard ground, caught in a murky half-sleep, half-wakefulness as exhaustion battled with the mosquitoes, the night cries, and bodies aching in every bone and joint. Finally, the night would depart as suddenly as it had come, the halfhearted light of morning would sift down through the trees and waken them, and another weary day would begin.

In the morning, at the midday rest break, in the evening, Ovono forced them to eat no matter how tired or unhungry they were. They needed food to battle the heat and the exertion of the journey. Barbara gave thanks more than once that Ovono had volunteered to come with them on the final leg of the journey. They never could have managed this trip on their own.

Now, on the afternoon of the third day, they were so tired they didn't realize it at first when they came across the edge of an old slash-and-burn field, so overgrown that the furrows and rows were barely visible. It was Ovono who called out and pointed to the burn-over. "We are most close now," Ovono announced in French. "All is just as our two informants said it was." Instantly, Barbara felt the adrenaline pumping through her veins. They had to be close!

Ovono grinned mischievously for a moment. "So let us keep an eye out for the *tranka* they warned us of." Then he turned and started walking again.

Rupert cleared his throat and glanced at Clark. They had never really managed to make it clear to Ovono that the *tranka* were presumably real, and were the animals they were after. He shrugged to Clark and followed Ovono down the path.

Half an hour later, Barbara held up a hand for silence. As soon as they stopped walking, they could all hear it—the unmistakable sound of wood being chopped, shouts carried by the wind, a fire crackling, and a dozen other tiny noises that only came from a human settlement. Barbara sniffed and realized she had been smelling cooking meat, and the slightest hint of wood smoke carried by the wind.

There was a tiny flicker of movement visible through the endless wall of trees, and the travelers instinctively crouched down and froze.

Another flicker of motion. Another. Now it was clear that something was moving down a path that ran parallel to their own. A man. No, several men, the leader clothed in a simple breechclout and carrying a walking stick, the others naked—

—No, not men. Just one man. Barbara gasped. The figures behind the leader weren't human. On two legs, yes, but not human. Not human at all.

Chapter Fifteen

Jeffery Grossington opened the package marked *Strictly Personal* with no particular emotion or premonition. He noticed the Gowrie postmark and thought perhaps Barbara's great-aunt was sending along some papers he had left behind. It was with a dull, leaden sense of shock that he pulled out the photographs and realized what they were, and it was with a feeling of something close to despair that he read the story this Peter Ardley person had written. Grossington had expected the story to leak some time, but not this soon, and not this completely. And with the telegram that had arrived from Barbara yesterday saying they were off to find the Utaani and might be out of touch for weeks—it was the worst possible time for this to happen.

But had it really happened? Had the news *really* gotten out far enough so the whole world would pay attention? This Ardley character just seemed to be a reporter for the local paper down there. Maybe the story would stay local. Perhaps it would be some time before the national press got hold of the story—if they believed it all it.

With a shock, Grossington realized *he* was treating the story as if it wasn't true, as if it was a rumor he could and should deny, squelch before it reached widespread attention. The trouble was, Ardley's story told nothing but the exact truth, though God only knew how he had arrived at that truth. So what to do now? He felt as if his brain were stuck, with no useful thought or idea able to find its way out. He stared long and hard at the exterior pictures of his examination of Tail-End Charlie, trying to think of a way to undo the damage that had been done. He found the only notion he could summon up, ridiculously enough, was that the photos really were very good likenesses of him.

He pulled himself together, picked up the phone and pressed the intercom key. If the story was out, his job was to get the facts out as accurately as he could. "Harriet, talk to the Public Affairs people and see about arranging a press conference in the next day or so. I'll want to notify the long press list, not just the local science reporters, so we'll need a large room. But first, see if you can't get me through to the Secretary's office. It seems the boss is going to hear about what we've been doing, so he might as well hear it from me."

▼◆▼

Barbara's heart was pounding in her chest as they entered the village. What, if anything, was there to prevent these people from killing them all? What would the natives and visitors *say* to each other?

That was not the only thing that frightened her. She had seen that line of figures walking a few minutes before, seen the way they were led, seen, in a few seconds' glimpse, a hundred tiny details of action and behavior that told her what she was seeing. It had never really dawned on her that the Utaani kept the australopithecines, the *tranka*, as slaves. She had imagined the Utaani as simply *knowing* about the *tranka*, perhaps being able to find them, able to tell Barbara where they were, share some woodsy lore so she could find them to study. But *slaves*. It was so obvious, now that she considered it, that she wondered how she could ever have thought otherwise. But slaves did not exist anymore in her world. How could she have known? And in any event, could animals—even animals in human form—*be* slaves?

They reached the central clearing of the village and stopped. Barbara looked around nervously. The village was a miserable spot, a degraded, colorless, spiritless place of grey, cloying mists. The smells of rotting, spoiled food and decaying human waste were everywhere. No living thing grew in the grey, gullied mud of the village clearing. Most of the huts were ramshackle things that seemed to be threatening to collapse at any moment.

At first, as they entered the clearing, the village had seemed empty of life, silent in spite of all the sounds they had heard from the trail. But now, slowly, faces were appearing from around the doorways of huts, children were peeking out from behind their mothers' legs, men were sidling in from the fields.

Barbara was glad she could see no weapons, but she took no real comfort from that. They could be hidden anywhere.

Monsieur Ovono was even more rattled than Barbara. He had never believed in the *tranka*, had never understood, or even cared, what the party was looking for. He had been far less prepared than the others for the sight of those inhuman apparitions on the path. But *he* was the one who would have to speak for the visitors. No one else knew the language—assuming he and the Utaani shared a mutually intelligible dialect.

A small knot of Utaani villagers was slowly forming in front of them. One, a tall, muscular man with greying hair, stepped forward. He was wearing an ornate necklace that looked like it had just been hurriedly put on for the ceremony of meeting a stranger, judging by the way the beads were tangled up.

Ovono recognized him as the chief and stepped forward himself, holding his hands out, palms up and pointing at the sky. He bowed and spoke a few works of Eshiri. The chief answered back, and Ovono smiled nervously at him. Ovono turned to Rupert and spoke in French. "I have said hello, we mean no harm, and the chief has said no harm will come to honest visitors, and that he has never seen skin and hair like yours, though he has heard there were such people. He asks why you come here. You are here to see those creatures, of course, but would that be the wisest thing to tell these people?"

Rupert turned to Barbara, Clark, and Livingston. The situation would have been absurd, if it had not been so frightening. They were surrounded by a whole tribe of edgy Africans, with a trusty guide translating for them, and the very clear sense that if they didn't talk smoothly enough, they were dead. "Okay, gang, now what?" Rupert asked. "The natives are getting restless, if you'll pardon the expression. What can we say that won't freak them out? Should we ask if they'll have us for dinner, or what?"

Clark stepped forward. "Let me," he said, and went on in French. "Monsieur Ovono, ask if there are not tales that tell of people like us coming before?"

Ovono relayed the question. The chief consulted with some of the men standing with him before he answered. He spoke, and Ovono nodded. "Yes," Ovono said, "but not in the lifetime of this chief or his father. But they came, and were peaceful traders who did no harm and did not come to pry."

Clark thought quickly and said, "Tell him *our* legends tell of just such a meeting, and *we* have come in the footsteps of that trader."

The idea seemed to appeal to Ovono, and he translated it hurriedly.

The chief smiled and gestured for them to step closer as he spoke. "In that case," Ovono translated into French, "all is well." As the

Utaani pressed around them, Rupert hurried relayed what was going on to Livingston and Barbara. They moved toward the center of the clearing, and their hosts clustered in around them. Caught up in the middle of a crowd of tribesmen curious to get a look at these strange new people, Livingston found himself wondering just how well all was going to turn out to be.

▼◆▼

With a nice calculation of how fast the mails traveled, Pete picked up the phone to call Grossington a hour after the scientist had received the package. This was going to require delicate handling, but Pete had thought it all out beforehand. With all his notes carefully arranged in front of him, he dialed the call.

A secretary at the other end answered. "Dr. Grossington, please," Pete said.

"May I tell him who's calling?"

"Pete Ardley from the Gowrie *Gazette*."

"One moment," the secretary said, and there was the quiet *clunk* of a hold button. After the briefest of delays a gruff old man's voice came on the line. "Hello?"

"Dr. Grossington?"

"Yes."

"This is Pete Ardley of the Gowrie *Gazette*. Have you received my package?"

"Yes, I have," Grossington replied, his voice betraying some degree of nervousness. "Might I ask why you are calling me?"

"In a way, to apologize, Doctor. I wanted to talk with you before we went to press on the story," Pete lied, "but my editor said no. He felt the whole thing was a hoax and you shouldn't be given any warning about it being blown. As it stands, the story I sent you will appear in tomorrow's edition. Already at the printers."

"I see. Well, it appears the damage is done," Grossington said. "I really don't see the point in discussing it further."

"I'm afraid that the damage goes a bit further than that," Pete said. "The story is also going out on the wire, along with several of the photographs I sent you. And copies of the package you've got have gone to the Washington *Post* and the New York *Times*. I apologize for that, as well," Pete said, "but I'm afraid there was no real way around it." That last statement, as far as it went, wasn't a lie, but it was as close as the truth could get to being false. True, if the goal was to further Pete Ardley's ambitions, there *was* no way around it.

Pete knew the first rule of effective lying—tell as much of the truth as you can. Right now the goal of his lying was to get Grossington to feel as if Pete was on his side, so he might be willing to talk. But even so, he felt a little bad about it. Grossington seemed a decent enough old guy, and Pete was giving him trouble. He reminded himself that this story was important, and that if it was true, it belonged to the world. No bunch of scientists had the right to parcel out the facts when they saw fit.

"Your apology doesn't do much to make my position any easier," Dr. Grossington said irritably.

"No, but *maybe* you can help me patch things up for you," Pete said in his most earnest voice. He was betting that Grossington had little experience of reporters. If that were so, his trick might work. "Nothing has reached the public yet on all this, and you can bet the *Post* and the *Times* are going to do some fact-checking before they publish. *If* you can give me a credible denial, something that explains what really happened down here and accounts for the facts we've got, I should be able to get my editor to print a withdrawal and send word to the other news organizations that it was all a misunderstanding. The only published report in that case would be in one tiny little hometown paper. *Can* you give me a good denial to take to my editor?"

There was silence from the other end of the phone, and with each denial-free second it lasted, Pete felt more jubilant—and more guilty. He didn't like playing these games on the old guy, but that silence made him even more certain that the whole improbable story was true. He had gone out on a limb, and it wasn't going to be cut off. Finally, Pete heard a long, unhappy sigh.

"No, Mr. Ardley," Grossington replied, "I'm afraid I can't deny it. For the simple reason that it is true. We don't know how, we don't know why, but about a hundred and thirty-seven years ago, at least five members of a nonhuman hominid species, a species that was supposedly extinct these last million years, were buried in Mississippi. And we've just dug them up."

"I see," Pete said, trying for a sympathetic tone to his voice. "I'm afraid that changes the situation, doesn't it?"

"Don't try to play games with me, Ardley," Grossington snapped backed irritably. "You're a reporter, and a reporter wants a story, and my saying 'no, it's all a mistake' is no damn story at all. You've got the biggest scoop of your life, and you're trying to figure out how to run with it."

"Of course it's a hell of a story," Pete said. "I ought to know. I wrote it. But that doesn't make it impossible for me to sympathize with your predicament. The word is out now, and there's nothing that can be done about that. Now the question is, how do you handle it now that it's out there? I think I can help."

"I'm all ears," Grossington said. "I'm sure you've got nothing in mind but my well-being. You're just chasing a story, Ardley, and you don't care who gets hurt."

"Sure, right. Look, think what you want," Pete said, starting to feel annoyed. "But this is my *job*, Doctor. Getting the truth to the public quickly. Maybe I'm a little sneaky and dishonest in the way I go about things at times, but I have to be that way if I want to get the job done. And before you sneer at me, let me ask you a question. If we waited until you were ready, how long would it be until the world learned about those skulls?"

"I honestly don't know. At least some months. Maybe longer. We need time to study the facts, follow the leads this has opened up—"

"Have you considered what that means? In the year or two or three until you're good and ready to talk, what happens to the rest of us?" Pete demanded, surprised at himself. Even as he spoke, he knew he shouldn't be handling a source this way. "This isn't some dry little gentlemen's scientific disagreement. It affects all of us. The people's right to know is important here. There's a big debate over creationism versus evolution in the world today. People are deciding whether schoolbooks should even be allowed to mention the *word* evolution.

"People are using that debate to push school boards around, yank books out of libraries, take kids out of classes for fear their brains will get polluted by an unapproved thought. I cover a lot of school board stuff, and I've seen it. *Thought* control is being practiced down here, and nine times out of ten it's the fight over evolution that's the thin edge of the wedge. That starts it, and then the censors find out how easy it is to stamp out books and ideas. Do you have any idea how tough it was for me to find any books on human origins in the stores and the libraries down here?

"You're sitting on an incredibly potent weapon up there, one that could strengthen the hand of people interested in teaching children the truth instead of what their parents *wish* was the truth. And every day you withhold your discovery, another little township school board is going to knuckle under and agree to use the sanitized, bowdlerized textbooks approved by people who think you can change the truth if you don't like it. Do you have any idea how much more damage could be done by the time you felt ready to tell the world what you've found?"

Grossington cleared his throat again. "Excuse me, Mr. Ardley. I'm surprised to learn you care about anything."

Pete shrugged, knowing it was a pointless gesture over the phone. He was a little surprised to learn it himself. "I beg your pardon, Dr. Grossington, I didn't mean to get so worked up. I hope you don't take offense. I just get scared at the mush they're putting in the kids' heads."

"It scares me too, Mr. Ardley, and we've argued that very same point in this office, I assure you. Just not quite so persuasively. So tell me, how can you 'help'?"

Pete hesitated for a moment. He had gotten a little off track and had to collect himself. "It's like this, Doctor. I've had some time to work on this. I've had a month to read up on the subject, I've interviewed an expert in the field, I've had a chance to think and to learn about the subject of paleoanthropology to the point where I know what I'm talking about. I can write a follow-up story about these skulls without calling them missing links or ape-men, without people thinking you're saying that something that died just before the Civil War could be their ancestor. I can make it clear what their relation is to human beings, what the significance of the find is.

"When the other news media pick this up, they're going to put general assignment reporters on it—reporters who were writing about the mayor yesterday and a burglary the day before that. They or she won't know any more than I did a month ago—and I didn't know *anything*. I can put the case for your find clearly, without falling into the traps those guys will land in. And since I broke the story, I'm in a position to sell freelance pieces and wire stories. *That* could set the tone for reporting on this whole thing. With a little luck, we can keep the debate fairly civilized. Will you help me?"

There was another long silence. Finally Grossington spoke. "You talk a convincing line, Mr. Ardley, but I still can't see where I owe you anything. However, I'm calling a press conference for two p.m. the day after tomorrow, and if you can be here then, I suppose you'd be welcome. Good day to you."

Pete already had the airline schedule out before Grossington had the phone handset back on the cradle. Pete had been hoping for a real interview, but he'd have to settle. Those were the risks of the game when you forced somebody's hand. Pete spread the schedule out and glanced at his watch. The real trick would be getting up to Jackson fast to catch an early flight. It would do some good to be on the ground in Washington before the news conference. He had some leads up there to follow.

Chapter Sixteen

In the movie-cliché version of Africa, there should have been a glori-
ous feast in their honor that night, with spectacular music and danc-
ing around a roaring fire, shouting and laughing people surrounding
the flames as the sparks flew up into the jet-black sky. The food should
have been wonderful as well, of course, with all sorts of delicacies
laid before the travelers.

However, the Utaani apparently hadn't been to the movies recently,
and didn't know about such things. The five visitors were crammed
into the chief's rather fragrant hut along with the chief and several of
the village's leading citizens. They sat on mats on the floor of the
hut, wedged into a tight circle of bodies alongside the great man,
choking on the smoke from the sullen little fire in the hut's center,
forcing down the bland, pasty glup that seemed to be the Utaani idea
of a feast food. Livingston found himself missing the canned-goods
elegance of the hotel at Booué.

Liv had seen a lot on this trip, seen a lot of ways for people to
live, but this was the first he had ever seen that just plain felt *wrong*.
There was nothing, exactly, that he could put his finger on, but this
was a bad place. Nasty, brutish. He had yet to see anything clean, or
orderly, or well-made, anything a person could be proud of.

Livingston turned to Rupert and nudged him in the ribs to get his
attention. "So what in hell goes on around here? What does Monsieur
Ovono think?"

Rupert shrugged. "I'll ask him." Rupert got Ovono's attention
and the two of them talked in French for a moment or two, both men
making a big show of speaking in a very animated way, very happy
and effusive. Rupert turned backed to Livingston. "He says he has
never seen such a miserable place or such uncultured people," Rupert
reported, still keeping his voice animated and excited, so the Utaani
would think he was happy. "None of the villages he has seen have
been as unhappy as this. Do not judge the jungle villages of Gabon

by this miserable example. They live like pigs here. So says Monsieur Ovono," Rupert finished up.

"Okay, I'll go with that, but what about the reason we're here?" Livingston asked, being a bit cryptic so as not to upset either their guide or their hosts. He wasn't quite sure how either would react to mention of the creatures they were there to find. He didn't want to mention the one Utaani word he knew, *tranka* and he didn't want to refer to them by the scientific name australopithecine either, as Ovono would be sure to spot it.

"Hold on a sec." Rupert and Ovono started talking again, and after a moment Clark joined in. Then the Utaani chief tapped Ovono on the shoulder and spoke, apparently asking what his visitors were talking about. Ovono replied, no doubt at least sanitizing what the visitors were saying in French, but more likely out-and-out lying, inventing something that would satisfy the chief. Then, of course, the chief had to tell the visitors something, which Ovono had to translate, and so on. Livingston sighed. By the sounds of things, it was threatening to be a rather long conversation. He had gotten used to not being able to speak French, but now he felt doubly out of it for not speaking the dialect of Eshiri that the Utaani spoke.

Barbara poked him in the ribs and laughed. "It's okay, Liv, I feel a little out of touch myself. So much for cultural relativism, huh?"

"I've managed to blank out most of my sociology requirements. What's cultural relativism?"

"It's sort of a soppy liberal thing, the idea that you can't view one culture as superior to another, because all cultures judge themselves by different criteria. A member of a purely agricultural society like this, living in mud huts, might view Manhattan as hopelessly backwards because there was no place to grow food, and by their sights, they'd be right. Einstein's theory of relativity told us there were no privileged points of reference in physics, that all frames of reference are equally valid, and no one point in the universe is better for observation than another. The cultural relativists sort of work from an analogy with that, saying that there is no culture that is better than another, since there is no objective measure for comparing one group against another. There are no absolutes."

"But these people are living in filth! And they must die young— I haven't seen anyone much older than 45 or so."

"Ah, but what you call filth is part of their cultural matrix, living closer to nature. And no doubt they are accustomed to dying young, and if their life expectancy was extended, it would unbalance all the social structures geared to the chief dying young, for example. And maniac terrorists who kidnap innocent people and blow up airplanes full of people who have nothing to do with their fight are by their lights engaging in honorable, even holy war by the only means possible. *We* are not so oppressed, how would we act if we were? Who are we to judge?"

"Yeah, well, I don't remember anything about Martin Luther King taking any hostages," Livingston said testily. "Killing innocent people is wrong. *There's* an absolute for you."

"How can you be so dogmatic?" Barbara asked playfully. "You're just not a good liberal. Suppose the innocent *wants* to die, and the death is a sacrifice that plays a vital role in the life of the community? Or to get back to our hijackers, how innocent are the people in that airplane, really? Aren't they all growing fat and rich off the system of oppression that denies the hijackers a homeland? Aren't they going to spend their paychecks, pumping money into the global war economy that is denying our poor, misunderstood hijackers their rights?"

"Wait a minute," Livingston protested, "you're halfway to saying that no one can ever do anything wrong, that nothing can ever be someone's fault—"

"And since Hitler sincerely thought the Jews were subhuman, by his lights, killing them was no more murder than slaughtering cattle," Barbara said, her voice tight and angry, no longer playful. "The further logic is that it's always *our* fault—poor old Western mainstream culture's fault—for not being understanding enough. Beyond that, there is no right, no wrong, no moral dimension, because no one— not Hitler, not the hijackers, not the bastards who bought our ancestors for slaves—ever thinks of himself as *bad*. They always find a reasonable argument to explain what they did as good and proper from their point of view."

"So no act can be evil, because the only one who committed the act can judge the act, and no one ever thinks of himself as evil," said Livingston. "Jeez, that's real sharp thinking."

"The relativists have a point, in that we can't judge everything by one standard," Barbara said thoughtfully. "Monsieur Ovono wouldn't fit in our world any better than we fit in his, but he's a happy, useful person. But even if this is a tribal culture off in a tiny clearing in the jungle, there's no reason we have to stand around in human waste in the middle of the village! Ovono himself said he had never seen a place like this. There are such things as right and wrong, and this place proves it. This is no way for people to live."

Livingston nodded. "I know. I get the same feeling. Right down deep in the gut. It's as if they don't give a damn about anything."

Rupert turned to Barbara. "If you two are finished being catty, Ovono has just gotten done telling the locals how much we love the place, and then asked the chief if we might talk of what the other white men traded for. The locals are debating that point now."

The chief and his cronies were talking energetically, and finally seemed to reach a conclusion. Ovono listen and relayed their agreement. "Okay, they say fine, let's make a deal, and want to know what we offer," Rupert reported. "Now what?"

Clark spoke up. "My goof, I'm afraid. It should have occurred to me that we might need to barter for information. I should have thought of things to bring along to trade. Now we'll have to cough up from the gear we brought along for ourselves." He shifted to French. "What sort of things would they be interested in, of the things we have with us? Don't ask it of them, just give me an opinion before we start to bargain."

Ovono shrugged. "Tools, I think. You have some handsome knives they might like. Rupert's machete, perhaps. And your watches—not that these savages keep time, of course, but they might think them elegant jewelry. Perhaps some of your clothes if you can spare them. Nothing too unusual. But I suggest you leave the bargaining to me. I know the traditions for bartering things in these parts. These fellows are brutes, but they seem to follow much the same rules. And I suggest we leave it until tomorrow. They are in a mood to eat and drink, not to bargain. They will become irritable if we try to press a deal now."

Clark nodded. "That sounds sensible. Tell the chief we wish to rest first, and ask where we might set our mosquito nets and sleep tonight."

Ovono translated and listened to the answer. He grinned humorlessly as he relayed it. "There is no need to bother. We are the guests of the chief, and have the honor of sleeping here, under his leaky, termite-infested roof, tonight, on the very same mats you are sitting on now. I would suggest we check each other *very* carefully for lice in the morning."

Barbara woke from a fitful sleep to find a pair of leering eyes staring at her. It was the chief, God damn it, and judging from the way he had his breech clout off—and what his condition was underneath it—he clearly had but one thing on his mind. He saw that she was awake, grinned, and reached out to touch her, but she jerked back out of range without thinking. *Superb situation*, she thought. *The chief wants to rape me. I can't afford to annoy him, and I'm sure as hell not going to let him touch me.* Livingston was curled up next to her, and that was some comfort. Liv would tear this yahoo limb from limb if he tried anything—but on the other hand, that wouldn't exactly help them achieve their goals—or even survive. "Monsieur Ovono!" she called out in as calm a voice as she could, struggling to recall some shred of French to save her. "*Savez moi!* Monsieur!"

Ovono snapped into wakefulness with the speed of someone who spent time in the jungle. He sat up and took in the situation in a moment. The chief seemed not at all abashed, but instead looked at Ovono and laughed, as if Ovono should think it all funny. "*Merde,*" Ovono said, quite distinctly. "*Apa,*" he said, switching to Utaani. It was one of the few words of the dialect Barbara had picked up—the word for no.

"*Apa,*" Barbara echoed, drawing as far away from the chief as she could. She backed into Livingston, who stirred sleepily and opened his eyes. Clark, Rupert, and some of the locals were waking up too. Barbara felt her heart pounding in her chest, as frightened as she had ever been in her life. How many kinds of danger were they in now?

Speaking in a low, calm voice, Ovono began talking to the chief in his own language. The chief answered back, joined by some of his friends, but Ovono ignored them and spoke only to the chief.

The chief was all smiles at first, as if he were trying to pass it off as a joke. But at last the smiles died and the grimy breech clout went back on. The chief's manner turned apologetic, but he ignored Barbara, speaking only to Ovono, and then, briefly, to Livingston before hurrying out of the hut, followed by the rest of local men, leaving the travelers alone.

Ovono spoke rapidly to Clark in French, and then Clark translated to Barbara. "Chief Neeri apologizes to you, Livingston, for his having tried to take your wife without your permission. Ovono told him Liv was your husband, Barbara. It was the only thing he could think of that fast. The slimy bastard thought he could just whip off his pants and have you right here in front of everyone, that you were brought here as some sort of gift for him. Charming people, aren't they? What Ovono said last night is right, Barbara. Don't judge jungle Gabon by these brutes. For the most part, they are very decent people out here, who wouldn't dream of treating a guest that way—but something is wrong around here."

Rupert shook his head. "That's for damn sure. Everyone remember we can't afford to offend these people just yet—unless we have to. But Barb, if anyone—*anyone* touches you again, scream bloody murder and we'll all come running, beat the hell out of him, and worry about the consequences later. Okay?"

Barbara nodded, and noticed she was shaking. "Okay."

Clark reached over as if to pat her reassuringly, and then seemed to think better of it, and stopped midway. Barbara was glad of it. Physical contact was not what she needed just now. "All right then, let's get out there and pretend everything is okay." He shifted to French. "Monsieur Ovono, I believe it might be best for the rest of us to go off by ourselves for a time and let you take care of negotiations. Our emotions run too high just now."

"You are wise, M'sieu Clark. Go down the path we came in on, and return in two hours' time. By then we will have the beginnings of a deal with these mongrels. Perhaps you should take your packs with you and have your breakfast meanwhile. But wait a moment, I just thought of something else." Ovono reached for his own rucksack and began emptying it. "Distribute my belongings among your own packs, and then everyone should put the things they are willing to trade in my pack."

Ovono's pack started to fill up. Watches, jewelry, pocket knives, U.S. and Gabonese coins, and even paper money. Ovono thought the U.S. paper might be of interest because it had pictures of strange buildings and the stranger-looking white men, while the Gabonese notes would trade because they were prettier. They dug deep into Rupert's gadget bag, too. A magnifying glass, a mirror, a collapsible fishing rod and some spare fishing line, a folding camp stool and a pair of binoculars. Livingston donated his class ring, a spare pair of boots he was tired of carrying, the sleeping bag it was too hot to sleep in, and a harmonica. Clark and Ovono, who had packed far more sensibly than the others, had much less to contribute. Clark threw in his tobacco pouch and Ovono a spare hat, and each of them threw in a spoon and fork. Just before Ovono closed the bag, Barbara thought of one more thing. She pulled off the wedding ring she was still wearing for some unexplainable reason and tossed it in the bag. God knows she wasn't going to need it again. The place on her finger where it had been felt very strange, being out on its own.

▼◆▼

The keeper watched the visitors move down the path, leaving their guide behind to talk. He shook his head. How could Neeri have been such a fool? Risking all the anger of these strangers just so he could have a woman! Wasn't it enough that he had had every woman in the tribe, angering the husbands, no matter what a chief's rights might be? A good ruler knew not to abuse his privileges. The keeper had never been away from the village—none of the Utaani had—but he knew full well that there were mighty tribes out there, who had great power. He had seen their guns, once or twice, brought along by the rare visitors to the village, seen the guns kill birds and animals from far away.

But the chief seemed a greater fool even than that—he seemed ready to break the law of many years' standing, and not only admit the existence of the *tranka*, but even trade in them again. It had been the hatred of the other peoples for the *tranka* that had kept the Utaani apart from them, far off in the darkest part of the jungle for so long.

All in the village knew that even the rumor of the *tranka* made the rest of the jungle fear and hate them. What anger did the chief risk now in openly trading in what the other tribes thought were evil spirits or the dead brought back to life?

Once, and once only, the keeper's father had dared tell him the real story of what had happened when the tribe had tried to trade *tranka* for other things—the real tale, not the storyteller's ravings where all Utaani were brave and bold and the trade-riches had made them all wealthy. Yes, the tribe had traded *tranka* to one of these strange, pasty-white men, and yes, for a time, the whole village had worn its fine new clothes made from the cloth the trader had brought, had used their fine new tools—and their fine new guns for hunting. Then the medicine men of the other villages had seen the well-armed trader parade the *tranka* down the jungle paths. They dared not attack the trader, but they banded together when he was gone and brought the wrath of a dozen tribes down on the Utaani for trading in imprisoned souls. All the tribes had long traded in slaves, in bodies, but they rose up against what they thought was a traffic in the reanimated dead.

Now not even the chief was told the true tale. Even he heard only the fairy tales.

But the keeper was a crafty man, and his father had told him that often two problems could solve each other. If he had to trade away one of his *tranka*, why not one they planned to dispose of anyway— a troublemaker who would make the deal look bad? And then, in the embarrassment of a trade disaster, perhaps this chief would need replacement. . . . It occurred to him that the other village leaders were being a bit too enthusiastic in supporting the chief's stupidities. Maybe they were letting him work his own destruction. And many a keeper of the past had been a chief. It could work.

He turned and walked toward the stockade and opened the heavy door. That one. The female who was acting strange, that no one could get any work out of. He looked at her and laughed. If she got rid of this chief for them, she would have done a lifetime's work right there.

▼◆▼

She sensed his eyes upon her and looked up. The hair on the nape of her neck bristled, and she bared her teeth in hatred. Of all the humans, this one was the worst—the harshest, the cruelest, the most punishing. She longed to leap for his throat, and her fingers twitched, and she let out a low growl. But the keeper just laughed again. He could control her long enough, this one. Just long enough.

▼◆▼

Ovono gave the others a few minutes to get down the path before he emerged from the chief's hut. Waiting would make the Utaani think he was planning something, make them a bit more anxious and ready to deal.

Finally, enough time had passed by his judgment, and he stepped out into the village square, carrying the satchel full of the smaller trade goods in one hand and Livingston's sleeping bag and shoes in the other. He squinted for a moment in the somewhat brighter light of the outside, and looked about for the chief and his chums. There they were, sitting around one side of the empty fire pit at the far end of the square. They looked a small bit nervous, Ovono thought. Good. Repressing the urge to smile, he walked over and sat down opposite his hosts. He considered mentioning the nasty incident in the hut, but decided that bringing it up again, even to dismiss it, might not be the best idea. Best just to ignore it. "Good morning once again," he said. "My friends have gone to stretch their legs, and asked me if I might talk with you for them."

The chief grinned cheerfully. "That is good. Without all the tiresome changing one talk to another, we can deal faster, and everyone will be happy."

Ovono nodded. There was no effort to apologize from their side. He would be willing to bet the chief had no idea he had done something wrong. Ovono promised himself to deal a little harder on that account. "Yes, I agree. Perhaps it would be best if we began. We are travelers and have brought mostly small things, of great beauty and value, but light and easy to carry. I have many things to show, but since we are both eager to save time, it would easier if you told me what you wished to have, and what sort of value you placed on it." *In other words, tell me your price before I let you look in my wallet.*

"But first, I must ask, precisely what are you after?" Chief Neeri asked. "You have spoken of wanting what the trader in the legends wanted, said you have interest in what interested him, but you have never come out and said precisely what you wanted. Come, it is time for plain words."

Ovono nodded his agreement and tried to think fast. It occurred to him that he *wasn't* sure precisely what the Americans wanted. That was not right or proper. He could not be an honest agent that way—but it was unthinkable that he should jump up and run to ask them such a simple question—he would look ridiculous to these crude boors, and they would raise their prices in contempt for him.

Well, what was it all about? *Tranka*, of course—that was obvious. There was no other reason to come here, and the Americans had seemed to talk of little else. He had caught the long English word *australopithecine* many times, and Clark had told him it meant the same as *tranka*. So they were interested in the creatures for some reason, and presumably had come here looking for them. They had not realized the *tranka* were not wild, and so had not come ready to trade for them. But the Americans had seemed reluctant to discuss the *tranka* with Ovono, perhaps fearing he harbored fears of the creatures, despite his denials. So what did they want with them? How many did they want?

Ovono realized he also knew nothing about the *tranka*, either. Could he tell a weak one from a strong one, a young one from an old one? Were some fierce, some docile, some smart and some stupid? His sum total of knowledge was based on one glimpse of a line of miserable-looking creatures through the trees.

All of this flashed through his thoughts in an instant. He had no information, and no good trader dared betray ignorance. What to do? Suddenly, a solution, a perfect solution, popped into his head. He spoke smoothly, after only a moment's hesitation, making it seem that what he was saying he had had in mind all along.

"We seek *tranka*—but first, we seek a beginning," Ovono said. "A wise man does not seek to gain his wealth in one day, but slowly and carefully, so he does not lose as fast as he gains. We expect to trade again here, many times, but our people have been away long, longer than anyone still living. We do not know the quality of your *tranka* compared to others." There *were* no others, of course, but these isolated tribesmen wouldn't know that for sure. Why let them know they had a monopoly? "We need to know your price, your quality. So, come, I will do a very daring thing and trade without looking at what I trade for! I want to have *one* tranka for now, your very best one. We want to know your finest quality first, and the price for it. Sell us a poor one, and today we will not know it—but tomorrow we will. We will trade well for the best, but overcharge us today and we will trade sharply the next time. We wish to show we trust you from the beginning by asking *your* judgment of quality and fair price."

Ovono stopped talking and looked over his audience. Once again, he forced himself not to smile, but instead looked as sincere, as trusting and wise as he could. They had not expected this! Perhaps they had been expecting a one-time sale, hoping to skin the Americans this once. Maybe they wanted to sell their surplus in one go and be done with it. It didn't matter. Now they were off-balance, which is the way a good trader wants his counterpart in a deal. Ovono felt tempted to say more, but he knew the dangers of overselling. Let them make the next move.

He smiled and settled back, politely waiting for their reply. The chief thought for a moment, then gestured for his cronies to lean in toward him and whisper with him. Ovono put the time to good use sizing up his customers, judging what they'd like to buy. The chief seemed to be the only one to worry about. His advisors were nowhere near as important, and seemed divided equally between those who eagerly agreed with everything he said and those who actually tried to give some sort of counsel, which was generally ignored. Ovono had the feeling that the chief's head had been turned by his power, that the right tack here was to appeal to his vanity. This was the sort of chief who ruled capriciously for a month or a year or two years until the tribe got tired of it and killed him or ousted him. Vain, unreasonably confident that his views were always correct, eager to agree with anything that made him look good. To a good salesman, there was no better prospect.

After a long discussion in low tones, the locals seemed to come to some sort of agreement. Finally, the chief spoke. "I agree with your proposal. My keeper of the *tranka* here tells me that he has just the one for you, a young, healthy female of great spirit and intelligence."

"Splendid. That will suit our purposes perfectly," he enthused, having no idea what their purposes were. But at least buying one, a sample, suited *his* purposes. It let him do limited damage if he was making a mistake, and gave him the chance to consult with the Americans properly before he did any serious dealing. "But we come to the price for such a fine animal. What interests you? Perhaps this sturdy and handsome pair of shoes?" he asked, touching Livingston's huge boots. No reaction. "A sleeping-mat of great softness and comfort?" he suggested, pointing at the sleeping bag. No apparent interest. "Clever tools?" he ventured, opening the rucksack. "Perhaps some fine and handsome jewelry?" *Aha.* The chief's eyes lit up at the mention of jewelry, and his henchmen exchanged worried glances, as if Ovono had touched on a very vulnerable weak spot. With a look of perfect innocence on his face, Ovono dug into the sack, appearing to fumble a bit as he brought out one or two of the lesser tools and the ugliest watch, along with the least interesting rings and trinkets. He would hold back on Barbara's gold ring until they were weakening, eager to buy. This was going to be almost too easy. Monsieur Ovono smiled his most unctuous smile and zeroed in for the kill.

Barbara rubbed her ring finger nervously, trying to make the empty-feeling spot around her finger seem a bit less strange.

Now she was at the end of her quest, it seemed. The Utaani were agreeable, and would let her get a look at their australopithecines, study them, if for a price. She found herself forced to face the question of what she was going to *do* with the creatures. Up until now, the quest, the search itself, had served to keep her from introspection. Now the last barriers to finding out were seemingly down, and she finally confronted the question: What would they be like? These were the descendants of animals who had come very close to becoming human, creatures whose evolution had shied back from that possibility. They and their ancestors had almost everything it took to become human—the upright stance, the clever hands. But they had never produced the last and most needed thing—a brain large enough to contain a complete mind. Why had they turned back? Had they found something better?

Barbara scratched her own head and sighed. That was foolishness. Evolution was directionless, and no creature ever decided whether to evolve into a new form. It simply happened. There was another thought that worried her, frightened and excited her. Humans liked to think of themselves as reasoning and rational, but she knew the "human" part of the brain was but a thin veneer over all the evolutionary past of the brain. Literally just below the uniquely human part of the neocortex were the structures of the mammalian brain, and below that were components which closely resembled the reptilian brain, the amphibian brain, the fish brain, all the way back to structures that harked from the first creature to grow a spinal cord. All the history of the phylum *Chordata* was etched in her skull and her spinal cord. In a very real sense, wild animals lurked in her skull, in all human skulls, and evolutionary ancestors dead a hundred million years whispered and hissed their reptilian counsel from the core of her brain. She knew from examining skulls what human-like structures were smaller, less developed, or missing altogether in the australopithecine brain. What would a near-human be like, with that thin veneer of humanity stripped away, and the past so much closer to the surface?

Put it another way: What would humans be like, without that thin layer of brain cells that made them into a completely different kind of animal?

▼◆▼

Ovono scooped up the pile of trade goods that was settled on as the price, took off his hat, and dumped the things into it. "Then we are settled on the price," he said as he put the rest of the thing back in the rucksack. "All is agreed. Now I must tell you of a small tradition in the American tribe, where my friends come from. They are willing to let agents do their bargaining, but they often claim the right to perform the exchange themselves, with no middlemen." It was a reasonable-sounding lie, Ovono thought, but could use some embroidery. "They feel that if the final trade is made face-to-face, buyer and seller will know each other better, and trust each other more. So, I will go and collect my friends, and perhaps you can bring their *tranka*, and then they can make the trade themselves, eh?"

The chief said, "Yes, that is fine," and gestured to the keeper to bring the beast. He seemed distracted, far more interested in the fine new things he would get than in anything else.

Ovono stood up and bowed politely to the chief before heading off to find his clients. He hadn't mentioned the real reason for having the Americans do the trade themselves, of course. They could hardly complain about the price he had negotiated if they paid it themselves.

Even an honest broker knows he must protect himself.

▼◆▼

They heard a noise in the underbrush, and turned to look down the path in time to see Ovono coming along, all smiles. *"Bonjour, mes amis! Allez, allez, vite, vite!"* he called out, and urged them to stand and follow him with a gesture of his hand before turning back toward the village himself.

Rupert scooped up his pack and hurried to catch up. "How did it go?" he asked.

"Very well, very well," Ovono said. "Here," he said, handing

Rupert the hatful of trinkets. "Your leader is the woman, no? Then give these to her, and tell her she is to exchange them for the *tranka*. But hurry, before the locals can debate the agreement!"

And before you Americans have time to argue with me, either, Ovono thought.

Rupert dropped back next to Barbara and explained. She looked in the bag. The harmonica, two of the watches, an inexpensive gold-plated chain—part of the jewelry she had brought to Gabon in case they ended up at an Embassy reception or something—Rupert's Swiss army knife, Livingston's class ring, and Barbara's gold wedding ring. "All this just to examine one creature?" she asked Rupert. "We're going to be bankrupt before we're done."

Rupert upped his pace to keep up with Ovono, who was still hurrying them on. "Well, I guess the locals knew more about trading than Ovono thought. But we can live with it for the moment. Let's go.

They hurried along, almost double-timing, with Clark and Livingston bringing up the rear, and soon came to the village clearing.

Ovono led them to the fire-pit, where the chief and his men were waiting. Ovono spoke rapidly and quietly to Rupert, and Rupert passed along the instructions to Barbara. "Walk over to the chief, and place each item, one at a time, onto the mat on the ground in front of him. Make a little bit of a ceremony out of it, and make sure everyone can see each thing as you take it out. Do a little dago-dazzling. When you are done, step back and join the rest of us. Don't kneel, just squat down as little as you can and still put the things on the mat grace-fully. Don't bow to the chief or anything. We trade as equals, and shouldn't kowtow to this geek. That's a fairly free translation, but it gets the spirit of what he said."

Barbara nodded, and did as she was told, pulling each thing out of the bag and holding it up high to be seen, gesturing grandly to the neatly displayed bric-a-brac when she was done. "What do I do with the hat?" she asked in a stage whisper, still squatting down in front of the chief, hoping she didn't lose balance and fall down flat on her face.

Rupert checked with Ovono and relayed the answer. "Throw it into the pot as a sweetener. Sign of good will. Now stand up and come back to us, and make sure you *do* turn your back on him—it's a sign of trust, and shows you don't hold him in any awe."

She turned and walked back to her friends, imagining daggers and spears sprouting out of her back with every step. She turned again and watched as the chief made a show of examining the goods, and his cronies made signs of approval, smiling and nodding. The chief gestured to one of his men, who bowed and left the group.

"Now what?" Rupert asked Ovono in French.

"Now the Utaani keeper goes to bring the *tranka* you have purchased. Make a show of examining it and saying how fine it is."

Rupert and Clark looked sharply at Ovono. "The *tranka* we *bought?*" Clark said. "We only wanted to study them, look at—"

"What's going on?" Livingston demanded, alarmed by the rapid French. "What's wrong?"

Rupert was about to answer when he chanced to look up. "Oh my God."

Barbara followed his glance and drew in her breath.

The keeper was walking back into camp, dutifully followed by—

Her eyes could not see it properly at first, trying to force what they saw into pigeonholes where it wouldn't fit. It walked like a human so it must be human, but it looked like an animal, so it must be an animal, but some tiny gesture was so human-like, its—her—eyes were so expressive and soulful—but the mouth was a muzzle and the nose was barely there . . .

She blinked, swallowed, and realized she had grabbed onto Livingston's arm, was holding him so tight it must have hurt, but he didn't seem to notice. She relaxed her grip and forced herself to look again, to really *see* what was there.

It—no, *she*— was a female, unclothed and hairy, and somehow her nakedness, her vulnerability, seemed greater *because* of the sparse covering of fur. She was hairier than any adult human male, but the dark, coarse fur didn't cover her even as thoroughly as a chimp's would. There was no fur on the black-skinned muzzle of a face, but around her chinless jaw the hair was thick enough to be a sort of beard. She was short and massively built, no more than five feet tall, the muscles on her body standing out like a weightlifter's. Her breasts could not properly be called by that name, but were so flat and flaccid they were more like a set of teats sagging against the muscular chest.

She stood quietly, solidly, her feet set a bit further apart than a human might find comfortable, but she was as thoroughly a biped as Ambrose's bones had said she would be. There was no grace in her short-legged stance, but no clumsiness either. She belonged on two feet. Her feet were large and splay-footed, the toes wide apart and looking capable of gripping things more effectively than a human's could. Her arms were nearly as massive as Livingston's, and the proportions of the arms looked a little odd. Her hands were large, callused things, the nails big, thick, yellowing a bit, and badly chipped at the end—closer to claws than to human fingernails.

But all that was strange, yet almost acceptable. It could have been the body of a stocky and unfortunate woman with a pituitary problem. Every detail was nearly human, close enough that it didn't matter. Humans could still have been human with that body.

It was the face, the head.

The all-too-human eyes, hazel-colored and solemn, stared at Barbara from below a massive shelf of bone that swept directly back into a low, hairless skull. The forehead, for all practical purposes, was not even there. Perched atop those massive superorbitals were an incongruous pair of bushy black eyebrows that moved and wiggled with the strong facial muscles, just like human eyebrows.

The front of the head seemed to jut out, and the massive jaw forced the mouth farther forward still. Her nose was a squashed-up thing, the flat, wide nostrils pointed out like a gorilla's, rather than down like a human's. The ears were tiny, folded back against the skull—but then they seemed to prick up to listen more closely.

It was not an ape's face. It was too erect, too alert, too expressive. In the eyes, in the intent stare and the purposeful set of the head, there was something no chimp had ever had. And that face was staring as intently at the Americans as the Americans were staring at it. The creature's eyes flicked back and forth from Livingston to Barbara, hesitated a moment longer on the strangely pale white men, Rupert and Clark, and began the inspection again.

Livingston finally collected himself enough to whisper his question again. "Rupert, was something wrong with the deal? What were you and Ovono arguing about . . ."

But Livingston saw the answer before he finished asking. The keeper smiled at them, stepped over to the australopithecine, and peeled back her lips to display her front teeth, then urged her jaw open to display the back teeth. The creature flinched away for a moment, grunted and drew back, and the fur on the nape of her neck stood up on end. But then, with a shrug of resignation, she allowed the keeper to do what he would. The keeper finished with her mouth and made the creature hold her arms straight out, and he patted the muscular biceps proudly. He made her turn around so he could show how strong she was. The keeper prattled on as he performed, smiling, telling them what he was doing, but for once, no translation was needed.

Every black American had a scene like this burned into his memory, into his past, would have recognized this eerie burlesque for what it was in a moment.

"Congratulations, Barbara," Livingston said, his voice filled with as much shock as horror. "You've just bought yourself a slave."

Chapter Seventeen

She did not understand. She did not understand anything. These were a new kind of people, dressed strangely, colored strangely—they even smelled strange. Somehow she sensed that these new ones were as surprised as she was. Staring at them, she ignored the rude probings and proddings of the keeper and strained to figure it out.

"Now what the hell do we do?" Rupert demanded. "Ovono, you *bought* this creature?"

"Isn't that what you wanted?" Ovono asked, almost in distraction, staring at the thing standing in front of them. He had never seen such a monster! He could suddenly understand why the surrounding tribes thought these things were imprisoned souls. His Christian God was barely bulwark enough to keep him from thinking the same. He shivered, crossed himself, and forced himself to listen to Rupert's words.

"We wanted to *look* at them, take pictures, that's all!"

"But what better way?" Ovono replied, trying to think his way out of this catastrophe. "You own this creature now. You can do with it whatever you like."

"Americans don't buy slaves anymore," Rupert said harshly.

"But a slave is a person, a human being! This is an animal!" Ovono protested.

"An animal these bastards use as a slave! I'm not sinking down to their level!"

"*Quiet.*" Clark spoke for the first time, in a low, forceful tone. "Let's remember these bastards *are* bastards and that we are in their place. Get them angry, make them think we're displeased, and we might not walk out of here." Sure enough, the chief looked rather worried already. The men behind him were backing off a bit, shifting their stance, and the two or three gripped the handles of their work knives unconsciously.

"What's done is done, Ovono," he said in French, "and we were too afraid of what you might think to explain ourselves well. It's a bad situation, but nobody's fault. Talk to them, lie your way out of this, think up some pleasant reason we'd be fighting." He shifted from French to English. "Barb, Liv, I don't like this any better than you do, but we appear to have purchased this young lady by accident. Smile and put a good face on it, or else these creeps might get nasty." He switched back to French and spoke again to Ovono. "Now, smile, talk to them, and make it convincing."

Ovono felt a nervous sweat starting to drip down his face. He ran his tongue around suddenly dry lips. "Excuse our excitement, gentlemen! A slight disagreement over who most properly has first claim over this fine *tranka*, and the right to escort her back along the path. Surely that right must belong to—to the owner of the most valuable thing paid for it! Yes, of course." He turned and grabbed Barbara by the arm, and spoke to Rupert in French. "Tell her she must lead the creature off from here, back down the path we came from." Ovono turned backed toward the Utaani and smiled. "We shall return later today, but my friends are most eager to examine our new prize. We will retire to our camp and come back later for more talk." Ovono bowed slightly to the chief—proper in an emissary, if not in a principal—and backed away a step or two. "We must leave now," he said to Clark. "I have told them we have made camp down the path, that we will be there for a time. We must leave calmly and gracefully. And tell Mademoiselle Barbara to do what I said and claim the creature, *quickly*."

▼◆▼

Clark shifted to English and relayed the instructions. Suddenly all eyes were on Barbara. Her heart was pounding in her chest, her stomach churning with fear. But still she stepped forward, walked past the keeper, who had finally noticed something was wrong and stopped his sales-patter.

Barbara stopped, standing face to face with—with the living, breathing embodiment of a million yesteryears, a black and hairy creature who stared back at her with eyes that seemed far too wise. She stood so close she felt the australopithecine's warm breath on her face. What to do? Impulsively, recklessly, she reached out and offered out her hands.

The creature stared at her for a long time, then, hesitantly, wonderingly, offered up her own right hand.

Barbara took the hand in both of hers. The strange flesh felt warm and strong, strangely gentle and familiar.

Barbara stepped back, tugging gently on the creature's arm, and the creature followed along, most slowly and tentatively. She let her own right hand drop, and held the australopithecine's right in her left. She fell into step with the poor frightened thing.

Hand in hand, side by side, the two of them walked out of the camp.

Hurriedly, almost furtively, the other visitors followed a respectful step or two behind.

▼◆▼

Dr. Jeffery Grossington stepped, rather unhappily, out onto the stage of Baird Auditorium and looked out into the audience. The Baird was a handsome old auditorium, set neatly into the basement of the Natural History Building, and Grossington had both given and attended many pleasant talks in it over the years. He did not expect today's little presentation to be pleasant. There was a low trestle table set in the middle of the stage and he carefully set the box holding Ambrose the skull down on it before sitting behind a small forest of microphones.

It had been a bad day already. The wire services had picked up the story, but only a few small, regional papers had run it. The *Times* had yet to use it, but the *Post* had run an inside-page piece. Several radio and TV station had run items, mostly funny ha-ha what-a-cockamamie-rumor things. There had been some very odd sidebars here and there already—and some of the people who had called for interviews were just plain strange.

He looked out once again at the audience. Not as much of a crowd as he had expected. Maybe twenty or so reporters, though his office had contacted many more than that. There were a fair number of museum employees present, too. *That* shouldn't have surprised him. They were no doubt eager to hear whatever truth there might be behind the rumors that had been flying about the building for days now.

Grossington glanced at his watch and grimaced. Time to begin. Might as well get it over with. He tapped at one of the mikes and cleared his throat. "Ladies and gentlemen, if you could take your seats, perhaps we might get started."

It took a welcome minute or two for everyone to get settled. Finally, the moment came when he could stall no longer, and there was nothing for it but to plunge right in. "I'd like to thank you all for coming, and also thank the Smithsonian and the Natural History Museum for providing facilities at such short notice. My name, incidentally, is Dr. Jeffery Grossington, and I am the head of the Anthropology Department at the Museum. Before I take any questions, I have a statement to make.

"I am sure that most of you, perhaps all of you, have seen or at least heard about the reports coming out of the town of Gowrie, Mississippi. I suppose that the rather sparse turnout today has something to do with the expectation that I've called this press conference simply to deny those reports.

"I'm afraid I can't fulfill that expectation. Although the news came out sooner than I would have preferred, and long before we have had the time to carefully consider the implications of what we have found, the news is true. Thanks to the determined efforts of Dr. Barbara Marchando, who cannot be with us today, a remarkable discovery has been made.

"But, before I discuss that discovery, I should like to pause a minute and say a word or two about Dr. Marchando. By rights, *she* should be up here telling you all this. It is her work, her determination, her time, effort, money, drive, and imagination in pursuit of something not only unexpected, but altogether unlikely, that brought to light the remarkable things I am about to discuss. I might add that she went in search of something quite different from what she found—which is the way a lot of good science happens. Had *we* chosen the time to make this announcement, she would be here to take the credit that is her due. I should also like to mention the signal efforts of Dr. Rupert Maxwell, who has made a great contribution, and also to a young man named Livingston Jones, who uncovered some extremely important facts.

"However, it seems the time has chosen us, instead of the other way around. Therefore, as the only member of the team present, it is incumbent on me to make this announcement and so insure that the discussion of this discovery is based on fact, rather than speculation and rumor.

"Briefly put, Dr. Marchando discovered a burial site, approximately one hundred and thirty-seven years old, in which no less than five extremely well-preserved and complete specimens of the genus *Australopithecus* were found. Those who have examined the find further believe the specimens are of the species *Australopithecus boisei*. As most of you should know, this species— and this entire genus—have been thought to be extinct for a million years. Therefore, the discovery of remains that were alive two human lifetimes ago is a most remarkable thing.

"At this time, I should like to present the skull of the first-found and best-preserved of the Gowrie specimens, cataloged as Gowrie Exhumation Project #1, GEP-1, but nicknamed Ambrose." Grossington gingerly removed the skull from its box, and there was a flurry of flashes going off and the whir of motorized camera winders as the photographers captured the moment. "I should like to note that we managed to recover every single one of Ambrose's bones. Obviously, it would be impractical to present them all here, but we have them in our possession—a few with traces of skin and fur on them. At the conclusion of the press conference, you will all be welcome to examine and photograph the skull as closely as you like, but needless to say, I must insist you not touch it. Tomorrow at noon I plan to present the entire skeleton, and indeed the entire GEP collection, for the close inspection of scientists and the media.

"There is clear and compelling evidence that the creature who owned this skull was buried no earlier than the latter half of 1851, probably in the summer of that year. As I have said, since his species was supposed to be extinct as of a million years ago, this is certainly a remarkable discovery. But I should like to dispose of several other supposed mysteries before I take questions on that and other aspects of the discovery.

"Chief among these alleged mysteries is that the creature was found in America, in Mississippi, and was deliberately buried. The announcement of their existence is less than thirty-six hours old, and I have already heard speculations to the effect that a band of australopithecines ventured to these shores across some sort of land bridge from Asia, or constructed some sort of vessel and crossed the ocean, and that the australopithecines then survived in America while becoming extinct in Africa. In fact, several rather enthusiastic theorists have already called me, asking to confirm what they regard as obvious: that the legendary Sasquatch, or Yeti, the abominable snowman allegedly seen from time to time in this country, were in fact members of this remnant population of australopithecines.

"Furthermore, the fact of deliberate burial for Ambrose and friends has been embroidered into the invention of a whole sophisticated culture for these creatures. More foolishly still, several people, especially in the Deep South, have already reported seeing strange man-like creatures since the discovery of these bones. None of this is supported by the evidence we have found, and I will state flatly that none of these reports has any basis in fact. They are nonsense. What is more, the people reporting those stories *know* they are nonsense, and will, no doubt, continue to report them anyway, even when confronted with the evidence that destroys their theories. I mention these reports only in the hope that the more rational members of the press will know they are false.

"As I have noted, we did not choose the moment to make this announcement. For that reason, we are not as yet prepared to release all our evidence, as we have not completed our analysis yet. But from our preliminary work, I can state with absolute confidence that these creatures were brought to these shores by perfectly ordinary human means, not by australopithecine sailors. I can further state with perfect confidence that human beings, and not their fellow-creatures, buried these australopithecines, not out of religious necessity, but out of fear of contagion. In short, the presence of these creatures in America, instead of Africa, can be wholly and satisfactorily accounted for by the actions of *humans*, without recourse to wild surmises or lost civilizations of ape-men. I would venture to say that the truth is fantastic enough in this case that the invention of scurrilous stories is quite unnecessary. And, I am grieved to say, I deny these false reports now in the full expectation that others will follow. I would therefore urge all of you who will be following this story to be most cautious, to examine *all* claims and statements as thoroughly as possible. This is a complicated topic whose implications could be tremendous. It requires thoughtful and responsible reporting. I'll take the first question now."

▼◆▼

Pete Ardley wriggled down deeper into his chair and grinned. Beautiful. Absolutely beautiful. Grossington was doing his best to hide exactly the stuff Pete had left out of the first article, no doubt for the same reason: If he released the text of the old newspaper ad, the clues in it would have everyone and his cousin chasing the story in Gabon. Since Pete had already paid a visit to the Gabonese Embassy, the precaution wasn't going to do Grossington much good. He checked his watch. His follow-up story should be hitting the wire in about an hour if Teems kept on schedule.

A reporter in the first row stood up. "Dr. Grossington, Cindy Hogan, Los Angeles *Times*. This skull here, this hundred-odd year old skull, if I understand this, you're saying that it's an ancestor of mankind. How could that possibly be?"

DR. GROSSINGTON: Very simple: It *couldn't* possibly be. (Laughter.) Things are more complicated than that, and maybe I should go back a step or two. *Australopithecus boisei* was last seen about ten thousand centuries ago, at which point it vanished without a trace. Now he pops up again. What this amounts to is a million-year gap in the fossil record. Any paleontologist will tell you that is not at all uncommon. Look up the coelacanth when you get back to the office. That's C-O-E-L-A-C-A-N-T-H. But what makes this case so unusual is that the gap happens to end so recently, and that it involves a species closely related to our own. But there is no great mystery about the gap.

"The odds against a given creature dying in such a way that it leaves a fossil, and then the odds against that fossil later being found, are astronomical. If there was only a small population of these creatures, and if they happened to live in a climate where it was unlikely for their remains to fossilize, then all that is required to explain the gap is that we simply haven't found any of the very small number of fossils left by that small population.

"However, there is another point I need to clear up. *Australopithecus boisei* is not considered an ancestral species to mankind, and has not been for decades. The human and australopithecine line do share a comparatively recent common ancestor. As was noted in the first news story, Ambrose is our cousin, not our grandparent. The chimp and gorilla are also living species with which we share a fairly recent ancestor species. Ambrose here stands in a similar, though closer, relationship to us. Having said that, I must fog the issue a bit more by pointing out that there is no particular reason ancestor and descendant can't coexist—it probably happens all the time. A parent species splits off a descendant species, which comes to occupy a slightly different niche in the environment, leaving the parent species and its unchanged niche undisturbed. In such circumstances, both species, parent and child, can live side-by-side indefinitely. However, that isn't the present case.

"Yes, you in the back."

QUESTION: Dr. Grossington, given Darwin's theory of evolution, how can you account for this, ah, *Australpithcoos boyse* surviving unchanged for a million years? Aren't all species supposed to be slowly evolving all the time?

DR. GROSSINGTON: I'd suggest you work on your pronunciation, young man. (Laughter.) You've hit another misconception square on the head. There is a growing body of evidence that *most* species remain largely unchanged over long periods of time, so long as environments remain stable. They have no reason to change. But when, for whatever reason, the environment shifts, there is a greater chance for a mutation to be better adapted to the change. Many scientists—including myself—now believe that most evolution occurs in short bursts during these periods of environmental upheaval. For the record, the idea is called punctuated equilibrium. There is a series of interesting correlations between the dates of major shifts in the environment and the key speciations that eventually resulted in human beings.

QUESTION: Do you mean to say that these creatures are exactly like animals that lived a million years ago?

DR. GROSSINGTON: No, no more than you are exactly like the other people in this room. Human beings are widely variable, as we all know, coming in all shapes, sizes, and colors—but we are all one species. There are minor differences between Ambrose and the remains we've seen from a million years ago, but they are fairly minor ones, not enough to warrant the naming of a new species. In fact, I would go so far as to say this discovery will improve the standing of *Australopithecus boisei* as an independent species. The most notable change is that the creatures we found would appear to be a bit larger than the million-year-old *boisei* remains we have seen heretofore.

Ambrose probably stood about 172 centimeters tall—say, five foot seven or eight—several inches taller than his ancestors. He is also somewhat more lightly built, as best we can tell.

QUESTION: I understand the meaning of most of the other species names in hominid evolution, but what does *boisei* mean?

DR. GROSSINGTON: It means that the species was discovered and named by Louis Leakey, who received research money from a gentleman named Charles Boise. (Laughter). Yes, in the third row.

QUESTION: Dr. Grossington, if these animals did not evolve into humans, why is this discovery so important?

DR. GROSSINGTON: When most people sit down to ask what it is about human beings that makes us different, what it is that lets us build buildings and write books and create a civilization, they come up with a very short list of things that distinguish us from other species. Our hands, our upright posture—and our brain. The average size human brain is about 1,500 cubic centimeters, though it ranges between 1,000 and 1,800 cc's—with no correlation between brain size and intelligence of a healthy individual, I might add. Now the average chimp brain is about 380 cc's, and the earliest generally accepted fossil member of our own genus *Homo*, a skull called KNM-ER-1470 had a 775 cc brain. Ambrose here had a 560 cubic centimeter brain. There are other issues of brain function, of course—his brain was different from ours, not just smaller—but in a very real way, Ambrose was teetering just on the *edge* of the human range, a range his kind never crossed in the millions of years since his line divided from ours. They did just fine with a smaller brain. It's fascinating to wonder what life was like in that sort of twilight world, in between animal and human. We may be able to learn a lot about ourselves by looking at someone so similar, and yet so different.

QUESTION: I don't know any better way to ask this, but what were the australopithecines *like*? How smart were they? Could they use tools? Could they talk? Did they walk on two feet or four?

DR. GROSSINGTON: Taking those in order—we don't know, we don't know, we don't know, and on two feet, just as well as you can. Chimps are smart enough to use tools, which suggests that the australopithecines were capable of it—but we can't prove it. There is some evidence that the structures in our mouth and throat that make speech possible did not develop until very late in the game, so my guess would be that they could not talk in the way we do. Certainly they must have made cries and calls of one sort or another—every animal does.

QUESTION: If they *could* speak, Doctor, and there was one here to ask, what would be the first question you'd put to an australopithecine?

DR. GROSSINGTON: I'd ask the same question my entire science has been asking since it was founded: What is a human being? That is the central question of anthropology, and in a way, the central question of all religion and philosophy as well. What is it that makes us what we are? What is it that makes a man? Over and over again, we have asked that question—but always of ourselves. We have given ourselves some fascinating answers, but I'd be most interested to know what someone else thinks. What perspective would another kind of mind have? Yes, over there in the brown dress.

QUESTION: Dr. Grossington, couldn't a case be made that this discovery actually puts the lie to the whole theory of evolution? Wouldn't Creation Science better explain the appearance of a species in what evolution theory says is the wrong place at the wrong time?

DR. GROSSINGTON: I see a Creationist got in. Normally, madam, I am polite about such things, tolerant of your point of view—inaccurate, misleading, self-serving, self-contradictory, and anti-thought though it might be. But not here, not today. This is *my* house, and my work, my career, and you are here at my invitation, and I will not stand here and let you call my whole life's effort a lie. What we have found in no way contradicts a single particle of the *fact* of evolution. That life does evolve, no scientist with a shred of integrity or objectivity could deny. How it works, what the processes are that cause that evolution—*that* is what is still under legitimate debate. I might add that this discovery doesn't affect that debate either. It neither proves nor disproves anything, but is simply a dramatic event that nonetheless fits quite comfortably inside evolution as we understand it. So go peddle it somewhere else.

"You know, there's a joke, or maybe it should be called a parable, I've heard about you people, concerning a little boy who doesn't know how babies are made. He asks around, and none of his friends knew either, and so they conclude that babies *aren't* made, since none of them knows how it happens. They confuse the question of how the thing happened with the question of whether it happened at all, and decide that not understanding the process proves the process doesn't exist, despite the overwhelming evidence to the contrary. Later on, our little boy finds out a few details about what Mom and Dad did together to make a baby. He's so upset by the thought of his parents doing any such thing he rejects not only that answer, but the whole question of his own origin, and decides that story about the stork makes sense after all. Moral: You can't know the truth if you aren't willing to believe it. But we try not to think that way here. So kindly tell your readers that the stork did not bring them. Next question. Over on the left side there.

QUESTION: I'm going to have to remember that analogy. Dr. Grossington, I have a question, and perhaps a follow-up. I have noticed that you have referred to this fossil species in the present tense more than once. Is there a reason for that? If there were a skull in 1851, might there not be a living animal somewhere in the world today? Are you researching that point?

DR. GROSSINGTON: Ah, yes. Well, that's an excellent question. As I am sure you know, many species have become extinct between 1851 and today. There is no guarantee that *Australopithecus boisei* survives today. But it is a point we are looking into. Next question.

QUESTION: Yes, Doctor, I had a follow-up. Where, exactly, *are* Dr. Marchando, Dr. Maxwell, and Mr. Jones?

DR. GROSSINGTON: I can't answer that question, for the very good reason that I don't know, exactly. At the moment, there is no way to reach them. I can say that they are in seclusion of their own choice, so they might work further on this whole issue. But, I must admit that even if I did know where they were, I wouldn't tell you. They are at a delicate stage of their work, and I think it would be not only unfair but counterproductive to disturb them now.

QUESTION: Doctor, I'll let someone else get a chance in a moment, but one last thing: There seem to be a number of areas you aren't willing to go into—how these creatures got to where they were found, how you came to excavate them, what the rest of your team is doing. Considering the importance of this find, and the right of the public and the scientific community to know, shouldn't you be a bit more forthcoming?

DR. GROSSINGTON: Young man, I have been bludgeoned over

the head for the past two days with the public's right to be told things I don't even know myself yet. I will not be forced into making statements that could seriously damage the course of our researches.

▼◆▼

Pete just sat back and let his recorder take it all in. He glanced at his watch again. His story was safely out by now. He hadn't asked a question yet, but his flair for the dramatic was getting the better of him. Maybe it was time to drop his little bombshell. He stood up and called out, "Dr. Grossington, Pete Ardley, Gowrie *Gazette*." All eyes and cameras instantly turned on him. Already, either his name or his paper's name was already well known. "Regarding the whereabouts of your partners, could you at least confirm the information I have obtained, that they received visas to enter the African nation of Gabon, and are currently in the interior of that country, searching for the home of the australopithecines?"

Grossington opened his mouth and shut it. Abruptly he stood up, placed Ambrose back in his box, and announced, "This press conference is concluded." He stood up and walked off the stage, but already Pete was surrounded by other reporters, demanding to know more. Maybe the press conference was over, Pete thought, but the fun was just beginning.

▼◆▼

Barbara sat and watched the creature. Nothing else was important—nothing else existed for her but this not-quite-human. Her new friend sat across from Barbara, just as fascinated with her, the creature's expressive brown eyes locked on her.

The others busied themselves setting up some sort of a camp on the trail, comfortably out of earshot of the village, but everyone kept glancing over to look at the strange newcomer—and to glance down the trail toward the village. Were they safe from the Utaani? What did the Utaani think the Americans were doing here? What the hell could they do with this beast that Ovono had dumped in their laps? Why was the critter still around? Why hadn't it rushed off into the jungle at the first opportunity? Vague, amorphous, and yet insistent questions that led nowhere but back to themselves.

Nothing was clear anymore, Barbara thought. The knowledge that *Homo sapiens sapiens* was not alone seemed to mean nothing else could be certain.

We are not alone . . . Out of the blue, Barbara remembered with sudden, perfect clarity a moment from her past. She could recall every tiny detail of the moment, as if her mind were rebelling against the confusion of the present by presenting the past in perfect solidity.

She was curled up in her childhood bed, the cotton sheets crisp and clean-smelling, fresh out of the drier. It was late on a dark, impossibly silent night, and she had her head under the covers, reading *Robinson Crusoe* by flashlight. And then, suddenly, she wasn't just back in her childhood bed, she was inside the book, riding on Robinson's shoulder as he walked his island. She was on that bright, clear, windswept island, walking along the surf with him when he saw that shocking, solitary footprint. Robinson knew, impossibly but irrefutably, that he was not alone. He found the man who left that footprint, named him Friday after the day he was found, and made him his servant—

There was a noise in the trees, some tiny creatures leaping loudly from one branch to another, and Barbara gave a violent start, coming back to herself. She looked over to the creature, saw that she had spooked the poor thing by jumping like that.

"You need a name, my friend," Barbara said. "We can't just call you *it* or *she* or *australopithecine* and I'm sure as hell not calling you a *tranka*." The creature cocked her head at Barbara, listening to the sound of her voice and the strange shape of the words these people used.

Barbara thought for a moment, working out how many days they had been out here, what day it was. "Thursday. You are Thursday," she said, feeling quite pleased with herself. The name suited her, somehow.

"What'd you say, Barb?" Livingston asked as he sat down next to her.

"I just named her. I'm going to call her Thursday. Wanna know why?"

Livingston thought for a second. "Yeah, I know." He began reciting.

"Monday's child is fair of face
Tuesday's child is full of grace
Wednesday's child is full of woe—"

"*Thursday's child has far to go . . .*" Barbara finished. "Yeah, she sure as hell does. But read *Robinson Crusoe* when we get home. So now what do *we* do?" She stood up and crossed to Thursday, being careful not to get too close or make any sudden moves. She reached out her hand again, and Thursday put out her own hand to touch it, lightly, as she stared deep into Barbara's eyes. "And what do we do with you, Thursday?"

She sensed that this strange human was talking to her, and some small part of her recognized that the new sound 'Thursday' was suddenly being repeated, directed at her. She rocked back and forth on the log she was sitting on, and made a friendly, snorting noise at this strange one in hopes of making her feel better. All these new ones were so strange. But they seemed so interested in her, paid so much attention to her, moved about her so respectfully, almost as if they were afraid of her. They did the work while she sat still. It occurred to her that she could run away from these people easily—they had not tied a rope about her neck, or put her in a stockade, or even hobbled her legs. For so long she had thought of escape, of getting away, out. Now, for the first time, she wondered what she would do when she got there, got 'out.' She looked at the jungle, which seemed so much closer and bigger here. How would she live there? Could she find things to eat? The things that made so much noise seemed so much more frightening here.

And she was curious, most curious. These people were so different! What were they going to do? She had to know more. She listened for a moment more to the jungle calls, and then turned her back on them forever. She would stay with these people.

Barbara shook her head as she looked at Thursday. She thought of the whirlwind they were going to reap together. Thursday grunted again and reached out to give Barbara's hand a reassuring pat. It was going to be all right. Somehow.

▼◆▼

Dr. Michael Marchando wearily pushed the hospital's pasty version of green beans around his plate, too tired to be hungry, too much in need of food not to force the stuff down. He had already survived the meatloaf more or less, and it sat on his stomach like a mid-sized lump of lead. He needed food, and sleep. Thanks to some inept shift-trading on his part, he had managed to draw the graveyard shift in the

Emergency Room, then the following midday shift, after four hours sleep—and now that he was clear of that, he was due to start On Call duty in an hour.

Mel Stanley sat down far too cheerfully next to him. "Mike! So how's it feel to have a mystery star for an ex?"

"Huh?" Mike asked.

"Jeez, where have you been? Haven't you seen a paper or the news or anything?"

"No, I've been here up to my armpits in gunshot cases. Haven't had a chance to look up in twenty-four hours. What are you talking about?"

"Just a sec." Stanley popped up and went over to search the empty tables until he found a newspaper. He came back and handed it to Michael. "Here, this morning's *Post*. Page A-3. But that's old stuff. There was some wild stuff at a news conference today. She's supposed to be out in Ghana, or Gabon or something. Looking for that thing."

Michael opened the paper, saw the headline, and felt his blood start to race. *Scientists Discover Pre-human Graves in Mississippi.* There, alongside the story, was a photo of her boss, her cousin Liv, and Barb looking over a skull in what looked like the backyard in Gowrie. "Jesus. I knew some about this but I . . . . What do you mean, she's *looking* for it in Gabon?"

"I mean they think it's still out there, alive. Pre-humans roaming the jungle. And some reporter claims your wife is out there, trying to find them." Stanley looked down at his friend. "Hey, you okay? C'mon, snap out of it."

But Michael did not even hear him. He didn't believe it, couldn't believe it. How could she go off to the *jungle,* for God's sake, without telling him? Suddenly, he was afraid, afraid for her—not because she might be hurt, or lost, or killed, but because he might have lost her forever. He felt, for the first time, that he was not any part of her life. It was a shock to realize that something besides himself was that important to her. But why should *that* be a surprise? God knows he had done enough to drive her away.

He had to get back to her. He had to make it up to her. What the hell was going on? He stared at the newspaper page, as if looking for answers that weren't there.

Chapter Eighteen

Things, it seemed to Livingston, were happening too fast. Everyone on the team had been prepared for a long, drawn-out search for the australopithecines. They had envisioned the wise native guides leading them to the nesting-sites of the shy, secretive creatures, so they could photograph them from half a mile away and gradually gain their confidence, or something. No one had bargained on having Thursday dropped in their lap so quickly. No one knew what to do about it. They were all in a slight case of shock.

Livingston, though he didn't speak up and say so, was all for heading back at once, perhaps taking Thursday with them, if possible. After all, they certainly had what they had come for, and getting the hell away from those Utaani scumbuckets sounded like good policy. What was hanging around going to get them?

Livingston held his peace that day. Barbara was too busy to pay any attention anyway, and she was the only one who mattered, really, as far as decision-making went. After all, *she* was the one who owned an australopithecine. Even if that wasn't strictly so, there was no denying this was her call.

But Barbara didn't seem much interested in making decisions. She spent the day doing little more than staring at Thursday, taking occasional notes now and then. Since Thursday wasn't doing much besides wandering around the makeshift campsite, it seemed unlikely that the notes would tell anyone much. Maybe, Livingston thought, note-taking was good therapy—a comfortable, familiar thing to do in the midst of so much that was unknown.

Thursday spent a lot of time poking through the campers' belongings, never hurting anything, merely indulging her curiosity about all the unfamiliar objects, grunting and grimacing, and seeming to make some sort of hand-signs to herself now and then. At first she was a bit hesitant about moving about, glancing over at Barbara as if to seek permission for whatever she did. But she quickly got it into her head that she was allowed, probably for the first time in her life, to do whatever she wanted. Once *that* got into her head, she seemed remarkably unwary and relaxed. Obviously she was more used to humans than these human were used to her. The big moment of the morning came when she wandered far enough out of camp to dig up a few tubers—fat white roots far too big and tough for a human to eat. She chomped them down in a few massively powerful bites. The highlight for the afternoon came when she found a small, fast-running stream and leaped into it with obvious delight, eagerly splashing about. The humans were just as glad afterwards. Once the shock had worn off a bit, it was quickly apparent that an unwashed Thursday was pretty gamey.

Rupert at least had the presence of mind to take pictures, lots of them. Shots of Thursday walking, sitting, yawning, splashing in the water; close-ups of her head, feet, and hands. Rupert took a lot of notes, too—the same sort of careful, copious notes he always took. Maybe he got the same therapy from it Barbara did.

Ovono and Clark returned to the Utaani village in the afternoon for a bit of fence mending, making sure the chief was happy with the deal, assuring the villagers that they had never seen such a fine *tranka* (which was certainly true). They ended up staying for a brief afternoon meal and a tour of the *tranka* quarters and the crop fields, which seemed to leave them both a bit shaken. Neither of them was willing to say much about it afterwards. The day slowly petered out. The humans prepared dinner, a rather subdued affair, and in the process made the signal scientific discovery that Thursday was fond of canned beans, hot or cold, and understood fire perfectly well. She sat quietly next to Barbara, staring at the flames, keeping a respectful distance from the heat, but showing no fear. It was nice to have *some* things clear and certain, Livingston thought.

After dinner, they sat about the campfire for a long time, speaking little, talking of inconsequential things. All the humans found themselves staring constantly at Thursday, endlessly fascinated by her human-ness and her alien-ness. Thursday's self-assurance was off-putting to all of them. She seemed to feel she belonged here now, that there was no question of that.

Livingston concluded that someone had to get them started talking about the situation. "Listen, we can sit here like we're on a hike roasting marshmallows if that's what you want, but I say it's just about time we decide our next move. This isn't what we planned, granted, but we can't sit here for the rest of our lives. I vote we get the hell out of here, and take Thursday with us. We've got what we came for, and a hell of a lot more than we bargained for, and we should get out while we're ahead."

"I want to stay here for a while," Barbara announced crisply, as if she had made up her mind on that point long before. "We have Thursday here to study, and I'm sure the Utaani can tell us a lot we need to know. We need what they know."

"I think," Clark said, "that I don't want to deal with our hosts anymore. I understand them a bit too well now." He poked a stick into the fire and watched the sparks shower out. "Monsieur Ovono and I had quite a visit over there. All of us, right along, have felt there was something very *wrong* with this place. Now I know what, and we should have known it right along." He nodded toward Thursday. She looked up from the fire and returned his glance. "Slavery. We saw today, firsthand, how they treat their slaves, and I've been thinking, all day, how that must affect the slave masters."

"Grandpa Zeb said a lot about that in his journal," Liv said. "He kept saying he felt sorry for the slavers, having to crush their own better feelings enough to let them live with slavery."

"Yes, but it's worse here," Clark said intently. "Your slave masters could lie to themselves, tell themselves their slaves were inferior, just animals that could be worked to death—but here, that lie is true! Their whole economy is based on *tranka*-slavery. They have dumb brutes to do all their work—and so work is something for dumb brutes. The women do domestic things, but the men do virtually nothing themselves. All their routine work is done through their slaves. There is no dignity of work because work is something your slave animals do for you—and those animals aren't really capable of doing a lot of things properly. Work is something for the stupid, the clumsy, to do.

"And they spend their lives staring into the eyes of creatures that aren't *quite* human, but very close to it—so close that the Utaani must *know* how close to animals they themselves are. They haven't tried to raise the *tranka* up toward the light, they've dragged themselves down into the mud. They've brutalized themselves, and I don't have the stomach for it. I saw one of them whipping a *tranka* today. The poor beast was screaming in agony—and the man with the whip just looked bored. Not angry, not full of hate or seething with the need for vengeance, or forcing himself to go on even though the cries horrified him—he was *bored*. He could have been weeding the crops for the amount of feeling he showed. No more for me. I want out." He looked up again at Thursday. "And I'm not saying no to it, necessarily, but I think we should think long and hard before we take a slave-beast back with us. What will it do to *us*?"

"She's not a slave-beast," Barbara objected. "She's a . . . I don't know—a beast, a creature, a near-human, a person, a *something* that has been used for a slave. My ancestors were used for slaves—does that make us slave-people?"

"Let's not get too riled up there," Livingston said. "The australopithecines dropped out of sight for a million years. And even before that, we know next to nothing about them. A few scraps of bone, that's all. No real idea of their behavior. Then somewhere in the last few thousand years, these Utaani got hold of them somehow. Maybe in the last century, maybe in the time of the Pharaohs. We don't know. How do we know they haven't been bred for slavery? We bred wolves into dogs, and you could make an argument that dogs are pretty slavish. Thursday here seems incredibly docile. How long have the Utaani and their ancestors being killing all the *tranka* that showed any spunk? Certainly they've bred them, domesticated them. We've domesticated a lot of animals. Doing it to australopithecines is different, somehow, yes, but why, and how, and by how much? But as far as your question, Clark, I can't quite see how one australopithecine is going to contaminate Western civilization. Rupe, what do you think?"

Rupert had been whispering a translation of the conversation to Ovono and listening to Ovono's whispered comments. He looked up and said "Mmmm? I don't know. There's a great deal to learn here, but I'd say we've got our hands more than full already. For the record, M'sieu Ovono wants to get the hell out, but says we paid for Thursday, she's ours, and we should keep her. He says it's nonsense to think of releasing her to the wild. She has lived with men, and would not know about fending for herself. She would die if left behind, or else be captured and put back to slavery. Ovono says he would shoot a dog rather than be so cruel as to let it suffer that way. He's got a few points, and I'd say they all cloud the moral issues just a bit more."

"Hold it here, just a second," Livingston said. "Let's assume we're all agreed that we have to take her along—for ethical as well as scientific reasons. But has anyone thought about the logistics? We can't just stroll into Makokou with her—we'd cause a riot. And what, exactly, are the export rules for removing a hominid from Gabon?"

Clark raised his eyebrows for a moment and nodded. "Mmmph. You've got a point. Requires a bit of thought."

"I'll say one more thing. Thursday can go with us—but only if she wants to," Barbara said. "She can't possibly be made to understand moving to a new place, and how different it will be, but at least we can give her the free choice to stay or go. I can accept that we'd have to restrain her for part of the trip—during the flight home, say—but whenever we leave *here*, if she follows us, fine. If not, no one is to try to compel her in any way. Is that understood? If she comes, she comes of her own accord."

Rupert chortled. "'Look Dr. Grossington,'" he said in a little boy's voice. "'She followed us home, can we keep her?'"

"Shut up Rupert, I'm serious. But before we plan how to leave, we have to decide how long to stay," Barbara went on. "And I still say we need to stay and learn more. I don't like the Utaani any more than you do, but surely we can save some time and learn more by staying here."

"But we're not equipped for that sort of study, Barb," Liv protested. "This was all put together in a hell of a hurry, and I don't know that anyone really considered what exactly we were to do at this end— but this is a small survey team. We're not prepared to wade in and study a whole culture. And do you really think the Utaani will tolerate us hanging around all day watching their slaves? How would you learn more? What would your procedure be?"

"I don't know yet," Barbara said hotly. "I haven't had time to think it through. But we can't lose this chance."

"Barb, I guarantee this isn't our last chance," Rupert said. "Once the scientific community knows about this place, the Utaani and their *tranka* are going to spend the rest of their lives up to their wazoos in anthropologists. And I for one would be happy to leave these bastards to the eternal torture of being studied—as long as I don't have to do the studying. We're not abandoning the quest if we head back now."

Barbara said nothing more, but sat, her arms wrapped around her knees, staring at the fire. Her companions looked at each other, and reached an unspoken agreement. There was no real point in arguing further tonight. One by one, they bedded down.

▼◆▼

Monsieur Ovono insisted that they stand watches in the night, and Barbara drew the last shift. Liv poked her awake a little after three in the morning, and she spent the last hours before dawn watching the darkness, and watching the dark, huddled form that slept next to her.

Thursday woke up once, opening her eyes abruptly and sitting bolt upright, the very picture of a disoriented child waking up in the wrong bed, confused by strange surroundings. Barbara watched her intently, wondering what she would do, and instantly resolved that she would not prevent Thursday from running away. Maybe she would die in the wild, but she at least had the right to die free. If the morning came and the others woke to find the australopithecine gone, Barbara could claim she had dozed off. Barbara watched eagerly for some sign that Thursday would run, make a bid for freedom, but instead, the australopithecine grunted and scratched her crotch as she looked around. After a moment, she seemed to remember where she was, and lay down and went back to sleep.

The incident depressed Barbara, and left her with a sense of obligation to her new charge—she could not, would not, use the word 'slave'. The moment made it clear that Thursday had decided she trusted Barbara, and chose to stay with her rather than make a bid for freedom.

What was the old Chinese idea? If you saved a man's life, you were responsible for that life, that person, from then on. Something like that. So what claim did a near-human have on a person who accidentally freed her? And what claims went the other way? Barbara didn't want any part of those obligations, but it was too late to refuse them now.

She gave it up and stared into the jungle. The jungle at night was not the best place or time to try and resolve such things.

▼◆▼

The next morning snapped into existence with the usual disconcerting speed of dawn in the tropics. It seemed to Barbara that she blinked once and the sun was up. She looked up to see what sort of day it was going to be. Directly above their trailside camp, a tiny patch of sky peeked through the trees, startling blue and bright to eyes used to nothing but grey and dark green. One by one the humans woke up to the new morning. Thursday managed to sleep later than any of them. It made sense, Barbara decided. This was probably the first time in her life that the poor thing hadn't been jolted awake by her keeper.

It was well past seven before Thursday stirred. By that time the rest of the camp had long been up and about. It was a beautiful morning, the air clear and bright, the humidity down, and there was a freshening, almost cooling, breeze. Everyone woke up in a good mood, and the baffled gloom that had hung about the night before seemed forgotten, as unthreatening as a nightmare that hadn't come true.

The coffee was on the fire, the birds were singing, and all seemed right with the world. Rupert even managed to get the BBC World Service on the short-wave, and picked up a music program.

Finally, Thursday woke up, coming alert very quickly. She stood up, stretched and shook herself, getting the kinks of the night out. Then she turned and walked out of camp, hurrying just a bit, disappearing into the wall of forest. Every eye in the camp was on her, wondering if they had just witnessed an escape. One by one, they all turned to look at Barbara. Should they go after her? Should they let her go?

Suddenly, there was the sound of a small, fast stream of water striking the ground. The men got it first, of course, and roared with laughter. Then Barbara understood, and found herself blushing—and that set her laughing. Thursday was answering a call of nature, not escaping to it.

The sound ended, and a moment or two later Thursday reappeared from the trees. She stopped at the edge of the trail and looked at the humans, all of them still laughing out loud. She hesitated, looking just a bit alarmed, and even stepped back a foot or two.

"Thursday," Barbara said. "It's all right, it's all right."

Thursday looked at Barbara and cocked her head. "Come here, Thursday."

The australopithecine raised her arm and pointed to herself. It was an unmistakable gesture. *Who, me?*

"Jesus, she's learned her name already," Rupert said. "And no one even tried to teach it to her."

"Let me try something," Barbara said. "Yes, Thursday, come," she said, gesturing for Thursday to approach. She spoke slowly and carefully, enunciating each word. With only the slightest hesitation, Thursday walked toward her. Barbara raised her hand and put it on her own chest. "Barbara." Livingston was standing nearest to her, and she needed to point to someone else, to show "Barbara" wasn't the word for human. "Livingston," she said, and then pointed to the others. "Rupert. Clark. Ovono." Thursday followed her pointing finger, looking to the person indicated, and not instead staring at the tip of the finger, the way a cat or dog might. Then Barbara put her hands at her side and said "Thursday?" Barbara looked from side to side, as if looking for her.

Thump. Thump thump. Thursday patted herself on the chest, solidly, confidently. She had no doubt who she was. There was something eager in her face and her bearing, something that looked most proud and pleased. Barbara understood. Thursday had something she had never had before—a name, a symbol for herself. For the first time in her life, in a strange way, she *was* something.

Barbara walked toward her, reached out and touched her on the shoulder. "Thursday—yes." She kept her hand on the warm, furry shoulder and said "Barbara—no." She put her hand on herself again. "Thursday—no. Barbara—yes."

"*Es.*"

Everyone in the camp froze, stunned once again. She had said it, most emphatically, if not clearly.

Barbara tried it again, another way. She touched herself again and said, "Thursday."

"'*O.*"

Barbara touched the australopithecine again. "Thursday."

"*Es, es.*" Thursday rocked excitedly back and forth on her feet for a moment, and the fur on her neck stood straight up. She snorted happily and did it again, pounding herself in the chest. "*Es. Es. Ur-ay.*"

Thursday looked around to their faces again, worried that she had done something wrong. "Good! Yes, yes!" Barbara said anxiously. "My God, she's quick."

Rupert sat down slowly next to the fire, reached out for the coffee pot and poured himself a cup. "Great," he growled. "It isn't as if we didn't have enough to think about already."

▼◆▼

They settled down to eat after a bit. Barbara was eager to continue the language lessons, but once Thursday got it into her head that the food was for her, too, she wasn't much interested in words anymore. She gulped down the freeze-dried glup and bland canned food as if she was starving. Livingston couldn't help thinking she'd be a big hit in the no-fresh-food hotel restaurant at Booué.

Barbara got the radio and set it down next to Thursday, expecting her to be fascinated by the music coming out of it, but she seemed to have no real interest in it.

"It makes noise, so what?" Rupert said. "So does the wind and rain and fire. What's she's supposed to do, recognize Beethoven's Fifth?"

"She likes voices," Barbara said. "Maybe she'll respond when someone starts talking. Pass the coffee, will you?"

Not long after, the music did end, and the BBC news reader came on. Barbara, watching intently to see what Thursday did, wasn't really listening to the words herself at first—until she heard her own name in the lead story.

"—ara Marchando and her colleagues are reported to be in the west African nation of Gabon, possibly in search of living examples of the species. As Dr. Grossington noted at that news conference, the first fossil of *Australopithecus boisei* was discovered by the famous paleontologist, Dr. Louis Leakey, a native of Kenya, the son of a British missionary and graduate of Cambridge. . . ."

"How do they *know* about us?" Rupert demanded.

"Oh my God, it got out," Barbara said. "The story got out. Now we *have* to get back. They'll eat Jeffery alive back there."

Thursday didn't notice the commotion. She was too fascinated with the box that had begun talking. She picked it up and shook it, tried to find a place to peek into it.

The radio, quite unimpressed with being shaken, went on. "Despite the impressive nature of the evidence offered in the form of the skull called Ambrose, several experts at the British Museum of Natural History expressed grave doubts that such a creature could have survived into historical times."

   "*Now* they tell us," Rupert muttered. "Someone want to tell Thursday?"

Thursday. Thursday. *Her mouth and throat could not form the sound clearly, but she could hear it, and recognize it, and know that it meant* her, *and no one and nothing else. There was magic in that.*

There was magic, too, in her new people—in the foods they had and the things they did and the way they acted.

On the day after her first night with them, there was a great flurry of activity. All of them got upset suddenly, for no reason that she could see. At first she thought it might be because of something she had done, but none of them seemed angry at her. If anything, they ignored her a bit in the big rush of activity. After their morning food, which they seemed to eat in a great hurry, they packed up all their belongings, put them in bags that hung on their backs, and started walking down the path, away from the village. Then she thought she understood. They had to get away from the village, from the bad men there. But none of them looked back at her, not once, not at all, as if they had made a rule not to look at her. She chased after them, and ran fast until she was alongside Barbara, walking with her. Barbara looked at her with a face so happy and sad at the same time that once again Thursday feared they would not let her come with them. But they did let her come—and didn't even make her carry anything.

They walked all that day, and another, and another, sleeping at nights, until at last they came to a place where there was a very large and strange box, unlike anything Thursday had ever seen before. The humans seemed to know what it was, and they knew how to make parts of it swing open and shut. They seemed to play with it for a while, climbing in and out of it, and the small dark one—Ovono?— seemed to put some small thing into the front part of it. She tried to stick her head in the box through a hole in the side, and bumped her head on it, and so discovered that the clear parts of the box were there, even if they were invisible. Barbara, who was always telling her words, more words than Thursday could dream of remembering, told her the box was called a car, *and the clear parts were called* glass *or* window. *Thursday did not remember that for long, but some-how it helped even to know a thing had a name, even if she did not know what it was.*

They watched the men play with the car-box for a while, and then, after a time, Barbara led Thursday a long ways away from the car-box and stood there with her, watching it.

The other humans climbed into the car-box and sat down in it. Suddenly the car-box made a terrible roaring noise, and let out a horrible-smelling puff of smoke. It frightened Thursday very much, but Barbara held her hand and made soothing sounds. Then the box began to move, not walking, but going about in a strange way with-out lifting its feet at all. It moved around and around the clearing, and the men inside leaned out of the windows, smiling and waving at her. Thursday, in a burst of understanding, realized that they were all trying to show her not to be afraid of it. Barbara led her toward the box-thing, and Thursday understood that she was to get into the thing, and ride in it as well.

It was almost too much for her, but her trust in Barbara made her fight her fear. With her heart racing, and every tuft of fur standing erect, her fingers trembling with fright and excitement, she got into the—yes, it took a moment, but she recalled the name, and felt very proud of that—she got into the car. *The car moved again, this time with her in it, and for the first time in her life, Thursday moved with-out doing the work of moving for herself. It was a scary thing, and exciting.*

For days they drove that way, until they came to a place where a huge swath of the jungle was not there anymore. In its place were men—many, many men— huge, noisy, frightening machines, trees fallen down, and endless sights and sound and smells she could not understand. The one called Ovono made the car move fast past there, and the humans tried to hide Thursday from view, as if they were afraid of her being seen. Perhaps these men would want to take her away from Barbara, just as Barbara had taken her away from the others. Thursday did not want that, and so she let them hide her, even though she was curious about all the things they were moving past.

On and on they went, until they came to a big place, like the old village grown and grown and grown bigger and bigger, with the huts made of strange things, and the air full of odd smells. Again Barbara and the others tried to hide her, and again she let them. They came to a broad, open place near the big village, with many strange machines standing about on it.

Thursday began to notice new words that sounded alike in the conversation—airplane, airport, airline. She wondered what they meant. She wanted to see everything, but they kept her hidden under a blanket in the back of the car. It was hot there, but there was a hole in the blanket she could peek through, and Barbara stayed with her. Peeking through the blanket, she saw Clark talk to a man, and give him some flat things that the man folded up and shoved in a pocket.

When night came, the car moved again, and stopped alongside one of the biggest of the strange machines. The back door of the car opened, and Barbara urged Thursday to step out and come with her.

Thursday saw a door in the big machine, and realized they wanted her to go through it. She climbed inside it, with Barbara following after. Barbara sat down on the floor of the machine, and patted the floor next to her, signaling Thursday to sit down next to her.

Thursday did, and shivered, for the strange floor was made of something very cold and hard. She wondered what would happen next.

Then she felt a jabbing in her rear, like a bee sting.

She was asleep before she knew to be afraid, thank God. Barbara reached over and stroked the coarse fur on her head, and did her best to arrange the unconscious creature into a comfortable position. She wrapped a blanket around Thursday's body and took the hard, callused hand in her own.

The old DC-3 coughed into life, and the well-bribed pilot took them up into the night sky, out of the seedy airstrip of Makokou toward Libreville, and whatever transport Clark could improvise there.

Chapter Nineteen

TOP SCIENTISTS AGREE:
APE-MAN SKULL IS HOAX

(UPI) Is Ambrose the ape-man skull for real? The first reactions from the worldwide scientific community are in, and the answer is a resounding "No." While few scientists were willing to comment on the record, a dozen experts in the field interviewed for this report expressed incredulity at least, with most suspecting outright fraud. It proved impossible to locate a disinterested researcher who believed in Ambrose.

Several independent sources speculated that the "skull," presented to the press by Dr. Jeffery Grossington of the Smithsonian Institution three days ago, was actually a forgery made of dental plaster or a plastic composite. "If it's for real, why hasn't Dr. Grossington let outside scientists see it, examine it closely?" asked Dr. William Lowell of Harvard's biology department, the only scientist who agreed to talk on the record. "Where are the other skulls and post-cranial bones Grossington reported? Why have there been no follow-ups to the first press conference?" A planned follow-up session, at which Dr. Grossington claimed he would display voluminous evidence to prove his claim, was cancelled without explanation.

Other critics were even harsher. "Not only is it a hoax, but Dr. Grossington must be an active participant in the hoax, and no mere dupe, much as it grieves me to say that," one scientist said, on condition that he not be identified. "It is flat-out impossible that a genuine skull of that kind could exist, and while it might be possible to manufacture a fake that would look believable from a few feet away, no working scientist would be fooled if he touched it, or even got reasonably close to it. You'd have trouble fooling most of the general public, for that matter. Jeffery Grossington had to know Ambrose was fake when he presented the skull in that press conference."

Dr. Grossington declined to be interviewed for this story, and has not spoken publicly since his press conference.

Observers agreed that the showman-like nature of Grossington's press conference weighed against him in their evaluation of the skull. "The first people to see that skull should have been Grossington's colleagues—people qualified to examine it and understand its significance. Instead of such legitimate peer-review, we had to read about it over our cornflakes in the morning papers. He leaks it to the press and then stages a dog-and-pony show for the media," Lowell said.

"There's really only one mystery involved here," another researcher commented. "Why on earth would anyone try to pass this off? How could they dream of getting away with it? There is no way this fraud could hope to survive public scrutiny. Australopithecines in Mississippi? It's absurd. Why not dinosaurs grazing in front of Grossington's museum? It's like trying to pass your kid's drawings on the refrigerator as the Mona Lisa. I hear they were staging an expedition to Africa to bring back a live one. I just wonder who they're going to get into the gorilla suit for that press conference."

▼◆▼

The Air Force made lousy coffee. Barbara shivered slightly as she took another sip of the foul brew, wishing to be anywhere but on the windswept flight line of Andrews Air Force Base. At least the overcooked battery acid was warm, and heat was something she could use right now. Twenty-four hours after sweating in the humid furnace of Makokou, Washington in February was *cold*. Sleep was something else she could use, but that would have to wait.

The big C-130 transport that had carried them from Libreville squatted on the hardstand while the maintenance crew swarmed over it, a lumbering sky-god being tended by its acolytes. Jeffery Grossington humped up his shoulders against the cold and puffed out a cloud of smoky breath. "Why haven't they brought her out yet?" he asked.

"I don't know," Barbara said. "Soon. Things always take a long time to get on and off airplanes. Law of nature. Don't worry. Livingston and Rupert are in there, keeping an eye on her. She should be all right. But she's been sedated for most of the last day or so, and I don't want to give her another shot if we don't have to."

Neither of them took their eyes off the airplane, watching and waiting. "So how did you get out?" Jeffery asked. "All I got was a message to be here, brought over by a State Department courier."

Barbara shook her head. "I don't know, exactly, myself. Give Clark White the credit—he's quite a guy. Our guide, Monsieur Ovono, drove us into Makokou, the closest town with an airfield. Thursday wasn't too afraid of the Land Rover, thank God. We got to the airfield and bought a ride on some old rustbucket that flew us to the coast. We landed in Libreville about midnight, and then just sat there on the tarmac while Clark took our passports, went into town, and did his thing. Eight hours later, a USAF Military Airlift Command aircraft lands and taxis up next to us. Flown in from West Germany. Clark reappears with our passports all properly stamped and a license to transport 'one ape of uncertain species' out of the country. He hands us the papers, herds us onto the MAC bird and waves goodbye. We refueled in the Azores and landed here. And let me tell you, the Air Force has one surprised doctor aboard that airplane." She took another sip of her coffee and made a face. February had already sucked every drop of warmth from the cup. She poured the rest of it onto the immaculate concrete of the tarmac, crumpled up the styrofoam cup, and jammed it into the pocket of her borrowed coat.

"It hasn't been much more fun around here," Jeffery said. "I don't know how much you've heard, but our cover got blown but good."

He pulled a newspaper out of his pocket and handed it to her. "Page one story all about what a charlatan I am. A reporter from Mississippi broke the story, and like a fool, I decided to go public. The sharks have been circling ever since. I'm a fraud, or a gullible senile fool taken in by hoaxers. You name it, I've been called it. I was going to lay out every single bone on the trestle tables in the Digger's Pit— ah, that is, in the main anthropology office," Grossington said, plainly embarrassed to have used the office slang. "I was going to set up a slide show of your excavation, have photocopies of Zebulon's journal and the ad from the 1851 Gowrie *Gazette* available—the whole chain of evidence. But then the reporter who broke the story in the first place found out you were in Gabon and announced it, and I got the cable that you were headed home. I decided to keep mum until you were back. All I've said was 'no comment.' I realized the publicity was going to be so heavy that I couldn't let you in for it without consulting you. It's going to be rough, and you need to decide how to handle it. Besides, who knows what sort of trouble you would be in it if the Gabonese knew what you were doing? Oh, one other thing— the secretary of the Smithsonian let it be known my resignation would be accepted, until I barged into his office with Ambrose this morning—just the way you barged into *my* office. He's starting to believe. He'll back us. I think."

"I'm sorry, Jeffery. Truly." She shut her eyes and rubbed them for a moment, and then looked back at the big airplane. "Have you figured out where we're going to put her?"

"I think so," Grossington said. "I don't know if you'll like it, though."

"Where?"

"St. Elizabeth's."

"A *mental* hospital? Jeffery, she's not crazy or dangerous—"

"I'm sure that's true, but that's not the point," Grossington said wearily. "Saint E.'s is at least partially a federal facility, which makes it a bit easier for another part of the federal government to prevail upon them. It's here in Washington, but secluded. It has good security, and a staff that's used to dealing with the press—they still have John Hinkley locked up there. It's a big medical facility, spread out over a large, secluded campus. They have labs, observation equipment, all that sort of thing—and the staff there is experienced in some of the things you're going to need help in. Cognitive studies, motor coordination, language skills, that sort of thing. It makes sense for us." He nodded to an Air Force Medevac van waiting behind them. "I've got an ambulance waiting to take her there."

Barbara let her shoulders droop, and she let out a deep, heavy sigh. Livingston and Rupert came off the plane, carrying Thursday's still figure on a stretcher between them. Barbara tried to get a look at her, but she was so wrapped in blankets that no part of her was clearly visible. Thick straps held her to the stretcher. If she should wake, she would not be able to move at all. "Okay, okay. I guess you're right. Let's go lock her up."

▼◆▼

Now, Jenny-Sue, I know all the good folks out there watching our special prayer-vigil broadcast today are just as concerned as we are with the need for a decent, Christian education for their children. That's why I want to take a moment from our usual fundraising this morning to talk about a *challenge* to all of us—a mighty challenge that could well produce an equally mighty triumph against the creeping secular humanism that pervades this nation's classrooms. (Applause.) Now, we've all seen and heard the reports of this amazing new skull that's been found right here in America. The scientist who found this skull tells us it belongs to a species of so-called ape-men that he says has been dead a million years, a species of ape-man that's supposed to be your grandparent. The scientists say it proves their theory of evolution. Certainly this new evidence *looks* like a challenge to all the study and research of our friends at the Creation Science Institute who have *proven* the Earth to be a mere ten thousand years old, who have laid that old devil evolution to rest with all their work.

You *might* think this report means that slippery old devil evolution has risen yet again, but it's not really so. That's what they *want* you to think, but friends, it's just not true. They are putting a new set of clothes on that naked old emperor evolution, but *we* can see it's really just the same old rags. Think again. Think, friends, for a moment, of the disarray, the dirty old mess, the evolutionist secular humanists have gotten themselves into here. You almost have to admire them for trying to use this amazing discovery to 'prove' evolution. They try to hide the obvious truth behind a smokescreen of complicated logic, but it just won't work. How could it be, friends, that humans are the descendants of a monkey that died just before the Civil War?

You know it can't be, and so do I, and so do they. And they're ready for a fight. Are we? Are all you good Christians ready for a fight? I'd like you all to listen to Jenny-Sue now, and then contribute to the Defense Fund she's going to describe, to be used in the fight to scourge every textbook in the land, cleanse them all of the lies of evolution. So do contribute what*ever* you can . . . .

▼◆▼

Firmly, resolutely, pointlessly, Barbara decided not only that she had to be with Thursday when the australopithecine woke, but that she, Barbara had to remain awake until then. Now she sat in a spare but comfortable room, all whites and dulled grey linoleum, in a small outbuilding at St. E's. It wasn't a luxurious room, but it was not an unpleasant one either. Indeed, it would have seemed almost homey if not for the bars on the windows and the too-solid door that locked from the outside.

Thursday lay on a bed in the corner, right where the baffled orderlies had left her. They had wrapped a sheet and a blanket around her, for want of something more to do for her. Her breathing was regular, her heartbeat seemed strong, and there really was nothing *to* be done until she woke up. Logically, Barbara should have been resting herself, but she had gotten it into her head that Thursday should not awaken all alone, and that was all there was to it. She would not eat, would not sleep, until Thursday was awake in this new world.

Barbara even knew, deep inside, that what she was really doing was performing a penance—punishing herself with hunger and sleeplessness for the sin of kidnapping Thursday and transporting her across the seas. Guilt had always been a powerful motivator for Barbara—so strong that she sometimes invented a cause for it when none was around. Was that the case now?

Should she feel this guilty? Not if she had simply brought another kind of ape from Africa back for study. Most paleoanthropologists worked with chimps or gorillas at one time or another, and Barbara saw the necessity of such study. So long as the animals were treated well, and not caused needless fear and pain, she felt no great shame in using them. But as engaging as the great apes could be, as bright and personable as they often were, they were indisputably *animals*, not people.

She had bought Thursday as a *slave*, and every other slave in history had been a person someone had treated like an animal. How could she be so sure she wasn't doing the same thing?

Her great-grandfather Zebulon was the only other person in history to report any real information about the creatures, and *he* had flatly stated they were not people.

So, Barbara thought, *All I have to do is decide if she's a person or not.*

But there was another question to answer first, of course.

What, exactly, makes a person a person?

Thursday whimpered in her sleep, thrashed about for a moment, and kicked the blankets off before she settled back down and began to snore.

▼◆▼

Pete knew they had found themselves an australopithecine. and also where they had stashed it. He had stumbled onto that one by tailing Grossington for three days when the story seemed to be dying as suddenly as it had appeared, when he had run out of leads. Grossington's press conference had started out to be all that Pete could have hoped it to be, but when Grossington had stalked out, and then shut down any further access to his evidence, canceling the follow-up conference as well, that had smelled enough like fraud to convince everyone. By the second day, even Pete was starting to wonder if Ambrose was for real.

But there was no turning back now. Ambrose *had* to be real, or Pete was dead. He'd be out of a job, a laughingstock in his profession if anyone remembered him at all, suited only for work on the *National Enquirer*—and working *there* was his worst nightmare. So he set off on the desperate chance of tailing Grossington, with no clear goal in mind.

But sometimes even desperation pays off. Pete was on his tail when Grossington drove out to Andrews. Pete sat in his rental at the main entrance gate, and then, grinning with relief, tailed Grossington's car on the way out as it followed an Air Force ambulance through the unfamiliar city, to some place called Saint Elizabeth's—a mental hospital, apparently.

Obviously, Grossington had met a plane, but why would he be interested in a plane landing at an Air Force base, and why would they need an ambulance, and why drive directly to an insane asylum? He had collected the Gabon expedition and their cargo. What else could it be? What better place than a mental institution to stash a wild ape-man? Either someone had really cracked up, or they had found something. Pete sat in his rental and stared at the entrance to the expansive grounds of Saint Elizabeth's. He *knew* that the ape-man was in there.

There was something else he knew—knew by feel and not by fact: Grossington was not the real key to this story. Barbara Marchando was. Pete had missed that because Grossington had the rank and the reputation—and because Marchando was a black woman and that still counted against her in Pete's southern male-chauvinist subconscious.

But she had found the skull—and found it on her own family's property. She had gone off to Africa to search for more, had been the one Grossington had singled-out for praise. All of which meant she was inside those gates in some outbuilding with the ape-man right now. He *knew* it, but he couldn't prove it. And he couldn't get much further staring at this gate.

And no one outside the operation besides himself would know where she was. That was an interesting point, and it gave him interesting ideas. He turned the key, started the car, threw it into gear and headed back downtown.

▼◆▼

Thursday woke up. She felt weak, sick, stiff, as if she had not moved in a long time. Slowly, she sat up and tried to stand. She nearly fell—

not because she was dizzy, but because she was sleeping on a strange, soft sort of ledge or box, and not on the ground. Carefully, she swung her feet around and put them on the floor.

Nothing smelled right. The ground here was grey-white, impossibly flat and smooth, lifeless. She was in a hut—a big, empty hut, and quite alone but for a human who was staring at her. Where were the others? Where was the keeper, and why wasn't he crying out for them to get to work—

With a shock, she remembered. The newcomers, the journey, the strange machines and wondrous things. Where was she? She looked again at the human who was watching her. B—B... Barbara! She remembered. And she remembered, no, more than remembered, she knew her own name. She knew it to be a part of herself, like her hands. She stood up and looked at Barbara. "Urs-ay" she announced. Barbara smiled and nodded, and Thursday felt better. Thursday walked across the room to the window. She remembered the idea of windows—clear stuff that was still there even though you could see through it—though she could not remember the word. She looked out across the flat, barren, cold fields of February, the grounds of the institution looking grey and forbidding. She reached up and wrapped her hands around the iron bars set into the window frame. Bars on doors and windows were something else she knew without having to remember.

Where was she? How had she gotten here?

▼◆▼

". . . You may recall that we opened the Nightly News a few nights ago with a report of a remarkable discovery in the study of early man. A skull named Ambrose, reputed to be about a hundred years old, and allegedly belonging to a pre-human species said to be extinct these past million years, was trotted out for the press. For those of our viewers eager for an update, we're sorry to report that Ambrose has come down in the world since then. Amid cries of fraud, the scientist responsible has refused to defend his claim. Meanwhile, Jan Werkner, a Hollywood special effects man, took just two days to create the skull pictured on your screen now out of plastic and plaster. Result: a dead ringer for Ambrose. Werkner said he made the fake to demonstrate how easy it would be to commit such a hoax—provided no one was allowed to get a good close look at the skull. How have the mighty fallen. That's our report for this evening. Good night."

▼◆▼

Pete came up out of the subway entrance and looked around. There it was, across the street, pretty hard to miss. George Washington University Hospital. They had taken Reagan here when he was shot, he remembered.

He crossed the street and hesitated at the entrance. But this was the only lead he had. It had to go somewhere. Thank God there were only three Marchandos in the phone book—Barbara's separated husband Michael had been easy to find. Pete was frankly amazed that Dr. Michael Marchando had agreed to an interview, but with the bad press the australopithecine story had gotten in the last few days, he would take what he could get. None of the principals in the case—Barbara Marchando, Maxwell, Jones, Grossington—were answering their home phones or returning messages left at their offices. He went inside.

There's an unwritten law saying hospitals are easy to get lost in, and it took Pete fifteen minutes to find the cafeteria. Once there, however, Dr. Marchando was easy to spot—a black man in a doctor's coat, sitting alone, a little bit nervous, glancing at his watch repeatedly.

Pete went up to him. "Dr. Marchando?"

"Mr. Ardley?" Michael asked politely.

"Yes. Thank you for agreeing to see me." Pete sat down across from Michael, and wondered where to begin.

But Michael beat him to it. He picked up his coffee cup and took a fair-sized swig. "Listen, I want to come straight down to it. Do you know where she is? You hinted that you might on the phone."

Pete looked his host straight in the eye. "Yes, I do. At least I'm fairly certain I do."

"Then what do you need me for?"

"For a few reasons. Maybe you know something about what's going on. Maybe, if you knew where she was, you'd be able to help me get in to see her."

"Maybe. We're not on the best terms at the moment. Besides, why should I help you—" Michael looked up, past Pete's shoulder.

Pete was suddenly aware that two people had come up behind him. He turned around in his chair, and got a sinking feeling in his stomach. He knew the faces of the two grim-looking men.

"Mr. Ardley," the blonde one said. "I'm Rupert Maxwell and this is Livingston Jones. May we sit down?" The two of them sat down on either side of him, not exactly aggressive, but certainly not in a way you could say no to, either.

"Hello, Liv," Michael said. "Nice to meet you, Dr. Maxwell."

Pete suddenly felt that he wasn't in control anymore. "What are you two doing here?" he asked.

"Dr. Marchando was good enough to call us and say you had contacted him," Rupert said. "Liv and I thought we might sit in. In fact, I think you and I need each other."

"So, Mike," Livingston said. "Getting interviewed by Jimmy Olson here?" He turned to Pete. "Sell lots of newspapers since you did me the big favor back in Gowrie? You know, we were in Africa when we found out you had broken the story. What with all the publicity, we decided we had to drop everything and get the hell home," he said, glaring at Pete. "Isn't it a terrible thing, Mr. Ardley, the way a little headline-chasing can screw up so much important work?"

Rupert leaned in toward Pete, not saying anything, obviously doing his best to intimidate. Pete glanced nervously from Rupert to Liv. The two of them looked awfully damn big.

"He said he knew where Barbara was," Mike said, "that he'd tell me where she was if I helped him get in to see her."

"He's lying," Liv said coolly, "trying to trick you into something. He's good at that. He doesn't know squat, Mike. He doesn't know where she is. No one could."

Pete realized he was sweating heavily. "Saint Elizabeth's," he blurted out. "And not as a patient. She's there watching over your new pet. I followed Grossington's car until he went there." Pete watched the newcomers' faces as he spoke, and felt a little thrill of triumph as he read their shocked expressions. He was right. Knowing it for *certain* was worth losing his interview with Michael Marchando.

Besides, his little revelation seemed to have thrown Jones and

Maxwell—and they were angry enough with him that deflecting that anger was extremely worthwhile. And the best time to pursue something was while the other guy was off balance. "But you said we needed each other, Dr. Maxwell. How so?"

Rupert cleared his throat and spoke, clearly a bit disconcerted. "Because we'll all be out of a job if things keep up the way they are. On our side, our entire team is looking like a bunch of idiots and frauds. No one is that interested in listening to us, to put it mildly. And it's not just reporters—our colleagues in the field are practically ready to burn us at the stake for putting the entire discipline in disrepute. We need to prove that we're not lying, that Thurs—that, that *Ambrose*—is real, that we know what we're talking about. You heard at the press conference that the National Geographic was supporting us—well, even they're pulling back. To be blunt about it, we need a mouthpiece. And right now, you're even less believed and look like even more of an idiot than we do. You need a story. If you get us decent coverage, we'll cooperate, give you everything you need. You'll win, and we'll stop losing."

"Barbara doesn't know you're here, right?" Michael spoke with flat confidence, knowing it was true. "You're here behind her back, or else she'd be here with you."

Rupert and Liv exchanged glances again, and then Liv shrugged. "Yeah, you're right, she doesn't know. But I doubt she'd care if she did know. She's pretty far gone. Oh, she's okay, she's all right, she's not hurt or anything," Liv added hurriedly. "I just meant she's so damned wrapped up in—in what she's doing, she doesn't know what's going on."

"She does have an australopithecine with her," Michael said, wonderingly. "You didn't deny it when *he* said it," he went on, nodding toward Pete, "and you've both almost said it yourselves. My God."

"Yeah, she's got one," Liv said. "Calls her Thursday. But I don't even much care about that just now. Yesterday's news for me. I'm worried about Barbara." He turned to Pete. "I might as well tell you this stuff. You'll hear it soon enough, anyway. I think she's convinced herself that Thursday might be a kind of human, and she feels guilty as hell for bringing her here. I don't know why. Maybe because guilt is supposed to be for humans, and to Barb, at least, Thursday is a person. Barbara *bought* Thursday—so if Thurs is human, that makes

Barbara a kidnaper, a slave owner."

"Well, *is* it—is she, Thursday—human?" Pete demanded. This was a touchy moment, but he had to know.

"We don't know, Mr. Ardley," Livingston said absently. "We're in sort of a grey area there, to put it mildly. Human, ape, something in between. You look at her, say words to her, watch her move and act and *think*—and you still don't know. But right now I don't even much care about that. I'm just worried about Barbara. She's in a bad way."

Rupert nodded. "It's not just my job I'm worried about here. It's her. She's a friend, and she cares a lot about something that's tearing her up inside. I figure at the least, we can get her mind off things if there's some publicity and hoopla to distract her—and she won't have to handle this alone anymore. At first we thought it would be better to work in private, but Jesus, even without Barb's problems, we'd need help. This is too big. Other people, specialists in all the pertinent fields, have to weigh in, examine the evidence. We need some positive publicity to pull them in." Rupert leaned in close to Pete again, grabbed his shoulder hard enough that it hurt. "So we need you to help. But Barbara is very fragile right now. Play nice with her, play gentle. Or I'll rip your lungs out."

Pete swallowed hard. "You drive a interesting bargain, Dr. Maxwell. Look, ah, this isn't the right place to talk, and we're all a bit riled up. Why don't I meet you at your office at the Museum at noon? That'd give us all time to cool off, and you'll have the materials there I'll need to do the job you want."

Rupert glanced from Liv to Mike and nodded. "Fair enough. Besides, I think we three have a few things to talk about in private anyway. But make it at Saint E's. Barbara will want to stay there. Ask the guard to direct you to Dr. Marchando in Building 3-K. I'll have all the materials and information you'll need. Right now, why don't you take off?" he asked blandly. "Mike and Liv and I need to talk."

Pete nodded, stood up, and pushed back his chair. "Fine. Fine. I'll see you there." He found his way out of the cafeteria, out of the hospital, greatly relieved that they hadn't beat him to a pulp.

▼◆▼

It was not a comfortable silence at the table. "Mike, she's not in good shape," Livingston finally announced. He pushed back in his chair a bit and drummed his fingers on the table top. "She's torturing herself with worry, wondering if she did the right thing, wondering what else she could have done, what she *should* have done. She's got herself convinced that Thursday is just going to be tested and tortured and studied to death, that she's brought the poor thing back here to be a slave to science or something."

"I don't understand," Mike said. "This is a big discovery for her. She should be happy and excited. Why is she upset?"

"Because—" Liv sighed and drummed his fingers on the window glass. "I don't know. But I can tell you some stuff—stuff you ought to know already. She went off to Gabon in a pretty fragile state, thanks to the kind treatment of a certain person. You had her tied up in *knots*. I dunno what was in your letters, what you said in person when you saw her, but they sure as hell didn't make her happy. You two are separated, Mike. You have no claim on her, no right to say thing to make her feel bad. She did her best. Over in Africa, she *seemed* okay on the outside, but inside, I think she was just barely holding together. *I* think you had her convinced she had failed in some obligation to you, that she owed you something big.

"And then Thursday comes along, a poor miserable creature that needs a very clear-cut kind of help, instead of demanding some vague kind of endless support. I think she's taking all the pointless guilt you made her feel about you and redirecting it onto Thursday."

"Listen," Mike said abruptly, nervously. "I let this reporter guy come here and talk to me because I thought I could find out what he knew and pass it on to you guys, because I wanted to help, because I was worried about Barbara. I let you guys come and talk to him—I didn't have to tell you when or where we were meeting. I'm trying to help. I *know* I treated her bad," he went on, talking rapidly, wondering if he was babbling as much as he thought he was. "The last few weeks, I've thought about a lot of stuff—all those damn fool whining letters I sent her when you guys were in Mississippi. They were bad, I know, really unfair. And they didn't help *me* any.

"I spent our whole marriage pushing her away and then demanding things. But the first time Barbara really rejected me, instead of just walking away from a mess, was after those letters, just *before* she left for Africa.

"The last I saw time I saw her, she was happy *because she was leaving me.* I had thought I could bring her around again, get her to see things my way again, but none of the old crap was working. I couldn't understand it. It hit me, really hit me how much I must have hurt her if leaving me felt that *good.* I owe her. And she still feels something for me—you guys both know that. I don't say she should feel it, or that I've earned it, or that I've got rights here. I'm just saying maybe I can help because of how she feels. Let me help her. Let me give back some of what I took."

Liv shook his head. "You got one thing right. You've got no rights here. But Barb needs help, and we need help. Act like a decent guy, and you're in. Doing what, I don't know exactly. None of us knows what happens next. But we'll need some warm bodies, that's for sure."

Mike offered up his hand, and Liv took it after a moment's hesitation. Rupert looked at both of them and shrugged. "I predict," he said, "some interesting times ahead."

Chapter Twenty

Barbara glared at Pete Ardley as she led Thursday out into the visitors' room. No doubt she had been told all the sensible, logical reasons why they had to tolerate the man who had caused them so much trouble, but she didn't have to like it. And her ex-husband Michael was here, too. Plainly she had no idea how she should handle her former husband. From what Pete understood, there hadn't been a chance for the two of them to talk alone since Gabon. Judging from the expression on her face, she was glad to see him—but also pretty upset by it as well.

At least so far as Pete himself was concerned, her emotions were clear and uncomplicated. At a guess, there were lots of worse things she wanted to do to him, but she contented him with a look that should have killed at twenty paces.

Pete took all that in within half a heartbeat, and knew he ought to worry about soothing Barbara Marchando's feathers—but he found his attention otherwise occupied. He had eyes only for Thursday, the reality, the creature, the ape-man—no, make that ape-*woman*—at the center of the fuss. He felt a strange twisting in his stomach as he looked at her, a sense of fascinated revulsion.

This creature walked *almost* the way a human did, and the difference was—disturbing. He remembered the feeling he had had as a child when he saw some poor misshapen person, twisted by disease or injury, hobbling or lurching along on limbs that didn't move in quite the right way. You tried not to look, you tried not to pity, you tried to treat the unfortunate person as a person, not a crippled freak or a monster. You worried about trying too hard to be solicitous . . . Pete shook his head and blinked, pulling his eyes off Thursday's strange and graceful stride. But this *was* a freak, *was* a monster. Not a human being. Look at that head, that face, the forehead that sloped back to nothing, the apish muzzle. Not a human. Remember that. Thursday pulled up a hard wooden chair and sat down in it, a bit awkwardly. *Sitting in chairs like that is what people do, isn't it?* Pete asked himself.

"Here she is, Mr. Ardley." Barbara's voice cut into his reverie, harsh and angry. "Your front page story. Your headline. Feel up to exploiting her?"

Easy now, Pete thought. *She wants to fight, but you don't. Remember that.* He was disconcerted enough by Thursday without picking fights with Dr. Barbara Marchando. "No one's interested in exploiting her, Dr. Marchando. Your own team invited me in here to do a story, and that's all I want to do." Pete took a good hard look at Barbara, and decided she looked bad, besides looking angry. She hadn't had enough sleep or food for a long time.

"We need more than a newspaper story, Mr. Ardley." Dr. Grossington looked no happier to see Pete than Barbara did, but he was in better control of himself. "We need your sage advice, your public relations work to get the rest of the press to pay attention. We're like the little boy who cried wolf. You have to get them to believe us again."

"Right, right. I know. We need to put together a press kit, then. Photos of—ah, Thursday here, bios of all of you, a statement explaining where you found her, that sort of thing. But the key is the photos. They have to be the best possible. Sharp, clear, no blurred-out stuff that could have been faked up. We release that material, *then* schedule a second press conference and bring her out, present the skeletons and other evidence, and issue an open invitation for the media and the scientists to study it all as closely as possible. And, ah, we have to prove that Thursday isn't simply someone in a really good gorilla suit."

Barbara seemed ready to explode. "*Gorilla suit*! For God's sake, look at her! How could you possibly fake that?" Thursday looked around nervously, wondering what was wrong.

"Easy, Thurs. Easy, it's okay. Barb, you go flying off the handle like that too often, poor Thursday is going to have a nervous breakdown," Livingston said. "But someone could fake Thursday—the same way that Hollywood guy faked the skull to prove Ambrose was a fake," he said gently. "Didn't you ever see *Planet of the Apes?*"

Pete hesitated a moment before going on. Barbara didn't look happy, but she didn't say anything more. "Okay, then. We'll have to stand ready to provide tissue samples, hair, blood, that sort of thing. I realize that we've got to control it or else she'll be sampled to death, but we have to be prepared to cooperate with that sort of request. I think the best we can do to *absolutely* nail it down is a CAT scan—one of those high-tech super-duper x-rays. These guys are going to be *suspicious*. Dr. Grossington and I agreed that camera flashes might scare Thursday, so we're going with bright TV lights and not allowing flashes. They're even going to resent *that*, assume that we're hiding a gimmick a flash would reveal. We need all the proof we can get, and a CAT scan showing she's real is pretty damn good proof."

Mike cleared his throat. "I think I can get us that, get you into the George Washington University Hospital, use the machine there. People have used the CAT machine before for research, Egyptian mummies and so on. I bet I could get us in—one of the radiologists owes me a favor. There's a hell of a waiting list for the machine, though. I could call now and try to schedule it, if you like."

Pete shook his head. "No, not yet. We don't want the scan done now. We wait until we've got a panel of impartial experts lined up in the room, making sure the scan's done right, with no chance of fraud. Maybe it's not too soon to make some polite inquiries. But the photos are the main thing. Give me photos I can distribute, and we can pack them in."

"Photos we got, and I suppose we can take more and rush the processing, but, ah, I must ask an indelicate question," Rupert said. "In these photos—does she wear *clothes*? Let's face it, we want to get these pictures into family newspapers. And I guess we've got to think about dressing her for the news conference, too."

Barbara seemed about to have another outburst, but she restrained herself. "I don't really see how that matters," she said. "But I'm afraid it's a moot point. It's pretty cold here for her, and we've tried to get her to wear warm things, sweaters or smocks, anything—but she won't. She just tears them right off. In time, I think we can get her used to them, but that'll be weeks or months, not days."

Rupert shrugged. "Okay, that settles it then." He turned to Thursday and said "Looks like you're going to be a nudist at your own coming-out party, kiddo." Thursday cocked her head to one side and pursed her lips, an expression that seemed to be her equivalent of a smile.

"Fine," Pete said. *People wear clothes*, he thought to himself. *Nice to have some distinctions left.*

Pushed, prodded, led this way and that, Thursday numbly followed Barbara into yet another box that moved, a *car*, this one without any place to see out, and rode the car to yet another strange place. Barbara talked a lot, said a lot of words that Thursday did not understand at all, speaking in a low, soothing monotone. She could hear the sounds of the words better and better, though, even if she could not understand them. But there was more to understand than just the words themselves. Thursday suddenly realized that Barbara was trying to encourage her, to soothe her, to make her feel better—and started to wonder what there was to soothe her about.

They arrived wherever it was they were going, and Thursday allowed herself to be led from the truck. They were in some sort of short tunnel, and Barbara immediately led her through a door in the side of the tunnel and through a series of hallways to a small, cluttered, odd-shaped room.

Barbara sat down in a chair, and pulled on Thursday's arm, guided her down into the seat next to her.

The small room had two doors, and Thursday could hear strange noises from the one they had not come in through. She heard rustlings and thuds, voices and laughter. After a time, the noise settled down a bit, and she heard a single voice, speaking very loud. She recognized the voice. It was Grossi—Grossington, that was the name. She heard him speak her name, and her ears pricked up. Barbara took her arm, opened the second door, and led her out into a big, noisy, brightly lit room.

She could not understand what she saw or heard. There was Grossington, and Barbara, standing in a broad empty place. In front of them was a wall of dazzling lights that made it hard to see anything but the vaguest shapes beyond. She could just barely make out people, lots of people, moving about behind the lights. There was a babble of voices, and a whole tangle of strange noises, clicks and whirs and hums, that seemed to come from black machines that some men were putting up to their faces.

She was scared, but Barbara held her hand and said the same soothing words, over and over. The men with their black boxy things came closer, and each of the boxy machines had a huge, dark glassy eye at the end of it. Other men and women started talking into sticks with puffy ends, and then would shove the sticks into her face.

"She can't talk! She can't talk! Get those cameras and mikes back! You'll scare her!" It was Barbara's voice, shouting something at the strange people, but they didn't seem to notice at all. They kept on shoving and pushing, struggling to get close to her. Barbara grabbed Thursday by the arm and pulled her back, put herself between Thursday and the mob, holding her arms up to urge them back. At last, the people settled down a little, and went back behind the lights, but they all kept talking at once, shouting at Barbara or Grossington or one of the others, barely listening at all when the people with Thursday said anything back.

After a long time, they led her out of the room and down the long hall to the car. But there were more people with the same kinds of machines there now, some chasing them down the hall, others appearing from around every corner. They rushed in around the car, and made it hard for Thursday and Barbara to get into it. Hands sprouted out of the crowd and grabbed at Thursday, and she snarled and slapped them back with a wave of her arm.

The crowd drew back a bit then, and they climbed into the car. They took her back to the place she knew, the room with the bars on the window. She did not understand what had happened.

"This is Penny Wambaugh broadcasting live from the Natural History Museum in Washington D.C. What all expected to be a clumsy fraud waiting to be exposed has turned instead into the story of the century. Reporters turned out once again for a press conference conducted by Dr. Grossington, drawn this time by what appeared to be photos of a living ape-woman. Good as the photos were, no one expected them to be authentic—until an australopithecine named Thursday was brought out on stage. To confirm that there is no fraud, Thursday is to undergo a CAT scan at George Washington University Hospital later today. But for those of us who saw her, there can be no doubt. She is no actor in a gorilla suit, but instead a living, breathing and non-human creature. As one scientist put it, quote, She is so close to being human, and yet so far, that we can no longer say for certain what a human being is, unquote. We'll have film of her on the five o'clock news, coming up next. Stay tuned."

"What Clem here says makes sense, don't it? This Thursday critter is from Africa, ain't it? And where the hell are nigrahs from? *Africa!* You see the pictures of that ape—black as the coal scuttle. The Klan's been warning the rest of the country for years the kind of trouble we're gonna get with the mixing of the races—and now we got proof, 'cepting it's a different set of races. It's gotta be that this monkey blood got in with the nigrahs some time back. You kin see the resemblance, and that blood's been the cause of all our troubles. Hey, darling, another round a' beers here if yah please."

More things, strange things, began to happen. They took her to another place, and made her lie on a flat white table. They strapped her down on it so hard and tight she could not move, and then the table began to slide slowly back through a hole in a white wall. The table slid back the way it had come, and then the whole thing happened again. And again. Finally, they took her home again, but even there she had no peace.

People, many people she had never seen, came to look at her, to pry open her mouth and look at her teeth, to poke needles into her arm and draw blood, to glue wires to her head and her body and hook her up to machines. Half the time it seemed she felt sleepy, listless, woozy. She would suddenly fall asleep and wake up in a new place, or back where she started, but with the feeling that she had been taken somewhere, that something had happened to her. The whole day, her every living minute, had the strange, shifting, floating, ephemeral feeling of a dream. Her real dreams became more vivid, bright images of the jungle, or Barbara's face, or whatever frightening things the humans had done to her that day running through her mind again. She was never quite sure if she was awake or asleep anymore.

She began to get snappish and moody. She began to growl at people and bare her teeth at the people, try and frighten them.

Barbara was the only one she would let come near. Barbara was with her, always, for those long days, always holding her hand, saying kind words. Barbara would take her to a big, bright room with nice things, and one wall with a big shiny window in it, a special window Barbara called a *mirror*. Thursday quickly learned that the *tranka* she saw in it standing next to Barbara was herself, and spent long hours staring at her own image. But they played games in the room, too. Barbara would strap a little box to her belt, and take a wire from it, and stick the plug on the end of it into her ear. Now and then, the plug would fall out of Barbara's ear and Thursday could hear a tiny voice come from it. Once she had the wire in her ear, Barbara would show her games to play, like stacking blocks or matching shapes and colors, or teach her new words. Those were the happiest times of day for Thursday. Yet she could tell there was something sad about her friend Barbara, as if Barbara wanted it to stop and couldn't make it happen. Barbara would glance at the mirror, frown at it.

Finally, one day, in the middle of a game, Barbara got mad. Right in the middle of showing a picture to Thursday, Barbara jumped up out of her chair, yanked the wire out of her ear, threw the picture cards up in the air, and turned to scream at the mirrored wall. "Stop it!" she cried. "Stop watching!" She picked up her chair and threw it through the mirror, smashing it to bits and revealing the watchers hiding behind it. She pulled the box off her belt and threw it on the floor. "Stop telling me what to do! Go away! Leave us alone."

Thursday was scared, astonished, bewildered. She stared at Barbara, wondered what she should do. Barbara sagged down onto the floor and began to cry, wailing as if her heart was breaking.

Slowly, gently, Thursday sat down on the floor next to her and wrapped her shaggy arms around her friend. Barbara threw her arms around Thursday and sobbed into her chest. Thursday, frightened and confused, hugged her friend harder and rocked her back and forth, making the most soothing noises she could.

And still, through the broken window, the watchers watched.

"Okay, so she cracked," Rupert thundered back at the bland-faced doctor. "No real sleep or decent meals for a week—a week where she had to watch someone she feels responsible for being tortured and tested like an animal, a week of *helping* in the testing and torture in the name of some vague scientific ideal. She has every reporter on planet Earth breathing down her neck, and then some pencil-necked geek in the observation room tells her to try *lying* to Thursday about what the pictures on the cards are, just to see what happens. So she yanks her radio pickup and throws a chair through the snoop-mirror.

I just wish she had managed to hit one of the little bastards back there. And just because it happens in your laughing academy, you lock *her* up in one of your rubber rooms. We don't want any crap— we want her out."

Mike Marchando nodded his head vigorously. "Damn straight we do. I'm a medical doctor, and I'm prepared to sign any release you want to get her out of her. There couldn't be *anything* worse for her right now than being locked up."

"Dr. Maxwell, Dr. Marchando, she is not being locked up." The psychiatrist, a round, heavyset man with a sincere manner, spoke in a steady, calm voice. "She is sedated, yes, and in one of the hospital rooms here. Where else would we have put her? In fact, it's the same room she's been using right along. You'll concede she needs rest. That is all we are giving her—a chance to actually *sleep*, instead of staring at the ceiling all night, knotted up with guilt, then waking up to another day of, as you put it, torturing a friend. The sleep comes out of a needle, yes, but it is still restful, deeply restful. We're not regarding her as mentally ill, just exhausted. She is not officially registered as a patient. When she wakes tomorrow morning, she will be rested—and free to go."

Mike worked his jaw, clenched and unclenched his fist. "Okay. Good. But I'm still a doctor, and I'm going to sit up with her—keep an eye on her, and on you guys. Where is she?"

The psychiatrist nodded. "All right. Nurse—could you take this gentleman down to Dr. Marchando's room? Make sure he has everything he wants."

"Later, Rupert," Mike said, and left, following the nurse.

Rupert watched him go, shrugged and scratched his unshaved face. "I'm sorry, doctor. I shouldn't have flown off the handle like that—but we're all in pretty raw shape."

"You ought to be, with what you've got to handle. If you people didn't feel the pressure—*then* I'd start to worry. Good luck, Dr. Maxwell."

"Thanks, I guess. So long." Rupert turned and walked back down the hallway to the very temporary office space the Saint E's people had loaned to the anthropologists. He had a government-issue steel desk of his own, wedged into one corner of the back office of the suite. He threaded his way past the other desks to his own little nest and tried to get a start sifting through all the paperwork.

They had wanted to be accepted by the press, and they had certainly gotten their wish. Every newspaper, every TV and radio network, every magazine and rumor mill, had featured Thursday. And, as they said in the business, public response was overwhelming.

Telegrams, express letters, telexes, faxes. telephone messages scrawled in unreadable handwriting littered his desk—missives from every corner of the civilized world; and then some. All of them urgently requesting information, or asking that this or that sample be drawn from Thursday, or that a certain test be run on her, or else requesting—or out-and-out demanding—permission for the writer to run experiments personally on the poor old girl. Barbara was constantly occupied with Thursday, and Grossington was up to his eyeballs trying to get their paper out while running his long-ignored department *and* wining and dining the hordes of potential contributors. Livingston had gotten himself signed up with some crowd doing DNA studies, and *he* wasn't around. It all left Rupert as the only member of the team able, if not altogether willing, to deal with all the incoming queries. Michael was willing to help, but he didn't know the politics of the profession. Crudely put, he didn't know who it was safe to snub and who to suck up to.

It certainly wasn't going to be a straight case of judging the requests on the merits. Some requested tests were as simple as getting her to touch her finger to her nose with her eyes closed. Some would require vivisection to perform, and some were just out-and-out ludicrous—like the grad student who had sent along a copy of the Scholastic Aptitude Test to see how Thurs would do. Rupert shrugged. Maybe they *should* give her the SAT, just to find out what colleges would take her.

Some requests were just plain weird. "Please inform as to precise extent of webbing between test subject's fingers and toes (and enclose calibrated photos), and report on degree of streamlining visible in her fur/hair covering." What were they looking for, a swim-team captain? Rupert knew he wasn't being totally fair on that one. It must be from one of the groups trying to prove humans evolved at the waterside and still retained a few semi-aquatic traits. The idea was a little weird, but you could at least call the people involved legitimate scientists—as opposed to the gen-ew-wine, accept-no-substitute, industrial-strength kooks who were writing in. The whole Thursday/ Ambrose case had attracted droves of them.

"We have PROOF that the so-called ape-man came from a sector of Africa WELL KNOWN as refuge for alien spacecraft. TWELVE SITINGS of ALIEN EXTRATERRESTRIAL UFO space vehicle have been made their. We must assume so-called ape-man is ALIEN! DESPITE Project Blue Book coverup, USAF our best hope. We Urge you to contact them (Air force) at ones with ALL details of CRETURE..."

"I have a suggestion to explain the creature you have found. May be it is the result of a prehistoric atom-bomb mutation, like in the old movies. If so, may be a dose of the opposite radiation would cure it. Hope you can tell what radiation cause it, so opposite can be found . . ."

"Was the prehistoric australian pithacine alive when the dinosaurs were here? Maybe he can tell you what they were like..."

But the shortest was also Rupert's favorite.

"How can you PROVE the australopithecine is alive?"

He sighed and got back to logging in the last of the day's mail. Supposedly, he was to write in who had written and what action was taken. Rupert had always enjoyed listing things, organizing things, but this was ridiculous. It was impossible to read them all, never mind answering them, or trying to comply with all the more useful tests. For most of the letters, he just noted N.A.T.—No Action Taken. Just trying to handle a few of the most reasonable and sane requests— and accommodate some of the scientists who had come in person— had driven the whole team to distraction, and practically given Barbara a nervous breakdown.

Thursday herself was not in much better shape. She had been tranked or knocked out altogether for one reason or another so many times that she seemed to be losing touch, forgetting things.

It had been a pretty tough week all around. His instinct was to stop it, but that wasn't a realistic solution. He knew there had to be better controls put on the experiments, or they weren't going to have a sane and living australopithecine to run the experiments *on*.

Something had to give.

MARCH

Chapter Twenty-One

The Question of Thursday
(New York *Times* Editorial)

All human beings are persons. Are, therefore, all persons human beings? At first glance, the answer is so obviously 'yes' that none of us even considers the question. Yet, this is the age when the phrase Artificial Intelligence is bandied about, and computer scientists confidentially predict the construction of a thinking computer. We have learned that chimps are more closely related to us than ever suspected, learned that chimps certainly use tools and possibly have the capacity to learn languages, learned of the impressive mentalities of dolphins and whales. This is the age in which our radio-telescopes began patiently to search the skies for signs of intelligence—seeking for signs, if you will, of personhood beyond the Solar System. In such a time, we are forced to concede at least the possibility that the indefinable something that makes us persons could also belong to a new kind of entity we are about to create, or to the great apes or cetaceans, or to beings not of this Earth. But these fascinating and disturbing possibilities have remained comfortably unrealized, and we have not been forced to confront the issue.

But now, suddenly, nonhuman personhood is more than an academic possibility, but an issue of such overwhelming importance that we devote not only this editorial of unprecedented length, but the entire Science section to the question.

Out of Africa comes a mystery named Thursday. The flabbergasted scientists who at first denied that she could possibly exist now have conceded that much. They are busily redrawing humanity's family tree, and eagerly studying Thursday for clues to our own past appearance and behavior. These are laudable efforts, but they sidestep the main question, to wit: Is she a person?

Thursday is not a human being. So much is clear from a glance at a photograph of her, or a cursory examination of the Gowrie skulls. But as we have noted, the modern world has long since conceded that a nonhuman could be a person. Therefore, her non-humanity is no bar to personhood.

It has been demonstrated that she can think and reason, that she can understand; that she can use and learn language to a limited degree; that she can use tools, that she shares with us a whole constellation of communicative gestures, expressions, and sounds. Are these enough to make her a person?

There is no debate that her general intelligence and her language abilities are far below human-normal levels. But there are hundreds of thousands, perhaps millions, of mentally disadvantaged human beings whose abilities are far below Thursday's, and yet these unfortunates are unquestionably one with ourselves—they are us, they are people.

No newborn human baby can reason or speak, and senility robs many elders of their faculties, and yet no one could or would deny the right of all these people to be called—and treated as—persons. Can we claim Thursday is not a person because she, too, lacks such skills? Obviously not.

Indeed, there is no objective measure of personhood wherein a bona fide human being could not be found who scored lower than Thursday. Is she, therefore, a person? Is she one of us—strangely different, but imbued with that spark a less secular age would not hesitate to call a soul?

The outside world is beginning to deal with Thursday and her species. Already, new expeditions have been dispatched to Gabon and the tribe that breeds these creatures. We must deal with them. But deal with them as what? As apes that walk upright, or as persons whose intelligence is somewhat limited and of a different nature than our own?

All human beings are persons. It has taken untold bloodshed—the catastrophe of the American Civil War, the war against Hitler, and a thousand other battles large and small, to force humanity to accept that idea. Recent history, from Ethiopia, where the starved were driven like cattle, from Cambodia where entire generations were destroyed, to Central America and its bestial violence, to the Gulags of the Soviet Union, to the United States and the hate-addled ravings of the Ku Klux Klan—that simple idea is still challenged, still fragile. Now it might face new danger, posed by a new question: Are all persons human beings?

To put that question in sharper focus: Is Thursday a person?

Our answer will affect every field of human activity from biology and psychology to religion and philosophy, from politics and labor policy to the civil rights movement and education. It is an answer we cannot afford to get wrong.

The world has learned of the strange incidents in Mississippi in 1851, and of the western world's first contact with *Australopithecus boisei*. That contact came in the midst of slavery and the degradation of human life; in short, in the midst of treating humans like animals. What upheaval awaits us if Thursday is a person and we treat her kind with such arrogance? And yet, if she is an animal, what storm gates of hatred might we open by treating her like a person? It is too easy to imagine how the hatemongers might use the precedent to claim, as our ancestors did, that certain human beings were not people.

Is Thursday a person?

A more delicate and dangerous question in human relations can scarce be imagined. Misjudge Thursday's personhood, and we threaten our own.

▼◆▼

Amanda Banks reached out once again to take Thursday's hand, gently moving the fingers into the correct position one more time and then held up the object under discussion. "Ball," she said, and signed the word with her free hand. "Ball."

Thursday drew her lips back from her teeth, the very picture of concentration, and made the sign herself. "*'Awl. 'Awl*," she said. Barbara watched intently, and patted Thursday on the shoulder to reassure her. Thursday turned to her and repeat the sign without trying to speak. *Ball.*

"Good, very good," Amanda said, echoing her own words in sign language. "Thursday learn fast. More next-day."

"*'Ore*." Thursday agreed. "*Kood, ve-ey kood.*."

"Bye for now. Bye bye." Amanda forced a smile and stood up. Thursday and Barbara both took her cue and rose from their chairs.

"Dr. Marchando, could you stop back here after you see Thursday to her room?" Amanda asked. "There are a few things I'd like to ask you about."

Barbara nodded, her face betraying no emotion at all. Leading Thursday by the hand, she left the room. Amanda closed the door behind them and instantly scrabbled in her pocketbook for a cigarette. It was tough to find the time and place where it was socially acceptable to light up around the people she worked with back in Atlanta—and even more so with this crowd up in Washington. Amanda was a language specialist at the Yerkes Primate Research Center in Atlanta, on a road trip to work with this new-type primate, Thursday. Amanda liked to think of herself as a tough cookie, hard to rattle, but this crowd got her nervous. It was just as well they had gotten space at Saint E's—they *ought* to be in a loony bin. She finally found the cigarettes and dug them out. She put it to her lips, flicked her lighter, and found she needed both hands to hold the lighter steady. Great. Now *she* had the shakes.

Hell, the atmosphere around here was enough to drive anyone nuts. Amanda had sometimes worried that she and her fellow primatologists were playing God or Frankenstein with their apes—teaching them language, capriciously reshaping their behaviors just to see what would happen. But compared to what was going on here, the Yerkes crowd wasn't involved in any issues at all. Amanda had arrived a week after Thursday made her debut. The pressure on these people—a lot of it self-imposed—was enormous. In the last few days maybe, just maybe, it was all starting to let up a little. Perhaps humanity was getting used to the idea of its new relations.

Amanda considered herself in the newly replaced one-way mirror. Since Thursday clearly understood that the people on the other side could see her—she waved to them—Amanda couldn't quite see why they had bothered to fix it. She took another look at herself and wondered why she had bothered herself. She glared at the mirror, cataloging her flaws. There was something wrong with the buttons on her white lab coat, and it kept falling open to reveal the baggy jeans and sweatshirt underneath. Her luxuriant red hair was once again escaping from the tight, professional-looking bun she was trying for. She had dispensed with makeup again today, and her pale face seemed a featureless blank under the unforgiving fluorescent lighting. And, of course, there were the usual ten or fifteen pounds that she could do without. Not what the teacher of a new race was supposed to look like, but what the hell.

The door squeaked open behind her and Barbara came back in. "You wanted to talk, Amanda?" she asked, her voice flat and neutral. She looked bad, Amanda thought, worse every day. She had stopped losing weight, but she hadn't gained any back, and she had stopped paying much attention to her appearance. Her clothes were often wrinkled, her hair was mussed, and she wasn't worrying about makeup anymore. Amanda had never put much stock in such things, but she knew it was a bad sign when someone who thought they were important gave up on them.

"Yeah, Barbara, I did." Amanda hurriedly stubbed out her cigarette into the ashtray she carried around and sat down in one of rickety wooden chairs. "You're the boss here, but your group brought me on board to do two things—to find out how significant Thursday's language abilities were, and to teach her as much language as possible. When it's time for language lessons, this is *my* shop—and you're getting in the way, to put it bluntly. I am trying to teach Thursday a simplified American Sign Language, and you're slowing the process down, simply by being here. I teach her a sign, she tries it and then she looks to you for approval. You don't know ASL. You nod yes and tell her very good when she's done it wrong—and she's picked up a new bad habit to unlearn."

Barbara sat down facing Amanda and grabbed the seat of her chair on either side, as if she were afraid of being pulled off it. She twined her feet around each other and looked down at them for a long time. "But I need to learn it, too," she said at last. "If Thursday can talk, I need to be able to talk to her."

"But you're a—" Amanda stopped herself. She had been about to say her "you're a person, a human being," but there was no point in starting up *that* argument again. "You're aware of what a language is," she went on smoothly. "Thursday isn't. As best I can tell, what she learned back with the Utaani was on the level of commands you'd teach a dog. 'Come. Go. Fetch.' More sophisticated than that, but not by much. She has to learn how much more language is *capable* of— which is something you already know. When you learn ASL, you're just learning a new set of symbols that closely match up with what you already know. The ideas of grammar and syntax and word order are burned into your head already—and since ASL is patterned on English, you don't have that many new rules to learn. Thursday has to start practically from scratch. Not just words, but the *idea* of words, the idea of abstractions. I can just show you the sign for 'love' or 'justice' or 'danger,' and you'd be all set. It might be months, or years, before Thursday has enough vocabulary to understand those concepts—if she ever does learn that much. I don't know that she is capable of it.

"But that's another issue. You, and all the other workers here, could learn more, better, faster, by letting me hold a regular, daily, ASL class—a class designed for people who can hear and understand English. You'd be doing Thursday more good that way. She'd learn faster if she just had one teacher, and no one distracting her."

Barbara didn't say anything.

"A separate class. Is that okay?" Amanda asked, as gently as she could.

Barbara nodded absently. "Yeah, sure. But can't I stay here with her for her own classes with you?"

Amanda sighed and found herself wishing for another cigarette. This was getting to be like the old days, back working in special education. "Barbara, I know what you want for Thursday. You want her free—you want to find some way for her to stop being a laboratory animal. You know she's been a slave, a work animal, all her life. But you can't teach her to be free and still walk around holding her hand every moment. You need to let go. Leave her in class with her teacher, and trust me."

Barbara shrugged, and seemed to relax a little. "Okay. I—I *know*, intellectually, that you're right, but that doesn't make it any easier. I brought her into all this, and I just feel so *responsible* for her." She paused and then spoke quickly, as if she were afraid of the question she was asking. "Do you think she's smart enough to learn?"

Amanda cocked her head to one side for a moment. "Slippery question. Language—language is a window on the mind. There are cases of normal, even brilliant men and women, losing all ability to speak or communicate. They were still as smart as they ever were, but a stroke or accident had taken out the parts of the brain in charge of talking, reading, writing. And there are plenty of idiots out there who can talk, God knows. Thursday could be smarter, much smarter than we think, and yet not have the tools to tell us about it. She could be full of fascinating insights we'll never hear about."

"Amanda, don't get into philosophy," Barbara said, her voice urgent. "Tell me straight, without the grey areas—*how much can she learn? Is there any chance she can learn enough for meaningful communication?*"

"Christ. That takes me back." Amanda stood up and started walking around the room. "Before I got into this line of work, I used to work teaching special ed—retarded kids, deaf kids, bright kids with learning disabilities that meant they couldn't ever read past the first-grade level. Kids who were brain-damaged in accidents, dying kids. And they all had mothers. Mothers who wanted to know, 'How much can he learn? Will he ever have a normal life? Can he learn to dress himself and tie his shoes? If we keep trying will he start to remember. . . ' And, except for the parents who finally accepted the reality of their situations, none of them really *wanted* straight answers, would accept straight answers—or even hear the straight answers. They wanted *hope.* They wanted some tiny little shred of a possibility that Timmy might wake up tomorrow and be a normal, perfect kid.

"And the way they *got* that from me, the way they forced me to give that hope, the way they forced me to give them the cruel, unfair, unrealistic hope they *needed,* was to find something unknowable. So, finally, I'd have to admit that yes, the tumor might respond to treatment, or yes, he might regain motor function, or yes, the hearing loss *might* be temporary. After all, they'd tell me, you don't know what *caused* the problem, so how can you say it will never be cured?

"And now *you* come in here like one of the saddest of those parents, and ask me that. And I know and you know that *any* answer I give you might be wrong, because I *can't* know for certain. After all, we're dealing with a whole new *species* here. How *could* I know?"

The hell with it, Amanda thought. She pulled the cigarettes out of her purse and lit up. Filthy habit. "On the other hand. On the other hand. Besides my special-ed work, I'm fresh from Yerkes and all sorts of work on language ability on apes—real hands-on stuff, years of study and experience concerning language and learning among primates. And now I've had a month working with Thursday, enough to get a feel for the situation, enough for a reasonable assessment. And that assessment will in large part determine what kind of life Thursday will have, what kind of life she is capable of. Will she be a lab rat or a very rare and special kind of person? If she can demonstrate intelligent use of language, we have no right to treat her as an experimental subject. But if she can't demonstrate that intelligence . . ." Amanda shrugged. "So do you want the tenth-of-a-percent hope, or the ninety-nine-and-nine-tenths truth?"

Barbara shifted in her seat and didn't speak.

Amanda grinned. "Yeah. Loaded question. I wouldn't answer it either. So I'll tell you the truth anyway. She certainly understands a large number of spoken words, more than any other non-human could. She has some problems with retaining what she has learned, but that shows signs of getting better. I can't say whether or not she's got good enough vocal folds or a good enough larynx for forming speech.

Her speech apparatus is certainly not like human-normal, but I've seen people who learned to talk with worse equipment. However, teaching her to use the vocal equipment she's got is probably not worth the effort. Forming speech is an extremely complex process, and at best it might take her years of very slow progress to get much past where she is. She tries very hard to speak, yet it's clearly difficult for her.

"But if she doesn't know how to use her voice, she *does* know how to use her hands. Simplified ASL is probably the best bet, because hand-signals should be simpler for her to learn. Unfortunately, she seems to have some sort of resistance to learning a signed language, and prefers spoken word-symbols—though that behavior might just be starting to break down. You may have missed it, but she didn't try to vocalize 'ball' the last time she signed it today—which is the first time for that.

"So there is hope that she can learn more words. But can she learn *language*, something that goes past learning responses and parroting them to get a hug or a treat? Rover the dog rolls over and plays dead in order to get a dog-bone. Does that make the roll-over-play-dead movement the doggish word for dog bone? Obviously not—though it took us years to realize that the chimps who learned to ask for a cookie weren't connecting the sign for 'cookie' with the object. Mostly, they had learned that the gesture would be *rewarded*—with a cookie. Just about all of their gestures could be linked to that kind of reward training or pain-avoidance. There's good evidence that the chimpish language ability past that—chimps inventing words, for example—was really the human researcher imposing his interpretation on what the chimps were doing.

"Can Thursday go past that? I don't know. I can say for certain that she will never, never, never be as smart as you or I. She will never have a large vocabulary. She just doesn't have a brain big enough to hold many words. She also doesn't have the brain structure, the sophisticated language centers we have. In some ways she behaves like a patient with partial aphasia—partial speech loss. She reminds me of patients whose languages centers— Broca's area, Wernicke's area, and the smaller speech loci—have all been damaged somehow. Those patients can improve, but they can't come all the way back.

"Her brain isn't really built for speech, for language. Can she overcome *that*? I don't know. Can she get past asking for cookies? Can she express an idea? Someday, she might. Never as well or as clearly or as complexly as we do, but she might do it a little. I don't know. I really don't know. *Maybe* she can. And that's an honest, fifty-fifty chance maybe, not a million-to-one shot."

Barbara smiled, for what looked like the first time in a long time. "I can't ask better than that."

Amanda tried to smile back. But she could see that look, that tragic look of a parent who has found hope—pointless, unfair, unfounded and sustaining hope—in Barbara's eyes.

▼♦▼

GABON APE-MAN EXPEDITION SET TO GO
Walter Pinkman, Boston Globe staff

An expedition to collect more specimens of *Australopithecus boisei*, the same species as Thursday, the famous so-called 'ape-woman,' is making final arrangements for departure from Boston. The expedition, delayed by prolonged negotiations with the Gabonese government, is being led by Dr. William Lowell of Harvard University.

When the evidence for *A. boisei* surviving to modern times was first reported, Dr. Lowell was prominent in the ranks of scoffers. Now, he has enthusiastically changed his mind. "I can flatly say that I have never been happier to be proved wrong," Dr. Lowell said. "My chief regret is that I said some very harsh and unfair things about Dr. Grossington and his team when their work was first published. I now understand that the way it was reported was quite outside their control. I have offered my heartfelt apologies to the Grossington/Marchando team, and I am delighted to report they accepted my apologies with great kindness and grace."

Dr. Lowell still holds some strong opinions on the boiseans, as he calls them. "There have been endless discussions in the media about the 'rights' of these creatures, suggestions that they are people, and not simply another type of animal. These are patent nonsense. A boisean has no more—and no less—right to decent treatment than any other animal. They are a precious scientific resource that must be carefully managed, but they are not a fit topic for any discussion of human rights. After all, they aren't human."

Dr. Lowell hopes to bring back several breeding pairs to be housed in a facility now under construction near Dracut, Massachusetts. "If a population can be established here, the possibilities for research are endless. Not just animal behavior, but medical, psychological, and product-safety testing as well. Obviously, we are talking about a set of projects for twenty years or more, but I feel that now is the time to pursue this exciting opportunity for the future."

There is one other mystery Dr. Lowell is interested in solving. Briefly put, the boiseans were found in a place they shouldn't have been. "All the australopithecines, all the early hominids, were supposed to be savannah-dwellers, living in West African open plainlands," Dr. Lowell explained. "Now we find them in deep jungle in West Africa, a totally different environment. It could be that our understanding of the early hominids is way off. Maybe they did live in jungle areas as well, but we never found fossils there because it's tough for fossils to form in jungle, and even tougher to find them in a jungle. Or maybe this population is the only one to migrate into the jungle, which is why they survived. Or maybe the ancestors of the tribesmen who keep them migrated from the east a few hundred or thousand years ago, bringing the boiseans with them. Whatever the answer, we hope to find it out, and bring back some splendid research animals in the process."

▼◆▼

Dr. Grossington glanced at his watch as Livingston slumped into the daily morning meeting. Livingston was ten minutes late, and obviously ill at ease. It was the first meeting Livingston had gotten to for a while, thanks to the fussing about of the biochemists, who wanted to check everything eight times. Liv sidled in around the edge of the meeting room and scooped up a stack of doughnuts and a big cup of coffee. He probably hadn't had much chance to eat recently.

Dr. Grossington, free for the moment of the endless fund raising he had to do, was chairing the meeting. The original group had grown into practically a whole institute. The newcomers—the behaviorists, the language specialists, the support workers and assistants—had started to refer to the old timers as the "Gang of Four." Grossington was glad to hear the kidding. Maybe it meant morale was improving.

Pete Ardley had been signed on as press agent, on the theory of better the devil you knew. Besides, he was willing to work cheap, thanks to some book contract he had signed. A few strings had been pulled, and Barbara's ex-husband had been granted a leave of absence from his hospital, so he was on board too, overseeing the medical procedures done on Thursday—for example, making sure there weren't so many blood samples taken that she got anemia. Apparently, he and Barbara were back together again.

There was a certain amount of research that couldn't be done at Saint Elizabeth's. Analytic stuff for the most part. They farmed out the work to the labs equipped for it. The Saint E's staff was no doubt glad of that. Thursday and her entourage had already taken over two outbuildings and had designs on a third. But that was the sort of administrative problem he was supposed to solve on his own. He took another sip of his coffee as the various working groups went through the daily progress reports. The team approved the idea of a daily ASL session for the staffers, talked through a half-dozen other ideas, and went over what the outside world was saying about the project. Grossington came around to Livingston last, perhaps noticing that the young man was ill at ease. "If that closes the routine reports, I believe that Livingston Jones has some news for us. Mr. Jones?"

Livingston hesitated for a moment, and then rose from his seat. That in itself was a signal they had gotten some results. Important news required a bit more formality than slouching back in his chair.

"Well, as most of you know, I've been working with a group of biochemists who have been taking a look at Thursday, examining her at the cellular and molecular level—and they've got some news. But before I tell you what it is, I'd better give you some quick background. You'll all have heard the term molecular anthropology. The idea of M.A. is to compare proteins, antibodies, and DNA between various species of primates, and measure the degree of difference between them.

"It's been known for some time that there's sort of a molecular clock, ticking along in our genes. The clock works this way: tiny micro-mutations occur at a pretty constant rate in all our genes, from one generation to the next. It's of course a random process, so you can't predict when a *given* mutation when occur, but the overall *rate* of these random mutations *is* measurable, so that you can predict very well how *many* mutations will occur in a given time interval, a time interval on the order of thousands or millions of years.

"What the M.A. people did, some time ago, was measure the degree of difference between human DNA and chimp and gorilla DNA. They discovered that there is only about a one percent difference between ape and human DNA. By taking that amount of change and comparing it to the established 'clock' of random microchanges, they could learn how recently we split from the apes, how long ago we had a common ancestor.

"It's been established that we split from gorillas about seven million years ago, and from chimps about five million years ago." Livingston leaned down and pushed his papers around, stalling for a minute. "Now, needless to say, a lot of people had trouble with these ideas—that our DNA is ninety-nine percent identical to a chimps, and that we shared a common ancestor with chimps—for all practical purposes, *were* chimps—only five million years ago. But that's nothing. Now people are *really* going to go bananas." The people around the table laughed, and Livingston looked baffled until he noticed his own unconscious joke and smiled, wanly and awkwardly. The smile didn't last long. "I've been in the M.A. labs at UCLA, watching them run Thursday's blood proteins, antibodies, and DNA through the same sort of tests—as well as some new ones that were just invented a few months ago."

Livingston looked around the room, and something in his

expression tied Grossington's stomach into a knot. "The results are that—that she's human."

Barbara looked up sharply, suddenly attentive.

Livingston kept talking. "On the molecular level, the measure of DNA similarity—she falls within the range of human values. She is no more different from us than we are from each other."

"Livingston, that's ridiculous," Rupert protested from the far end of the table.

"Maybe so, but it's also true," Liv replied unhappily. "Let me see if I can make it a little clearer. Each of us is of course different from one another. Some of that's environment, and some of it is genetic. There are thousands of micro-mutations that decide whether you're black or white, what color your eyes will be, that sort of thing. If not for those mutations, we'd all look alike. You might say we're all mutants. The trouble is, a major mutation can look just like a minor one when you're down there, looking at the DNA. No one has even made a real start on actually mapping the entire human genetic code, and we still have no idea what the vast majority of DNA sequences actually mean. Crooked pinky fingers run in my family—most of the men have them. Obviously, there's a sequence somewhere in my DNA for that, but no one know which one it is. At our current state of knowledge, there's no way to tell it from the sequences that decide how curly my hair is, or the shape of my nose, or the relative sizes of my teeth—or how big my brain is."

"There are thousands or millions of micro-mutations in each individual's genes, but each of us has billions or trillions of DNA sequences. Compare the total number of sequences to the number of mutations, and you'll see that in spite of the many genetic differences between any two human beings, there are far more similarities.

"How can you say Thursday's DNA is like ours when no one's mapped human DNA in the first place?" Amanda Banks asked.

"Good question. Let me see if I can explain. When the molecular anthropologists compare two sets of DNA, they don't go through and compare every codon. If they tried, they'd be at it till doomsday. Too many codons. What they do instead is take strands of DNA from each animal, and divide each strand in half, lengthwise. That's easier than it sounds—the strands will split under gentle heating. So, let's say you have the left-hand strand from a human and the right-hand side from a test animal. You drop both of them into a test tube and basic biochemistry says they'll stick together at each point where the two strands have the same coding—and *not* stick where they are different. Measure the strength of the hybrid strands' bond and you've *directly* measured the overall similarity of the two parent strands. So we can measure similarity without having to read the code itself.

"Now, as I said, all mutations are not equally important, and a little genetic mutation can result in a big change in the organism. It's just one tiny change or two that causes such drastic disorders as sickle-cell anemia, or Down's syndrome, or some types of manic-depressive disorders.

"Somewhere in the genetic differences between Thursday and humans are a thousand or two equally tiny mutations that spell out the difference between her and us—but they are hard to find, camouflaged behind the billions or trillions of identical codings and the thousands or millions of unimportant mutations. The point is, there are DNA differences between Thursday and ourselves, but they are so small we can't spot them easily, and a key coding looks just like a meaningless little blivet of code for earwax consistency. Or else four or five widely separated bits of code could be working in concert to determine intelligence, or manual dexterity—-or toenail toughness. *But we don't know which are the key micro-mutations.* On a molecular level, the codings that make Thursday's brain a third the size of yours and mine are probably not much larger, or more important, or more detectable, than the codings that decide that one *human's* brain will be larger than another human's.

There was a dead silence in the room.

"There are two other findings," Livingston said quietly. "In spite of the closeness of the DNA match, there are other means, such as faster-mutating mitochondrial DNA, for dating the split, the time when Thursday's ancestors split from ours. It was between 2.5 and 3 million years ago, which shouldn't be much of a surprise. It fits in pretty well with the fossil evidence that has been gathered over the years.

"But the last thing. The last thing is the worst. Needless to say, the molecular anthropology team was bothered by the incredible similarity between australopithecine and human DNA. They expected it to be close, but not close as it was. They ran new tests examining nuclear DNA piece by piece, instead of long strands all at once.

They—they found some things in the DNA, long sequences, that aren't just extremely similar to human DNA—they are *identical* to human DNA. They *are* human. When they did go through, codon by codon for the sections of DNA they *have* mapped, there were *no* unknown codings in those sections of Thursday's genetic material. If those duplicate zones are factored out, Thursday gets to be a bit less similar to us, to be right where she should be, midway between humans and chimps.

"But those duplicate zones tell us something else." Livingston paused again for a moment. "Part of the reason there is so little difference between human and australopithecine DNA is that there have been what the M.A. people called human 'intrusions' into the australopithecine gene pool. They can't yet tell if it happened a hundred years ago, or two hundred thousand years back—or both. But it's happened, very clearly it's happened.

"Humans, true humans like you and me, have interbred with Thursday's fairly recent ancestors."

Jeffery Grossington found himself wandering again that night, lost in thought. Boiseans and humans interbreeding? His whole world was slipping away, again. He walked the grounds of the hospital, and found his steps leading to the outbuilding where Thursday was kept. On impulse, he went in, went upstairs to her room. He went in through the observation room, and looked at her for a long time through the one-way glass.

She was sitting on the floor, playing with one of the manual dexterity tests, putting the right-shaped block in the right-shaped hole. Her movements were smooth, practiced, skilled, and she wore an expression of calm thought.

Grossington opened the door to her room proper and she looked up, a bit startled. "*Hello, Thursday,*" he signed.

"*Hello.*"

"*What are you doing?*" he asked.

She gestured toward the blocks. "*I try learn. Learn blocks.*"

Grossington smiled. "*Me too. I try to learn.*"

Thursday cocked her head at him and looked puzzled. "*You know all. What you need try learn?*"

Grossington shook his head. Suddenly, he remembered a question at that disastrous first press conference. The reporter wanted to know what he would ask a live australopithecine. It occurred to him he *had* never asked it. *"I try learn answer to question. Maybe can you tell me. Thursday—what is a human being? What is a person?"*

Thursday stared at him again. *"I not know."*

Grossington shook his head sadly. "Nobody does," he said out loud. "Not anymore."

Chapter Twenty-Two

A PETITION

WHEREAS by their own admission scientists representing the Smithsonian Institution, and by extension, the government and people of the United States, did unlawfully kidnap and detain a person known as Thursday while in the Nation of Gabon, and

WHEREAS these same scientists, with the connivance and assistance of the United States Embassy to Gabon, the United States Air Force, and other United States government agencies, did illegally remove this same Thursday from Gabon to the United States in violation of international law regarding piracy and kidnapping, and

WHEREAS this same person Thursday has been held against her will, with no charges preferred or intended against her, and has been denied her right to legal counsel and representation when such representation was offered to her by the American Civil Liberties Union, the World Wildlife Fund Legal Defense Fund, Greenpeace, and many other worthy organizations, and

WHEREAS Thursday has been the subject of repeated and relentless so-called scientific tests conducted on her person without her consultation or consent and

WHEREAS the Federal Bureau of Investigation and the United States Immigration and Naturalization Service are charged with enforcing laws involving kidnapping and the illegal abduction of persons into this country,

WE THE UNDERSIGNED hereby petition the Federal Bureau of Investigation and the United States Immigration and Naturalization Service to assure Thursday the full protection of the law, to free her from her illegal and unjust imprisonment, and to provide her with all lawful assistance, allowing her to choose of her own free will whether to remain here or to return to her native shores, and to investigate and prosecute those responsible for this flagrant violation of federal civil rights laws . . . .

▼◆▼

Barbara hesitated before entering Thursday's room. Was today the day to try the first step? Thursday had made great strides in her signing over the past month, and for that matter, so had Barbara. She had some intelligence all right, but would it be sufficient to get the idea across today? Was Thursday up to understanding enough? Would she ever be? *Forget it*, Barbara thought. *There'll never be as many answers as questions in this business.* She took a deep breath and opened the door.

There was Thursday, sitting on the edge of her bed, looking with rapt attention at the drawings in a picture book—that she was holding upside down. Another intriguing mystery. It was pretty clear that she could see and understand that a flat picture was a representation of something else. She could see a kitten in a picture of a kitten—if you showed her the picture right side up. But she simply could not see it as the same image when she looked at it upside down. Could not, or perhaps *would* not. Some of the researchers thought there were times when she was just as happy to look at the shapes and colors as abstracts, and choose not to puzzle out a picture's meaning, whereas a human eye would insist on trying to fit the pictures to a pattern, an image. A human would match the upside-down picture to an upside-down image of a cat, realize the book was the wrong way to, and correct the error. Thursday didn't work that way. By choice or capacity, to her, one copy of Mother Goose was four equally interesting books—one each right-side up, upside down, and on its side either way.

Barbara made a scuffling noise to get Thursday's attention without startling her. Thursday looked up from her book, grunted with pleasure, and dropped Mother Goose on the floor. The whole room had long since lost its prison-barracks spareness and developed a sloppy, comfortably lived-in look, with the toys and gadgets used to test Thursday strewn everywhere, and bright-colored blankets and pillows scattered on the floor. It reminded Barbara of her own room as a teen-ager.

"Hello, Thursday," Barbara signed.

"Hello, Barbara friend," Thursday signed back. *"Work learn today?"*

"No, no. Today for rest," Barbara replied. It was Sunday, and there was only a skeleton staff on duty. That was all to the good, and part of the reason Barbara had chosen today for this little chat.

"Rest outside?" Thursday asked hopefully. *"Go out, see sky?"*

"Cold, cold today." Barbara cautioned.

"Thursday good. Thursday put on coat, promise."

"Not take coat off? Promise?" Barbara asked. This was a breakthrough of sorts. Not only was Thursday volunteering to put the coat on, which was a first—she had made the associational jump between it being cold and having to wear warm clothes. It had taken a month of daily wheedling to get that far. Progress with her was like that—sometimes so tiny and subtle that you could barely notice it. Every day a word or two more, every day the old words used a little better, every day a tiny surprise. And it all helped, it certainly helped. It made Barbara feel she was right, gave some purpose to the risk, focused her attention. It was good therapy for Barbara. She was taking care of herself again, paying attention to how she dressed and looked. That helped, too, gave her the confidence for what she was planning.

"Promise," Thursday said, nodding her head and looking most sincere.

"Outside, then."

▼◆▼

They dug Thursday's coat—an enormous army-surplus trenchcoat with a warm lining—out of the closet and got it on her. Thursday let Barbara fuss with the buttons and zippers, and waited patiently while Barbara buttoned her own coat back up. She watched her friend, and wondered again about her. Barbara was the only real link between her old place and this one. Thursday knew Barbara felt things about her that no one else did, though she did not know why.

Thursday did not understand many things, but that didn't bother her much. She had an almost fatalistic lack of curiosity about some things, among them why she was here, what this place was, why the people here did such strange things with her. She had never questioned why she had been with the others, the Utaani. That had been part of the natural order of things, the way it had always been. She had managed to transfer that attitude to new circumstances. It never occurred to her to question such matters, any more than she wondered about why the sky was blue or why the air smelled good outside. The world was what it was. It swirled around her, did with her what it would, and it never occurred to her she might have a voice in how it treated her.

Deep inside her the instinct for escape, for freedom was still there. That would be with her no matter where she went, whatever she did. But now, today, being all alone with these strange new ones, and in spite of their sometimes strange and cruel tricks, she was now freer than she had ever been. For the moment, at least, that satisfied her. Besides, the worst of the cruel times here seemed to be over. Barbara and Michael were always there to stop the others from doing things that scared her or hurt her too much.

She followed Barbara through the door, down the hallway, and then down the stairs. Stairs were still a little tricky for her, but she was getting used to them. Another hallway, another door, and they were outside. Thursday stopped on the threshold and closed her eyes, breathing deep, drinking in the cold, crisp, clean air.

▼◆▼

Barbara turned to watch her friend, and smiled. Thursday so obviously delighted in the outdoors, the spare beauty of a late-winter day. It must be so different for her, a whole new range of sensations impossible in the jungles. Barbara shivered a bit, and thought once again how the cold didn't seem to bother Thursday. In some ways, she was better adapted to it, of course. She had a built-in fur coat, for one thing, and her heavily callused feet seemed immune to the cold. That was probably just as well—it would probably be impossible to get Thursday into shoes.

At last, Thursday opened her eyes and looked about herself, at the empty trees and sleeping earth. Barbara reached out and took her hand, and the two of them began to stroll the grounds of the hospital. They made a strange pair, the carefully coifed and elegantly dressed scientist in her trim and stylish jacket, hand in hand with the gawky, ambling barefoot figure in an oversized trenchcoat.

They came to a wooden bench and sat down. Here, away from prying eyes, Barbara hoped she could talk—or sign, rather—to Thursday in private.

"Thursday, I ask question. Do you wonder why we do the things we do to you?"

Thursday frowned a surprisingly human frown that puckered up her forehead. *"A little. But what is, what is."* A typically fatalistic answer for Thursday.

"Let me try and tell," Barbara signed. *"Your kind and mine. They are different, are the same. Do you see that? Some ways same, some ways not?"*

Thursday nodded enthusiastically. *"Yes, yes. Look same, walk same, hands same. Not—"*she hesitated*"—not make words inside same."*

"Make words inside—that is called think."

"Not think same. Not do *same."*

"Not do same," Barbara agreed. *"That is why we do things to you. To see what we do same and different. Is blood same? Is hair different? Is thinking, making-words-inside, all different, or is some the same?"*

"Why must know? Why try you so hard?" Thursday asked.

Barbara hesitated, trying to find a way to explain, trying to make it clear without frightening her. *"I tell why, but it might scare you. Don't be scared. I not let them hurt you. Will you be not-scared?"*

"Not-scared. Tell why."

"We need know—are your kind like dog, like cat, like squirrel, like monkey—or like humans, our kind?" Thank God for flash-cards.

Thursday had enjoyed learning the names of animals, and looking at the pictures. *"Those animals—cat, dog, monkey, all others, not think, not make-words-inside at all like our kind."*

Barbara hesitated once again. They had got the idea of rules across to Thursday, but not right or wrong, and of course, they had not even tried to explain law, or justice. Thursday regarded good and bad not as ethical standards, but questions of how a thing tasted or felt. When Barbara needed to say a thing was good or bad, fair or unfair, right or wrong, the best she could do was to tell her what the rules were, and Thursday had a disturbing tendency to a knee-jerk, instinctive obedience to the rules—if there were a chance she would get caught. She would and did break every rule in sight if she could get away with it. So, instead of morality or ethics, Barbara had to explain the situation in terms of authority. It was a most unsatisfactory solution, but the best they could do. *"The rules say that humans can do things to animals that are not-humans. We can make them work hard, we can kill them and eat them, we can do a thing to them first to see if it would hurt humans. It is against the rules to do that with humans. Humans can go places, do things other animals not allowed to do. Those are the rules."*

"If I human, I do many things?"

"Yes, many, many."

"If they learn I not-human, rules say I be like old ones made me. Word is?"

"Word is slave." That summed it up pretty well. She and the other australopithecines would indeed be what the old ones, the Utaani, had made them—slaves, of one sort of another. Test animals, freak show gimmicks, who knows, maybe even real, honest to God household slaves. Damn it, right or wrong, mad or sane, she would not be a party to that. She would do what she had to, and damn the consequences. *"Yes, but not you. Never, never you. You will never be slave. I promise, like you promise to wear coat. I will stop that, even if I break every rule there is to do it."* Barbara stopped, got hold of herself. She was signing too fast, and the sentences were too complex. There was no way Thursday could follow it all. *I stop them making you slave. But I cannot protect all your kind. More people visit old ones, take more of your kind. Those others, I cannot break the rules for all of them.*

"No. Too many, lots of rules."

"Are you sad because your kind will be slaves?"

"Sad. Sad-sad."

"You can help. You make rules that your kind is human."

"Make rule?"

"Show you like me. Me human, so you human. Against rules for human be slaves."

Thursday stared at her for a long time, tilting her head this way and that, thinking, puzzling out the logic. "*Yes, yes,*" she signed at last. "*Make me like you. Good. Good.*"

Barbara looked at her friend. That was the first time she had described an intangible thing as good. Another breakthrough.

"Damn straight it's good," she said out loud, not bothering to sign what she was saying, simply talking so the sound of her own voice would make her feel better. "No matter what we have to do to get it done." Was she as brave as she was trying to sound? "No matter what," she repeated. "Come on, let's get back inside."

▼◆▼

THURSDAY A LEGAL HOT POTATO

(UPI) WASHINGTON, D.C. No one in government knows what to do with Thursday, the australopithecine recently presented to the public. Is she an animal or a person? That question must be answered before anything can be done about her, and pressure to do something is growing from a number of groups.

Neither Thursday herself nor the people who are, depending on your point of view, either caring for her or imprisoning her, think that anything much needs to be done about her, but that hasn't stopped the legal speculation.

If she is an animal, she was imported to this country illegally, and either the U.S. Fish and Wildlife Service or the Customs Service might claim jurisdiction and impound or destroy her, according to several legal scholars.

If she is a human being, a person, then, since she seems to have come to this country willingly but in apparent violation of the law, arguably she is an illegal alien, under the jurisdiction of the Immigration and Naturalization Service, unless she is a political refugee, in which case the Department of State is in charge. Even if jurisdiction were established, however, what action the responsible agency could or would take is not obvious.

It can be argued that she was gulled into following Dr. Marchando out of the jungle, and so was abducted by the Federal Government. Some legal scholars, following that line of reasoning, claim that she should be repatriated to Gabon and granted monetary restitution for her illegal abduction and detention. A petition demanding her release from federal 'custody' and repatriation to Gabon was circulated by the American Civil Liberties Union, the World Wildlife Fund, and several other organizations. Copies of the petition, with over 100,000 signatures attached, were delivered to the Immigration and Naturalization Service.

But not every one of Thursday's well-wishers want her sent home. Others, pointing to her willing departure from Gabon, regardless of destination, and also noting that she was held in a form of slavery in Gabon, have claimed she should be regarded as a political refugee and granted asylum, and indeed, papers to that effect have been filed in federal court.

Despite all the hypothetical legal arguments, no government agency seems at all willing to take the lead in this case. . . .

"Ahhh. God bless the man who invented the brewski." Rupert lifted his bottle again and took another long slug. "This is just what the doctor ordered, isn't it, Doctor?"

Mike grinned. "Actually, I believe I prescribed Heineken, not Bud."

"Don't bother me with details," Rupert said.

"This is a weird place, Rupert," Livingston announced, having taken a good look around. He settled back a little deeper into the blown-out springs of the booth's ancient bench seat. "Why the hell do they call it the Tune Inn?"

"'Cause it's got a jukebox, I guess," Rupert said.

"Every place has a jukebox," Livingston protested.

"Yeah, but not every place has surly help, big cheeseburgers, the decor of a backwoods cracker bar four blocks from the Capitol Building, or a clientele of yuppies who don't understand that they're not welcome."

"Or the wrong end of a deer stuffed and mounted on the wall," Livingston muttered. "So this is life in the big city."

The jukebox started up again, playing so loudly it was impossible to identify the song. "Shut up and enjoy the atmosphere," Rupert shouted cheerfully. The wizened old man behind the bar cursed to himself, came out from behind the bar and reached down the back of the jukebox. The noise subsided enough that normal conversation was just barely possible.

Mike Marchando grinned and took a sip of his own beer. In the midst of the turmoil over Thursday, he had found greater self-satisfaction, a better and clearer view of himself, than he had ever had. For the first time he could remember, his own struggling to get ahead was not, even in his own mind, the most important thing—and somehow, not being the least bit important in all the crises had taught him something without his noticing the lesson. Maybe it was simply that the grand questions Thursday inspired made his own endless struggles to prove himself and test those around him seem a lot less important. Maybe it was being part of a team, a group of equals all working toward the same thing, rather than one of a hundred medical students competing against each other. It didn't matter. For once, Michael wasn't interested in analyzing things too closely. He was happy with himself, and that was enough.

"So what's up at your end of the shop, Liv?" Mike asked.

"Same old thing we've been tossing around for weeks now. What to do with the information about Thursday's DNA. It's got a few pretty weird implications. According to the molecular anthro honchos, it requires us to regard *Homo sapien sapiens* and *Australopithecus boisei* as conspecific."

"What the hell does that mean?" Mike asked.

"It means we're all one big happy species," Liv answered. "The definition of a species is that it be a population capable of producing fertile offspring, reproductively isolated from all other species. The long human DNA-sequences in Thursday's genes say pretty clearly that there was at least one fertile union. We can tell there was an interbreeding at least a few generations back, and Thursday herself is pretty clearly fertile. Even if she wasn't, the DNA says she's at least as close to humans as donkeys are to horses. *They* can breed to produce a hybrid, a mule—but mules are sterile. According to definition, that means horses and donkeys aren't in the same species— but they are very close, plenty damn close enough to freak everybody out. No one has the guts to release that kind of information. I guess the most honest way to regard her would be as a subspecies *of Homo sapiens*. Call her *Homo sapiens boisei*—but are *you* ready for that? No one else is. If Thursday is a specimen of a subspecies of ours—then, if *she* is an animal, so are we all. *You* try selling that to John Q. Public without causing a riot."

"Can you get anywhere with the idea of chronospecies?" Rupert asked.

"What's a chronospecies?" Michael asked.

"A species is a breeding population, right?" Rupert said. "But you couldn't have kids with a woman who died two hundred years ago; her genes are no longer directly available. You also can't breed with a woman who hasn't been born yet. Both women are reproductively isolated from you by time. A chronospecies is a species projected through time, to take into account such cases. Of course, no one gets that persnickety about it. Obviously, a human being is still the same species across the distance of a few lousy centuries, and only the most anal-retentive among us would insist on saying 'chrono' species to talk about your grandmother.

"But if you go back far enough, enough parent-offspring cycles for some real evolution to take place, the earliest member of the line couldn't breed with the latest member, even if you could get them in the same room. In theory, you could trace my ancestry back through twenty million years of successful matings. If they weren't successful, I wouldn't be here to buy the next round. But ten million years ago, my great-great-great-and-so-on gramma looked like a lemur, and *no* one would say we were in the same species. Somewhere in between a hundred years back and twenty million year ago, we stopped being the same species—several times, in fact. So they cooked up the rather fuzzy idea of chronospecies to account for such paradoxes. Clear as mud?"

"Just about," Mike said. "You going to eat those fries?"

"Help yourself," Rupert replied, shoving his plate into neutral territory in the middle of the table. "Anyway, Liv, maybe you can call the boiseans an earlier phase of our chronospecies. It doesn't mean a hell of a lot, but it sounds better than saying it's okay for your sister to marry one."

Livingston grinned and reached for a few of the last remaining french fries. "I'll pass that suggestion along."

Sunday night was when Barbara liked to read the newspaper, lolling back in bed with the front page and the comics and the ads and the *Style* and *Outlook* sections strewn about the covers, slopping over onto the floor. For the first time in what seemed a long time, there wasn't anything about herself, or Thursday, or australopithecines in the *Post*—not even a turgidly written and inaccurate piece about evolution. It was nice to be a normal, un-famous, anonymous person again. Michael wandered in from the bathroom in his boxer shorts, toweling off his face. She looked up and smiled at him. "Hi there, big boy," she said. "Come here often?"

He smiled back and shoved the comics out of the way to sit down on the edge of the bed. "Not often enough. I've missed you."

"I hate to admit it," she said a bit sadly, "but I've missed you too. It's nice to see you—and nice to have a little bit more of the old you back. Not worrying about what other people are thinking so much, just relaxing and being yourself."

"Yeah, I know. It's kind of a relief in a way. But—I don't know. I've had a lot of time for thinking the last few months, and I'm not so sure this *is* the old me—or a new one you helped make, one that I lost for a while. Growing up, all I cared about was not getting trapped in that slummy old neighborhood. Fight, struggle, study, work late, work harder than everyone else, get that scholarship. It was always others who judged me, not myself. It was what *they* thought that mattered. Even the people who thought well of me treated me like a hot prospect, a great investment who would *probably* pay off—but maybe not. I had to impress everybody."

Michael reached up and stroked her cheek, tweaked her nose play-fully. "You were the first person in a long time who saw me, liked me, for what I *was*. You made me start liking myself the way I was, not for what I might be or should be. But then the residency started, and the compete, compete, compete, and the endless hours. I was judging myself by what *they* thought again—and I started judging you God knows how. Any which way, as long as you failed, so I'd be better than you." Mike shrugged. "Real true confessions stuff, isn't it?

"When you up and left for the dig in Gowrie, and then went off to Africa, I suddenly realized I had *really* lost you. You weren't coming back. I started worrying about you, off in the jungle, imagining all sorts of things that might happen to you. I worried that—that you might die. And I thought about how terrible that would be, how empty the world would be." Mike stood up and crossed to the dresser on the other side of the room. "I'm sorry. For all of it."

Barbara got out of bed and went across the room to him. She threw her arms about him, felt the strength of being wrapped in his embrace. "It's okay. I haven't been the easiest person to deal with either. We take it from here, start over."

"Maybe there are other things we could make another try at," Michael said. "Maybe we could try for children again. We didn't have to give up quite so soon. You want to call the fertility clinic again, give it another shot?"

Barbara looked up at his face, and thought she was going to cry. How could she tell him? "I've made an appointment already. For tomorrow." He smiled, a beautiful, happy smile, and she buried her head in his chest so she would not have to see it. How could she do what she was going to do? But there was no other way.

They made love that night, fierce, intense, gentle love, as if for the first and last time.

▼◆▼

The deeds, the acts themselves, were easy. She had no appointment, of course. What she had was a forged prescription, scribbled out on a sheet stolen from Michael's prescription pad.

She drove over to the hospital, parked, crossed the street, went inside, doing each of those routine, automatic things with preternatural care, watching over her own movements as if each was something special.

She knew exactly where she was going. She had been there often enough. She knew where in the hospital the clinic was, which was the only comfortable chair in the waiting room, what station the duty nurse played on her desk radio. She had learned all about that place in the course of her unsuccessful struggle for a baby.

The bored nurse took the prescription from her and headed back toward the freezer. Barbara knew just how long it would take her to get back. It should be enough time to get the other things she needed. Heart pounding, trying to watch behind herself every step of the way, she slipped into an empty exam room and scooped up the instruments she'd need. In thirty seconds, she had what she was after, and was back waiting for the nurse at the counter. Finally, the nurse returned with the small, cold package from the freezer, wrapped in insulation. Barbara was outside, on the street, in ten minutes, driving toward Saint E's. No problem.

Barbara had charted and timed her scheme carefully. The moment for the thing was right that same night. Even so, it would require some luck. Barbara knew the procedure by heart, through her own difficult experience. The sedative for the patient was easy to come by. *No problem*, she kept telling herself. Barbara felt a strange, dreamlike detachment as she worked, a comforting fog of unreality that settled over her and made the task seem less bizarre because it was not real.

A half-hour's work, and the job was done.

Barbara left Saint Elizabeth's quietly, unobtrusively, struggling to hold onto the fragile new composure she had built for herself. She wanted to cry, to scream, to confess, to vomit, but she refused to let herself. There was no turning back. If it failed this time, she would try again. And again.

For there was no other way.

Three weeks later, in the midst of giving Thursday her routine weekly physical, Mike noticed a few strange things about his patient, and ran some tests. He couldn't believe the results.

She was pregnant.

APRIL

Chapter Twenty-Three

"You can just sit there and placidly admit you did it? A month or so back, I was arguing on the other side of the point, Barbara. But Jesus, why the hell *shouldn't* they lock you up?" Rupert paced back and forth across the floor of the Digger's Pit, the overcrowded office at the Natural History Museum where he had first seen Ambrose, where this whole insane thing had started for him. Livingston, Michael, and Dr. Grossington sat and leaned against various chairs and desks in the room. From the window, the sounds of wet-rubbered tires on slick streets hissed into the room from the rainy night.

Barbara sat placidly at her desk, unperturbed by their anger. It seemed to her as if nothing could ever reach her, bother her, upset her again. The four of them had burst in on her while she was clearing up some paperwork. She had expected them to find out eventually. It was almost a relief that the waiting was over. Calmly, smoothly, she collected the papers into a tidy stack, slipped them into a folder, and dropped the folder into her out tray. She had found the courage to commit, and admit, the ultimate transgression, the ultimate sin. Nothing should frighten her anymore. She knew that she was lying to herself, that her mind was whirling and her hands were trembling, but she needed the lies to hold herself together. "Who knows?" she asked, staring with calm fixity at the desk top.

Rupert stopped and glared at her. "What the hell do you mean, who knows?"

"Michael told you." She turned to her husband. "Who else? Who else did you tell?"

"Livingston, Dr. Grossington, Rupert. That's it, so far," Michael answered, his voice hard and far off. No one spoke. "The fucking fertility ward," Michael said at last. "The one we used. That's it, isn't it? You got the semen from my own damn hospital, right? It's not enough that the damn ape is pregnant, not enough that it *has* to be by a human because she's menstruated twice since she's been here, but

308

you had to do it out of my hospital. Any idea who the daddy is?" he asked sarcastically.

She still did not look up, still stared at the blank center of the desk blotter. "You are," she said in a small, still voice. Inside herself, it felt as if the world were whirling away from her, the last hopes thrown away. "You are."

"ME?" Michael screamed out. He lunged across the room for her, and Livingston almost couldn't grab him in time, caught him just a step or two from Barbara. It took all Livingston's strength to hold him back. "Me? You've made me the father of an *ape*?" He strained against Livingston's grasp, leaned his face as close to Barbara as he could. She forced herself to look at him. Sweat sprang out on his forehead, and his eyes were wide and wild with anger. "*This* is going to be the child I've always wanted? You *monster*."

"I'm sorry," she said. "I'm truly, desperately sorry, but I needed to give them a registry number—and yours was the only one I knew! After all—" she broke down suddenly, at last, crying and laughing at same time "—where's a woman going to get hold of sperm by herself?" She felt the tears flowing and fumbled in a drawer for a Kleenex. "It's funny when you think of it. Isn't it?" She collapsed into full-blown sobs. Finally, the tears subsided.

"Let go of me, Livingston," Michael said quietly. He sounded back in control, but Livingston hesitated for a moment. "Let go."

Liv released him, and Michael stood over Barbara. "Right now I want to do something I swore I'd never do—I want to strike you, *hit* you. I don't even think anyone here would stop me. You deserve it. But I'm not going to do that. I'm not going to do anything, but walk away from you and your sickness. I don't want to get myself any *dirtier* by touching you or your work or your damn ape again." He stood over her, and Livingston thought for a moment that he *was* going to hit her. "Everyone always thought I was the one with troubles, that *I* was the sick one. But God and Jesus, now look. Now look. Goodbye, Barbara."

Barbara stared down at the desk, unable to took at him this time. He turned and left the room.

No one spoke for a long time.

Jeffery Grossington shifted himself uncomfortably in the hard wooden chair he found himself in. "Barbara, what in God's name possessed you to do such a mad thing?" he demanded. "How could you—you *pervert* Michael, pervert yourself, pervert Thursday this way? How could you breed humans with beasts?"

"Because, Jeffery. Because I care about human beings, and what happens to them."

"Yeah, what happens when you crossbreed them with animals," Rupert said. "Jesus, Barbara."

"I did it because I didn't want slavery back. You said it yourself, Liv, when you told us about the DNA comparisons. She is human— and there's no better way to prove it than what I've done."

"But what the hell does that have to do with slavery?" Livingston demanded.

"Have you read what Lowell is doing?" Barbara asked quietly. "Have you read about his setting up a camp for the boiseans?" she asked. "A camp with barbed wire fences and surveillance TV and dormitory barracks. He expects to have twenty boiseans, or whatever the damn word is, there by summer. He's laying plans for a breeding stock. There's another research team being set up in England, and another in Germany. Both of them will want captive boiseans to study. The British team plans to focus on seeing how educable, how trainable they are. Some of the scientists involved are already speculating about using them for manual labor, drudge work. Someone's even worked out hypothetical formulae for price points. I saw it in a supposedly tongue-in-cheek article in the *Wall Street Journal.* They're kidding about it now, but it's on their minds. One day they'll think about it seriously." She looked up, finally, at all of them. "Don't you get it? *Price points*, based on importation or breeding costs, training required, health maintenance costs, warranties, novelty value. The bastards want them for *slaves.*"

"Damn it, Barb, we've been through this," Livingston objected. "You have to be a person before you can be a slave—or are you calling every domestic animal on earth a slave, too?"

"Stop and think about, Liv. *Animals can't do human work.* Thursday *can.* Think about what will happen if we just slide into sharing the world with subhumans. Imagine migrant workers losing their jobs to boisean slaves. With a lot of training, with a lot of good, harsh beatings to punish mistakes, maybe Thursday could learn to be a janitor, or even an assembly line worker. Is that like any other domestic animal? But how could they be slaves, if they're animals? Can you *really* believe that?!

"Are you ready for anti-boisean riots ten years from now? And what will people think of *work* twenty years from now if it's something *slaves* do? Liv, Rupe, you saw what the Utaani were like. Do you want our society to have those attitudes?"

Barbara could feel her heart pounding, her body trembling with reaction and emotion. "And did you ever think about how those earlier 'intrusions' of human genes happened? You can bet *they* weren't through artificial insemination. Think about it. Could there *be* anything more degrading than that? It'd make normal pimping and whoring seem downright wholesome by comparison. This won't be the first hybrid born—but you can bet your ass it won't be the last unless *we do something.*

"The world needs a shock, something to make it sit up and think about this—before we all just slide down into a horrible social disaster without even noticing. This mess is our responsibility. *We* have to provide that shock, and I can't think of any other way to do it besides what I've done. We, the people in this room right now, have the chance to decide what the world will be like from now on. This is the time, this is the place, and we are the people. *I'm* not going to be the one who let them crowd these creatures into concentration camps in the name of science, or set them loose to insult honest work and bring back the nightmare that's in the back of every black person's soul. Do any of *you* want to go down in history that way?" Barbara stopped, and sat back down. She took a deep breath, and ran a hand over her hair, trying to smooth it down. "I honestly wish we had never found Thursday. But we did, and we have to deal with the fact. And that one poor unborn child is the best chance we've got for a decent future."

"Barb," said Livingston, "you don't *know* that the boiseans will be made slaves, and even if that might happen, you can't be sure that this birth, this stunt, could prevent it. This is a terrible, terrible crime— is it worth it just in case it might stop a hypothetical crime later on?"

"Oh, slavery will happen, don't you worry about that. Because if the boiseans aren't human, they are animals, and animals can't be slaves, just like you say. Anyone in the country or around the world who needs cheap labor could figure out that loophole. And if it's legal, it'll happen, believe me. So the question is, do you *want* slavery legal again, Livingston?" Barbara asked, venom in her voice. "Do you want to live in a world where it's okay to buy a hominid, legal to work the creature to death, or to torture it, or to run experiments too dangerous for 'real' people on it?" She opened her desk drawer and pulled out a slim volume. "And slavery isn't just bad for the slaves, Liv. Aunt Josephine mailed me the original of Zebulon's journal a while back. It was something in the journal that decided me I had to do this thing. *Listen* to it."

▼◆▼

. . . I was never beaten out of anger, but in a skilled, calm, scientific manner, nicely calculated to produced the desired results—as a blacksmith might pound a horseshoe on an anvil, bending the iron to his will without anger or emotion, without a thought that the metal he worked upon could possibly feel pain or fear or want. . .

Better the furious punishment of an enraged Master than a calm man methodically forming a tool to suit his needs. Our Masters treated us not as men and women, not even as dumb creatures, but as objects, tools to be used up, patched up if it seemed worthwhile, but otherwise discarded without a care or thought. . . . How crippling to the heart and soul for a young white child to be raised and trained and schooled to believe that a human being could be less than an animal. How vile, to force oneself to believe that pain did not hurt, that cruelty was blameless. How evil to learn—and then to teach—the techniques of stripping a fellow man of all dignity. . . . How horrible to know at the back of one's mind that all one's wealth, all one's peace and prosperity, had its foundations set on Blood, on the Lash, on barbarity carefully hidden from view beneath the most elaborate civility and courtliness. Guilt hung like a heavy, funereal shroud over the white man's plantation."

▼◆▼

She closed the book and put it away. "Do you want to live in a world like that one, the one your ancestors lived in? Do you want to live like one of the white men, the *slavers* in that world? Do you want to explain to your child why it was wrong that *we* used to be slaves, but go ahead and beat the boisean if you feel like it? Do you want to raise your child to think a creature that walks like us, looks like us, can talk with us if we teach it to, is an animal? Do you want to let him loose on a playground with kids who'll notice *he's* the same color as the boiseans? What would *that* alone do to black people?"

She stood up and looked at each of them in turn. "Have any of you thought about the corrosive, degrading effect on society, on the world, on *each of us*, if we hold an inferior human race in bondage?"

No one spoke.

"If Thursday is an dumb animal, then so are all of us!" Barbara almost shouted. "Her kind is so close, so frighteningly close to ours. It's just the *littlest* bits of DNA, one or two molecules built that way instead of this, that keeps *us* from being shambling, inarticulate, language-less, bipedal apes that can just about figure out how to dig with pointed sticks, who have trouble making sentences. One or two tiny gene changes, and our species would be like her—we *were* like her, not so very long ago."

"But Thursday is *not* a human being," Grossington said. "She is not a person."

"Prove it," Barbara said. "Point to the part of yourself that makes *you* a person, and I'll look and see if it's missing on Thursday."

"How can you point to a man's soul?" Grossington demanded.

"You can't. But before you tell me it won't matter if her kind are treated like soulless, expendable robots for our dangerous work and experiments, first you prove to me she doesn't have a soul. She might not be a human being, but I *know* she's got a soul."

"Come on, Barb," Rupert asked. "How do you know? Have you touched it?"

"No, but it's touched me," Barbara snapped. "I know she's got a kind heart, know she can love, and talk, and break the rules and try to get away with it. I know she loves me, trusts me. Trusted me when I promised her she'd never be a slave. She's been a slave all her life, no question about it, and she's just beginning to learn how to be free. I wasn't going to let her turn back to slavery."

"So you made her a mother, instead," Rupert said.

"If we can breed together, then we are the same kind of creature. That's the definition of a species," Livingston said quietly. "And we then have the choice between saying that we are animals or that the boiseans are human. Neither choice is terribly pretty, but I think I'd like to go on being human. If there are consequences to that, okay, I'll pay the price. Let justice be done, though the heavens fall."

Barbara looked her cousin in the eye and smiled sadly. "Thank you, Liv."

"Don't thank me yet. I'll accept Thursday as human only if it's a choice between that and my being an animal. But never mind that for the moment. Tell me something else: Why? Why did you do it?"

"Because there wasn't any other way," she said, her eyes passionate and sorrowful. "There was no other way to show *people*— not just scientists and molecular anthropologists and DNA mappers, but *people*—that she is like us."

"But you don't know that she is!" Rupert said. "She got pregnant, yes, but is that a baby or a monster growing inside her?"

"There have been other interbreedings," Barbara said defensively.

"In Thursday's genetic background there is evidence of interbreeding, yes," Livingston said. "But there could have been thousands of attempts for every success—and the last attempt might have been thousands of years ago. We don't know. On the other hand, subsequent generations of the hybrid *did* manage to breed back into the australopithecine line, we know that much. The offspring survived and had descendants. If they hadn't, their DNA wouldn't show up in Thursday's genes. Will this kid survive? It's a crapshoot. As to what the child will be like—there is absolutely no way of knowing. But there is a very good chance that, if it is allowed to be born, it will lead a misshapen, deformed existence. It won't be 'normal,' that's for sure."

"That child is going to be born," Barbara said. "No one is going to prevent it. If I have to, I'll take Thursday away, hide her until it's her time. You'll *have* to lock me up to stop me." Her voice faltered for a moment, then grew stronger. "I know this is wrong. I know it's a violation—of Thursday, of myself, of—of 'decency,' for want of a better word. But I'm not going to be the woman who brought back slavery, and worse!"

Rupert turned and stared out the window. "So what you're saying is that we've got a choice," he said. "There's no doubt that we're going to bring an abomination into the world—the question is, which one? Is it going to be dehumanizing slavery and hatred—or one little hybrid baby? Good or bad, we don't know what kind of life the kid will have, or if it will live at all. It's playing God the worst possible way. But the way you put it, Barb, committing the grave, terrible, criminal sin of letting the pregnancy continue is the best shot at keeping the whole world from getting much worse than it is already. I wish I could argue with that, but I can't."

Livingston shook his head. "Neither can I. But the kid—the child, the poor little baby. For that, for him, I'm sorry."

Dr. Grossington had been listening, and thinking hard. "I see," he said. "I think I begin to see. What you've done is mad, insane, perverted, Barbara—but I'm starting to wonder if there were anything else you *could* have done." He cleared his throat and thought a minute more. "But if this strange little birth is to have the desired effect—if it is to have the shock value to stop exploitation of the boiseans, it will have to have maximum publicity. First, though, we'll have to keep it quiet while some ground is prepared. The people will have to be educated, got ready for the news. Public revulsion is going to be strong anyway. If Thursday *is* to be a mother, instead of being burned at the stake, it'll take some extremely careful planning and maneuvering."

"It'll be tricky," Rupert agreed. "I can't believe I'm going along with this—but given what Barbara had said, what choice do we have? But, anyway—we four can just about accept it—after all, we know Thursday. But will the world accept it?"

Somewhere in the long night of talk, they worked out a plan, went from opposing the pregnancy to discussing its merits to scheming how to make it work. They would wait until the molecular anthro paper was released, so that the public would at least understand that crossbreeding was possible. That might make the shock acceptable. Maybe wait until Lowell was back from Gabon, and had his colony of australopithecines well established in Massachusetts. With luck there would be some protests of that, and maybe a sympathetic back-lash. They knew they could not rush the announcement. They would have to wait until the moment seemed right. They went home that night with what seemed a reasonable plan for releasing the information at a time and in a way the world might accept.

Except that two days later, Michael filed suit in Federal Court to have the pregnancy terminated.

▼◆▼

MAN-BOISEAN PREGNANCY REVEALED

(AP) The australopithecine brought back from Africa is pregnant by human sperm. This shocking development was revealed by Dr. Michael Marchando, estranged husband of Dr. Barbara Marchando. He brought suit against his wife, claiming she used his sperm to impregnate Thursday, the famous so-called "boisean" brought back from Gabon.

A source in the Smithsonian Institution confirmed that Thursday was indeed pregnant, and that recent research indicated that impregnation by human sperm should be possible for boiseans.

Barbara Marchando, who resigned her post with the Smithsonian Institution this morning, did not deny the accusation, but stated flatly that she would fight the suit and do all she could to let the pregnancy continue. . . .

▼◆▼

Barbara was astonished how at easy it was to explain to Thursday that she was going to have a baby. It was a lovely, early spring day, and the two of them were walking the grounds of the hospital again. It had only been a day or so since the news had come out, but already none of the researchers at Saint E's, none of her one-time coworkers, wanted to talk to her, or deal with her. That didn't matter, either, as long as she could see Thursday. Although Barbara had quit her job to spare the Smithsonian any further embarrassment, she was still allowed on the grounds of Saint Elizabeth's—for the moment, anyway. There were more than a few who thought she ought to take up residence there permanently. Maybe they were right. Never mind.

She had lost her job, her husband, her career, and nearly all her friends. Maybe they'd find some way to put her in jail. It didn't matter. Nothing did, except Thursday's child. She took Thursday's hand and led her to that same park bench they had sat on before.

"*Thursday know what is in Thursday?*" Barbara asked, patting her friend's stomach.

"*No,*" Thursday replied.

"*Baby grow there. Baby grow, you will be mother.*"

"*Mother? Mother, with baby?*" Thursday asked eagerly. Her signing was getting better all the time, more expressive and precise, and her use of words was more sophisticated—though she seemed to have reached some sort of capacity limit on learning new words.

"*You be mother, with baby,*" Barbara assured her. "*But long time from now, must wait long for baby to grow inside.*"

"*Happy! Like baby. Want baby come!*"

"*Baby come, but not soon.*"

"*What baby be like?*" Thursday asked eagerly.

"*I don't know,*" Barbara replied truthfully. What sort of creature were they conspiring to bring into the world? A monster? Some genetic disaster that would die before it could be born? A healthy baby that would simply look and act a little strange? What sort of life could it lead? Barbara had wondered all those things when she had plunged in the injector full of sperm, but the mysteries, the moral ambiguities, weren't getting any clearer.

Now there was little else to do but wait.

SUMMER

Chapter Twenty-Four

[Excerpt from an article in the June 26 Washington *Post* "Outlook" section]

. . . . The legal maneuvering in this case has gone on for some months now. Dr. Michael Marchando's suit to have the pregnancy terminated lost on its final appeal on Friday. The judge ruled that, under the terms of his agreement with the hospital fertility clinic, Marchando had surrendered the rights to control the use of any of his sperm stored by the clinic, and further that there was no existing civil or criminal law against the acts Dr. Barbara Marchando committed, other than forgery of the prescription, and the theft of the sperm and the hospital equipment she used to perform the insemination procedure. She pled guilty to that crime and received a suspended sentence.

Now free of the Marchando vs. Marchando suit and the attendant temporary restraining orders, it would seem that authorities can confront the question of what to do about this strange pregnancy directly. But no one seems eager to tackle the question. Various interpretations of one issue or another in the case could be made, assigning jurisdiction to the Fish and Wildlife Service, the Customs Service, the Immigration and Naturalization Service, the State Department, the FBI, or even the U.S. Civil Rights Commission. There are also several District of Columbia government agencies that could be involved. But no one seems to want to be the one to decide if the pregnancy should be allowed to continue.

Even if a federal or local bureaucrat decided to try and terminate the pregnancy, there are a few legal problems in the way. Federal funding of abortions is of course illegal, and Thursday is presumed to be under Federal jurisdiction, even if the specific agency can't be identified. She is at a federally funded institution, was imported to this country by government scientists and government aircraft, and has been fed, housed, cared for and studied with federal funds.

A second problem: Thursday is past the first trimester of her pregnancy, and therefore, past the time when most clinics and doctors are willing to perform an abortion, although terminations are legal in the District until the twenty-first week, which in this case would be about July 15. Further complicating the issue is the fact that Thursday has clearly indicated she knows she is pregnant and that she wants the baby. All indications are that the fetus is developing normally—whatever 'normally' might mean in this situation.

In such a case, and assuming she is regarded as a person with rights under the law, it is virtually impossible, from a legal standpoint, to compel her to have an abortion, and by the time the legal issues could be resolved, the 21-week deadline would certainly have passed.

If she is an animal, of course, her rights or wishes do not have to be consulted, and there seem to be no pertinent statutes regulating abortions for animals.

At issue, then: is she a human or an animal? This question was being argued long before her pregnancy was discovered, but the changed and unique circumstances give them renewed urgency and focus.

Since no agency of government wants to take on this case, many expect that the pregnancy will be allowed to come to term. No one can decide what to do—and that temporizing will likely continue until the point is moot, and Thursday's child is born. . . .

JULY 5

A BILL establishing the legal rights and status of australopithecine persons in the Commonwealth of Massachusetts.

1. All australopithecine persons resident in the Commonwealth on the date this bill becomes law shall be declared wards of the Commonwealth, and legal guardians shall be appointed by the Governor for their protection.

2. The further importation or introduction of australopithecine persons into the Commonwealth, save for temporary importation of such persons in need of humanitarian or medical assistance, is hereby banned. The secretary of State is hereby authorized to issue licenses for such temporary importations. During such temporary importations, such persons shall be temporary wards of the Commonwealth.

3. No australopithecine person who is a ward of the Commonwealth shall be confined against his or her will without due legal process, or otherwise be denied due process, or be the subject of medical or other sorts of experimentation . . .

JULY 20

[Statement from the President's Office, Republic of Gabon—translation from original French]

It has been determined that the individuals known variously as *tranka*, boiseans, australopithecines or *Australopithecus boisei* have been illegally held in a state of servitude by the tribe of the Utaani, and further determined that any additional removal of these individuals from the Republic of Gabon would constitute kidnapping. The australopithecines liberated from the Utaani by the government last week are hereby declared an endangered species and displaced persons. Pending further determination, they will be under the joint care and protection of the Gabonese government, UNESCO, and the World Wildlife Fund. . .

SEPTEMBER 4

[Excerpt from an interview with Dr. Rupert Maxwell, *60 Minutes*]

. . .*Question:* But isn't there a danger that the child will, for example, grow a human-sized brain inside a boisean-sized skull?

Dr. Maxwell: That is a far less likely outcome than you would expect. There isn't one gene for brain size and another for skull size. There is instead a whole suite of genetic coding that works in concert to develop whole systems of the body. In this case, there is a lot of evidence that the skull is stimulated to grow by the shape of the underlying brain. It's like Abe Lincoln's joke that a man should be tall enough so his feet touch the ground. It's not the skull that decides the shape of the brain, but more the other way around.

Question: So you anticipate a normal, healthy child being born? No problems?

Dr. Maxwell: Healthy, yes, but not normal. Actually, below the head, the body-plans of the two subspecies are so similar the kid should look normal—if a little stronger and hairier than most. The one thing I'm worried about is the teeth.

Question: The teeth?

Dr. Maxwell: Have you ever gotten a look at the back teeth on an australopithecine? Crossbreeding between them and human teeth might well be trickier than getting the brain right. This kid is probably going to run up some real orthodontist bills.

SEPTEMBER 26

Barbara shifted uncomfortably on the hard chair and tidied up her notes again. She should have been used to this by now, but public speaking always made her nervous. Testifying before a congressional subcommittee was even worse. She took a sip of water and waited.

The chairman finally arrived, gaveled the committee into session, and went through the usual opening formalities. Barbara didn't listen, not really. After months of being trotted out before every public forum in the country, she had learned what she could safely tune out.

"Dr. Marchando, are you ready to begin?" the chairman asked.

"Ah, yes, Mr. Chairman, thank you, and thanks to the committee for inviting me."

She swallowed again and picked up her notes. "What seemed unimaginable a year ago, and unthinkable a few months ago, has now not only happened, but, in large part, been accepted by the American people. There are still some months before the main event, but Thursday's pregnancy is progressing well, and every day we have more reason to be hopeful about the outcome.

"There are, quite understandably, a lot of people who still vehemently resist the idea that we could interbreed with a lesser kind. But that is a misconception. This pregnancy shows she is *our* kind, by all the rules of science and common sense. *Australopithecus boisei* must be considered a subspecies of our race. It was to demonstrate that fact that I took the actions I did, and accepted the consequences of that act. As the committee is aware, my legal expenses have been large, and the disruption of my life significant. None of that matters. Proving Thursday to be human is more important.

"Thursday bears a human's child, and I am certain will bring it to term. Therefore, Thursday must be human. But even if the child is born malformed, as now seems unlikely, or is stillborn, an even more remote possibility, it must be clear that are dealing with a close relation. We must look into her face and see our own. She is a less intelligent, less cultural, less linguistic kind of human—but she *is* a human.

"We can no more send her off as a test animal than we could send off a mentally retarded child for vivisection, no more consider her a fit slave—and let us not mince words: slave is what she was, and what some would make her kind again under new and pretty euphemisms—we could no more consider her a fit slave than we could consider a Down's syndrome victim proper fodder for the salt mines.

"I am pleased to note that many states have already passed laws banning the importation and exploitation of boiseans. This congressional committee is considering similar legislation, as are many foreign nations. The General Assembly of the United Nations is expected to consider the issue soon." Barbara paused for a moment, and put her notes down.

"But there's more to it than that. Thursday and her child have done more than merely get laws written. They have taught us something. Even the tiny genetic differences between her kind and ours result in great changes in behavior and ability. She *is* different from us, dramatically so. Surely that proves that all the races of *Homo sapiens sapiens* are exactly the same, that the differences in skin color, facial shape, hair texture and the rest are all completely meaningless.

"We have found our long-lost cousin. May the experience teach us that we are all brothers and sisters."

Big bellied, gravid, moving slowly, Thursday walked the now-familiar grounds of the hospital with her friend Barbara. Fall leaves were swirling about her feet, and the strangely shifting weather of this place was changing once more. She was getting cold again.

Barbara had warned her once again that the baby might be sick, or strange when it was born, or might grow up to be different from Thursday. That scared her a little, but not so much as it might have. Thursday was a fatalist.

Barbara had also told her about the others being set free from the Utaani, and told her it was because of her. She could not understand how that could be, but she was proud, nonetheless. But not so proud, she sensed, as a human might have been. It did not seem possible she could do such a grand thing.

Thursday couldn't imagine being able to change the world.

Perhaps, thought Barbara, as she looked at her friend, *that* was the real difference between their two kinds.

DECEMBER

Chapter Twenty-Five

It was time.

The sonogram made it look like the child's head might be too large for a safe delivery: a cesarean was required. They anesthetized her, and wheeled her, blanketed in white, into the operating room. Barbara went in with her. Even if Thursday was unconscious, she might want a friend with her.

▼◆▼

Livingston, Rupert, and Jeffery Grossington sweated it out in the waiting room, in the long tradition of, if not expectant fathers, at least expectant uncles.

Liv and Rupert were up and pacing, but Jeffery seemed not only calm, but actually at ease, and happy. It was more than Livingston could put up with. "Jeffery, why in God's name aren't you climbing the walls?" he demanded. "Don't you know what's going on in there?"

Dr. Grossington smiled. "I know. I've been thinking, that's all. Maybe we are a lot closer to being beasts or animals than we thought— but we really haven't done so badly, in spite of that.

"If we are close to the australopithecines, then *they* are close to *us*—and look how much the tiny differences have meant. Our kind, our precise species and subspecies, has only been around for about 35,000 years. Perhaps eighteen hundred generations in all. That's not much time. *All* the other hominid species had longer than that. Hundreds of thousands, or millions of years. The australopithecines have been on earth for over four million years. None of them even made a start on what we've done.

"In all their millions of years, none of them tracked the stars, smelted metal, grew crops in a field, built a city, wrote a history or a song or a poem. None of them invented the wheel, or discovered fire, or created culture. None of them wondered so hard where they came from that they searched the world for their honored ancestors, buried beneath the millennia.

"We *did* search, and we found a poor relation, an orphan of creation, still with us, to remind us of how much we have done, and with how little.

"It was that *difference* in us that made us go out and look, to find out how much the same we are. If we find it humbling to be Thursday's relations, think how humbling it must be for her to be ours. Her kind can claim no more than slavery in the jungle. *We* have the world, and the stars beckon.

"After all, we're orphans too. God and Nature left us here to fend for ourselves, without any of the divine intervention we thought we had, and thought we needed. We've done all right on our own. Well enough that we can accept our poor relations, even if we don't know quite where to put them yet."

Rupert was about to answer when he heard a noise behind him.

It was the door opening. Barbara stepped into the room, and pulled down her surgical mask. "It's a girl," she said. "And she's all right."

POSTSCRIPT

She was a very ugly baby. Her skin was not dark enough, and there was not enough fur on her limbs or body. Her nose was not flat enough, her chin was too pointed, and her lips were too wide, with no real muzzle to speak of. She didn't have a single tooth grown in at birth, and her whole head too big and round.

But she was Thursday's, and even as she was cataloging her faults, Thursday forgot them, and looked again—at the prettiest baby she had ever seen.

Barbara sat down beside the bed, smiling. *"Hold her?"* she signed.

"Yes," Thursday signed, a bit awkwardly with the hand that wasn't holding the baby. Her stomach hurt a little, from where the doctor had cut her to take the baby out. But that didn't matter.

"What name for her?" Barbara asked. *"You must give baby name."* She took the strangely and wonderfully made babe in her arms and cuddled it.

Thursday thought for a long moment. *"Can I give two names?"*

"Yes, as many names as you like."

"Barbara-Thursday. Name Barbara-Thursday. Because she like both us."

"Yes, yes, she is," Barbara agreed. *"Thank you for name."*

"Grossington—he ask me long-time-back, when just learn good hand talk—he ask what is person, and I not know." Thursday reached for her daughter, and Barbara carefully handed her back. *"Now I know. Will you tell him answer?"*

"Yes, I will tell him. What is person, Thursday?"

Thursday stroked the tiny baby's furry head, her gnarled, hairy, callused, chip-nailed hands infinitely gentle. She pointed to the baby, and looked up at Barbara. *"Tell him, this is."*

THE END

Author's Note

Updated and revised for the FoxAcre Press edition.

There is perhaps no other major science wherein so little is known for certain, or wherein so much thought and study is based on so little evidence, as in paleoanthropology.

In it, we seek to read our history in anonymous scraps of bone, and the wonder is not only that we succeed at all, but that we succeed so well. It has been said that all the bones of our ancestors from a million years on back could fit onto one or two trestle tables. This paucity of evidence is hidden by the mold-maker's skill, affording the illusion that there are enough Lucys or Zinjs or Mrs. Ples's for every museum to have one. In reality, few curators would dare display an original hominid skull even if they possessed one—and most don't. The 'skulls' on display are all but invariably accompanied by a small placard which states, in very fine print, that the skull are reproductions.

The fragility and irreplaceability of our ancestors' remains make public display far too risky. The accidental jostling of a display case could reduce a cherished old fossil to powder.

The average australopithecine skull is therefore likely to be in an custom-made storage case, with every scrap of bone nestled in its own separate, hand-shaped niche, carved into the chemically neutral foam rubber, the whole case lovingly packed away in an environmentally controlled, underground, bombproof vault inside the borders of its nation of origin. Few are ever exposed to the common view of the vulgar public. The Smithsonian Institution dares to display the real Hope Diamond—but not any real pre-human hominid skulls.

Except for the exciting and sometimes unnerving results of molecular anthropologists, these fragile, pampered bones are the *only* physical, tangible evidence we have of our own remote past. The molecular anthropologists and primate researchers have made great contributions, but nearly all of our scanty knowledge of our distant ancestors is based on these few bones. Small wonder that the unknowns are endlessly greater than the certainties.

No rational person, examining the evidence, could doubt the essential fact of human evolution—but no sane person could claim that we have the full story. I have done all I could to conform my story to the known facts, and I believe in large part I have done so. Furthermore, there are, unquestionably, undiscovered species, not only in the inaccessible reaches of Earth's dense equatorial rain forests, but in every environment of the planet. To the best of my knowledge, there is nothing in taxonomy or the consensus view of humanity's beginning that would make this tale impossible.

But, speaking of the impossible, a word about creationism. A few friends have expressed disbelief that creationism and its fraudulent offspring "creation science" are actually forces to be reckoned with. Rest assured that they are. Scratch the surface of any number of otherwise sensible folk, and you will find frightened, threatened people unable to cope with the idea that humankind was not always as it is.

These good people will throw up misquotations from prominent scientists, toss out flatly wrong misstatements, dredge up old and wholly discredited hoaxes and doctored "facts" and evidence, deny the voluminous evidence of paleontology (for many animal types are far better represented in the fossil record than the hominids are), misinterpret evidence to suit themselves—and, at times, out-and-out lie—rather than admit that a beautiful, ancient, poetic, poorly translated, self-contradicting creation myth is not the exact truth and literal word of God. Most of these people are not lying, but genuinely believe what they are saying. On the other hand, *someone* had to have doctored the quotes and faked the phony evidence they cite. For starters, *someone* deliberately carved footprints alongside fossil dinosaur footprints to "prove" the two species lived side by side.

There is a large body of creationist "thought" (I use the word advisedly) which at least acknowledges the existence of a complex and self-consistent fossil record in all the strata of Earth's sedimentary rock. Unfortunately, this "theory" (using *that* term advisedly) actually suggests that *God deliberated placed those fraudulent fossils there*, as bogus evidence of a nonexistent past (after all, the world was created in 4,004 B.C.). God, it seems, is testing us, seeing if he can trip up our faith in His revealed word by salting the mine, placing forged fossils in the Earth, and generally giving the place that lived-in look, making the 6,000 year-old planet appear to be billions of years old. These good people suggest God is testing our faith—by lying to us. If so, I for one must at least applaud His thoroughness. After all, He not only created fake plant and animal fossils; He also threw together seemingly eroded mountain ranges, bogus extinct volcanoes, huge simulated erosional canyons, and even ersatz coprolites—fossil feces. It was a messy job, I suppose, but it had to be done right if it was going to be done at all.

It would be funny if it weren't so sad. Sheltering behind these and other patently absurd claims, put forward with all earnestness and seriousness by the creationists, is a desperate determination to deny our links to and our oneness with the rest of nature's wonders, an urgent need to keep from admitting the terrible truth—that humankind is today better than it once was.

But what is so terrible about knowing we are an improved model, that in our brief tenure on this Earth we have accomplished things never before done in four and half billion years? Why is that a source of shame rather than pride? I wish I knew.

But the silly theories, patently phony evidence and trivial misquotations are mere pop-guns, creationism's lesser defenses. When they need heavy artillery, they wheel up the deadliest weapon of all: ignorance.

All the battles for sanitized biology texts that don't explain biology, all the suits claiming religious persecution over books that say children should respect other religions, all the flapdoodle rulings that *not* being religious is a religion and therefore all public schoolbooks that *don't* support religion are efforts to establish a State religion (I'm not making any of this up)—all of these are battles for the right to be ignorant.

Misguided parents, teachers, and principals, aided and abetted by lawyers and judges who should know better and probably do, are trying to stamp out ideas. They seem to be afraid that children will pick up strange, foreign ideas that do not coincide with the orthodoxy presented at home. One of those ideas might get lodged in the kid's head. Next thing you know, she'll be having ideas herself, God forbid. Then, inevitably, she'll throw off a lifetime of ethical training and moral guidance to go act like a Godless heathen who smokes rock and roll and plays drugs with the volume up really loud, or something. After all, decent people don't ever do their own thinking—they just do what they're told.

What is so threatening about allowing more than one idea into the world? Why must we all think the same way? Why is anything short of a state-imposed orthodoxy considered religious discrimination? If these parents are so concerned, why aren't they spending an hour a night with the kid in Bible study? Wouldn't that be some bulwark against outside ideas?

To me, it all suggests the faithful are showing a distressing lack of faith. Is the revealed word of God so weak and fragile a thing that it can't survive contact with mere human ideas? Can the lifelong care and guidance of a devoted parent who teaches a child decency, kindness, courage, and tolerance be overthrown by mere facts and figures in a book? Is religion so delicate a flower that learning can destroy it? I don't think so. The people who are so afraid of knowledge seem to have formed an opposite opinion. They're wrong.

I should like to thank the people whose collective patience was above and beyond the call of duty during the writing of this book—starting with the original editor, and now long-time friend, Betsy Mitchell. She continued to have faith in me and in this book when there was no objective evidence (or manuscript) upon which to base that faith.

I would also like to thank my mother for egging me on; and my father for vastly improving this book with his editorial skills, and for insisting that I not chicken out on the ending.

I owe a further nod of the head to Shariann Lewitt for loaning me reference books that I kept far too long, Charles Sheffield for pointing me toward a dishearteningly large literature in the field, and to Van and Ellie Seagraves, for their accommodating attitude that gave me the time—and the hardware—to get this book done. Likewise, my thanks to Jim Baen, the book's first publisher. And, finally, my thanks to Dr. Kathleen Gordon of the Smithsonian Institution, who took the time to give me a behind-the-scenes tour of the anthropology department there. I would like to emphasize that I did not seek and she did not offer any advice or opinion on the subject matter of this book, or on any technical issue. Whatever errors I have committed, I have made without any outside help.

▼◆▼

Addenda to Author's Note for the FoxAcre Press Edition.

This book was originally published in 1988, to very strong reviews, and very marginal sales. There was exactly one edition, from Baen Books, and, when it went out of print no so very long after publication, it stayed that way. There were British and German editions, but the book vanished from its home market. I have tried from that time to get it re-issued in the United States. The desire to get this one book back in print was the main driving force behind my decision to start FoxAcre Press, and behind FoxAcre's primary mission: bringing back science fiction and fantasy titles that belong in print.

Things have changed in paleoanthropology since 1988. More fossils have been discovered, and various species of hominid and humanoid have been newly discovered, newly denounced, newly named, and, in some cases, newly withdrawn. The creatures once called *Australopithecus*, some would now call *Paranthropus* (literally, near-human). The Black Skull, WT-17000, is called either *Australopithecus* or *Paranthropus aethiopicus* these days, though some still call it *bosei*. The details of humanity's family have been rewritten countless times over the last decade and a half, as the scientists argue over which species is ancestral, and which is not, and as new evidence, and new dates, come in. We learn more, and understand more—and discover, over and over again, how much there is still to learn. In short, the more things change, the more they stay the same.

Several other things remain much as they were when I wrote the book There still just aren't that many sets of pre-human remains out there. A lot of science, a lot of very good science, is based on a relatively small amount of physical evidence. But the evidence that has accumulated make it more abundantly clear than ever that our ancestral line leads back to Africa. It seems quite likely—indeed, all but certain—that several hominid species shared the continent for millions of years. We are alone today, but we were not always alone. In fact, the present day situation is unusual precisely *because* there is only one hominid species in the world. We tend to view that circumstance as the normal rule—but it is in fact the exception.

When I first sat down to look over *Orphan of Creation* for the new edition, I was tempted to update the book, and the science, and recast the book in the year 2000 or thereabouts. However, it soon became plain that an update wouldn't work very well, wouldn't accomplish much in terms of getting the science right, and would not improve the story. This story belongs in the time it was written.

I have, however, tidied up a few things here and there in the text, but in this I have acted as a line-editor, not as a rewriting author. The changes I have made are intended to fine-tune the existing writing, to improve some turns of phrase, to make some points more clearly, and to clear up some small patches of pointless muddle. This is essentially the same book as the 1988 version, but with a number of minor errors and bits of poor writing cleaned up.

This new edition, however, does sport one significant change: the dedication. I want to explain it here, for a very simple reason. When, as a reader, I spot something like an change in a dedication, or a name vanishing or reappearing from an acknowledgement page from one edition to the next, I am enough of a snoop that I want to know the story. I hate it when writers leave that sort of little mystery dangling out there. I find it deeply annoying when I am told there's a good story out there, but that I am not permitted to hear it for myself.

Therefore, a brief word of explanation. The 1988 edition was dedicated to Joslyn Read, my girlfriend of the time. Well, as it turns out, Joslyn and I are now happily married—to other people. Joslyn and I are still in touch, and on good terms, but it didn't seem quite appropriate to leave the previous dedication in place (I can think of two spouses who might object, for starters). But I still wanted to acknowledge the previous dedication, for another very simple reason, and one that is consistent with my objections to the Creationists: I hate it when people try to pretend that events in the past, now rendered slightly awkward, didn't happen. Therefore, please consider the previous dedication duly noted.

But that left me with *another* problem. I couldn't bear the thought of sending a book out into the great wide world without a dedication, and yet it seemed awkward in the extreme to assign a *new* dedication that, however sincerely felt, might appear to be something merely stuck on to cover up the hole where the first dedication had been. When I dedicate a book, I want it to mean something, and I want to make it plain that it means something.

I have been thinking about doing this new edition for years, and have been brooding over the problem of an appropriate rededication for nearly as long. Finally, less than a week before I planned to release the FoxAcre edition, the solution, the obvious, utterly appropriate, solution popped into my head: Harry Turtledove. The choice was so obvious that I can't understand why I didn't think of it before. There are good and sufficient reasons to dedicate this edition to Harry. And because it is based on things that happened after *Orphan of Creation* was published, and indeed that happened *because* it was published, it can't be construed as being a second-best choice. The book had to be published first before *this* dedication could happen.

Back in the spring of 1988, about a week or so after *Orphan of Creation* came out, I got a phone call from Harry, whom I had never met. Still, it was plain even from the tone of a stranger's voice that something had thrown him for a loop. Harry told me that he had just published *A Different Flesh,* which was *his* science fiction novel about humans encountering another hominid species. The novel was based on stories he had published (in *Isaac Asimov's Science Fiction* Magazine, as I recall). Since my novel had not been serialized, Harry had no idea it was coming. This meant I was at a slight advantage, as I had known about *his* stories—at a distance. As with many writers, I try not to read something that's too similar to what I'm working on, for fear of being unduly influenced, and/or demoralized. As I recall, I read part of the first of the stories, and then backed off because the stories were based on a theme that was a little too close to home.

Little did I know how close. What Harry was calling to talk to me about was the quotation from Stephen Jay Gould that appears at the front of the book you are reading at present. Harry, it turns out, had been inspired by *precisely the same words.* Gould's work had set *both* of us off to explore a fascinating what-if. At the same time, Gould's work had produced as striking an example of divergent evolution as one could wish for. Harry and I, starting from precisely the same jumping-off point, had told two totally different stories. And Harry had just opened up a book by a total stranger, and there read the paragraph that had set *him* thinking hard enough to produce a book. No wonder he sounded a bit spooked.

I suggested to Harry that we both sue Dr. Gould for incitement to fiction—and hence the new dedication. The lawsuit never came off, but that was how Harry and I met. It was the start of a longtime friendship—one that, I have no doubt, will continue to evolve as the years roll by.

Roger MacBride Allen
Takoma Park, Maryland
November, 2000

About The Author

Roger MacBride Allen was born in Bridgeport, Connecticut on September 26, 1957. He graduated Boston University in 1979 with a degree in journalism, and published his first novel in 1984. From that time to this, every work of science fiction that he has completed has been published. He has written seventeen novels to date, (three of which were New York *Times* bestsellers) and a modest number of short stories.

In 1994, he married Eleanore Fox, an officer in the U. S. Foreign Service. In March 1995, they moved to Brasilia, Brazil, where Eleanore worked at the embassy. In August, 1997, Eleanore's next assignment took them back to the United States. Their son, Matthew Thomas Allen, was born November 12, 1998. They live in Takoma Park, Maryland, just north of Washington, D. C.